MW01128437

Destiny

Chris Johnson

ISBN: 1-4392-3875-8
ISBN-13: 9781439238752
Visit www.booksurge.com to order additional copies.

Cover art courtesy of Waldo Bender

For Ruby Louise Johnson, 1939-2008.

Chapter 1 - Carnival   1

Chapter 2 - Mama Thea   41

Chapter 3 - Hooks and Crooks   81

Chapter 4 - Long Gravy   105

Chapter 5 - New Orleans   127

Chapter 6 - The Delta   161

Chapter 7 - Best Laid Plans   209

Chapter 8 - Lady of the Moon   239

Chapter 9 - Destiny   263

Chapter 1 - Carnival

August, 1969

A scorched yellow fingernail of moon crept below the vague horizon. Three people in a sweaty teakwood skiff puttered up to a small, nameless marsh key six or seven miles off Azalea, on the Mississippi coast, in the northern Gulf of Mexico.

Two men stepped onto the unsure surface. The bigger, younger one made a quick scan around, seeing nothing. The unusually gentle surf lapped against the gunnels of the wide, shallow fourteen foot flatboat; only the syncopated ratatat of its idling little gas engine interrupted the ambient hum of millions of mosquitoes.

The marsh smelled like dead fish. The short stop was necessary, and the two pissed under the same shimmering constellations that made sailors the first men to understand insignificance. They did not talk.

Before stepping back in the century-old oystering craft, the big one kicked its side with each foot, one after the other, knocking off sandy mud. The little old one did the same, hoisted his bad leg into the boat, then pushed off the key with his good leg, hopping in the front. A semiconscious young lady laying in the middle of the floorboard moved, periodically moaning.

"Tide's extra low," said the man in front. "Must be that hurricane."

"That hurricane's off Cuba. It ain't affecting our tides," the big one snorted, steering. "Camille. What kind of candyass name is that for a hurricane? It'll probably go to Texas, won't amount to nothing."

"Sort of a coincidence, don't you think?"

"What?"

"You know, Hurricane *Camille*?"

"Don't get stupid." The big one glared at his partner, which did no good, in the light. "Besides, like I said, that little old squall's gonna peter out, or go to Texas. Maybe Mexico."

They headed south. The older one was in the square bow seat, facing backwards. There was no wind, just a small breeze from the movement. Both men swatted mosquitoes.

"You sure you want to do this?," said the one in front, just loud enough not to have to say it again.

"Shut up, you old fool," said the big one, looking around, a little nervous. He let go of the handle of the outboard motor for a second, checking his .44 magnum revolver in its holster, the ivory handle inlays slick with salt water spray. "And check them ropes."

The older one leaned over, fiddled with knots that bound the young lady's hands behind her back. She wore a light, white linen dress, which was damp from the humidity and occasional splashes. The old man could see her underwear through the wet spots, and her pregnant belly protruded. A second strand of rope knotted her feet together, attaching them to two concrete cinder blocks. Blood trickled down the side of her pretty face, from under her dark, curly auburn hair, which he could barely see. By starlight, the blood was perfectly black.

Humidity caused lights at the Azalea harbor, on the northern horizon, to twinkle. It was almost midnight, and the temperature was still in the high eighties.

"This'll do," said the big one, shutting off the engine. "Help me get her up." The young lady only weighed a little over a hundred pounds, even as pregnant as she was. The big man was just about drunk, and almost fell out of the boat, cursing, stumbling over the middle seat. He hoisted her up. "Grab the damn bricks," he said, "they go in first."

The little old man did not move.

"Goddammit," the big one said, listing the boat, "this whore ain't getting any lighter. Grab them bricks!"

"I ain't doing it."

The big one dropped her, like a bag of ice. She bounced once on the old teak, unconscious. "What the hell is *your* problem?" He jabbed a big scarred finger through the humidity toward the girl. The old one could make out two black tattoos on the big one's veined white forearm, an eagle and a crucifix. "This bitch *threatened* me! Hell, she could *ruin* me, and you know it! That what you want? Where's that going to leave you? Now pick up them bricks!"

The old man sighed. "I ain't doing it, Raymond. This ain't right. It ain't the fifties no more. We can't just…it just ain't right."

"What, are we having a fucking *meeting* here? This girl ain't white! In case you forgot, I *am*! You starting to agree with them damn Kennedys, now?"

"Well, that ain't no issue. I believe y'all already killed them two."

"I already told you, '*y'all*' didn't kill *nobody*. It was the damn New Orleans Mafia."

"Hell, Raymond, I remember you bragging about making the introductions."

"Shut up! That never happened! And quit calling me Raymond. I hate that name. Besides, they only shot the first one. Bobby, that was pure luck."

"Well I just don't care anymore who done what to who or why. I do know *this* ain't right. Them two brothers getting shot wasn't right, either. People can't just keep on… we can't just keep killing people, Raymond. *Any* people. Besides, this girl don't even *look* black. Hell, she's as white as you and me. Whiter, even."

The big one plopped down on the boat seat, the one he had stumbled over. "Well, ain't this interesting," he said, pulling a bottle of beer out of the aluminum cooler, popping the top off on the side of the boat, "seems like we ought to have talked about all this back at the pier. Hell, since we're at it, let's talk about all the ones *you* were in on killing. Let's see, there was..."

"I don't need reminding, Raymond. That was a long time ago. This is nineteen sixty-nine. Things are different now, gonna *be* different. What we're doing tonight ain't right... it wasn't right back then, neither."

"Well, I'm happy we had the chance to have this little talk. We'll have to take time to discuss this further, when we ain't out here in the middle of the fuckin' ocean. In the meantime, this one," he waived his beer at the girl, "is going in the gulf." He gulped down the rest of his beer, throwing the empty bottle in the water. "You can tell it to Jesus later. Now get your gimpy ass up, and help me." He leaned over to pick her up.

The old man grabbed Raymond's crucifix arm. "Stop it," he said, "leave her alone. She's too young. Hell, she's about to have a baby, Raymond. *Your* baby."

Raymond slapped the older man's hand away. He drew his pistol, pointing it in the dark at the old man's forehead.

"Don't you ever talk to me about that bastard kid! And stop calling me Raymond, goddammit! Nobody calls me that!"

The older man gradually pulled a cigarette out of the pack in his shirt pocket, took his time lighting it. "Well?," he said, "which one you planning on shooting me for, Raymond?"

"I'm tired of your old mouth!" He dramatically cocked the huge revolver.

The old man snorted. "You ain't got them kinda balls."

Raymond drooped a little, uncocked his gun, slid it back in its holster. They sat silent for a moment, then the girl started stirring.

Raymond said, "One of these days, I *am* gonna shoot your ass." He nudged the girl with his boot. "Now, you gonna help, or not? Aw, hell, I promise this'll be the last one."

The older man just sat smoking, silent.

Raymond reached for the bricks, and the girl suddenly started kicking, screaming. In a single motion, Raymond scooped her up, threw her over the side. The ropes connecting her feet to the bricks, two or three feet long, momentarily suspended her upside down in the water, kicking, flailing. The older man tried to catch the girl's feet, but Raymond grabbed the bricks, threw them over. She snatched under.

Raymond coughed, caught his breath, steadied himself and the boat, scanned the horizon. He took another beer, did not offer the older man one, clomped over the middle seat to the back, plopped down. "Well," he said between heavy breaths, "you can sit up there and think your hands are clean, if you want to. But they ain't."

Raymond cranked the motor, and turned the skiff north, toward Azalea.

Today

Lee Farrell's hangover was so bad it deserved a name, like a hurricane. He and his best friend Jake Carter leaned against a portable bar, under a white canvass dome, among massive live oak trees on the Mississippi Gulf Coast. Just outside a portable fence, thousands of people streamed out of sight along a Mardi Gras parade route in the small town of Azalea, Mississippi. Scores of floats, each equipped with a blaring sound system, produced a cacophony of competing tunes that vibrated Lee's chest, agitating his headache. He decided to attack it with a Redeye. The bartender wrinkled her nose when Lee told her beer and tomato juice, with a shot of hot sauce.

A drunken insurance executive whom Lee vaguely knew staggered up, shouting to the bartender, "We need more whiskey!" Having been served in a giant plastic cup, he turned and announced to no one particularly: " I *guarandamteeya* we ain't got enough whiskey!" He staggered away.

Most of the parade floats, pulled by tractors or large pickup trucks, were elaborately decorated flatbed trailers. They carried fifteen or twenty Crewe members, whom hurled colorful beaded necklaces, candy, flying disks, panties, miniature Bibles, superballs, and beer huggies on the crowd. The crowd threw back what they didn't like.

Jake stretched his lean torso back against the bar. His curly reddish blond hair wisped in the wind, shining in the afternoon sun. He shouted out into the crowd at someone.

The February weather was typically warm on the edge of the Gulf of Mexico; most of the people shuffling through Lee's view wore shorts and light cotton shirts under their Mardi Gras accessories: oversized, garish hats, face and body paints of all description, pounds of Mardi Gras beads glazed with various spilled concoctions. Lee and Jake's clothes were standard gulf coast: cotton button-down shirts, khakis, loafers, no socks.

The parade shut down part of Mississippi Highway 90 for a couple of miles along the beach. Cat Island spread along the gulf horizon to the south. It had been deposited eons ago by the meanderings of the Mississippi and Pearl rivers. Lee remembered that it had been named three hundred years earlier by the French, whom mistook its population of raccoons for cats. He also remembered another horrible picture from Cat Island, a terrible scene of fire and death. He involuntarily winced at the thought. He noticed black rain clouds forming on the southern horizon.

Between the island and shore was a shallow sound, seven or eight miles wide, full of shrimp and oysters, game fish and sharks.

It lay in cool, smooth, gray-green repose; a serene backdrop to the madness of the Mardi Gras parade, which some of the old folks more properly called Carnival.

Lee imagined Hurricane Katrina, which not long ago had surged completely over Cat Island, and pushed a four story wall of water through that sound, over this spot. It went miles inland in places. He shook his head, trying to forget. He had resolved to cut down drinking, and had been doing so since New Years, but had profoundly backslid during the endless stream of Mardi Gras parties leading up to the parade, which was the last Sunday before Fat Tuesday.

A burst of noise from the parade route diverted his attention. An obviously inebriated college-aged Crewe member on a float was flashing the crowd her bare chest; they howled approval. Lee chuckled at the thought of how, when she was sober, that young lady would explain this to her snotty sorority sisters at Ole Miss or LSU.

Then, he saw Diana. Even now, she made his breath catch, like a crying hiccup. She was perfect. Blonde, lean, gliding through the crowd, still possessing runway-model looks. He had secretly loved her the first time he saw her, in New Orleans, at the Endymion Ball. Back then, she was only sixteen, about to be one of the hottest debutantes in the South, and Lee was the top high school quarterback on the Mississippi Gulf Coast.

She had been with her parents. Her father was a big lawyer in New Orleans; Lee's group and Diana's parents had been seated at adjacent tables in the massive Superdome. He had asked her to dance, but her mother said no and he didn't even feel stupid.

Lee had met her again during his second tour in college, when they were both students at Tulane; they had driven off into the night, and married in Las Vegas. When Diana's mother found out, she had a nearly fatal attack of embarrassment, and the couple had agreed to another, "real" marriage, a re-enactment that was taken to be genuine by all but the primary participants.

Jake was still blathering about politics to two guys at the other end of the bar. Lee lost sight of Diana for a moment. He loved her more than anything, and he was pretty sure she still loved him. They just didn't talk about it anymore. It was either the baby thing, or the law school thing, or boredom, or the damned hurricane.

Katrina had been a perfect calamity, destroyed everything in Azalea. She had hundred foot waves out in the blue water, in the deep part of the gulf, then churned up old oil sludge and wells, boat wrecks, and ghosts of the shallow parts before she reared back and slammed the shore, erasing houses and trees, roads and people. More than anything, Lee thought about the smell afterwards. In the hundred degree heat of late August, death. Katrina did not just wipe everything out, it stirred up the mud in everybody's lives. Everybody's.

Bam! Bam! Jake had slapped the bar with both hands. "*Damn,* boy, looks like you need another beer." He tussled Lee's dark hair, then resumed talking up a clutch of tipsy lawyers.

"Hell, why not," said Lee to himself, chuckling at this own lack of resolve.

They were attending a private party. Set among centuries-old Live Oaks, tough trees that had somehow survived the hurricane, Lee's hosts had cordoned off, with portable fencing, a section of public park adjacent to the parade route. People lined the narrow street as far as Lee could see in either direction.

He thought about how long people had been gathering under these old trees. Some of the lazy, ancient oaks had been living when the French landed here in 1699. They later shaded idle U.S. forces which occupied the area during the War Between the States.

They survived thirty-five feet of raging seawater during Hurricane Katrina.

Space along this part of the parade route was rare. There probably weren't more than a hundred people fenced in at the at the party, but the crowd immediately outside was packed, intertwined. They madly scrambled and fought for trinkets cast from the floats. Inside the fence, Lee's group enjoyed catered food, a full, tended bar, live jazz trio that no one could hear, comfortable seating, shade, and the all-important portable restroom facilities. A private compound in the middle of a public park. Lee thought, *the Mafia sure knows how to throw a party.*

Jake was talking loud and laughing with another group under the tented dome. Lee had always said Jake was going to be a politician. And Jake had done the requisites. He had gone through law school, done his time in the trenches, assisting the old District Attorney. Gotten his face on TV at the right times, in the good cases. Still, how the hell had that knucklehead actually gotten elected D.A.? He looked just like he did years ago, when they were freshmen at Mississippi State, up in Starkville. *More than twenty years ago*, thought Lee.

Now, he really wanted to find Diana, whisper to her how much he loved her. He tried to see her through the crowd again, but couldn't.

Diana was so good at hosting, entertaining, nursing conversations, and talking about fashion and decorating, she was commonly considered a necessity at parties. Even though the Cronus Casino was the official host of this party, Diana had taken over the hostess slot, which made her and everyone else happy.

She read a lot, and not fluff. She was ready to talk about politics, religion, history, science. Anything really, as long as she thought it was appropriate for the situation. She was carrying on traditions; her mother had always reminded her she was raising a *lady*, dammit, and a southern lady too, who requires much more finesse than uptight northerners, or sloppy westerners.

Lee was used to seeing people fall in love with her at parties, mostly men. She was an erotic social philosopher, a siren who understood the vague promise of love some men think they see in the eyes of all beautiful women. In that way she was the ultimate tease, but only because of the predictable conclusions of boring people. And she was perfectly comfortable with breaching some of the more ridiculous rules her mother had taught her. You were expected to *know* so little. She knew she was pretty, but she knew she was smart, too

Lee always wanted to be around her at these things; she never got stupid drunk, and transformed over the course of many a social event from hostess, to siren, to vixen, finally to house mother, who got everyone rides home.

Lee saw her standing with a group of six or eight people that included Nicolas Bonacelli and his wife. Bonacelli had recently been profiled in the local newspaper, The Mississippi Sound. He was the new Chief Operating Officer of the Cronus Casino, the largest and newest Biloxi casino and hotel, and sponsor of the present party. Lee had heard rumors that Bonacelli was a cousin of the Bardinos, the old Mafia family that still supposedly ran much of the New Orleans French Quarter, and possibly controlled the Cronus. He didn't feel like joining their conversation.

The parade passed slowly, with fitful stops and starts, as the floats alternately got left behind, then overcompensated by roaring ahead, causing shrieks from Crewe members fearing rear-end collisions.

No one at the Cronus Casino party seemed particularly interested in catching beads. Hundreds lay on the ground, trampled. Seeking better positions, members of the outside crowd pressed between each passing float, miraculously avoiding being crushed by the parade's sporadic flow. Small skirmishes erupted as more favorable beads were hurled; they quickly dissipated as attentions turned toward the next volley.

Jake turned to Lee. "Looks like Diana's made more new friends," he said, gesturing toward her conversation cluster with his beer. "Bonacelli. He's supposed to be in the Mafia, too."

Lee looked around to make sure no one was listening. Diana's group was far enough away; the bartender was preoccupied with the parade. "The guy's supposedly a cousin of the Bardinos. Is that true?"

"Don't know, don't care."

Lee momentarily studied his loafers. "I don't get it. If everybody knows he's in the mob, how did he get licensed to run a casino?"

"Nobody *says* he's in the mob. He's not been ID'd by any informants, nothing. No arrests of any kind."

"Has he ever run a casino, before?"

A little one in Indiana, or Illinois. Somewhere."

"Aren't they afraid he'll screw it up?"

"Who?"

"The Bardinos?"

"How the hell should I know? Besides, there's nothing he can screw up. Security and floor bosses run the casino operations - all he has to do is show up at parties. As far as the licensing - well, I understand the feds wanted this guy waived through the Gaming Board, and they didn't bother to tell me why."

Lee smirked. "These damn casinos. Snowbirds, traffic, and now feds letting in the Italian mob."

Jake rolled his eyes. "Actually, *Sicilian.* Used to be, anyway."

"I've got TV too, counselor." Lee poked him in the ribs.

"They've been here all along, babe. It's a common understanding among D.A.'s around here to let the feds fool with that kind of stuff. It's healthier." Then he remembered some things an FBI agent told him at the golf course recently. "Bonacelli supposedly dropped his Polish last name and took 'Bonacelli,' the last name of his adoptive mother, who just happens to be a Bardino cousin. The Bardinos pick on him about it, Polish jokes, like that, and it's supposed to be a tender spot. They call him Bonehead, but he's supposedly smart as shit. Harvard MBA."

They were drowned out by an outburst from the adjacent crowd. The parade had halted; a float somewhere down the road had a flat tire. A thirty-ish bleached blonde on a nearby stationary float was teasing, raising her shirt halfway.

"SHOW YOUR TITS!," someone yelled.

Lee glanced back toward Diana's group. Bonehead was talking, gesturing, oblivious to the crowd. Diana seemed the only group member paying attention to him. Lee turned back to Jake, shouting over the racket. "Carter, *granted*, you're an incompetent son of a bitch, but you are, in fact, the District Attorney. Are we just going to have to live with the Mafia running things now?"

"Like I said!," Jake shouted back, "they've been here all along. Ain't my headache!" He held up both hands, and faked wiping them clean. "Besides, look at Bonehead's wife. Should I run her out of town?"

Lee stared. Teeny cotton dress, jet black hair, cobalt blue eyes, private-trainer body. Diana caught his stare, and retaliated by conversationally placing her hand in the crook of Bonehead's arm. Bonehead visibly puffed out his chest in response, and continued talking, with more elaborate gestures. Mrs. Bonehead seemed more interested in the girl on the float than her gesticulating husband.

"Marvelous," said Jake, pointing over Lee's shoulder with his chin, "speaking of boneheads…".

Charlie Roark stumbled toward the bar, drunk, grinning. Charlie was an investigative reporter for The Mississippi Sound, and a particular annoyance to anyone in politics or the casino industry. He miscalculated the distance required for his last couple of steps, and stumped his sandaled right foot on the metal base of the bar, spilling what was left of his drink. "Dammit!," he squealed, hopping.

Lee said, "So, Roark, you hate the casinos, but you can drink their liquor?"

"Itza free country," Roark slobbered, ordering a drink.

"That's debatable. But this is a private party. How did you get in?"

"My friends." He pointed to nowhere particularly.

Lee said, "Let me guess: 'Ecology Democracy'? 'Mothers for Mother Earth'? 'Mean for Green'? Charlie gave the "thumbs up" sign on the last choice, though Lee had made it all up. Charlie attempted to wink, along with his thumb gesture, but he could only manage to blink both eyes instead, like a lizard.

Roark said to Jake, "Mister Carter, what're *you* doing atta casino party?"

"No comment."

Roark said, "Offa the record, isn't, ah, whatsis name? Bone…"

"Bonacelli," said Lee.

Roark said. "Exactly!" He thrust his hand toward Bonacelli, pointing, forgetting the scotch drink in it, which flew ice-first into the brand new purse of a newly blue haired party patron, who somehow didn't notice. "Isn't Bonajelly in the *Mafia?*"

Lee, pulling Roark aside, said, "Roark, let it rest. It's Jake's day off. Besides, with the Hog Roundup coming up soon, shouldn't you be focusing on *it?*" A year earlier, Roark had gotten cornered by a group of motorcycle riders at the annual Hog Roundup after they caught him secretly recording interviews with female participants in the "Birthday Suit Salute."

Lee, an occasional motorcycle rider himself, had found the reporter surrounded by a group of bikers, pleading for his life.

Lee knew some of the bikers, and had "saved" Roark. He knew the bikers had no intention of harming him, were only trying to scare him. Ever since, Lee and Roark had an unspoken understanding that Roark wouldn't harass Lee's friends, and Lee wouldn't tell everyone that Roark had pissed his pants, begging.

Lee ordered two more beers and a scotch for Roark, who was temporarily subdued by dark memories. "You're right, Lee," he said, "is's my day off, too. Happy Mardi Gras!" He raised his glass, then strolled away, swaying.

Lee glanced back at his wife. She and Nick Bonacelli were apparently engaged in a fascinating conversation. In response to some missive, Bonehead playfully put his arm around her waist, which, from Lee's perspective, definitely placed his hand too close to Diana's behind.

Lee nudged Jake. "Does Bonehead have his hand on my wife's ass?"

Jake pondered, cocked his head, shrugged. "Depends on where her ass starts."

Lee studied Bonacelli. Mid-forties, average height, maybe even short. Hard to tell, with dress shoes. He was in decent shape, but no threat. Of course, Diana would never forgive him for making a scene. Still, he thought, he had to do something. "So, Mister His Honorable Carter," Lee said in his best television-fake southern drawl, "as a taxpayin' citizen, I suggest you perform your *sworn duty*, go over there, and arrest the yankee scoundrel who's trying to charm my good, southern wife."

"Mister Farrell," he said, picking up the fake drawl, "I shall never interfere in the bidness of the Federal Bureau of Investigation, but I will *not* stand by while yankee scoundrels try to impress our *flowers of the Confederacy*. Let us defend her honor." They snickered, and headed toward the Bonacelli group.

The parade was still stalled, and the bleached blonde on the float still had not shown her tits. That part of the crowd, mostly high school kids, but a few seasoned paraders, drew the attention of a walking group of a dozen amateur evangelists known as "The Holy Strollers." Sponsored by the Southern Family Council, the Strollers attended any public function in Mississippi where sinners were likely to congregate, converting them to Council President Reverend Joel P. Tarnation's particular program for Christly forgiveness and salvation.

The group entered these dangerous frays armed only with hundreds of postcard-sized handbills, outlining a "Ten Step Plan for Salvation" program, and unbelievable tenacity. Their squad leader also had a bullhorn.

They thrust handbills upon every person they met. Unfortunately, "Step One" of the program was "Stop Drinking Alcoholic Beverages"; consequently, the handbills veritably carpeted the parade route, and the group was not popular with the crowd.

The Holy Strollers' leader, who was employed as manager of a collection agency, marched the group between the stalled floats, next to the teasing blonde. He raised his bullhorn, cranked the volume all the way up, turned toward the main body of the crowd, and announced, "You people are all going STRAIGHT TO HELL." This abated the crowd, momentarily. "Unless," he paused for effect, "unless you turn your back on SATAN"- he dramatically pointed toward the blonde - "put down the devil's alcohol, drop to your knees and BEG GOD'S FORGIVENESS!"

"I ain't Satan!," screamed Bleached Blonde, starting to cry.

"Yeah, she ain't Satan, SHE'S PURTY!," someone in the crowd shouted.

"STRAIGHT TO HELL!," bullhorned the debt collector.

"Have a drink, preacher!," someone shouted, and launched a newly opened sixteen ounce can of beer, which struck Debt Collector between the eyes, spewing foam in an arc over the entire Holy Stroller flock. At that moment the parade lurched forward, and the Strollers retreated from between the floats, to the gulf side of the road. The parade now separated the Strollers from the hostile part of the crowd. Debt Collector was leaking blood from the bridge of his nose.

Diana saw Lee coming, not thrilled by his careful gait; at least he could handle his liquor, unlike most of his lowlife friends. But she could never quite wrest that stubborn Mississippi Delta redneck streak from him, even though it rarely flared up any more. When it did, it was always in these type of contrived social situations, which he scorned. Still, she could never stay mad at him, even when he was being impossible, or lazy, or rude, or … *unambitious.*

Lee and Jake arrived at Diana's group, which was down to Diana and the two Bonacellis. Lee started to introduce himself, but Nicolas Bonacelli was speaking.

"So I said, 'you want me to move *where?*' I mean, who would actually move to *Mississippi?* No offense, but I'm sure you understand. I was ashamed to tell our neighbors. I could have said I was going to Florida, which is bad enough. But," he shrugged, "I gotta admit," waiving his free arm around, "it ain't so bad." He grinned at Diana.

"Well, I can't speak for everyone, but I know that I'm relieved that you find our state minimally acceptable," said Lee, maybe a little too sarcastically.

Bonacelli's gaze slowly left Diana, and made a deliberate path from Lee's feet to his eyes. "And you are?"

"Lee Farrell, Diana's husband," said Lee, fake smiling, delivering an overly-firm handshake to Bonacelli's freshly ass-free hand. "And you are?"

"Nicolas Bonacelli. You and your wife," he cut a look at Diana, grinning again, "are certainly welcome at my party."

"Thank you so much, Nicolas. I didn't realize it was *your* party. My invitation said it was Cronus Casino's."

"Which I now run, Mr., ah, Farrell, is it? That's Irish, isn't it?" He smirked. "Anyway, there was an article on me in your newspaper the other day. A huge spread, actually, you may have seen it…"

"Sorry," Lee interrupted, "but, as you might have suspected, most of us can't read."

"Lee! Stop teasing Mr. Bonacelli - he may not understand our southern sense of humor!," interjected Diana, with a fierce look at Lee, re-clutching Bonehead's arm.

"Oh, I'm sure Bone-, uh, Nicolas understands our humor perfectly, Diana," stated Lee.

Jake interjected, "Hello, Mr. Bonacelli, Jake Carter. And this must be Mrs. Bonacelli?"

"Sarah," she said, presenting her hand. Jake made an exaggerated formal bow, and kissed it.

"May I present my uncouth friend, Lee Farrell?" Jake passed Sarah's artificially tanned, perfectly manicured, diamond and emerald ring-laden hand to Lee.

"Nice to meet you," said Lee, shaking her hand, then dropping it.

Thunder suddenly shook the ground; everyone reflexively looked toward the weather to the south. The dark clouds had moved to the edge of the water, nearly over the parade route. Across the road, Debt Collector had recovered sufficiently from his beer injury to get back on the bullhorn. "STRAIGHT TO HELL!," he shouted during and between float tunes. "STRAIGHT TO HELL!"

The crowd on Lee's side of the road, still irritated that the Strollers had interfered with the blonde before they could see some tits, were steadily launching beer cans and other refuse over the parade, onto the offenders. The barrage only steeled the Strollers, whom collectively took up the mantra, "STRAIGHT TO HELL!," rhythmically chanting in unison. Music from each passing float intermittently drowned out the chant, which increased in volume and fervor with each volley of beer artillery.

The crowd started its own chant: "SHOW YOUR TITS!," shouted at each float, each walking woman, anybody in general. "SHOW YOUR TITS!"

Lee nudged Jake. "Go find some titties for that bunch, and you're guaranteed to get re-elected."

"Oh, I should have mentioned before," said Diana, "Jake is our local District Attorney." Nicolas Bonacelli knew this already, but Sarah didn't, and they both acted suitably honored to meet him.

Sarah said, "Mr. Carter, you don't think these people are going to riot, do you?"

"Only if they run out of beer. And call me Jake."

Thunder momentarily drowned out the crowd and the parade, but the Strollers and the tittymongers immediately rejoined:

"SHOW - YOUR - TITS!"
"STRAIGHT - TO - HELL!"
"*SHOW -YOUR - TITS!*"
"*STRAIGHT - TO - HELL!…*"

Buck Carter strode up with a friend, and clapped Lee on the back. The jolt caused Lee to spill some beer on Buck's cowboy boots, which Buck did not notice. He was six-foot-five, seventy-something, still in good shape, and obviously intoxicated.

"Dad!," said Jake Carter, anxiously, "meet my new friends."

"First things first," slurred the old man, turning to Diana, snatching her hand away from Bonacelli's arm. "You're prettier than the day I met you, and almost stole you away from this sorry husband of yours." He slapped Lee on the back again, causing Lee to spill the rest of his beer. "And if he ever gives you any trouble, I'll take care of his ass right away." Buck tried to kiss her on the cheek, but got her in the ear, instead. "I want y'all to meet my new friend," said Buck, clapping the young man with him on the back, making him take an involuntary step forward. "This here's - ah - ," he bent over, whispered to his guest, rejoined, "this here's Zack Ellis, new agent over at the FBI office in Gulfport, moved here last summer, and the very first, ah, African-American agent in that office." Buck slapped his own thigh, like he just heard a good one.

"Actually, I don't care to be known as the first black person to do anything, Sheriff, just a good agent."

Buck said, "Hell, we don't put up with no false modesty around here, son, we know how hard your, uh, *people* have had to …"

"Jake interjected, "Dad, I don't think we need to get into any history lessons, do we? Why don't you get Zack a Coke, or a beer, or something."

Buck scowled at Jake, said, "I'll get him a damn beer in a second, son, now be quiet while I'm talkin'." He grinned at Diana again, said, "Anyway, like I was saying…"

Zack Ellis interrupted, saying, "I appreciate it, Mr. Carter, but I can handle it from here." He introduced himself around the group, physically recoiled when Diana air kissed near his cheek. He was genuinely embarrassed, and quickly moved along through the crowd.

Buck watched him walk away, said to no one in particular, "Good boy. I always tried to get along with them federal cops, even if they did have to bring in the n-, uh, African Americans."

Lee was ignoring Buck, having unconsciously become fixated on Sarah Bonacelli's body, which was truly amazing, up close. He jumped as Diana pinched his side, unseen by the others.

"Now," said Buck, "Let's hear about this one," jabbing a huge, gnarled finger through the air toward Nicolas Bonacelli.

Jake said, "Dad, this is Nicolas Bonacelli, just moved to Mississippi, I believe, and his wife Sarah. He's the new head of Cronus Casino over in Biloxi, which is the coast's biggest one, I think?," he looked at Bonacelli for confirmation; Bonacelli nodded in agreement, proud. "And this is Nicolas' wife, Sarah."

"Please," Nicolas said, "everyone call me Nick." He extended his hand to Buck. Buck ignored it.

"Well, ain't *this* nice. Another fuckin' Italian." Turning to Jake, he said, "Plus, I hear the sombitch is in the Mafia." Turning back to Nick, he said, "Well, lemme tell you, boy, we ain't impressed. I'm *Buck Carter,* dammit. I was the *sheriff* o' this county for thirty-something years, and let me assure you that my boy" - slapping Jake on the back - "ain't got no reason to be intimidated, and won't be! I've had some dealings with your kind, and none of you wop bastards can be trusted…"

Diana glared at Lee, expecting him to do something.

Jake grabbed his father by an enormous arm, and pulled him away toward the bar. The old man ramped up his cussing of Bonacelli as he allowed himself to be led away.

Nick tried to appear unruffled, chuckling. "Well, Sarah, it appears we've had our first encounter with an authentic redneck." Sarah seemed amused.

Diana said, "Please forgive him, Nick and Sarah, he's a little drunk. He doesn't mean harm, does he, Lee?" She fake smiled at Lee, plaintively.

Lee said, "Mr. Carter's from another generation. He doesn't speak for the rest of us." Now somewhat embarrassed, he extended his hand to Nick. "I… guess I should apologize for Buck and, well, the rest of us, too. Welcome to the Mississippi coast."

Nick shook his hand, while saying to Diana, "Thank you, Miss Farrell, but there's no need to explain. I can handle the rednecks."

Lee said, "Actually, of course, it's *Mrs.* Farrell, Mr. Bonacelli. And maybe I should warn you, a lot of people around here are a little sensitive about the whole 'redneck' thing. It's hard to explain. It's funny to Southerners, but not necessarily if anybody else says it. It… depends on the context, I guess."

Nick said, "I'm not overly concerned about what rednecks think, Mr. Farrell. But since you've mentioned it, what, exactly, does 'redneck' mean?"

"Technically, it's a term for farmers of Scots-Irish ancestry. But, as I said, people are sort of touchy about it, probably because of the way Southerners are portrayed on television. You know, drunken, violent, uneducated, incestuous…"

"Well, at least no one can say you don't have pretty sisters," said Nick, chuckling, gazing at Diana again.

Lee was rapidly tiring of trying to please Diana by being nice to this prick. He said, "I'm sure you understand, being of Italian descent. You *are* Italian, right, Nick? What does the term "wop" mean?"

"It means some ignorant bastards disrespecting my people when they came to this country," he snapped.

"Yes, so you do understand." Lee fake smiled. "Besides, didn't I hear you had changed your name to Bonacelli from a Polish one? What does that make you, a *wopski*?"

Diana stepped between the two men. "Lee, that's enough. Please, let's all go get a drink." She glared at Lee, steered Nick and Sarah toward the bar.

Lee spun, and walked away. He passed through the private party, past the food tent and the jazz trio, through cigar-smoking groups of businessmen and their wives or girlfriends, past rich, weekend environmentalists, and concerned garden club

members, around the old and wealthy, whom viewed the parade
as an invasion of their pampered privacy. He went through the
temporary gate, past the sheriff's deputy hired for the occasion,
into the mass of common people, where he preferred to be.

As Lee stalked by, he did not notice his old high school
acquaintance Flounder in the crowd. Flounder's real name was
Isaiah Fourcade. He was from Pearlington, Mississippi, down in
the swamps along the Gulf of Mexico on the Mississippi side of the
Mississippi-Louisiana line. Pearlington was a sparsely populated
fishing community; Isaiah had spent his first few years in a poor
family that tonged oysters and trawled for shrimp for a pitiful living.
After struggling through elementary school, he was chosen by St.
Thomas Academy to attend on a scholarship for the underprivileged.
There, he had met Lee. They were in the same grade.

From the beginning, Lee's teachers remarked how much Lee
and Isaiah looked alike. Same age, same height, weight, brown
hair, brown eyes. Both of the boys were excellent athletes. There
was one decided difference. Lee found academics easy, almost
boringly so. Isaiah had a tough time with his classes, never quite
overcoming the lack of academic interest in his home.

The kids at St. Thomas, especially the boarders, were in all
manners unmerciful. It was a local joke that a stupid person was
a "flounderhead," meaning that they were so inbred, both eyes
were on the same side of their heads, like a flounder fish. The kids
picked up the expression, and, mindful of Isaiah's economic status
and academic difficulties, started calling him "Flounder." It stuck.

Flounder was never friends with Lee; he regarded all rich
people, practically everyone at St. Thomas, as enemies. He had
grown from being shy young boy to a surly, brawling young man
by the time he and Lee became seniors in high school. That year,
he and Lee had competed for the starting quarterback job on the
football team, the job having been vacated by graduation.

Both had been starters on the team a year earlier, in different positions. Though both had the physical skills, Lee had a better grasp of the coach's complex passing schemes, and won the job. When the coach announced his decision a week before the first game that year, Flounder walked off the field, out of St. Thomas, and never returned. Lee went on to set several school records, winning in the process all that year's games, and a college football scholarship, to Mississippi State University, that he did not financially need.

Flounder had spent the intervening years on the coast in various labor jobs, sometimes shrimping, sometimes working on docks in Gulfport, or in the bait houses. He was always in association with the floating group of low rent hustlers, the Dixie Mafia, and liked to brag about it when he got drunk. He had spent a little time on various occasions in the county jail, mostly for drunk and disorderly, or misdemeanor assault.

Flounder glared at the rich boy Lee, who of course had not noticed him, even though Lee had walked right by. As Flounder jostled in the masses outside the fence all the rich bastards and their snotty women pranced and giggled inside the fence. He knew that he would never get in. He believed that every rich person screwed him out of his destiny, somehow. He was, by pure chance of birth, left out. Over the years, he had cultivated his hatred of Lee Farrell and people like him into a kind of madness.

The asshole Farrell made Flounder think about his old girlfriend, a bartender he met when he was working on the docks in Gulfport. All the rich kids had gone off to college, while he sweated. He met a girl, dated her for a year. More even. He loved her. Hell, he bought her a ring, over in the mall.

Then Farrell and his buddies showed up for summer break, with their fancy cars, and football scholarships. Farrell took her away. He didn't even keep her, just used her like a whore and tossed her aside, like all rich people do. Well, Isaiah had fixed her little wagon, and Farrell's time would come soon enough. Flounder emitted an animal growl, threw his beer into the air above the crowd, and stomped off to his truck. Nobody noticed, which made him even madder.

Lee walked toward his cottage on Gulf Drive. Some of the multi-million-dollar columned mansions had been rebuilt and restored along the road; large areas still lay stripped bare by Katrina. United States presidents had wintered on Gulf Drive; ancient and modern leaders of industry lived there; prominent politicians held unpublicized fund-raises there. The crowd thinned considerably as Lee moved further east, against the flow of the parade. Groups of disapproving residents lounged on verandas, viewing the end of the parade, as it passed their gates. The sky darkened still. The Holy Strollers and tittymongers still chanted, fading in the distance. "It's gonna rain," someone said. "It hasn't rained on the Azalea parade in a hundred years," another answered, "God won't allow it." That was the local legend.

The last float in the parade carried the Azalea Mayor. Suddenly, it skidded to a stop. A small child had run in the street to pick up beads, as its mother screamed. The drunken mayor stood up from her throne, perched high above the trailer, to view the disturbance. The child retreated, the driver lurched forward, and the mayor toppled onto the float's deck. Lightning struck the beach, a hundred yards to the south.

A furious gust of wind stung the crowd with sand. Two seconds of perfect calm were followed by an explosion of rain, wind, and lightning. A few blocks behind Lee, in the heart of the small city, floats, picnic blankets, beer kegs, and spouses were abandoned as the crowd scattered before the furious storm. Lee sprinted.

Running up his driveway, Lee leaped, soaked, onto his small front porch, nearly landing on Iris, his dog. Iris, a territorial, intelligent, and ferociously loyal Australian Shepherd was, as always, waiting for his return.

Lee yelled inside the front door, "Kiger! Please throw me a towel!" While Iris busily licked the water from his legs, Kiger appeared at the door with a towel.

"Sounds like a hell of a storm," said Kiger, "I thought Ja did not allow rain at the Azalea Parade." Kiger was a naturalized American, native of Jamaica. He chuckled, moving his massive body aside, allowing Lee and Iris to enter.

"Well, I heard God was mad about all the titties this year," said Lee, now relaxed.

Many of the houses along Gulf Drive were constructed in the antebellum South, with slave quarters. Modest housing for a number of servants, some of the quarters became spacious beachfront bungalows in later years.

Lee's house had been converted from a slave quarter to a two bedroom home, with ample room for entertaining, and a long, narrow, Bermuda grass front yard, which ended at Gulf Drive. Lee's next door neighbor, to whom Lee had never spoken, was a retired investment banker from New Orleans; his father had bought oil leases around the Gulf of Mexico during the Depression, for pennies an acre.

He owned the massive mansion to which Lee's slave quarters had once been appended. Both houses had been devastated by Hurricane Camille in 1969, and by Hurricane Katrina in 2005. Both times, their owners patiently salvaged, rebuilt, and restored the original style of architecture and materials. Lee's view of the gulf was dominated by one large Live Oak on the edge of his property line, and Cat Island, on the horizon.

Entering, Lee skipped across the hardwood floors, through the front room, with its twelve foot ceilings and crown molding, past the French doors, opened to his small brick courtyard.

Emerging from the bedroom in dry cotton clothes, Lee took in the aroma of fresh, hot Jambalaya, and plopped on his couch. Iris piled into his lap. The den, furnished in comfortable coastal style, airy, with dark red leather furniture, featured a large brick fireplace, rarely used, but comforting to see.

Above the fireplace hung a large framed charcoal drawing of Keith Richards, cool and violent, a cigarette dangling from his lips, squeezing a homemade chord out of his Telecaster. Lee had bought it in New Orleans, on Jackson Square, from a white haired old black man, an artist named Ody. Lee had it framed, and won the skirmish with Diana about hanging the picture in the main room of the house. Ody had told Lee he was from Belzoni, Mississippi, in the heart of the Mississippi Delta. His skin was as dark as Delta buckshot mud, and his eyes were birthstone blue. Ody had said that Keith was the only white man who ever truly understood the blues.

"So, where's the crowd?," said Kiger, moving behind the breakfast bar, into the kitchen. Lee hosted an after-parade party annually.

"They'll be here soon enough, wet and thirsty. Think we have enough supplies?"

"Feels like plenty to me." Kiger, who was blind, lifted the lid off a huge black iron pot, checking the consistency of the jambalaya rice with his hand.

"Please remember, my friend, you're not working today. Let the drunks get their own." Kiger was a bartender; he worked at a nightclub called The Blue Stone, where Lee was the manager.

"I don't mind helping the helpless, boss."

Diana, Nick Bonacelli, and Sarah had arrived at the Cronus Casino party's portable bar just before the storm struck.

"Repent before the WRATH OF GOD!," broadcast the injured head Stroller. "REPENT NOW, or all you people are going STRAIGHT TO…". His bullhorn crackled, and shorted out in the rain. Lightning struck the beach, several hundred yards away. It startled him so, he jumped straight up, splay-legged, like a cheerleader. Dropping the bullhorn, he screamed "mother*fuck!*," and took off running, losing his hairpiece.

The parade froze, and the mostly drunken crowd busted into an incompetent stampede. Diana and the Bonacellis huddled at the bar. The wind uprooted stakes tethered to ropes supporting the adjacent entertainment tent; a dozen tipsy octogenarians were temporarily trapped in the fallen canvas, but struggled free, shrieking. Nick ran for his car, leaving Diana and Sarah alone under the bar's canopy, which had survived the initial wind. The bartender had abandoned her post at the first big lightning strike.

Moments earlier, dozens of people had been mingling around inside the fenced area; now, only Diana and Sarah remained. The wind quickly settled, and rain poured.

"One hundred years," said Diana, marveling at the intensity of the rain.

"One hundred years?," asked Sarah.

"This parade has been held for a hundred years, they say, and it's never been rained on - until now."

Sarah said, "So this is, like, a Biblical event. Pity. At least we're safe," she moved behind the bar, pulled out a bottle of red wine, poured two glasses. "And supplied," she added.

Stragglers ran down the street, shouting for kids, wives, whatever. Diana and Sarah were perfectly dry.

Diana walked around behind the bar as well, taking her wine from Sarah. "What do you do, do you work?," she asked.

"Me? Work?," she laughed sarcastically. "Mob wives don't work, dear, though we are expected to cook, and screw. And I can't cook. So…".

They both laughed. Diana said, "I heard the rumors about Nick. Are you allowed to talk about the - the Mafia, or whatever it is - like that, in public? I mean, what if I was an undercover cop, or something."

"Please. The cops know damn well who is in the mob, and who is not." Besides, I talk about whatever I want." She raised her glass, in a toasting gesture. Diana responded in kind. They drank, and watched a few wet stragglers hustling down the street. Sarah poured more wine.

Diana said, "It must be an interesting life - and dangerous. Aren't you afraid for Nick?"

"No."

Diana looked at her closely, curiously. Sarah had the prettiest eyes Diana had ever seen, but she wouldn't say so.

An emptied float slowly passed, pulled by a truck. Its paper and chicken wire facade was drooping, pieces falling into the street under the driving rain.

Sarah said, "Nick and me - we aren't exactly Antony and Cleopatra. He needs to have a good looking wife, and I require lots of money. I've got the goods," she stepped back, presenting her body, like a model, "and he's got the cash. Perfect marriage."

The rain fell steadily. The wind and lightning were gone.

Sarah said, "What do *you* do?"

"Nothing, really. I studied graphic art at Tulane…, then I married Lee. And we've been sort of stuck here."

"Do you love him?"

"Yes, but…"

"Then you're lucky. That's better than money, I think. Well, I heard. But enough of all that." She took Diana by the arm, gently turning her around, patting her behind.

Diana, startled, said, "What are you doing?"

"Admiring your butt."

Embarrassed, Diana pulled away.

Sarah said, "Oh, come now," affecting a fake southern drawl, she continued, "are all you southern belles so *modest?*" Then, in her regular voice said, "Seriously, I'm an artist. You will have to model for me."

"Really? What medium?"

"I paint. But I prefer sculpture."

"Oh, I've *always* wanted to do that. I did some sculpture in college, but I never pursued it."

"Then you'll start tomorrow, at my place." Sarah set her wine glass on the bar. "You have such a perfect form." She placed both her hands on Diana's chest, as if she were examining her breasts. "You are *so* beautiful. First you model, then you sculpt."

Sarah's hands on her breasts shocked Diana. Her pulse raced. Sarah stepped closer, without removing her hands. Diana felt a rush of panic, but did not move. In the space of a heartbeat, the panic turned to thrill, and she nearly fainted.

Diana spun away, stumbled. Sarah caught her, and helped her steady herself.

Sarah said, "Maybe I've had too much to drink. I should apologize."

"No! No, please, it's just, no one's ever, I mean, *I've* never …"

"I'm sorry. You're so beautiful. I just got carried away." She leaned over, kissed Diana on the cheek.

Diana composed herself. Looking directly into Sarah's eyes, she said, "Don't be sorry."

Nick stopped his Mercedes sedan at the curb, tooting the horn at Sarah and Diana. As they moved toward his car, Nick thought: *what a fine piece of ass this Diana is.*

Lee Farrell had one thing in common with most of his Gulf Drive neighbors: he had inherited his house. His parents had bought the place when he was a child; it was an unusual luxury, a departure from his father's usual leathery habits. Lee and his parents had spent vacations and holidays in the bungalow for much of his youth. After his parents' sudden deaths, Lee had shuttered the place, and many years passed before Lee and Diana moved in.

Lee and Kiger were in the kitchen, Lee watching, and Kiger listening, to the howling weather outburst. Between echoes of thunder, several voices could be heard out front.

"Sounds like you need more towels, Lee," said Kiger, opening the door. The old house instantly filled with the din of Carnival, as several of Lee's wet friends rushed in. He retrieved towels from the back, and dispensed them to the crowd. Music came blasting through stereo speakers; Kiger served jambalaya, beer, and drinks to the helpless.

Iris, the Australian Shepherd, was so protective of Lee that she could not be trusted around a crowd. Lee took her in the master bedroom, where she would remain for the rest of the party. As he emerged from the room, he nearly ran over a beautiful redhead, who was about to enter the bedroom. Her real name, unknown to Lee, was Elizabeth; Lee knew her as Dahlia. She was a stripper from New Orleans. Lee had foolishly invited her to the party the last time he and Jake went to new Orleans on a "business" trip, and wound up on Bourbon Street, in the titty bars.

"Dahlia!," blurted Lee; she placed a finger over his mouth, reached behind him, opened the door, and pushed him back in the room, following. Iris decided not to bite the strange woman, and settled in a corner. Dahlia grasped Lee behind the neck with both hands, and kissed him passionately. "There," she said, "you've been wanting that for a while, I believe."

Lee's head swirled.

She pecked his cheek, then skipped out of the room. Iris growled. Lee shushed Iris, took a deep breath, steadied himself, and rejoined the party. Guests continued to pour in, and after some time, the rain abated. In the back courtyard, several people had gotten into Lee's hot tub, in their clothes. Walking through the French doors onto the patio, Lee was greeted by Remy Lafitte Richelieu du Bois, who sat in the tub, balancing a cigarette in one hand, a frozen margarita in the other, and a strange young lady on each knee. Lee did not know the girls; neither did Remy.

Lee knew Remy Lafitte Richelieu du Bois' real name, but hardly anyone else did; they all called him "Boot." He was probably in his thirties, and of the race of jolly, sinewy people whose ancestors had spread along the lower edge of the North American continent, and whose first language was French, and whose second language was recognizably English. People called him a Cajun, but he always referred to himself as a "Coonass."

Boot said, "Lee, glad you got to come and see me! I t'row a good god-doggone party, yeah?"

One of the girls said, to Boot, "I love your place, ah, what's your name?"

"You are the King of Mardi Gras, Boot," said Lee. "Nice place. By the way, how's the fishing been?" Boot ran charters on Lee's boat, a thirty-six foot Sportfisher.

"Oh, not too good, Lee. West wind." Westerly winds generally ruin fishing in the northern Gulf of Mexico, according to local tradition.

"West wind. Uh-huh. More like a beer flood, no?," Lee said, referring to Boot's well-known affinity for skipping work and drinking beer.

"No, no, boss, bad wind. But the fishing," - he cut his eyes back and forth between the two girls - "it's getting better, yeah?"

Lee laughed, and headed back inside, just as Diana entered, with Nick and Sarah Bonacelli in tow. Fighting a surge of adrenaline, Lee purposefully ignored Bonehead, and spoke with his other guests. Most he knew, some not.

Diana led her guests to the kitchen area, where Kiger had a blender of frozen margaritas going, and was intermittently shaking martinis, pouring liquors and mixes, and serving jambalaya in plastic party bowls. Diana secured drinks for the Bonacellis, and nearly bumped into Dahlia on her way through the party toward Lee. She gestured toward the bedroom, and Lee followed her in.

"I do not want to argue, Diana," said Lee, "I know that look."

"Lee, I don't want to argue either, but I can *not* understand how you always manage to offend the most important people."

"How *I* manage to offend? Was it my imagination, or did Mr. Bonehead insult the whole state, while managing to feel your ass in front of me *and* his wife?"

"Oh, Lee, you're so dramatic. And he did *not* feel my ass." She thought, *OK, maybe his wife did.* "Besides, it takes time for people to get used to the South, and you can't act like a redneck, then complain about people thinking you *are* one."

"Oh, so I need to perform up to the expectations of some greaser from the mob?"

"That's just a rumor."

"What, are you this clown's publicist, now?"

"Lee," said Diana, lightning flashing behind her green eyes, "you will not be rude to our guests. These people are very important. Mr. Bonacelli runs the largest casino in this state, for God's sake. If you can't be civil, just avoid him. But," she poked him in the chest, "you will *not* embarrass me in our home."

Lee knew better than to fool with her when she had the lightning-behind-the-eyes thing going. Besides, he was tired of the argument. He grasped her around the waist with both arms, pulled her close.

"Alright, Mrs. Farrell," he said, "you win. I'll leave your boyfriend alone. Always the debutante, trying to impress the rich folks," he teased.

"Oh, shut up," said Diana, pushing away. "By the way, who invited the titty dancer?"

Lee's mind flashed through several possible responses. "What titty dancer, darling?," was the unfortunate choice.

"Oh, give me a break, Lee, the one that practically has 'Titty Dancer' tattooed on her forehead. Out there, by the couch."

"I honestly have no idea, sweetie. Should I tell her to leave? I mean, we can't be rude to the guests, can we?"

Diana sighed. "Lee, it's bad enough that you run a bar, with all the lowlifes that hang out there, but you have to keep going to these strip joints, too? You're a long way from twenty-five. When are you going to grow up?"

"Jesus, Diana, are we having a full-blown crisis here? I mean, I know I've been horrible, but if you can just suffer through the beachfront home, the big boat, the Mercedes, and the money, I'm sure I can work on improving. Oh, and did I mention the lifetime Sailing Club membership, and the fact that you don't work?"

"Don't be dramatic. You know what I mean. And did I hear you mention money? Have you checked your balances lately?"

"Gee, let me think," said Lee sarcastically, "only when I have to pay the hair dresser - excuse me - hair *designer,* the manicurist, the pedicurist, the massage therapist, the tanning salon, and, let me think, oh yeah, did I mention the *yoga* instructor?" He stopped, but with the beer-influenced belief and satisfaction that he had hit all the pertinent points.

Diana went to the door, spun around. "Like I said, Lee, you're so dramatic."

Late afternoon sun emerged from behind the last black cloud of the gulf squall that had ended Azalea's one hundred year rainless Carnival tradition. A flight of gulls patrolled the deserted downtown parade route, screeching. Abandoned floats, piles of Mardi Gras trinkets, food wrappers, drink containers, handbills, occasional clothing, and all matters of human festival refuse littered the small city in every direction.

Traffic clogged the highway along the beach; the police patiently waived through all but the most hopelessly hammered drivers. People gradually reentered the parade route, searching for their stuff. "Looks like a tornado came through, or a waterspout," someone announced, and that became the new legend.

Lee's party overflowed his house, into the front yard. The neighbors whom had not joined the party made their annual calls to the police, complaining about parking, noise, life. They were ignored.

Kiger dispensed drinks with machine precision. Sarah and Diana sipped wine in the kitchen, behind Kiger and the thirsty crowd. "How does he do it? Isn't he blind?," whispered Sarah to Diana.

"It's magic," said Kiger, over his shoulder.

Unfazed, Sarah said, "Sorry to talk behind your back, Mr. Kiger, but, you must admit, it's a fair question."

"It is," said Kiger, pouring. "The trick is to be organized."

"Don't you ever make a mistake?"

"Yes. Sometimes, some smartass switches labels on the bottles."

"But how…"

Kiger turned, filled her and Diana's glasses, laughing.
"Asshole," said Sarah, and she laughed, too.

The noisy crowd occupied all available space in the house.
With the stereo still blaring its way through Lee's rock and
roll collection, conversation outside the kitchen was only
accomplished by close-quarter yelling. Lee, having now consumed
a few shots of tequila, was drunk enough to be conciliatory. He
noticed Nick Bonacelli pull a cigar from his linen blazer pocket,
and walk out the front door.

Lee wove through the crowd, and followed Bonacelli onto
the front porch. The sun had disappeared; its last light faded
over the white beach, brown waters of the sound, and Cat Island,
crouching ominously on the horizon. The front yard was deserted.

"Nick," said Lee, "I'm sorry about, uh, whatever I said at the
parade."

Bonacelli set his drink on a porch rail, lit his cigar with
deliberation, then stared at Lee, insolent, silent.

Lee said, "I'm offering an apology, Mr. Bonacelli. And
welcoming you to my home, and the coast."

Bonacelli drew the cigar, letting the smoke curl from his
mouth. He picked up his drink, sipped, still not responding.

Irritated, Lee said, "Look, pal, I'm *trying* to be nice, because
Diana asked me to. If you want to be a jerk, you can leave."

Bonacelli leaned close, spoke directly into Lee's face, "You
have no idea who you're fucking with."

Lee moved Bonacelli back, with his forearm. "Yeah, I heard
the rumors. I'm not scared."

"You rednecks, you're too stupid to be scared. I can make you
disappear."

Lee sighed. "Here we go with the dumb Southerner thing
again. Well, let me tell you something, Bonehead. I can make *you*

disappear, too." He snatched Bonehead's drink away, and pushed him toward the porch steps.

Bonehead glanced around for Sarah, then prudently left alone.

A couple of hours later, Lee changed into a swimsuit, and jumped in the huge hot tub. Boot had long since left, along with most of the crowd. The patio lights were off, and the night air was cool. The sky was perfectly black, dotted with millions of stars, planets, galaxies. In the east, the moon had risen, full and glowing white. Lee could see its craters. He cranked up the bubbles, and floated alone, until Dahlia slid in. "Mr. Farrell, am I causing trouble for you?," she said, removing her shorts under cover of the roiling water, and placing them with her foot into one of Lee's hands.

Lee said, "Well, no, what makes you think…," her panties arrived in his other hand.

Dahlia said, "Because, the *last* thing I want is for you to have trouble with the wife." She took Lee's foot, placed it on her crotch. Manicured bristles tickled the bottom of his foot.

Lee closed his eyes, tried not to think.

"Lee!," Kiger yelled, from inside. Lee bolted upright, guilty. "I'm headed home, my friend."

"I'll drive you!," Lee called back, jumping out of the tub.

Kiger walked to the open French doors. "No need, I've called a taxi. I also took the liberty of seeing the rest of your guests out. Diana and Mrs. Bonacelli are all that are left. So, good evening, young lady - Dahlia, isn't it miss?"

How the hell does he know Dahlia's in the hot tub?, he thought, and said, "Thanks, dude. Um, exactly where are Diana and Sarah?"

Kiger said, "In the bedroom, chatting. Intending to get in the tub themselves, if I overheard correctly. This situation looks dangerous, even to a blind man."

"You're my eyes, babe."

"Just doing my job, sarge." Kiger left.

"I guess I should leave?," said Dahlia.

"No. Stay."

"So how come Kiger calls you 'Sarge'?"

"Long story. Not a good one."

Lee reminded himself not to talk too much, and eased back in the tub. Expecting Diana at any time, he was careful where he put his feet. He lay his head back on the edge, staring at the stars. His head swirling from drink and fatigue, he closed his eyes. His thoughts rambled, settled on his most comfortable memory: sixth grade. He was one of the smartest kids in class. Star athlete. Every boy, every girl, all his teachers loved him, told him so. Expected him to grow up to be a congressman, a senator. The governor.

It was the last pure time in his life, before he found out that other people are scared to make their own decisions, that they want you, push you to lead them, then resent you for it. Why had his father never told him that? Did he know?

Who was his *real* father? He thought about the fire that killed his adoptive parents. An assistant coach had come to Lee's door at the Mississippi State athletic dorm, sophomore year. The look on the coach's face - Lee knew at that moment that the good part was over.

In Lee's mind, years raced by, indistinguishable. The Army, the Contras, the drug runners, the stupid, deadly night at Cat Island, marrying Diana. Finally getting his undergrad degree from Tulane. A half-assed attempt at law school. Dahlia.

What an idiot, thought Lee. There is one single, inviolable rule of titty bar patronage: do not, under any circumstances, fall in love with the dancers. They provide material for your fantasies, you provide money for their insatiable consumption, and everyone goes home at two a.m. The view and the results are the same,

whether you spend five dollars, or a thousand. Every man knows
the rule, and thinks he is the exception. Lee was no different.
He had met Dahlia at a strip joint in New Orleans. Over time, he
had given her tons of money.

He peeked at her across the tub. She was gazing at the stars,
too. She was perfect. Beautiful, accessible, never bitchy. Never
had a chance to gripe about underwear on the bathroom floor.
She was the girl in his secret life's story, the one that always ended
with him heading off to South America. He had never seen her
outside a titty bar until today.

And now here was Dahlia, in his hot tub, under the stars.
With Diana right around the corner. And Dahlia was now
grabbing his foot, pulling it toward…

"Lee."

Eyes springing open, Lee jumped, sloshing water out of the
tub. It was Diana.

"Diana! Darling! I was - I was just about asleep, and…"

"Oh, hush. Help Sarah and me."

Lee's eyes re-adjusted to the darkness. Diana and Sarah were
each wearing one of his white t-shirts, and apparently nothing
else. Diana had a bottle of wine in one hand, was clutching glasses
in the other. Lee hopped out, helped them in, then got back in on
the other side of the tub. Diana was as drunk as Lee had ever seen
her, though typically still in control.

Diana said, "Elizabeth, no need to get re-dressed." She took
off her shirt, flung it over her shoulder, it splatted onto the bricks
of the patio. Sarah and Dahlia did the same.

Lee thought: *Elizabeth?*

Diana said, "Lee, I understand you and Elizabeth know each
other?"

Lee's mind paused, like a recording.

Dahlia said, to Lee, "My real name is Elizabeth."

Lee said, "Real name? Well… yeah, I may have seen Elizabeth somewhere…"

Diana said, "Before you start fibbing, Lee, you should know that Elizabeth and I had a long talk earlier this evening."

Lee would rather have left the tub, as Diana paused and poured wine for everyone. Diana resumed, "She tells me you two met once in New Orleans."

Cautiously, Lee said, "Well, Diana, you know occasionally the guys and me, we go down to the city, and… well, I've told you all about this before, haven't I?"

Dead silence.

Then, all three ladies burst out in laughter. Diana, Dahlia, and Sarah slapped hands. Realizing the three had planned this little conversation, Lee laughed too, but not comfortably. The enormity of any type of collusion between his wife and his favorite titty dancer was more than his mind was willing to process, under the circumstances.

The night air grew cooler. Steam from the tub billowed, creating an illusion of isolation for its inhabitants. The ladies conversed, while Lee gently repositioned his body, conscious of avoiding foot contact with anything human.

When he had been in the U.S. Army, Lee had been trained to kill men. Yet, as a regular man, he was completely defenseless against three beautiful, inebriated, naked women. His experience in both roles led to the same conclusion: retreat.

Relaxing on his side of the tub in a molded recliner, Lee drifted toward sleep. His final coherent thought was: *my wife, Dahlia, and the local mob boss's wife, naked. It can't get any weirder than this.*

He was wrong.

Chapter 2 - Mama Thea

Once
The morning came
To chase away dreams

In the cool gray of first light, Lee stared at the cross-stitched, wood-framed, and aged three line poem perched on his desk. Its author was Lee's childhood nanny, an old black lady from New Orleans named Althea Jones. When Lee learned to talk, he called her "Mama Thea." After that, so did everybody else.

As a child, Lee had been plagued with nightmares, afraid of sleep. When he was three or four Mama Thea wrote the short poem, telling Lee it represented hope. "Hope," she said, "is God reminding you that morning's on the way." She never said what nightmares were a reminder of.

Mama Thea found the little frame in her house in the Delta after Hurricane Katrina had wiped out Lee's house on the coast. She gave it to him, he supposed, to cheer him up. Now, it rested on Lee's desk in the guest bedroom, where he spent many sleepless nights, trying to write a novel.

Writing is what he had always pictured himself doing. There was a story hiding on the edge of his consciousness, where it had developed, and remained hidden, for years. He sat before an empty computer screen, staring out his window, watching the sunrise, hoping Apollo or Poseidon or some bored muse might rear up and tell him what to say, or at least light a fire under his ass.

He had even written fifty or sixty pages before the storm, but Katrina had destroyed all his references, and it was useless, even if he could reconstruct his computer files, which he had not, for some crazy hurricane reason, gotten out before the storm. So if he had started the rock rolling up the long hill, then Katrina had rolled it back down, crushing him and any fire he once had. For Lee, the meaning of Mama Thea's little poem had changed. He had come to think of it as his epitaph.

In the distance, the eastern end of Cat Island became fully illuminated. It was summer, months since the annual farce of Mardi Gras. Pleasant wintertime warmth had been swept aside by an onslaught of palpable gulf heat. Humidity made the air alive, and through it Lee could see the outriggers of twenty or thirty shrimp boats. Campfire smoke rose from the island.

The smoke on the island reminded Lee of high school days. His school was an ancient all-male Catholic college preparatory institute sitting on the edge of the Gulf close to Azalea, and New Orleans. Saint Thomas Academy's pupils were sons of the rich from across the nation, the largest part of whom were cunning, immoderate progeny of New Orleans. He and Jake, and many of the kids around the coast, had spent lots of weekends out there, sailing out in small, single sail vessels, camping, fishing, trying to entice girls. He let the faint, sweet recollections wash through his mind: the smell of surf, the taste of freshly cooked speckled trout. Youth.

Lee's parents had been the preeminent plantation owners in Farrell County, Mississippi, owning fifty thousand acres in the Delta, up Highway 61 between Vicksburg and Rolling Fork, in the heart of the flood plain of the Mississippi, Yazoo, and Sunflower rivers.

The Delta, formed by eons of the great Mississippi river's flood deposits, was the most fertile farm land in the world - thirty feet of rich, black topsoil. Lee's adopted father farmed cotton, corn and soybeans in it, and Lee's blood, like all Delta residents, was rich and dark like the land.

Lee's late stepfather had been an amateur historian. From Lee's earliest memories, he had hammered into Lee the history of the family around the supper table, or after church on Sunday. His predilections passed along, apparently, and Lee was an occasional student of history, himself.

The Farrells were one of hundreds of families across the Delta - some of them remote cousins, whom could trace their lineage through ages of farming the Delta mud. Their ancestors - Scots-Irish immigrants - had fled the cruel English in the early eighteenth century, sailed west, settled in what would become Virginia and the Carolinas. Hard dirt farmers, indentured field hands, and trappers, they mustered along with their rich neighbors against the English in the American Revolution.

The extended Farrell clan spent two generations migrating to Indian territory, and free land along the Mississippi River. The Mississippi Delta as a farming concern was, in those days, a mere concept. The terrain was a great tropical swamp, only minimally cleared. As they expanded their fields, the Farrells would engage in new battles, as interlopers, with the locals: alligators, moccasins, black bear, and mosquitoes. As they cleared the forest canopy, they would wonder at the giant earthen complexes of mounds left by earlier generations of the Delta's human inhabitants, grown over in the timeless flood of history.

When Mississippi became a state in 1817, Farrells lived there. They struggled against heat, flood, and malaria, working the fields, adding small tracts of land each year, growing the family legacy, inching forward. Some of their sons had only recently returned from New Orleans, having followed part-time Mississippian General Andrew Jackson to defeat the English again, at Chalmette, on the banks of Lake Pontchartrain, north of the great river city, at the end of the War of 1812. When the U.S. fought Mexico in 1847, young Farrells served under Mississippi General John Quitman, part of the command of general Winfield Scott. Farrells in that war fought beside young United States Army officers named Lee, Johnston, Jackson, Longstreet, and Grant.

In 1861, gray old Samuel Farrell was the head of the family.
He was among the last living Farrells whom had been born in
South Carolina, after the Revolution. He had served under
General Jackson, and stayed in the Delta when a brother and some
of his cousins went to Texas. He was a gentleman farmer, had been
a representative in the legislature, had help establish "Ole Miss,"
the state's university and law school at Oxford.

In recent years, he had heard the secessionist "fire eaters," men
like eventual Mississippi Governor John Pettus - whom would
gladly destroy the United States to perpetuate slavery - make their
arguments for southern independence. Sam Farrell was a slave
owner, a circumstance he regarded, uncomfortably, as simply a
matter of God's will. Yet, he knew that God's plans sometimes
changed over time, and that the concept of slavery, as a practical
economic concern, was in its last days. As a matter of morality,
Sam Farrell, like his late father's Virginia farming friend Thomas
Jefferson, believed that God's patience with the evil institution
would soon run out.

Sam also believed the existence of the United States itself
was God's will. Only miracles could have been responsible for
the results of the American Revolution, and the War of 1812,
when a bunch of untrained farmers, merchant sailors and city
dandies defeated the unmatched might of England *twice*. His
blood, the blood of the Farrell family, had helped form the bonds
of the United States. He loved his country in a manner that
only parents of a child who has nearly died, but survived, can
understand.

A rich man, Sam Farrell had sailed from New Orleans to New
York and London, witnessed the awesome beginnings of mass
industrialization, of machine replacing man. He understood that
industrialization would one day render the institution of slavery
obsolete, destroy it completely. Prior to the presidential election

of 1860, the southern states had called a meeting in Atlanta to discuss secession; he was one of Mississippi's delegates.

Like most educated Americans, he believed that the Northerners and Westerners in the United States Congress would never initiate a war, sacrifice the Union just to end slavery. Yet, he believed, they would expend all the country's considerable resources in a war to prevent the South from seceding. He also knew the English craved a third opportunity to defeat their descendant rabble in New England - finally to sail into Boston conquering, triumphant.

Sam Farrell believed northern factories and citizenry would eventually overwhelm any nation in the world through production of war machines and soldiers. He had seen their numbers, inhabitants of their cities, teeming. He also knew that the proud yankees, undefeated by any European power, indeed, by any nation, would die to prevent subjugation by an inevitable Confederate military, political, and economic alliance with England, or France, or both.

And, unlike most of his white Mississippi neighbors, Sam Farrell had met educated, articulate men of color. Men of African descent, some of them former slaves, whom were intellectually equal or superior to their former masters, a condition not considered possible by earlier white generations, European or American. In his secret heart, Sam Farrell knew that slavery really was evil, and must end soon. When the hotheaded fire eaters in Atlanta voted for secession, he voted against it.

Young Farrells did their duty in the war. They died at Corinth; some died during Mississippi General William Barksdale's mad charge upon the Union battlements at Gettysburg; others starved or died of cholera at the siege of Vicksburg. When Mississippi was hopelessly occupied, their decimated companies elected new officers, and headed east to the Carolinas and Virginia, where their ancestors had fought for independence nearly a century earlier. There, they joined the straggling remnants of Lee's Army of Northern Virginia, still defiant, fighting for an honorable armistice, or death.

Samuel Farrell did not live to witness the inexorable course of history he had foreseen. Nor did many of his extended family. One of his grandsons, a senior at Ole Miss when the war started, was killed. So was his entire senior class.

After the war, Farrell family lands were taken away by the crude military occupation of Reconstruction. Sam Farrell's heirs endured the governmental exchange of pre-war fools for post-war reconstruction thieves. The cruel military government, whose officers were bent upon revenge, caused much of the Farrell clan and their neighbors to quit the Mississippi Delta. Like their Scots-Irish forefathers, they moved West, ever fleeing the damned English and now their New England progeny. Some joined the victorious United States Army, participating for the rest of their careers in its ghastly attempt to eradicate the Native American Indian. But some stayed, endured the military occupation, pooled their monies, and got their lands back, just before the end of the century.

The big river flooded every two or three years, replenishing the land, erasing some of the blood, burying things. The Farrells flourished. They sponsored great bear hunts, hosted politicians. In bad years, during drought and pestilence, they endured. They adapted from mule to tractor, from steamship to truck. In 1927, When the Mississippi River breeched a levee around Greenville, a wall of water fifteen feet high slammed through their houses and lands, eventually leaving thirty feet of roiling muck for nearly a year. They returned, reestablished, planted, lived.

In 1973, the old river breached its levees, coursing down upon the Delta in the second Flood of the Century that century.

In between, Farrell men had volunteered, fought, and died for the United States in Korea, World War II, and Viet Nam. The survivors always returned to their farms; family lands quietly, efficiently, grew.

Lee could remember the '73 flood. He was a little boy then, catching crawfish by the hundreds. When the water finally overwhelmed the house, the Farrells headed to a Memphis hotel. He remembered the grownups crying. His own mother cried then, the only time he had ever seen that. Mama Thea said the flood was God saying the land needed cleansing. Mama Thea knew all about God.

After that great flood, many resident farmers of the Delta simply gave up. Cousins, friends, whole communities sold what was left, moved to Memphis, Vicksburg, New Orleans. The ones whom stayed then faced a new kind of disaster: withdrawal of government support. After decades of forcing farmers to produce and trade within an artificial market, the federal government simply walked away.

By the early 1980's, Lee's father had bought out all the uncles and cousins; he was the lone remaining Farrell farmer after well over a century and a half in the Delta. He had learned to survive the disastrous loss of government subsidies by becoming an expert in banking and insurance. Now, in addition to coaxing cotton, corn, and soybeans from the black buckshot mud, he wrangled loans and made investments in equipment and commodities futures; he prayed for rain while balancing equity, production, indemnity, debt. He often railed about how the Republicans had come to destroy Mississippi a second time; first Lincoln, then Reagan.

When Lee went to Saint Thomas for high school, the consolidated Farrell family lands were among the largest in the Delta. While his father fought the banks, markets, and government, Lee's life was less complicated. Perhaps his father did not want Lee to suffer the hardening desperation that is a Delta farmer's lot; maybe he just didn't want Lee in the way. In any case, he was sent to board at Saint Thomas starting in the ninth grade, and there he spent his high school years, except summers.

As the sun rose further, completely illuminating Cat island, Lee remembered those days in high school. He had met Jake the first day. The two spent the next four years in constant company. Lee was shy, athletic, with a secret love of reading. Jake was the loud, crass son of a local sheriff, with no secrets, and a love for everything, especially drinking, and girls.

Lee learned much at Saint Thomas, most of it extracurricular. He discovered beer and pot, and developed the ability to lie with perfect composure. Students at Saint Thomas were obsessed with family financial status - a quality which conferred in direct proportion, social status upon the students themselves. Lee always fared well in these inquiries, since he was the only child of a rich Delta farm family. Perhaps as a result of the immutable family scrutiny, Lee began to question his own origins.

He did not look like either parent. He was tall, they were average in stature. He had brown hair and eyes, they, red and blue. His father had been accessible, instructive, but never overly boastful of Lee's athletic accomplishments, the way southern fathers are. His mother had been neither compassionate nor neglecting. She made sure Lee had the best clothes and birthday parties, and that he attended church and elementary school on a fairly regular basis. Lee was expected to garner such information as was necessary from these associations to survive and prosper academically, socially, and otherwise. But she never showed the avaricious pride of most southern well-to-do mothers. Even when Lee earned top grades, his parents failed their expected duty to overreact.

Lee's curiosity developed into suspicion that he was not the natural child of the Farrells. He got a copy of his birth certificate from the school administration, which indicated his birthplace, Greenville, Mississippi, and his parents, the Farrells. Still curious, Lee called his one true, unconditional ally: Mama Thea. Mama Thea would not answer any questions over the phone. She visited Lee, and his life changed.

Mama Thea said the Farrells could never have their own children, that Mr. Farrell had some condition that prevented it. Lee was adopted, she had actually gotten him from a poor family in Memphis; God had sent him to the Farrells for some great purpose, known only to Him. That was in the spring of his junior year. Lee had refused to go home that summer. He stayed on the coast, living with Jake and his dad, Buck, the sheriff. Jake and Lee had spent much of that summer camping on Ship Island.

Lee's wandering thoughts rested upon Mama Thea. She had long since retired; the Farrells had both been killed years earlier when their house caught fire. She had been set up with a home and lifetime living expenses by the Farrell estate. Far more than his adoptive parents, Althea Jones had been the nurturing force in Lee's youth. Lee's dispassionate adopted mother had been completely preoccupied with her tennis team at the country club. Childless herself, Mama Thea had resided with the Farrells, cooking, cleaning, and raising Lee.

From Mama Thea Lee learned to read, to think, to argue, when to show compassion, humility, and anger. When he violated the rules of the house - Mama Thea's rules - it was she who spanked him. When the preacher's stories about Hell gave Lee nightmares, Mama Thea held his head in her lap until dawn. Remembering, Lee could smell her hair, and the sweet dried gardenias she used to scent her clothes. He remembered the absolute comfort and protection of her embrace, being held to her massive bosom. He had trusted her to protect him physically, and her intimate dealings with God had guarded his soul.

He thought of the irony of his youth, of children of wealthy white Southerners. Even though Mama Thea had long since had the right to enter department stores and restaurants previously reserved for whites, she still could not join the country club, or any of the ubiquitous ladies' societies interminably marking the change of southern seasons with luncheons, teas, and debutante balls. Yet, she was Lee's true mother, his source of unconditional love, his teacher of morals. How could society relegate his own mother to inferior status? How could he allow it? How could *she*?

That disturbing thought was followed by another, more timely observation: Lee was a member of the local exclusive Sailing Club, which was over a century and a half old, and without a black member. How could he countenance such a thing. Yet, how could he change it?

Diana slept in the bedroom down the hall. Since Katrina, She and Lee had steadily become distant. Not fighting, just not talking. Diana was spending most of her time with Sarah, so she said. Iris, laying next to Lee's feet, yawned, stretched. Lee had forgotten whatever it was he wanted to write that morning, what had seemed so important during the night. Turning again to the empty computer screen, he quietly, sadly, turned it off.

Six days a week, Lee Farrell drove to The Blue Stone, a nightclub he managed in Biloxi. Moving east down Highway 90, he passed miles of manmade beach the state had pumped in half a century earlier, and doggedly replenished every couple of years, despite ever hostile subtropical weather. Azalea and all the little towns along the beach between were essentially distant suburbs of New Orleans, without the muggers.

Katrina had destroyed all the coast casinos, but several
had already been built back, this time on land, and the tourists
appreciated the change. As Lee drove in midmorning, he passed
scores of buses. The trip from his home to The Blue Stone was
only a little over 20 miles, yet it sometimes took him nearly an
hour to make it. The road, indeed, the entire coast had become
clogged - *inundated* - by tourists since the advent of casino
gambling in the early 1990's.

From Chicago, Minnesota, New York, Florida and everywhere
else the weekend gamblers poured in, aloft discount airlines,
onboard overloaded tour buses, benefactors of "Special Group
Rate Discounts," possessors of coupons proclaiming "$2.99
Seafood Buffet!!!," or "Ten Dollars of *FREE** Slot Tokens," readers
of any number of "insider" manuals such as "The *Real* Way
Professional Gamblers Make a Living Off the Casinos."

He was surrounded by busses at one particularly congested
intersection when he thought about something he had recently
read - one of Roark's stories in The Mississippi Sound; it had said
that hundreds - *hundreds* - of busloads of retirees, mainly from
Florida, supplied the casinos each week, forming a base of income
without which the casinos could not survive. The article was
titled: "Feds Supply Sheep for Fleecing," and had opined that, since
most of the retirees were on fixed, governmental supplemented
income, and that statistically well over ninety percent of casino
patrons lost money, the casinos were de facto beneficiaries of
federal subsidies. Given Roark's anti-casino history, the article's
content was of suspect veracity; however, Lee had found the
sheep metaphor amusing, and the stream of tour buses and their
wrinkled cargo was undeniable.

Entering Biloxi, Lee passed through what was once known as
"The Strip," an area of backroom gambling houses and collateral
businesses: strip joints, ragtag nightclubs, x-rated video arcades,

adult bookstores, and assorted local dives populated by hustlers plotting ways to separate tourists from their money. Many of the small time crooks who used to crawl the Strip, like Flounder, had liked to refer to themselves as "The Dixie Mafia," a designation which belied their status as an organization, and one which the real Mafia in New Orleans tolerated as a bemusing diversion of attention from *their* local activities.

Legalized casino gambling had subverted the Strip; the cops had been forced to run off illegal gambling, which had been a fundamental segment of the area's economy for decades. Next went the arcades, the adult bookstores, the nightclubs, and finally, the hustlers. Remnants of the Dixie Mafia whom had not the sense to leave voluntarily were persecuted. Jail, relocation or, in rare cases, assimilation into the newly legitimized gambling economy were their stark choices.

The Strip had eventually become a conglomeration of ridiculously overpriced t-shirt and souvenir shops, low quality hotels, and gas stations, all decorated in the most garish lights and paints their budgets would allow. It was thus transformed from a place where patrons of illegal gambling houses were ripped off, to a place where patrons of *legal* gambling houses were ripped off. But Katrina had exacted another cleansing on the strip, and most of the whorehouses and massage parlors that popped up in its aftermath were kept off the beach, because they could no longer afford the beachfront real estate.

The new Biloxi Strip was further east, and composed of great multistory hotels, each with a casino. Land based casinos were made legal by the state after the floating ones had all been destroyed. Old casinos companies and new ones, like the Cronus, salvaged what they could, tore down the rest, and entered a building race that still raged. The result was hulking, multistory, garishly lighted behemoths balanced on the very shore of the Gulf of Mexico, with police officers, private security, and armies of valets marshaling hoards of vehicles in, out, through and around the hotels and casinos to the south of the only thoroughfare, highway 90, and to the parking garages and businesses on the north side.

Into this mass of activity passed Lee Farrell. At eleven a.m., the traffic was sluggish. At one of the traffic lights along the row of casinos, a dozen tour busses were in the turn lane, preparing to enter acres of asphalt parking lots surrounding "The Golden Palace" casino; a dozen or so others were pulling out the other side. Lee chuckled and thought: *sheep for the fleecing. Baa, baa, baa.*

Directly across highway ninety from Cronus Casino, set among the parking garages and hotels, and billboards proclaiming: "94% Slot Returns , GUARANTEED!," was a relatively dignified old movie theater building which had somehow survived the initial casino-related development of the nineties, then Hurricane Katrina. Now, it was a nightclub called The Blue Stone.

Lee pulled his '69 GTO convertible around back, the side facing away from the gulf, and parked. Entering The Blue Stone through the backstage area, he emerged alongside the stage, where decades earlier an enormous, partially parabolic screen had hung, displaying *Gone With the Wind* to teary locals. The theater had been built, according to legend, with federal money funneled away from a Biloxi military base, so that congressmen and senators visiting the city and its fiefdom of gambling and whorehouses would have a decent place to see a movie.

Lee strode through the darkness of what was once ground-level seating, the squeaking of his boat shoes on the black and white checkerboard marble pattern dissipating into massive indoor airspace. Emergency lights along the distant wall provided enough light for Lee to discern successive steps of each ascending level of the dance floor. It had been constructed in cascading levels to compensate for the gentle back-to-front slope of the original floor.

His office was in the old projection room, above a curved balcony. The balcony was now stadium seating of carpeted steps three or four feet wide, where the seats used to be, and where Lee was constantly dispatching bouncers to interrupt illegal or inappropriate behavior. The office was accessible by an old service elevator, another requisition from the military base, which arrived in the towering projection area near the entrance to a private screening room, built to congressional specifications. The current owners had converted the screening room to a private lounge area, with wet bar. Couches lined the walls.

Across a narrow hall, Lee's office was where the projection room itself once stood, a sizable forty-by-sixty foot area gutted from an array of old closets. The office, as well as the next door private lounge had one full wall, floor to ceiling, constructed of tinted, one-way mirrors overlooking the interior of The Blue Stone. The effect of standing over the balcony, looking three stories down upon capacity crowds of fifteen hundred was dizzying. But for vertical supports framing the one way mirrors, it looked like nothing was there. This was especially disturbing when the drunks stood five feet away, smoking joints, oblivious.

Lee flipped on the house lights at the end of the hall, and entered his office. It was designed and equipped like an efficiency apartment, with desk, computers, security video monitors, and requisite office files and machinery in one area, the balance occupied by a sitting area with couch and chairs, and a kitchenette with stove, refrigerator, and microwave, a breakfast bar with several stools. In the back was a restroom with shower.

The existence of the Blue Stone was the result of an odd conglomeration of circumstances involving federal law. First, in an effort to gain any small victory against the casinos, which coast "environmentalists" regarded as simple evil, they pounced upon the way the United States government administered its

environmental laws, and succeeded in the early days of casinos
by suing to delay the destruction of the abandoned theater, on
the contrived basis that subsequent construction on the site
would cause untold, irreparable damage to the delicate Biloxi
peninsula. They were aided in this effort by a local "historical"
society, a group of ancient gadflies whom apparently believed that
all buildings which approximated their own ages deserved to be
preserved in perpetuity.

The environmentalists had long since discovered that any
half-assed "environmental lawyer" could hold up a multi-million
dollar development for years. In the madness of 1990s investment
expectations, such delays were often not acceptable to real estate
investors; consequently, the environmentalists won a number of
relatively cheap victories. The building's former owners, a group
of local Realtors, had intended to sell the dilapidated building
to any insurgent developer associated with the casinos, thereby
converting their collective fifty thousand dollar investment to
millions. Unfortunately, the well-funded environmentalists sued,
and the Realtors quickly tired. After Katrina somehow failed
to destroy the building, they took what they could get from
insurance, and donated the damned thing to the city, who had
leased it to the current owners for a hundred years, a dollar
a year.

An apparently legitimate business entity, whose stockholders
included an accountant, an attorney, and a privately owned
Louisiana corporation, bought the building. Local officials, if they
thought about it at all, simply regarded the new owners as the
latest bunch of crazy developers funding a boondoggle. In reality,
the new owners were the Bardino crime family of New Orleans;
the accountant and attorney were its employees. A Biloxi
accountant working for the company had hired Lee, and handled
all the club's money. Otherwise, Lee was in charge.

Lee knew the rumors about the Bardinos. He had not been told any of it, but had pieced the scenario together from things he had read in the paper, things he had heard in the club, and pure unqualified conjecture.

Lee did not necessarily need the job; he had never been without money in his life. Though he was the owner of his parents' huge farm, the whole thing was in a trust that paid him. It still was run by his father's old foreman. But after a childhood of watching his father worry about the rain, he never quite trusted the long term efficacy of farming. So he always tried to stay busy, just in case.

Lee had quit law school several years earlier, had started a charter fishing business. But it only generated enough money to pay for fishing trips, and Lee had turned the business, such as it was, over to Boot. He bartended here and there, managed a couple of local joints. He'd been told about the job at the Stone by an attorney friend, and never asked many questions. The Stone, as it turned out, paid very well.

The name "Blue Stone" came from the huge blue sapphire in a thick display case in the in the theater's lobby. Lee's primary duty was to keep the club full of people. That's all he had ever been told: keep it packed. It had to show a *lot* of income. So noon to 4:00 a.m., seven days a week, The Blue Stone was open.

Lee sat in his office, preparing to make another huge liquor order. Inventory did not really matter, he ordered the maximum allowed by the state every time. The Blue Stone had long since broken every Mississippi sales record, and was something of a legend among the state liquor police, who controlled the flow of whiskey for all of Mississippi since most of the state emerged from Prohibition.

Jake had told him once that the Bardinos probably used the Stone to launder drug money or whatever they were stealing. Lee had to order so much liquor, wine and beer to account for the volume of "sales," that much of it supposedly had to be carted to New Orleans, where it was sold in Bardino owned clubs in the French Quarter, or on the streets.

He looked across his desk, through the dimly lit expanse of the club. Cages with gold plated bars protruded from the walls on both sides of the room, far above the floor. They would soon be occupied by the squad of feature dancers Lee maintained for crowd entertainment. Dancers dressed in as little as the law would allow, usually less.

Years earlier, he had learned the singular axiom of the bar business: *bucks follow does*. The crude rule meant that the prudent bar manager should keep as many ladies around as possible, by whatever means necessary, to attract men. All men are vested with the hearts of suckers. Even the most accomplished, educated, or experienced of their number are reduced to alcohol-swilling, money-squandering idiots by the remotest chance of getting laid. The introduction of overpriced liquor into the environment was, Lee had come to realize, simple economic genius.

At the other end of the room below was the stage, where bands thrashed around on some nights, and which was part of the massive dance floor every other night. A huge deejay booth protruded from the upper back wall of the stage, where the top of the movie screen used to be, and where a parade of disc jockeys spun the most annoying dance music Lee could imagine.

The circular bar in the center of the floor was the core of all activity in the Stone, where businessmen and businesswomen, lawyers, secretaries, and assorted hustlers and losers would start showing up after work, then give way to the hard core all nighters, drug dealers and consumers, divorcees and late shift casino employees that made up the Stone's main clientele. It was headquarters for one of the Stone's famous attractions: Kiger, the blind Jamaican bartender, who had just entered the back door, the same one Lee had come in, and was going about setting up the bar in his preternatural way.

The club's most noted feature was a network of huge video screens which broadcast live, real time images from other dance clubs around the country. Each participating club had set up internet video, so desperate losers in one club could gawk at gullible posers in other clubs.

Lee checked his liquor order forms, then his messages. He had another one from Bonehead, which the bartender who took it had checked "urgent." That was about the sixth one he had gotten since Mardi Gras, and he threw it in the trash, like the others. If Mr. Bonacelli wanted to talk, he could come to the club. Bonacelli and the Mafia be damned, he wasn't going to be called on the carpet by anyone.

After a while, he had finished most of his immediate tasks. He idly watched Kiger go about his business, and the back door slowly opened again, shooting a knife of white light across the floor of the Stone. He looked at his watch: 3:30, time for Meat, the head bouncer, to be showing up. But the figure now silhouetted in the door did not resemble Meat's massive, muscular frame, and the intruder certainly was not one of the dancing girls. Lee slowly slid open the bottom drawer of his desk, reaching for the 9mm pistol he kept there. Then he squinted, paused, momentarily quit breathing. It was Mama Thea.

He rushed downstairs, hugged her, could feel that the solid mass of her body had somehow *diminished*. She was always short, but she had gotten shorter. Her gardenia smell was less like the green Delta, more like… a parlor.

"Mama Thea! What are you doing here?," said Lee.

"Baby," she said, "Mama needs to sit down somewhere."

"Here, let's go up to my office. What in the world are you doing here?"

"Hush, child, Mama's got to get off her old feet first. Then, we'll talk."

He led her to the elevator, up to the office.

"Baby," she said. "Sit down. Settle down." He did, at his desk. She slowly lowered into a small chair beside the desk, the one employees sat in when they were hired, or fired. Lee tried to get up, help her. She stopped him, gesturing, the palm of her hand toward him, like a traffic cop.

Her hair was now completely white, making the tone of her face even darker. Her eyes, the black pupil indistinguishable from the brown iris, were frightening in their calm resolution; Lee feared their fixation even now.

She said, "Baby, I'm dying."

Lee started to mouth something. She stopped him again.

"It's cancer, child, I didn't want to tell you on the telephone."

He slowly stood, went to her, took her worn hands in his, stooping, he kissed her on top of the head, hugged her, felt himself welling up.

"That's enough, Lee. Come on, get up." She pushed him away. "I didn't raise you to be acting like a little boy. Get up."

Lee went back around the desk, plopped into his chair, nearly overturning. "Is there any chance?"

She smoothed her linen dress where Lee had wrinkled it, around the bottom. "No chance, son."

What about the doctors? I can get you over to Houston, they've got the best …"

"Ain't gonna help. The doctors in Greenville know what they're doing."

"But Mama, they've got better facilities in Houston, better research."

"Lee, I'm old. Tired. It's my time. I ain't goin' to any more doctors."

Lee said, "When…?"

"Right away, child. You won't be seeing Mama after this, after I go home today."

Lee absorbed this. "How did you get here? You didn't take a stupid bus?"

"No, child, one of the men from church, the Youth Minister drove me, he's outside waiting."

"Tell him to come in, I'll get Kiger to…"

"Lee. The Youth Minister will not come in here."

Lee looked confused.

"In this place. A place like this," she said, gesturing.

Lee understood, had a flash of anger at the hypocrisy he remembered from his youth, how the good white Delta Baptists would never drink in front of each other, or dance, but would run off to Memphis, or New Orleans, thinking that no one would know, briefly forgetting that God knew everything, even the number of hairs on their heads.

But Mama had faith. She was always exempted from Lee's religious scorn, even when she misquoted the Bible because her preacher did, or when she responded to Lee's young skepticism about what *his* preacher had said - she was black, and therefore not welcome in his church - by trying to explain how God was perfect, and created man from dirt, but that man was *imperfect*, and invented sin, and that God was not responsible for sin, because He didn't invent it, man did. Or how Jonah could actually live inside a whale without suffocating, or how two of every animal on the whole Earth had gotten on one boat, because these things were God's will, except for the sin, and part of God's Great Plan that humans were not to question, or try to understand, but to obey.

And ironically, all these years later, Lee knew that he was secretly still afraid to not simply obey.

"Child."

He snapped back to reality.

"Lee. I have some things to tell you." Her great black eyes were welling up, she pulled out a perfectly starched, laced cotton handkerchief, dabbed her eyes, something he had rarely seen. "I have not been truthful. Mama has lied… allowed you to be lied to. Baby, please don't hate Mama, or be mad."

"What are you talking about, Mama? I could never hate you."

"Lee." She drew in a breath, let it out slowly, fixed her endless gaze directly in his, which he could barely endure. "You were adopted, as you know."

"I know, Mama, Pop and Mom and you got me from Memphis. You told me."

"I lied," she blurted. "I found you, baby. I … got you from your real mama. They were going to let you die, or kill you."

"Who…?"

She was crying now, and pulled something, a big medallion with a thick leather string, out of her purse. "See? This was with you, around you, to scare off the spirits, they wanted to hurt you, to kill you, and I couldn't stand it, I had to take you back to the Delta, to the Farrells, because I couldn't keep you, I was too young, and had no money, and the Farrell's didn't have no children, and were rich."

Lee stood up, she stopped talking.

"Mama, come over here, sit on the couch," said Lee. He directed her toward the leather couch, turned on a lamp next to it. He went to the bar and got a glass of water, gave it to her. She composed herself. He sat down. "Now," he said, "tell me. From the beginning."

She had settled down, was through crying. She fixed the gaze upon him, but this time he did not waiver. His eyes were now upon hers, commanding. This time, she diverted her gaze, and she appeared to shrink into the leather, if only a little.

"Child. Lee." She looked at him again, her eyes, soft, without menace, or mystery. "You did not come from Memphis. You came from down here, from over in New Orleans. Your real mama was a young lady, a beautiful young girl, and she was only fifteen or so when you were born."

"How the hell do you know…?"

"Child, don't curse. Let Mama finish. Your real mother was what we - what they used to call a *Mamissa*." She stopped, hoping for a question, or an interruption. None came. "A … hoodoo priestess. What white folks call voodoo."

Lee got up, couldn't really feel his legs, forced himself across the office to the bar, poured himself a glass of water. "Go ahead," he said, like a question.

"Baby, are you mad?"

"Go ahead," he snapped, then: "I'm sorry Mama, please, finish."

"She was … beautiful. They called her Camellia, because she was so white, like the flower. Just like her mother, and *her* mother, maybe - they said. They were all Creole. And they were very powerful people."

Lee slumped into the couch, looked at his feet.

Mama Thea paused, considered how to tell it. "Lee. Your folks, at least your real mama's folks, are all, were all… well, lots of folks in New Orleans thought your mama, she was a kind of witch. And they were afraid of her, 'cause she could supposedly call up the spirits…"

Lee snorted, stood up. For the first time in his life, he looked at Mama Thea like she was, well, superstitious. Or senile. He said, "Aw come, on, Mama Thea, who told you this? Hell, every silly tourist in New Orleans gets told some damned voodoo story the first ten minutes they're in the French Quarter."

"Son, I wish you would quit using that language."

"I'm sorry, Mama. It's just, there are dozens of places in New Orleans where you can go and get a spell put on your boss, or your landlord, or whatever. It's just stuff they tell tourists to make money off 'em, sell trinkets. Who's the famous one? Marie Laveau? There are probably six or eight different places in the French Quarter that claim to be where she used to live. It's all a bunch of baloney."

"It is true that they make up stories, lie to the tourists, like you say. But what you call voodoo is *real*. Your mama, Camellia, was *real*. She lived in New Orleans, and she was one of them. A hoodoo. A *Mamissa*, which is a kind of priestess, like I said, and very, *very* powerful."

"But Mama, if what you are saying is true, if my real mother was some kind of, of Mamissa … a Creole, or whatever, well, wouldn't that mean she was a black person?"

"That's right, son. That's what she was considered, by the law. She had some African blood in her, and French, and Indian, probably. Mostly white. She was white as you. But don't you think it's crazy that any of that matters? That a person like your real mama could have ninety-nine percent white blood and still be considered black? You know what that meant in the South, back when she was born?"

"But then, that would mean that I was a … black person to."

"Yes, baby, that's right."

Lee let the thought seep through him.

"Camellia was a black person, Lee, but real light. There's several generations of black folks in New Orleans that look white. They used to call them, ah, quadroons, and octoroons - meaning how much white blood they had in them. White men always did like those ladies, creoles. All your real grandfathers, goin' way back, were white, I guess. By the time your mama came along, she was what the creoles used to call *pas blanc*. So white that even white folks thought she was white.

"It means that even though a person is really black, they can pass for white, in the white world, if they want to. You're the same way. You've only got a drop or two of African blood in you. All the menfolk in your real mama's line had to be white, since before the war." She meant the American Civil War of 1861-1865, and he knew it, without asking. "But the crazy thing is, even counting all those white people in your family, white folks would still consider you black, if they knew."

"Mama, how do you know for sure any of this about my real mother is true?"

"Let me finish, child, I'm tired, and I've got to go home. Here's the whole thing: your real mama had the art, had inherited the reputation for power from *her* mother, who was a Mamissa, too. Everybody knew who Camellia was. And she figured out young how to make a living off it, like her mama did, like anybody would.

"Folks back then - this was in the nineteen sixties - they practiced a lot of hoodoo in New Orleans, black folks, and white folks, too. Still do. They had these big get-togethers, out by Lake Pontchartrain, and people believed… some of the people there were taken in by the spirits, and could do miraculous things."

"And you saw this?"

"Don't stop me son, I can't tell this twice. Anyhow, Camellia, she was always up in the middle of these gatherings, and could do… well, wonders. She could heal people, make people go crazy, they said she could fly, or walk on the water, if she wanted to, but I ain't saying that blasphemy is true. And she was just a young thing, a girl really, but she was beautiful, and she looked liked she was a lot older than she really was." Mama Thea took a drink of water. "Well, she had another line of business, which was something she learned from her mama, too. She…, well, she would get all dressed up, and go out on dates with these men, white men from New Orleans, or Baton Rouge, in the government, or rich folks, important men, mainly, and she would take them around, eat dinner with them, show them the city, the nightspots, show them where the best places were…"

"She was a prostitute."

"They didn't call it that. She was there to make the men look good, feel good, and they paid her a lot of money for it. If she went home with them after, that was her business. Anyway, there was a lot of gamblin' back in them days up here, on the Mississippi coast, over in Biloxi, different places. There was another place, out there on the west end of the coast, by Azalea, on that big bay, that had a bunch of gambling houses. I heard about this, everybody knew about it, but I never did go there. Miss Camellia, she would go with the men sometimes up the old highway, Highway 90, I believe, right out of New Orleans, up to Ladnier Point, where they would gamble. They would get out of New Orleans to do it, because many of them were important government men, and didn't want to get in the papers, if the police came. Some of them were scared of the Italians, the Mafia, and wanted to get out of town, away from them. Some of them *were* the Mafia. Anyhow, that's where they went, most of 'em, and that's where I heard your mama met your real daddy."

"You know who…"

She stopped him with her raised hand. "He was a man on the Mississippi coast, that's all I know. She got pregnant, and he wouldn't have nothing to do with it, with you. I heard he was going to kill her and you, too. At least that's what *she* said. She had to get rid of you, to keep her and you both from getting killed. She didn't want to, it 'most ruined her to do it. She told everybody you were dead."

Lee was more skeptical than when she had started. He said, "OK, suppose all this is true. How did you find me, get me, or whatever?"

She did not look at Lee, closed her eyes for a minute, could have been praying. She then handed the necklace she had been gripping to Lee. "I got you from *her*. Camellia."

"*How?*"

"The rest of the hoodoo people, some way older, and more powerful in the community than your mama Camellia, were afraid she was going to get them all in trouble with this business about your real daddy. They were going to make her get rid of you. So she came up with this plan. She fooled them into believing she had killed you, up by Lake Pontchartrain. I took you back to the Delta. You had that" - she pointed at the necklace - "wrapped around you when she gave you to me. She told me I could never come back to New Orleans, and I ain't been back since."

"She gave me to you, just like that?'

"Well, I didn't see her, exactly. It was too dangerous. She left you in a place we had agreed upon."

"Out by Lake Pontchartrain."

"Yes."

"Alone."

"Yes, for a while. It couldn't be helped, baby, and it saved your life."

"I don't mean to seem ungrateful, Mama Thea, but this is a little... much. I can't believe you wouldn't tell me before now. It makes me wonder, well, if this is true."

"Baby," she sighed, "child, your Mama Thea is very old. I am probably senile. But what I am telling you is true."

"How did you know this Camellia?"

"From New Orleans. I grew up across Esplanade from the French Quarter. I didn't have no brothers and sisters, and my mama was a widow lady. My daddy got killed in some kind of knife fight down by the river, by the French Market, when I was just a little bitty baby. That's what I heard from other people, mama never said nothin' about it. I grew up there, and I married a young man from Memphis when I was barely a young lady.

"We went off to Memphis, and he died, right off. Back in them days, lots of folks got the fever every year, and he got it and died. Well, I couldn't move back home with *my* mama, being myself a widow lady, I was ashamed, you know, so I went down to Greenville, Mississippi, in the Delta, 'cause I heard they had rich families there, and liked to hire young black ladies to take care of the house. I did that, and I worked for some of the families around there, and when I got time off, I'd go back to New Orleans, to see mama, and my friends." She smoothed her dress, patted an imaginary errant hair.

"Baby, we grew up with hoodoo. People believed that the African spirits followed African folks over here in the slave days, to protect them, to stay with 'em because they were ancestors, spirits of ancestors that had been with them all their lives, since the beginning of time. The black people, the Africans, believed these spirits could be called up in certain ways, to do good. Some folks could get them to do bad, too, if the spirits wanted to. Anyway, I was raised to believe these things, and whenever - back in the days I'm telling' you about - I would go back to New Orleans, I would go and consult with the Mamissas to see, well, to get advice, stuff like that."

"And these big gatherings out by the lake?"

"I went to some of those, too, baby, but I ain't here to talk about that."

"So you really believe in that stuff, Mama?"

"Lee, I believe in Satan, the devil himself, but I don't believe in what he says, or does. Jesus Christ was put on this Earth by God the Father to fight the devil, and save us from the silliness we do when we mess with him, his kind. Some of the folks, the hoodoos, they call up evil, by accident, and they don't know what they're doing. I ain't got to believe what those hoodoos do is *right*, but don't *you* believe that what they do is fake. Most white folks don't know it, but the hoodoos started the Civil War, to free the slaves. That's how strong they were."

"Come on, Mama, you don't really believe…"

"Think about it. *White* folks went out, got *killed*, thousands and thousands of 'em, and the President, Mr. Lincoln got killed, too, because of it, and why? To let people like me go. Like us. Like *you*."

"Well, there was more to it than that."

"No, child. That's what happened. It happened, and the hoodoos did it. They were strong then, and they still are. That's why I had to come tell you about your real Mama." She gestured toward the necklace, which Lee held. "Hand me that thing." He did.

The amulet was dark wood, not perfectly round, convex on top, like an upside down dish, and ringed with an edge of dull metal. It was studded with a pattern of small rocks or beads, and different colored metal pieces, painted in a splash of faded colors. There was a twisted metal cross in the middle. Not a Christian symbol, but more like an "X" standing on one leg, that looked like it could be gold.

Mama Thea said, "This is what they call a hoodoo *hand*, or *gris gris*. It's to keep off the spirits, or people, or to remind somebody of something, or warn 'em. I don't know exactly what it means. But I know it's strong, and your real mama thought you needed some powerful protection." She held it up. "The marks on it all mean something to the hoodoos, to the spirits, and to you. She wouldn't have left it with you if you didn't need it."

"What do you think I need it for, Mama? You brought it here."

"Son, Lee, I honestly don't know if it means anything or not. I just couldn't… I did not want to die with a lie on my lips, in my soul. That's all."

Lee let his breath out slowly. He said, "You said this Camellia, my - mother - had a plan. What was it?"

"By the time Camellia found out she was pregnant, I had met the Farrells and was working for them, down that way. Your daddy hired me on full time to keep the house, and cook for him and Mrs. Farrell. They let me live in the old house, upstairs, and gave me all kinds of nice things, was very kind, let me take vacations twice a year. Anyway, I was down in New Orleans when all this business came up with Camellia." She stopped, took a sip of water, seemed to try to catch her breath, coughed.

Lee said, "Are you okay? Do you need to rest?"

"No, baby. This is why I came. I got to get through this, so I don't keep the minister waiting." She took a deep breath. "Camellia was in serious danger. Everybody knew that she had gotten pregnant by this man up in Mississippi, and that he wanted to kill her. They did things like that, back then. Anyway, she had put a terrible gris gris on him, a curse that was meant to kill him. The hoodoo people were afraid that if he found her, and you, it would make bad trouble for everybody. And they didn't want it. So Camellia was afraid for herself, and for you. She was afraid of the hoodoo people, that they might try to do something to you. So she came up with an idea.

"When you were still brand new, she told them she was going to take you up to the lake, which they naturally took to mean to kill you, to protect everybody from trouble. Killing people, the hoodoos don't normally do. Well, most of them. But they knew she had this power, and they were scared of her. Nobody stopped her, or followed. She went up there, and left you, out by the lake, just like we planned."

"My mama had died, and I was in New Orleans for her funeral. I was getting ready to go back home to Mississippi. Camellia told me ahead of time where you would be, and we had agreed that I would take you off with me. We had agreed to leave you out there for a while, in case somebody *did* follow her, so I wouldn't get caught. We were plenty scared of these people, the hoodoos, and of your real daddy, who they say would have shot anybody that got in his way.

"Anyhow, so I went by there and got you, right where you was supposed to be, out by the lake, and I was praying that somebody else, or a 'gator, or a moccasin hadn't got there before I did. But there you were, and you had this, this gris gris wrapped all around you, and so I kept it ever since."

"You know, that was right after that bad storm, Hurricane Camille, came through the Mississippi coast. Everything was destroyed, just a mess. Anyway, a lot of the hoodoos thought it was Camellia that somehow caused that hurricane to hit Mississippi, to kill your real father. That was the worst hurricane ever, at the time."

"Do you still believe this Camellia made a hurricane hit the coast?"

"I ain't got no arguments with your mama, then or now. She had the power to do it."

"You say 'then or now.' Where is she?"

Mama Thea picked up her glass of water, took a sip, placed it back upon the side table. "I'm sorry, son, but she's dead. Been dead for a long time."

Lee snorted. "Dead? Hell, she wouldn't be but, what, in her fifties, at the oldest."

I heard she moved up north, to Chicago, to get away from the other hoodoos. They wasn't happy with her, you know, because they thought she had made that hurricane, and killed you."

"Okay, so what happened to her?"

"They said she caught a fever, and died, Lee. That's all I know."

"They said? Who said?"

"The people, the hoodoo people in New Orleans."

"But you never went back to New Orleans, right?"

"Baby, news travels up the river, as well as down it."

"That's it? That's all you know?"

"That's it, son. She's dead."

Lee put both hands on his head, looked at the ceiling for a minute. "What about this man on the coast, my 'real daddy', as you say. What's his name - where is he?"

"I do not know, child."

Lee, getting agitated, said, "Well, what was Camellia's real name?"

"I told you everything I know, child. I don't know her first or last name. Never did."

Lee paced over toward the glass partition, looked out over the club, where a few early customers had trickled in. He turned back to Mama Thea. "How come you know all this other stuff - you grew up down there, in New Orleans, right? You don't know her name? Come on, Mama, please, tell me the whole truth."

"Honey. Baby. You've got to understand when and where we're talking about. Camellia learned her business from her mama. Camellia's father was a white man, probably a tourist from somewhere, and she never knew him. Who knows if that child went to school, or even had a birth certificate. This was back when we didn't have the kinds of rights we have today. People worked however they could. Camellia would naturally not use her real name, because of the police and so forth, you know. Plus, different folks used the same fake name. It's to confuse people, you know, if you don't need them to know who you really are. In the French Quarter, folks did not want to know each other that well. People had to get by, however they could."

Lee digested this. "Well…what about this voodoo stuff? You still doing that?"

"Oh no, child, I gave that up after I got you, I was, well, scared of Camellia too. Scared she might come looking for you, want you back some day."

"This is all… crazy."

"Son, I know this is hard on you. I wish mama could make it not be true. But it is, and you've got to trust me, stay away from the whole thing. And don't believe hoodoo doesn't exist. It does, and it's dangerous. When the Farrells sent you down here to the coast, to go to high school, I almost died, because, of course, they didn't know exactly where you were really from. I had told them I got you from a poor white couple. They were happy to have you, and we all decided not to tell you anything, until you were grown, because we loved you so much. Of course, you figured it out too soon."

Lee considered this for a moment, felt a wave of bitterness. "Mama, I do love you, but I honestly don't know if I believe any of this. Are you sure you are remembering things that really happened? And how come you don't know the name of this man from the coast? That doesn't seem realistic to me. Plus, it's worse than not knowing. Can't you think of anything else? It seems like you aren't telling me everything."

"That's all I know, son. I'm telling you now, because you're a grown man, and because I don't want to go to Jesus with these things on my conscience. Promise Mama that you will not try to find that man, your real father."

Lee looked in her eyes, could see her power fading. "So he wasn't killed in Hurricane Camille?"

"She didn't think so, son. That's how I got you."

Lee stared. "I can't," he said, turning. He noticed downstairs the jerk Flounder had walked in. He turned back to Mama Thea. "Please tell me. Is there anything else? Are you sure you don't know this person - my 'real daddy' as you say - did you ever hear his name? Think hard, Mama."

She looked up at Lee. "No, son, I do not know, I ain't ever known, the name of your true father. Maybe he's dead, maybe not. If you trust your Mama Thea, you will not try to find out. Camellia told me he was evil."

Lee had walked her out the front entrance, avoiding the small crowd at the bar. He kissed her, hugged her. She wouldn't let him help her into the car. They pulled away, and that was it. Lee was too numb to think about anything, headed back through the back door to the bar, forgetting momentarily about Flounder being there.

Lee had not seen Flounder, or heard of him outside the "Local Arrests" section of the paper in several years, until recently. He had heard through Diana, who was spending all her time with Sarah, that Bonacelli had recently hired Flounder to be on the Cronus Casino security staff, but that his primary job was to drive Bonehead's private car.

Though while in school Lee had never participated in teasing Flounder, and had never considered him an enemy, he was aware that Flounder considered *him* an enemy, and was necessarily wary. Lee marveled at how much he and the guy still looked alike. Without saying anything, he walked up to the bar.

Kiger turned around from his register, said, "You need any help, sarge, let me know."

"How the hell do you know it's me?," said Lee. "I never can figure that out."

Kiger laughed, poured a brandy, reached over, plucked a paper beverage napkin from the top of a pile, spun it in the air just above the bar. It landed in front of a young lady just off the early shift at the casino. Kiger set the snifter in the middle of it, then spun and leaned on the bar in front of Lee.

"Amazing," said Lee, trying to smile, as if it mattered.

"What's got you so sad, boss?"

"You wouldn't believe it. I'm not sure I do. I'll tell you about it later." He looked around, the crowd was starting to fill out with early drinkers.

"Did you notice your evil twin come in?," said Kiger.

"Yeah, I did. What does he want?"

"Says he wants to speak to the boss. That's you."

"Well, tell him to come over. I'm not moving."

"Just sit tight. I think he's coming now."

Lee looked over Kiger's shoulder, saw Flounder coming around the bar, looked back at Kiger, who flashed a grin, spun, walked away. Lee thought: *how the hell does he do that?*

Flounder walked up to Lee, wearing a double-breasted Italian suit, new shiny black leather loafers with tassels, and a fake gold Rolex watch, like tourists wear to the casinos, to get some *respect*, dammit. He said, "Well, hello, Mr. Star Athlete, how's the fuckin' bartending business?" He chuckled at himself. "Who would've guessed, a rich boy like you, big scholarship quarterback, reduced to bartending?"

Lee said, "I never said I was a rich boy, Isaiah, and I'm the manager, not the bartender."

"Oooooh! Sorry to insult you. The bar *manager*, not the bar*tender*. I forgot, you got the blind Jamaican to help you."

Lee noticed Kiger stop wiping the bar, several feet away. Lee said, "Isaiah, I can arrange for him to throw your ass out of here, if you like."

"You can call me 'Flounder' to my face, since you call me that behind my back, asshole. And who's gonna throw me out, this guy?" He thumbed over his shoulder toward Kiger, who had moved along the bar and was now directly behind him.

Kiger said, "You want this swine outside, boss?"

Flounder flinched, startled.

Lee said, "Isaiah, I mean, Flounder, it may surprise you to learn that I don't call you anything behind your back; in fact I haven't even thought of you in years until I recently heard, quite by accident, that you were the new driver for Nick Bonacelli. Hell of a career move. How did you manage it?"

"What do you mean, 'driver'?," said Flounder.

"Oh, I'm sorry, *chauffeur*," said Lee, turning to Kiger, "I'm alright Kiger, I'll let you know if I need anything."

Flounder snorted. "Yeah, he *better* back off. And I ain't no fuckin' chauffeur, either. I'm a *security specialist*, and I'm here to deliver you a message from *the boss*."

An outburst from across the bar diverted their attention. A drunk from one of the casinos had ambled in, demanded a drink, and Kiger was calmly refusing to serve him. The drunk screamed, "Are you *kidding* me? What do you mean, 'too drunk'? I'm from Las Vegas, mister!" He wheeled around to the handful of other patrons. "That's *Las Fucking Vegas*, you bumpkins! You *hillbillies*! We got *real* casinos, not these goddamn ..." he apparently lost his train of thought, which made him madder. "Goddammit!," he finished up, "I come down to Mississippi, lose a fuckin' fortune, and I can't have a drink? *Bullshit!*"

Lee walked around the bar, said, "Sir, you may not have noticed, but this is not a casino. Now, you've obviously had too much. Let me call you a cab."

"I will *not*! I'm not leaving here until I get at least *one damn drink*!" He slapped the bar, for emphasis. "Maybe two!"

Lee said, "Sir, I'm going to ask you one more time."

"You tell this guy in the shades, this big, ugly sumbitch right here ,"- he was pointing at Kiger - "to get me a drink *right n* -"

Kiger's right fist had popped him on the chin, just enough to knock him out, and so quick that Mr. Las Vegas never saw it. Lee caught him, and dragged him over to one of the tables, set him in a chair, his head on the table. Lee went back to the bar. "Good work, Kiger. Call him a cab, would you?"

"Already did, boss," said Kiger, hanging up the phone. A few of the bar patrons clapped, mainly the ladies, and Kiger bowed.

Lee returned to Flounder. "I'd love to sit around and catch up on old times, Flounder, but as you can see, I have other jerks to deal with, and I'm sure you have some laundry or something to pick up."

"Very funny, asshole. And don't think I'm scared of your blind bartender, either. Here's the deal. Mr. Bonacelli wants to see you. Right away. That's the message."

"Well, Flounder, you can tell your boss that he's welcome, like everybody else, to come on in The Blue Stone at any time, during business hours, and maybe I'll have a chit-chat with him, if I'm not busy. You can leave now."

"I am leaving, asshole, but not because *you* say so. You better drop by and see Mr. Bonacelli, and soon" He walked away, stopped, turned back. "Oh yeah, Farrell, since you mentioned it, I do want to get together and go over old times, one day soon. Real soon." He left.

Back upstairs in his office, Lee pondered the day. Incredible. Mama Thea, Flounder, Bonehead. What else? There was one knock on the door, followed immediately by it swinging open. It was Meat, the head bouncer. Lee said, "This better be good news, Clarence."

Meat looked back out the door, closed it quickly, said, "Come on, Lee, don't call me that."

Lee laughed. Meat had grown up in the Delta, close to the Farrells. Lee had known him since elementary school. He was from a family of famous ruffians named Brown, several boys, whose father had gotten whiskey drunk and run off to Vicksburg with a lady from another church. Many Delta boys paid the price of Mr. Brown's sins when the Brown brothers - there were eight of them, as far as anybody could tell - took up a tradition of pounding the hell out of anyone who asked where their daddy was.

Meat's mother had named him Clarence, an indignity his estranged father could not bear, not only because it was the name of her old high school boyfriend, an illogically perceived infidelity, but also because it was the all-time candy-assed name for a boy. Clarence picked up the nickname 'Meat' from his older brothers, who liked to see how much of it they could stuff into him at mealtime. He grew to be the toughest of all the Browns, went off to work on the oil rigs, and rode Harleys.

He was not allowed to park his current Harley at The Blue Stone, a general order of the mystery owners, so he drove his 1968 Camaro to work every day. It was black, had been customized in every conceivable way, had a huge yellow and red flame painted the full length of the car. It had eighteen inch wide back tires, and a florescent orange bumper sticker he'd gotten the last time he rode his Harley to Sturgis that said, "FUCK COPS." When Lee had been hired to run the Stone, he tracked down Meat, who had socked away plenty of money, and was ready to get off the rigs, anyway.

Lee was the only one who knew his real name, other than the mystery accountant who issued all their paychecks. Besides being as big as a doorway, Meat was a perfect bouncer, because he did not drink alcohol, and was levelheaded, for a Brown. This had saved the health of hundreds of men whom would have been maimed, or killed, if he had liked whiskey like his old man, and his brothers.

Lee and Meat had short meetings a couple of times a week to discuss security issues. Lee said, "I've already had a heck of a day. I'm going home. Anything new I need to know about?"

Meat slumped on the couch. "Nah. Threw a couple drunks out last night. One of the cage dancers, uh, Margaret, got drunk last night, and stripped butt naked. I got her out of there, but she damn near fell down the stairs."

"Still naked?"

"Oh, yeah. Still naked when she got in her car. Wouldn't take a cab."

"You fired her, of course."

"Of course."

"Hiring her back tomorrow?"

Meat laughed. "Already called her. She'll be in Friday."

"You're good. Anything else?"

"Yeah, one thing. There's this new drug floating around."

"What, some kind of speed?"

"No, this is something completely different. It's not ecstasy, but it makes 'em horny as hell. It's not acid or mushrooms, I don't think, but it makes 'em trip their asses off." He laughed. "Really. I was talking to a cop the other night- one of the guys from the narcotics task force came in, snooping around, checked a couple of ID's…"

"He find anything?"

"Nah, we're cool. Anyway, he was telling me, this thing, this drug is a pill they make out of - get this - some kind of a *frog.*"

Lee looked at him, curious.

"No shit." He giggled, an odd sound for a big man. "There's a frog down in South America, somewhere, this guy says. These

people, Indians, or whatever, they use these frogs, it gets 'em
fucked up, and they think they can see the future. Helps 'em hunt,
or something." He chuckled. "It gets better. He says, in addition
to the kids liking it - because it's the new thing, you know - the
street trade, the corner boys, everybody is promoting the thing as
an aid to beating the casinos."

"What, so the sheep can tell what the next card is gonna be?"

"Yes! The cop says, he tells me, these sucker tourists, and
old people, people who have never as much as smoked a joint are
buying it and taking it in the casino hotels, trying to see the future.
So this cop goes on, he says," Meat was giggling now, had to catch
his breath, "so he says, they've got all these regular tourists, you
know, the Clampetts from Salt Lake City, or old blue hairs from
the busses, running around, tripping their balls off, and talking
about seeing God, straight flushes, whatever."

Lee let that image settle in as Meat wiped his eyes. "So is this
a problem for us?"

"Yeah, well, no more than normal. Caught a couple screwing
in the balcony last night. I think the internet feed picked up on
them before I did."

"OK, well, keep me posted. Jeez, South American frogs. By
the way, what's the name of the drug?

"Hell, I knew you were going to ask me that. Let's see... what
did he say? It had something to do with... oh yeah, I remember.
It's name is *Destiny*."

Chapter 3 - Hooks and Crooks

Lee and Boot eased Lee's his 36 foot Sportfisher, the Miss Di, out of its slip, through the Azalea harbor, past piers of sailing vessels moored by the members of Sailing Club at the harbor's south shore. The club was rebuilt after being completely destroyed by Katrina. A few sunburned highschoolers looked up from the small sailboats they were preparing for an upcoming weekend regatta.

Some locals sat on the seawall, lines out, fishing for speckled trout, red drum, black drum, flounder, or sheepshead, or whatever else was biting. As Lee passed through the mouth of the harbor, out of the no-wake zone, light chop of the Mississippi sound rocked the vessel. Lee pushed forward her dual throttles, steering southeast for the nearest channel marker. Miss Di's twin diesel engines emitted a guttural roar sufficient to attract the attention of a few bored Sailing club members whom had gathered on the back deck to drink vodka sodas and complain about their maids, bankers, insurance companies, or pain-in-the-ass tax lawyers.

Iris did not often get to go fishing with Lee anymore; she was getting older, more grouchy. When she stayed ashore, she would lay on the pier next to Miss Di's empty slip, staring out to sea, awaiting Lee's return. She was never disturbed by adjacent slip owners, or even the Harbor Master, all of whom were familiar with her reputation. But today, Iris lay on Miss Di's foredeck, her favorite place, where she could keep a protective eye on Lee, and stay out of the way of the fishing. Her boat habits were always the same: she would stay there until dark, when she would quietly make her way outside the cabin, on its walkaround, a feat of balance for any animal, human or canine. She would then enter the salon from the back deck, burrow in the corner behind Lee's leather chair, sleep, and dream the dreams of seafaring cowdogs.

Lee entered the Gulfport shipping channel, turned south, set the auto pilot, and settled in for a twenty-knot-per-hour cruise which would take him past Cat Island, and in a few hours, bring him and Boot through Breton Sound. From there, he would steer through Baptiste Collette into the lower Mississippi River, to the river port of Venice, Louisiana, the last place below New Orleans accessible by automobile.

There, they would refuel, pick up whatever supplies they needed, then make the final thirty miles or so down the river past Port Eads, a small harbor and lighthouse accessible only by boat. After feeling their way through the river's shallow South Pass, they would enter the Gulf of Mexico. Floating, deep water oil rigs, lighted cities which were havens for tuna night fishing, were the ultimate objective.

Diana leaned the teakwood lounge chair back, all the way flat, allowing the late summer sun to baste her naked body. It was hot - nearly a hundred degrees, and an announcer on the radio beside her chair was saying that the gulf surface temperature was as hot as had ever been recorded. What's worse, he went on to explain, was that any tropical storm that got in the gulf would feast on the heat.

Having heard hysterical, inaccurate hurricane predictions all her life, Diana laughed to herself. She had more immediate distractions: puddles of sweat forming between the muscles of her abdomen, beside her protruding hipbones, then tickling their way by rivulets to the pool decking under her chair.

Her eyes closed, she was remembering the day she met Sarah, how the first seemingly innocent conversation with her had caused such an upheaval of - there was no other way to characterize it - *lust.* How she had met Sarah the next day here at her and Nick's house, under the legitimate pretense of a common interest in art; how she had, without hesitation, submitted to Sarah's sexual advances, and had that day entered a confusing, but purely joyful relationship that revolved around sex, untainted by pretexts of love, devotion, nurturing, or any of the requirements that existed between her and Lee.

Not that she necessarily wanted it that way. There was a time, at first, that she believed she was actually falling in love with Sarah. The situation was perfect. Nick was never home, constantly at the casino, or out of town; the two of them would go days without seeing him, alone, unimpeded. But Diana had learned that Sarah was inaccessible in the way of love; she was completely uninterested in anything permanent, any restrictions; it became clear to Diana that Sarah was incapable of love, had never even considered it, especially not with Nick. Over the past summer, Diana came to appreciate that type of freedom, the ability Sarah had to act without remorse, with pure alacrity, with utter devotion to self indulgence in a particular time and place. And during that same span of time, Diana realized she was not capable of such exclusion; she *was* affected by such distracting considerations as truth, devotion. Morality. Even if it was a vague morality, she thought, an extremely permissive one. She turned over, adjusting her towel underneath, letting the sun cook her back, now.

Her experience with Sarah had actually caused her to fall back in love with Lee. Not that she had taken the time to tell him, she realized, but that could wait. He was so busy. And her concerns with morality and newfound love were not enough to keep her from making an almost daily trip to her lover's house, where they had formed a perfect sexual partnership - one that required no questions or permission. Her Catholic upbringing, she thought, with its hellfire method of programming restraint, was not enough

to overcome the pure animal ecstasy of sex with an expert at
pleasure.

Sarah emerged from the pool, glistening, naked. She walked
over to Diana's chair, stooped beside it, ran her hand down the
middle of Diana's back, across her bare ass, between her legs.
Diana involuntarily gasped, raised her hips. Between a group
of azalea bushes and the cypress fence surrounding the pool,
Flounder involuntarily gasped, too. He was photographing the
poolside happenings through a knothole. He zoomed in on
Diana's chair, only twenty feet or so away, and hoped they could
not hear his pulse.

FBI Special Agent Zachary sat in the FBI's regional office in
Gulfport, Mississippi reviewing his notes. He had just entered his
office on the fifth floor of the eight story Beauvoir Bank building,
with no view of the Gulf of Mexico, which lay just a quarter mile
south. The FBI occupied all of the fifth and sixth floors; agents
with seniority or a history of sensational drug busts got the offices
with views; young agents like Ellis got the interior cubicles. But
Zack Ellis was not interested in an office with a view of the gulf,
or any office in Gulfport. He had been assigned one mission in
Mississippi: gather enough evidence to bring down the Bardino
crime family, and along the way, anyone else associated with
criminal operations at the Cronus Casino.

His professional journey to Gulfport had started at birth,
really. For Special Agent Ellis, the Gulfport assignment was a
logical next step in his personal progression toward greatness.
He had grown up in the Algiers area of New Orleans, and had
received, upon high school graduation, a full scholarship to
Georgetown University. Not an unusual accomplishment for
an African - American, but notable among his public school
predecessors, because his was academic, not athletic, and was

regarded as proof among his peers that he would indeed, one day, become President of the United States, as he had often declared.

He had graduated Georgetown in three and a half years, with a degree in history, and a minor in Social and Political Thought. He was accepted to Yale Law School, where he immediately fell in love with a young lady, an undergrad named Jonni Ford, from New Jersey. She was intelligent, slender, financially well off - and the granddaughter of a Republican U.S. senator from her state. She was perfect.

Zack's first family dinner at the Senator Ford's house - Thanksgiving, his first year of law school, was awkward. Everyone else at the house - the mansion, actually - was white. Though Zack and Jonni eventually lost interest in each other, Zack and the senator, over time, became close acquaintances. During law school, Zack visited Senator Ford occasionally; the senator made sure Zack's name was prominent on the lists of several influential D.C. firms when summer law clerks were selected.

Senator Griffin Ford was not of modern Republican ilk; he was of the generation of his party whom had supported the 1964 Civil Rights Act, had helped to make it possible for black men like Zack to emerge from the Deep South and prosper among the academic and social elite of America without negotiating racial obstacles. Not legal ones, anyway. Zack was the type of man the senator wanted to know. In Zack, he felt he had found a protégée' who would validate his continuing support of the social programs so many of his party colleagues hated. The senator had become an anachronism among his own; he knew he was accorded topical, even institutional respect in public, but that he was privately derided as a relic and an impediment to progress by the new generation of his party.

For the senator, Zack would be a Progressive for the next generation, one with a renewed sense of righteousness he was

sure would arise, if only after the passing of his political life. And
probably his natural one. He determined to help Zack in any way
possible. When Zack graduated from Yale, he had offers from
numerous Washington, D.C. law firms. The senator, however,
aware of Zack's political aspirations, felt that a background in law
enforcement would help him. Senator Ford therefore encouraged
Zack to apply to the FBI Academy, where he was accepted, and
completed the sixteen week course. After finishing his required
two year probationary period at a D.C. office, the senator made
sure Zack got assigned to a practically secret investigative unit,
also based in D.C.

In his desire to further Zack's career, the senator failed to
perceive in himself any trace of racial paternalism. The irony of his
belief that Zack must necessarily need his help blinded him to both
his own innate bigotry, and the possibility that Zack may be just
be a smart guy who could succeed without the benevolent hand
of liberal white folk. Or that Zack could be a common political
opportunist, one of legions that a United States senator must
suffer in his tenure.

For his part, Zack merely considered the old man a convenient
friend. The irony of the old man's life, Zack thought, was that he
talked all the time about social justice, and adherence to Lincoln's
ideals, but he had no other African-American friends or staff.
None. Zack believed the senator was trying validate his official
position, rather than any practical personal conviction, through his
patronage of Zack's career, without having to sully his safe social
life by experiencing any of the actual strife of emerging racial
equality. For that, Zack harbored a secret disdain. For a lot of
other reasons, though, he was willing to be used in that way, and
had always actually liked the senator.

Zack Ellis' D.C. investigative unit had been unintentionally
authorized under the quagmire of anti-terrorism statutes Congress

had passed after the September 11, 2001 attacks on the United States. The laws, intended to fight domestic terrorism without serious oversight from the courts or compliance with the United States Constitution, had some legitimate anti-terroristic functions, consistent with its original mission. But by the time Zack arrived, they were mostly employed by the FBI while investigating domestic crimes of a more traditional nature.

His boss in the D.C. office was a third generation Irish-American named Fahey, who was famous in the bureau for getting divorced and being shot. He had tallied three of both categories, surviving all six calamities with minimal scarring. Fahey had been an agent as long as anyone could remember. His one pure love was the Boston Red Sox. After Zack's first day in the D.C. office, he and Agent Fahey had gone into Georgetown, where they climbed into chairs around a tiny table in a bar Zack knew from undergrad, famous for pizza and Georgetown University co-eds. Baseball was on the small television, the Yankees and the Red Sox. Neither agent said much during the first two pitchers of beer, as the teams entered the fifth inning tied at zero. Fahey ordered a third pitcher, turned his Red Sox hat around backwards, and said, "I guess you heard about me getting shot a lot." He laughed.

"I heard," agent Ellis said, "Does it hurt?"

"Stings a little. It's something I try to avoid. And something you're going to have to try to avoid, too, where you're going."

"Where's that?"

Fahey grinned. "Somewhere tropical and exotic, practically third world, with good food, good music, and a history of lots, and I mean *lots* of interesting crime. Somewhere I can practically guarantee you have been before. Wanna guess?"

"What the hell is in the tropics?"

"Mississippi."

"*Mississippi*!" People spun around and looked at them, from the bar.

"Quiet, Ellis," said Fahey, chuckling.

"What…"

"Oh, bullshit! That wasn't a strike!," yelled Fahey, at the television. Turning back to Ellis, he said, "These fucking umpires. Anyway, where were we?"

"Mississippi, as I recall."

"Oh yeah. We got an investigation into the mob, the Mafia, La Cosa Nostra, whatever you prefer - going on down there; they run a casino, some other operations. We're close - close enough to get convictions now, but we need more local work." He glanced away at the television; the Red Sox had just hit into a double play, and he grimaced. Looking back at Zack, he said, "Believe me, for the Bureau, this is not a major fucking priority. We're talking about the Mississippi Gulf Coast, and New Orleans - not exactly the bright lights of Broadway."

"Who did I piss off?"

"Nobody, kid. Look, everybody knows the senator, Senator Ford, is behind you. He's been on the hill since the Civil War, for Chrissakes, so we have to give him what he wants. Which means good news for you, and maybe bad news, too."

"Great. More bad news?"

"That's up to you, smart guy. Anyway, it has been conveyed to me, in non-negotiable terms, that you are to be given a chance to make a splash. This set off a small donnybrook down the hall, what with seniority issues, and so forth. Feeling is, you ain't been around long enough to be getting the cherry stuff, blah, blah, blah. Eventually, a compromise was reached. So this is it. You get this right, you can get any assignment, go anywhere you want. Might even get to go in politics, with the publicity, and all." He chuckled. "But, you fuck it up, and if the mob don't shoot you, one of ours probably will."

Zack snorted.

"Don't laugh, kid, that last part I wasn't joking about. You know anything about the CIA?"

Zack shook his head.

"You don't? Well, get ready. The senator apparently thinks you want to be a politician? My guess is, before this is over, you're going to learn all you need to know about politics. Trust me. Head, down, gun loaded, put in your thirty, retire. Stay out of politics."

"Like you've kept your head down?"

"Yeah, well, that hasn't been shot, yet."

"Why the coast, and New Orleans? Hell, I'm from there. I grew up in New Orleans. I've been to the Mississippi coast a dozen times, at least. That was all we could afford. I left that area because I wanted the hell out. Why not send someone who *wants* to be there?"

Fahey slowly diverted his attention from the game. "Seems like I read a memo said you were from New Orleans. Let's see… maybe in your file? OK, Special Agent Ellis, let me ask you: would it be a good idea to send an agent to an area he was familiar with, but where he was also virtually completely unknown? Would it, Special Agent ?"

Ellis Didn't answer.

"Thank you, Mr. Rising Star. For now, let me do the thinking. When you get to be congressman, or president, remember that I've done you this favor."

Nobody said anything for another beer. Fahey winked at a college girl at the next table, raising his glass, as if to make a toast. She acted as if she did not see him, slowly shifting her gaze back to friends at her table. Fahey glanced at Zack, who had not noticed. Fahey said, "Anyways, Ellis, I'll give you the details tomorrow. You'll be in Mississippi by this weekend. So, you wanna hear about all my ex-wives?"

"No thanks. I'm still trying to figure out how being so well connected gets me sent to Mississippi." He got up.

"Aw, don't run off, Zack, have a beer. Believe me, I'm more fun than your new neighbors are likely to be."

Some college kids in the other end of the bar cheered; Fahey looked up in time to see a Yankee home run fly out of the park. "Dammit!" he screamed, and threw his hat.

"See you tomorrow," said Zack, who had always loved the Yankees, but decided not to cheer.

After several months on the coast, it seemed apparent to Ellis that no one in local law enforcement, either state of federal, were particularly interested in intervening with the Bardinos. There was no organized crime investigation, to speak of, ongoing. Ellis came to believe he was being buried in the department structure, probably because of jealousy. Who knew? Politics inside the FBI was as palpable as it was in Congress, and just as many good people got wasted in the process.

He had found a little modern information on the Bardinos in the files. All the old ones were, for some reason, classified and removed to the archives in D.C. Stymied, he decided to request an official visit to Washington, where he could get real some research done.

His time in Mississippi had not been completely wasted, however. He had spent much of it, on the clock and off, compiling information from the files, the library, the internet, where he found all types of mob information sites, from magazine articles to tell-all books by former wise guys, to obvious speculation. He had even managed a few informal interviews at the numerous local coffee shops, though direct contact with civilians, he came to realize, was not his forte. Despite the lack of official information, he had compiled a solid background on the Mississippi coast and

the Bardinos, and he did not see any urgent reason to share it with
his peers.

Ellis had learned that gambling and organized crime were part
of the fabric of the Mississippi Gulf Coast long before legalized
casinos opened in 1992. When New Orleans' famous brothel and
gambling district, Storyville, was shut down in 1919 by the United
States Secretary of War's illegal World War I era order, many
gamblers escaped the subsequent local outbreak of anti-gambling
and whoring sentiment by heading northeast fifty miles through
coastal swamps and fishing villages to the Mississippi Gulf Coast.
Azalea, Mississippi was the first dependable high ground, and
where they alighted. Ladnier Point, outside Azalea, was where
four or five outright casinos sprung up along highway 90; others
moved down the beach to Biloxi, along what would become the
Strip. Finding willing protection from well compensated law
enforcement, gambling rapidly flourished.

Biloxi added supper clubs, dance halls, and upscale hotels.
Ellis pictured with amusement scenes that undoubtedly occurred
in Mississippi's devoutly Baptist capitol of Jackson: howls of
objection to the sins of the coast muted by bails of intemperate
whiskey cash.

Apparently, in the 1920's, Al Capone had even used Ladnier
Point in Azalea for his Cuba-to-Chicago liquor running business.
Rum came straight out of Havana, was offloaded, and some of
it trucked to New Orleans. The rest went straight up old 51 to
Memphis, and eventually, Chicago. Liquor and gambling became
as much a part of the local economy as fish and shrimp. By 1932,
the end of Prohibition, Capone's booze, New Orleans' gamblers,
lax law enforcement, and the area's remote tropical climate
combined to make it a secret getaway for the naughty well-to-do.

After World War II, Biloxi emerged as a national vacation
destination, featuring famous nightclub performers of the

day. Championship golf, theme parks, and charter fishing, the
whole show. Ladnier Point and Strip gambling houses continued
to operate, primarily as an outlet for hard core gamblers and
prostitutes, until the state legalized gambling, and shut them
down.

Initially, Zack wondered how the Bardinos had remained
relatively intact, while most of the rest of the Mafia in the United
States sat in jail. It was an official report by Congress, its final
report on the Iran-Contra scandals of the 1980's, that completed
the process, in his mind, of understanding overall picture. Not
that the picture was unequivocally clear. Much of the information
collected by the United States was classified. Zack's task as an
investigator was to accept facts as they were presented, and to
make reasonable inferences where necessary. Gradually, he put
together as much of the Bardino story as he needed.

Nofio Bardino had come to New Orleans from Italy in 1895,
at the age of fifteen. By 1920, at the beginning of Prohibition, he
had become one of the most powerful Mafia bosses in the United
States. When organized crime leaders from across the nation
met in New York in 1931 to form The Commission, a nationwide
organization to coordinate La Cosa Nostra's nefarious activities,
he had already established control over the municipal government
of New Orleans, the city's Mississippi River port, it's illegal liquor
trade, and burgeoning street drug trade.

In 1940, federal immigration officials had Nofio deported,
and he returned to an opulent life in Sicily. His successors enjoyed
power in New Orleans unrivaled by their counterparts in New
York, Chicago, and the other twenty or so Mafia enclaves in the
United States.

In the early 1980's, federal prosecutors started dismantling La
Cosa Nostra across the nation, using RICO, a federal conspiracy
law which allowed them to penetrate the layers of protection

previously enjoyed by mob bosses, and prosecute the heads of families. Curiously, the New Orleans Mafia, which had always operated in consultation with, but outside the direct control of the organized crime Commission, largely escaped prosecution. After a token guilty plea and light sentence of its semi-retired leader, Tony "Two Steps" Bardino - a great nephew of Nofio Bardino - the United States Justice Department seemed, to the general public, satisfied with New Orleans' La Cosa Nostra.

Yet to Ellis it was apparent that the Bardinos were still heavily involved in drug distribution and money laundering. And he was following a new trail. He believed the Bardinos were involved in the investment banking industry, which actually provided some of the funding for Mississippi's first legitimate casinos.

When Mississippi casinos had still been on the horizon, quietly passing the Mississippi legislature in the middle of the night, the family had apparently formed a Delaware Corporation which gradually bought, over a couple of years, significant equity in numerous Mississippi casinos. Not enough to trigger a statutory investigation, but enough to position itself for a future move, if the government got friendly.

The family had made quite a good return on its investment. But it had gotten greedy, and the feds were just about to open an investigation of all Mississippi casino financing, until Hurricane Katrina came. The Bardinos' amazing luck had saved them again, and allowed them to waltz in to the new market legitimately.

In the days after the hurricane, the Mississippi legislature had been hustled by the casinos, who threatened to move out. All the casinos destroyed by Hurricane Katrina had been floating on enormous barges. The "dockside" principle had been necessary to get gambling legalized initially; it had proved disastrous in the face of the storm. The legislature capitulated, and new casinos were built on previously sacrosanct land.

The Bardinos slipped in during the resulting cavalcade of casino permit applications. Cronus Casino, an old downtown Las Vegas concern that had gone defunct, was bought by agents of the Bardino family, recapitalized, and qualified to do business as a Mississippi corporation. Just another old operation moving to greener pastures, or sunnier beaches. The Cronus Casino became one of the first hotel-casinos built entirely on land in Biloxi. The Bardinos also bought what became The Blue Stone, and had it renovated in a year. Nicolas Bonacelli had apparently been brought in to maintain the family's direct control over casino floor operations, and, Ellis believed, to be sacrificed in case any police agencies became too curious.

All of this was probably legal, even ingenious. But for the use of illegal money on the front end, Zack would probably be reduced to trying to make a case for mail fraud, or some such mundane issue. Mail fraud, Zack thought, does not springboard one into politics. No, the entire focus of this investigation had to be on the family's drug dealing, and money laundering. That was the key.

Zack's entire life's ambition relied upon exposing those operations, the result of which would be a nationwide domino effect of investigations and frozen assets which would affect a significant portion of the entire American gambling industry, and its international subsidiaries. It would be one of the greatest cases in modern FBI history, attracting national news media coverage for months. Hollywood would make movies about it. And there, on CNN, at the inevitable Congressional hearings, portrayed in the movies, would be FBI Special Agent Zachary Ellis, American hero, on his way to the U.S. Senate, eventually the White House.

For now, it was a matter of continuing the process with better tools. Getting to D.C. for a while would be no problem, he knew.

He submitted the travel request, then decided to make a surprise visit the Local District Attorney, Jake Carter.

Lee and Boot, having refueled at the Venice, Louisiana marina, reentered the main channel of the Mississippi River, headed south, where the massive river makes it final terrible charge to the gulf. From the elevation of Miss Di's flybridge, Lee could see heavily caned marshlands in all directions, dotted by grassy lowlands, punctured by manmade canals and bayous, products of decades of oil company intrusion into the formerly pristine terrain.

He instinctively scanned for any suspicious small vessels, didn't see any. The pirates whom formerly patrolled these waters - including Jean Laffite - had given way over time to a less illustrious group of locals: petty criminals and low-level felons who had figured out that most of the big private boats headed out of the river were full of rich, inebriated weekend charter fishermen, loaded with cash they would not leave in any hotel room in Louisiana. These latter-day pirates would storm up to fishing charters in airboats, john boats, skiffs, even motorized pirogues, waive shotguns, board the vessel, rob its passengers, then disappear into the shallow marsh where heavy vessels could not follow.

This activity, though still rare, was highly lucrative and effective, and Lee knew only a few of the sorry bastards had been caught. Fortunately, no captains or their passengers had been injured; even so, Lee had told Boot recently to equip Miss Di with a shotgun; he had found an old 12 gauge double barrel and sawed it off. It was loaded with buckshot. He felt under the flybridge's console to make sure it was still there, hidden. The weapon was not much for long fights, either in distance or time, but should be the last word in a close confrontation.

They soon arrived at a massive aquatic intersection, where the main channel of the river divided into three distinct passes. Here the heaviest river vessels, many of them two hundred foot or more oil supply boats headed for the rigs, turned down the Southwest Pass for the final few miles to the gulf. Lighter local vessels, fishermen mainly, might take Southeast Pass toward shallows, and hordes of speckled trout and redfish.

Miss Di took the middle route, South Pass, the ancient waterway familiar to generations of river men, from raftsmen to steamers, to a modern flotilla of shrimpers, commercial fishermen, and charter boats that traversed the waters daily. South Pass had been, for Europeans, the original river channel; the French explorer D'Iberville ascended it in 1699, meeting natives with whom his men traded beads and knives for bear meat. Lee had read that along this very stretch of river, D'Iberville had met an Indian chief who displayed a Spanish officer's jacket given to the chief's predecessors a century and a half earlier by the expedition of Spanish explorer Hernando de Soto.

At sunset, Lee, Boot, and Miss Di passed the mouth of the river, and the dike erected by the engineer James Eads over a hundred years earlier, and into the Gulf of Mexico. A few sunburned fishermen waived beers at them from small boats around the dike.

Passing through the mouth of the channel, Miss Di left the serene, rapid flow of the river, entered headlong the southerly breeze of the gulf, and its waves. Lee took a southeasterly heading, toward oil rigs scattered across the northern gulf, where they would feed Miss Di's holds a limit of yellow fin tuna, and probably amberjack, and a grouper or two. As Lee rocked in Miss Di's flybridge, he plotted a waypoint in her guidance system, set the autopilot, and sat back, reflecting on the evening he and Boot would spend, rigging live hard tails for bait, hauling in the brutal knots of muscle that are yellowfin. Diana, the Stone, the asshole Bonehead: all seemed a lifetime away. For the first time in weeks, he relaxed, and smiled.

Agent Zack Ellis lounged in a vinyl interview chair in front of a fake oak desk in Jake Carter's dimly lit office, located in a second floor corner of the two story Harrison County Courthouse, in Gulfport.

Jake Carter walked in the door expecting a friendly conversation with Ellis, who he had met at Mardi Gras. Ellis had his feet propped on the desk, on a pile of Harrison County Sheriff's Office investigation reports. Jake paused, to see if the FBI agent would move, or at least re-introduce himself. He didn't. Jake closed the door.

Jake punched his intercom, said, "Kate, call Ken and tell him I might be a little late for our meeting. Don't want to insult the Congressman, you know."

Jake picked up an envelope from the desk, ripped it open with his oyster knife letter opener. Inside was a form letter addressed to "Valued Member of the Mississippi Legal Community," and was a fund raising request. Jake perused it like it was an invitation to join the U.S. Supreme Court. After what he deemed a sufficient amount of time, he placed the letter in his desk drawer, and addressed his relaxed guest, saying, "Nice shoes. Now, why don't you get them off my desk, and tell me what you want?"

Ellis did not move, conjured up his most insolent gaze. He thought: *these crackers*. "Mr. Carter, this isn't *your* desk. It belongs to the voters - who might be interested in your apparent inability to prevent the Mafia from operating in their community." He allowed himself a superior grin, calculating Carter's shock, anticipating a delicious, penitent response.

Jake thought: *Oh, shit, don't look worried.* Then: *Wait a second, I haven't done anything wrong. A little whiskey; that one hooker during the campaign, which the feds can't possibly know about. And all campaign donations are cleared by the Secretary of State.*

He said, "If you're talking about Nicolas Bonacelli, that ain't my gig. I understood you guys were keeping tabs on him, officer, ah…"

"Ellis. *Special Agent* Ellis."

"Yeah, we met at the Cronus Casino Mardi Gras party over in Azalea. What can I do for you Special Agent Ellis?"

"I need whatever you have on the Bardinos, and access to your sources."

"What are in my legal files, or not, is none of your damned business. Around here, cops do their jobs, and leave the lawyering to lawyers."

Agent Ellis smirked. "That's a brilliant arrangement. By the way, I'm a cop *and* a lawyer. Yale Law, you may have heard of it." He omitted the fact that he had never tried a case of any kind, or even been licensed.

"Yale? When did you pass the bar?"

"I graduated four years ago." He had actually graduated three years previous, and had not applied to take the bar exam, yet. "And speaking of lawyers, your best friend Lee Farrell may be needing one soon. Want to hear some more?"

Suddenly, Jake did not feel like cheeky exchanges. "Sure, Ellis, what do you have?"

Ellis reminded himself not to say too much. "Bonacelli is a cousin, second cousin, by adoption, actually, of Petrino Mallini, the current head of the Bardinos. They control the Cronus Casino, through a group of apparently legit owners - an accountant, couple of lawyers, that form the primary ownership group, bought out the old Vegas joint. Bonacelli was brought in, we think, to take the hit in case any of the mob's operations are exposed."

"What operations are you talking about?"

"This much we know. The Cronus itself is highly profitable, a good clean income for the Bardinos. But we think they use it, and a number of other businesses around the coast - restaurants, bars, pawn shops, title loan places - to launder money for themselves and their friends."

"Friends?"

"Other organized crime scum. Drug money mainly. Plus, they do the normal stuff: illegal sports gambling, prostitution, also insurance scams, fake condo timeshares, you name it."

"OK, so what do you want with Lee?"

"The Blue Stone is owned by the Bardinos. We think it is part of the laundering network, and a major outlet for street level drug sales."

"And you think Lee is involved?"

"He runs the joint, doesn't he?"

"Oh, *come on*, he's responsible for what the owners do? What the fucking accountants do with the money?"

"What, Mr. Carter, you think he's deaf and dumb? Can the guy be so easily fooled?"

"Well, I can tell you he's not involved in anything illegal."

"You can? How is that? In fact, how could your friend, the D.A.'s *best* friend, be up to his ears in business with the Mafia, and the D.A. not notice? Say, how long have you and Mr. Farrell been claiming each other as best friends?"

"Well, *officer*, I'm going to ignore those last couple of comments, based upon your obvious lack of experience." He stood. "This has been interesting, but I'm busy. Do you have a point, other than making it clear that you don't have the slightest fucking clue about Lee Farrell?"

Ellis stood. "That's *Agent* Ellis. And yes, I do have a point. You need to deliver us Lee Farrell. I need him to get inside with the Bardinos. Otherwise, as far as I'm concerned, he's part of the conspiracy. I'm sure you've explained RICO to him?"

"Let's see? That's the one where any person associated with any group the feds don't like can be prosecuted for just about anything?"

Ellis chuckled. "Yeah, that's the one." He reached down, picked up a brown leather dossier, opened its shiny gold buckle, removed three large photographs, spun them on the desk in front of Jake. "If he needs convincing, you might want to show him these."

Jake, still standing, picked up eight-by-tens, looked at each one slowly. Very slowly - here was one of Diana Farrell, naked, outside by a pool; another of her indoors by a pool table, with a drink, a third of her emerging from a bathroom, wearing a towel around her hair, and nothing else.

"What the hell?," Jake said.

"Ms. Diana Farrell, at the residence of one Mr. Nicolas Bonacelli."

Jake had to sit down. Agent Ellis remained standing.

"But, how?…"

"We were surveilling Mr. Bonacelli, and guess who popped up? Good looking isn't she?"

"You can't mean to tell me, she and Bonehead are…"

"Gee, you tell me, Mr. D.A. Maybe they're just having nude Bible study."

"How do I know you're not mistaken?"

"Well, you could ask her. Maybe she has some reasonable explanation for hanging out at Bonacelli's house, butt naked. Anyway, maybe you should have Mr. Farrell call me. Soon." Agent Ellis placed a business card on Jake's desk, turned to leave. "You have a nice day."

"One more thing," said Jake, "How would they use a casino to launder money?"

"Simple. Bad guy walks in, loses money. The casino lets him or his buddies win it back."

"But what about taxes on the winnings?"

"What about them? Depending on the amounts, they might not have to report the winnings, or pay taxes at all. Even if they do, it still beats the hell out of the forty or fifty percent the bad guys *used* to pay for laundering. And this way, nobody gets shot. Yet." He opened the door, paused, turned back. "And, by the way, you might want to tell your assistant that the congressman is in the middle east this week, so *he* might be late, too." He strolled out, through the office, into the hall, along the worn carpet, chuckling. "*Crackers,*" he thought.

Diana drove west on Highway 90 along the beach, directly into the setting sun. She had the top down on her Mercedes convertible, and every man she passed made an exaggerated glance in her direction. Many, traveling the opposite direction, tooted their horns.

She was especially melancholy this afternoon; she had a glass of wine with Sarah before leaving the Bonacelli house, perhaps for the last time. Wine always made her a bit sad, at first. But she was sad for other reasons, too.

She was midway into her thirties, and gradually entering the shock of middle age realization that people do, in fact, die. All her life she expected life to be idyllic, easy. She was literally raised to think of herself as a princess; she had been one in every pageant she had entered since she could walk. But now she faced middle age without children, with a barely functional marriage. And then there was Sarah. Sarah had definitely given her some reason to laugh. She realized, as she drove, that she had nearly lost all her humor in the last few years. What was it she and Lee used to laugh about, hysterically? Some joke he knew, that an old cowboy from Waco, Texas had told him...she could not remember.

But whatever it was, it wasn't the joke, but the times they lived in. They laughed all the time then, back when she was young. In those days Lee was still, in her mind, the star quarterback, who all the girls wanted. He had gotten out of the Army, was finishing undergrad, was optimistic about the future. And he loved her. Lee got accepted to law school at Ole Miss. They had rented out their house on the beach, moved to Oxford, Mississippi, found a nice apartment. Lee enrolled, bought his books, started going to school every day. He seemed happy. She was happy.

But then something happened to Lee. Nightmares. At first, she thought it was just the pressure of school. But then she realized it was something different. Lee told her he had these dreams all his life, off and on. Something dark, even evil. Lee had started to tell her something else a few times when he had been drinking. Some terrible secret, but he never finished.

Lee had quit law school after second year. Second year! At first, Diana was humiliated at the thought of returning to the coast, average. Later, she had become callous, scoffing at the idea of law school, and lawyers in general, when any one asked about it. Now, as she drove, she realized that her reaction to the law school debacle had been incredibly selfish. What could possibly have been so terrible for Lee that he would give up something that he had worked so hard for? Why had she not been more concerned about him?

She hoped she was not too late, now. As she passed the Azalea Harbor, its smell of shrimp filling her convertible, she looked south. Lee was out there, a hundred miles or more. Boot was with him, and Iris. Suddenly, she wished she was, too.

It was dark outside, and Ellis sat in his office reviewing files and videotapes of the Cronus investigation. All the other agents had long since left, headed home to their wives, or out with their girlfriends. Agent Ellis did not have time for such frivolities, he had work to do. Since no one was around, he did not bother to conceal the video he was reviewing, or the fact that he was agape at its contents.

Sure, what he told District Attorney Carter had been basically true. The FBI down here in Gulfport had indeed been investigating Nicolas Bonacelli, and surveilling his house. They had consequently filmed Diana Farrell naked. But what he had told the D.A. about Mrs. Farrell's sex partner - well, *alluded to*, really - had not exactly been accurate. True, Mrs. Farrell had been incredibly prolific in her extramarital sexual activities, insatiable even. But the focus of her passions was not Nicolas Bonacelli - never had been. As these tapes indicated - and there were hours of them - Mrs. Farrell was very much content with Sarah Bonacelli, not Nick.

Ellis left his office, drove along the beach, following the moon west. Pulling into the cheap motel where he was still temporarily lodged, he laughed at his own Walter Mitty imaginations - delusions of grandeur that had him being ushered into Congress by a backwater investigation of a third rate mob family that may or may not functionally exist. Still, the case was all he had, and could be huge.

One thing he had told Jake Carter was perfectly accurate. He needed informants who had inside access to the Bardinos. Like this fool "Flounder," Bonacelli's chauffeur, who appeared in the FBI's tapes to be in the habit of making his own record of the goings-on between Diana Farrell and Sarah Bonacelli. And Zack needed someone else, someone with credibility, money, and a reason to help set up Bonacelli. Like Lee Farrell. The Diana Farrell sex tapes were therefore simply manna from heaven.

As he climbed in bed, too exhausted to read, or watch TV, he pondered the mess. As he drifted away, his last conscious thought was about Diana Farrell. Beautiful, naive, lustful Diana

Farrell, who obviously was not happy with her husband. She needed someone to help her, to protect her from the scum she was unknowingly associated with. She needed a real man, a *good* man. A man like Zack Ellis.

Chapter 4 - Long Gravy

When Big Ed walked through the rotating front door of the Cronus Casino, he had a plan. He had driven all the way from Picayune, Mississippi, an hour or so in his old Chevy pickup, which he had valeted. Unsure what to do, he had tipped the parking attendant five dollars.

Stopping in the garishly carpeted entrance, he carefully surveyed the table games off to his left. He had spent the last year or so, down at the co-op where he worked, reading up on how to beat the casinos at their favorite card game, blackjack. Having studied all the theories and methods of counting cards, of betting patterns, splitting pairs, doubling down, when to hit, when to pass - he was satisfied that he had made himself an expert, and now it was time to collect.

Big Ed had had enough of his boss, his wife, hell, even his church, where he himself had been a deacon - and a damned good one - for over twenty years. But did he ever get asked to coach the church softball team? Was he ever named employee of the month at the co-op? Did his ungrateful wife ever stop between her soap operas and cooking to think - much less say - what a great man he had been?

Alright, she *was* a damn good cook, but she didn't even put one of those embarrassing ads in the paper, with his baby picture, when he had turned fifty this year. If he had ever had kids, he bet they would have done it for their dad. And, she was fat as a cow, and mean if she missed her shows.

But that was all behind him. He had a plan, which he had been working on for a while. After he got through whipping the casino, he was going to fly off to Las Vegas, or New York, or wherever rich people go. Back home in Picayune they'd all be sorry, especially his ungrateful wife, who was probably just now getting her fat ass off the couch to cook his supper. Meatloaf, he thought. Tonight's meatloaf night. Twenty-two years of meatloaf, once a week. Until now.

And these snooty casino people were about to get a lesson. He tried to tip his enormous cowboy hat at the female security person working the front, but only knocked it off his head. Replacing his hat, he unconsciously felt to make sure his belt buckle was centered, then headed to the nearest bar, careful not to stumble in his brand new cowboy boots.

Zack Ellis entered the Cronus Casino with no particular intent, certainly no desire to confront anyone. He merely wanted to get a fresh feel for the place, before he went to D.C. The interior was a marvel: carpet so maddeningly patterned and colorful that it actually caused his head to spin; walls covered with Greek and Roman reliefs, murals, and paintings so numerous that a spoiled young child might have been the decorator.

Three stories high, giant crown molding, plaster sculptures, fake marble, huge chandeliers, gold brocade, innumerable small frescoes…*this*, thought Agent Ellis, *is what happens when people with no taste get too much money.* He found a spot along one of the casino's numerous bars, where tourists and locals were served free drinks, as long as they played the video poker machines, which were imbedded along the bar top.

"You need something, mister?," asked the nearest bartender.

"Diet soda," said Ellis, reaching for his wallet.

The bartender returned, placed the drink next to a poker machine. Ellis tried to hand him a bill.

"No charge, if you're playing," said the bartender, whose name, "Charles," was engraved on a fake gold badge, affixed to his Hawaiian -styled shirt.

"I'm not playing," said Ellis.

"You will," said Charles. "Name's 'Charles'," he added, helpfully pointing at his name badge. "Let me know if you need anything else."

Ellis tossed a dollar on the bar, which Charles grabbed and tapped on the bar twice, as an acknowledgment. He spun toward a tip jar, pretended to place the dollar inside, then slipped it in a book laying on the back counter. The book, Ellis noted, was drink recipes. Ellis also noted that neither the bartender, nor any other casino employees in his sight line, had pockets on their clothes.

Big Ed, whose name was not really "Big Ed" at all, but only Ed Harper, squeaked up to the bar in his new boots. Ellis noticed him a few feet away, and snickered to himself. The man could not have been more than five foot six, a hundred and twenty pounds. He was outfitted like a B-movie cowboy: crisp, new straw cowboy hat, blue jeans, a starched white western shirt with fake mother-of-pearl buttons, silver and turquoise watch band with matching necklace, boots with an extremely tall heel, and a silver, gold, and turquoise belt buckle that was so large it nearly covered the breadth of his tiny waist. The belt buckle said God, America, and Rodeo. The entire costume, Ellis thought, looked like it had been purchased that day.

Ed Harper, who had just taken to referring to himself as Big Ed, dramatically pulled out his wad of money, which was indeed impressive to the other bar patrons. As part of his plan, Ed had saved every coin, every extra dollar over the last couple of years. He had bought his new clothes yesterday at the co-op, eliciting smartassed questions from his boss and coworkers about joining the rodeo.

Just this morning, he had gone to his bank, cleaned out his checking and savings accounts, and cashed out a couple of cd's. All together, he had raised a little over ten thousand dollars, which he took in one hundred dollar bills. He had folded the bills, wrapped them in a rubber band, stashed the wad in his front pocket. He had seen Vegas high rollers in the movies carry money that way.

Big Ed announced to Charles that he wanted to buy the whole bar a round of drinks. Charles explained that no one at the bar had to pay for their drinks, since video poker players drank free. Ed already knew this, having snuck up to a couple of casinos in Vicksburg before, when his wife was out of town. He really just wanted everybody to see how much money he had, and it worked.

Ellis watched as Charles served the little cowboy a whiskey sour. The cowboy then boisterously got change for a hundred, gave twenty to the bartender, and squeaked off toward the table games. Charles flipped the twenty in his tip jar, which Ellis thought was curious, since he had earlier palmed the single. Ellis eased over a spot, where he had a clear view of the glass tip jar, and noticed that the dollar Charles had previously booked was on top of the pile inside; the cowboy's twenty undoubtedly had taken its place among the recipes. A baseball game was on a video screen behind the bar, and he ordered another soda.

After a while, Ellis decided to stroll around the casino. He passed the five and one dollar slots, some of which were dinging, some flashing. One had a red light spinning on top, like an old fire truck, and a middle aged woman with one shoe was jumping up and down in front of it, until she landed wrong on her one high heel, and went down. Security guards were on her almost before she landed, heavily.

He passed by some table games, one of which served the little cowboy, who was whooping it up over a double-down winner, and ordering everybody free drinks. Zack eventually stopped around a group of tables that seemed to be particularly popular to the tourists. Each game had a name that incorporated the word "poker," but none of them were any form of poker Zack was familiar with. Each had a small scrolling tote board which displayed ever increasing money totals, in the tens of thousands. Ellis surmised that these figures represented some sort of accumulating pot that the players - and likely players in other casinos, were competing against each other for.

A half hour later, he went up an escalator, and arrived among the poorest casino patrons, appropriately ensconced in a remote, upstairs corner. Here, gamblers bet dimes, nickels and even pennies in multi-denominational video slot machines.

Four stories above the casino floor, in a large, darkened room containing over a hundred flat video monitors, a fat casino security manager paced, drinking cold coffee out of a Styrofoam cup. Pointing to one of the screens, he instructed a nearby seated technician to train a camera on Zack Ellis. The camera zoomed in, scanning him, revealing astonishing detail: his scowling face, the embroidered emblem on his polo shirt, the time on his cheap digital watch, 8:10.

"Anybody recognize this guy?," said the security manager. Ten employees shook their heads.

"He's been hanging around video bar three, drinking diet soda," said one.

"Has he played anything?"

"Nope."

"Loop that tape on three."

The manager waited for the video replay, which was not on tape at all, but digitally recorded. He studied it for a few moments.

"He's up to something," said the manager. "Run him on all the logs." He opened a door to leave, stopped and turned. "And call downstairs. Tell them that prick bartender Charles whatever is skimming the tip pool again. And another thing. Tell them to get the midget cowboy on B-nine into the parlor. He's starting to draw a crowd. Gamblers, we need, not gawkers. Why do I always have to tell you people this?"

Zack Ellis had been standing around for a while, studying the people in the cheap section. He noticed a common look of what he first mistook for resignation, but he had come to believe was simple boredom. When one or the other hit a fifty or hundred dollar jackpot, they would whoop and scream, then bet the whole thing away. Eventually, he had enough of watching poor people bet pennies and nickels. These casino bastards, he thought, have got to take *everything* - even pennies. And they have the gall to brag in the news about how they increased employment and improved schools. He was going to enjoy bringing these people down.

Ellis walked through the whole casino, stopped at various game stations, watching people, learning. He was headed back toward the entrance to leave when he came upon a small gathering, surrounding the little cowboy. He could see between the spectators that the cowboy had amassed an enormous pile of colored chips. He heard someone say that the stranger had fifty or sixty thousand dollars out there, and had started with only a hundred bucks. Another said he heard the cowboy was really a famous Vegas gambler, come to town to clean out the casino.

Ellis decided that this was far more interesting than anything on TV at home, so he found a good spot to stand. The cowboy was now playing all six spots on the table by himself.

"My name's Big Ed!," he shouted to no one in particular. "And we ain't leavin' 'til everybody's *rich!*." He grabbed a handful of hundred dollar chips, tossed them over his shoulder into the growing crowd, causing a scramble. Standing beside the dealer, a floor manager leaned across the table, amid the cacophony caused by Big Ed's largesse. He whispered something to Ed, who got out of his stool. Standing actually made Ed shorter. He turned to the group, which was still growing, raised his hand imperially. They quieted.

"This man," Ed said, jerking his thumb in the direction of the manager, "has informed me that the casino does not *approve* of me chucking *their* money to you good folks."

"Bullshit!," somebody shouted, "It's *your* money!" Others shouted approval.

Big Ed took a big sip of his whiskey sour, one of the three he had on the table. He held up his hand again, gaining quiet. "They also want me to go back yonder in one of them fancy private rooms, so they can cheat me, 'cause they know they can't win *fair and square*!"

"Hell, no!," the crowd rejoined, "Don't let 'em do it, Big Ed!"

Ed spun back around, nearly falling, climbed back up in his stool, grabbed a wad of chips, threw them in the air, and said, "Now *deal*, or I'm taking my bidness somewheres else."

The dealer looked at his supervisor, who nodded. "Yes sir," he said, and dealt.

Lee Farrell pulled his GTO into the parking lot in front of Long Gravy Saloon on Ladnier Point, outside Azalea. The building that housed the Long Gravy was built in the early 1900s, and had been a gambling joint, at various levels, since the Capone days. It was on old Highway 90, formerly the only practical route from the Mississippi Gulf Coast to New Orleans. Buck Carter now owned the place, and had for the last several years. He rebuilt it a few months after the storm, using the old slab and crazily colored parquet floor, just like it had always been.

Even though Lee had been coming in since high school, he never knew what to expect. The bar was a classic watering hole for fishermen, both commercial and the type who were always somehow injured and off work during the best speckled trout runs. It was also a favorite of college-aged girls who knew that old Buck wouldn't dare risk losing their business - and the paying male customers they attracted - by quibbling over I.D.

A dusty old stuffed eight foot alligator gar was mounted over the liquor shelves behind the bar. It was what river and bayou workers and fishermen used to call a "long gravy," and Lee had heard Buck explain at least half a dozen different ways he caught it. It survived Hurricane Katrina by getting hung in the top of an old Live Oak about a mile away. Buck had retrieved it, hosed it off, and stuck it back on the wall in the new place.

The Long Gravy had hosted a few of the greatest bar fights Lee had ever seen, mostly over pool games, and was legendary for the semi-naked women that always showed up after the Azalea Mardi Gras parade. The Long Gravy's status as a haven for whiskey-lechers and general miscreants was continually renewed; every time the bar's name was mentioned down the road at the Sailing Club, a group of martini-addled female bluehairs reflexively suffered a collective case of the vapors.

Lee entered through the creaky front door, immersing in a smoky smell. Mississippi had not outlawed smoking in every building, defying the trend, and places like the Long Gravy were smoker havens. The Gravy did not serve food, officially, but Buck was known as the best Cajun food chef around, even though he was decidedly non-Cajun. He often set a big batch of gumbo, jambalaya, etouffe' or red beans and rice out on a hot plate, for free. Paper plates strewn across several tables, and around the nearest garbage can showed evidence of tonight's jambalaya.

The Gravy had a few pool tables, some dart boards, and the best jukebox in the county, which was softly rendering a blues song. Normally at least one local cop, attorney, judge, or even congressman would be dodging their wives, whom would never deign to come in, by having a drink with old Buck; but Buck wasn't around, and neither the constabulary, the government, nor the legal bar was represented this evening.

All the pool tables were empty, and except for a quiet couple hunched in a far corner of the bar, the only people present were Lee, Joe the bartender, and an old salt named James, or Bob, or John, depending on who you asked, but everybody called him "Cookie," a nickname which lent much suspicion to his blithering soliloquies about back when he was a high seas badass. Cookie only had one leg, and he could not really see, but he somehow drove to the Long Gravy every day, where he sat and drank scotch and milk until someone took him home. Every morning he got his car back.

Lee ordered a beer, and took a seat next to Cookie, leaving enough distance to dodge the gnarled, heavy braided greasewood cane he carried, and sometimes swung at other drunks. Lee said, "How are you, Cookie?" Cookie slowly wheeled around on his barstool, a cigarette trailing smoke from the corner of his mouth between his faded amber eyes.

"Hello, boy," he grunted, apparently unsure of who Lee was.

"I'm Lee Farrell, Cookie, I grew up with Buck's son, Jake." Lee had introduced himself to Cookie in the same way at least twenty times.

"I know you, boy. I ain't that goddamn old," Cookie said, though he knew he was.

"Where's Buck tonight?" Cookie had been Buck's best friend since anyone could remember.

"Somebody prob'ly finally shot the son of a bitch," Cookie said. He took a big slurp of his drink, finishing it. He waived the glass at the bartender, set it down heavily.

"Buck went home already," said Joe, who was busy adding up his uncollected tabs.

"I've got this round, Joe," said Lee, to the bartender.

Cookie adjusted the stump of his leg, which the Japs had shot off at Iwo Jima, or a shark had bitten off around Cuba, or he'd lost to gangrene after getting bushwhacked by fish pirates in the Louisiana marsh. "I ain't broke, boy. I can buy my own goddamn whiskey," he said.

Lee eyed the cane, which was safely propped against the bar. He made a quick scan around Cookie's belt line for the pistol he famously waived around on occasion, but which Buck had mostly prevented him from loading.

"I know you can buy your own whiskey, Cookie. Hell, everybody knows you've got that secret pirate treasure back at your house." Lee chuckled, but Cookie did not, and Lee looked for any signs of levity in the deep brown folds of the old man's face.

"All right, I'll drink with you. But I got the next one," said Cookie.

The next several minutes were spent in silence, as Joe tuned in a replay of an old football game, and the three stared at it. Cookie ordered his round. The couple at the end of the bar slipped out the door. Lee had come to the Gravy to ask Buck about this 'Camellia' that Mama Thea mentioned. He figured that if anyone knew what went on years ago, Buck would. As he sat next to Cookie, it occurred to him that the old man might remember something, too. Lee said, "Cookie, how long have you been coming around this place?"

"Long enough to know better'n to ask a man his business."

Lee fought the impulse to confront the old drunk's rudeness, but then had to laugh, quietly. He said, "What I *mean* is, I heard there was still a quite a bit of gambling, and so forth, around here, even up into the late sixties. Is that true, or were you around then?"

"What, are you writing a book?"

Lee thought *yes, well, sort of*, but he said, "No. Forget it. I was trying to find out about somebody named 'Camellia,' but I guess I'll just wait and talk to Buck."

Cookie turned toward Lee. His eyes seemed sharper now, and Lee noticed his lips were trembling. "Who you been talking to, boy?," he said. "What do you know about a Camellia?"

"Nothing, really, just that she might have used to hang out around here, and…"

"You forget about what you heard," Cookie growled, "there ain't no Camellia, never was."

"But a second ago, you acted like you knew who I was talking about."

Cookie lurched off his barstool, balancing on his cane, started a amazingly efficient two-point hobble toward the front door.

Joe said, "Whoa, Cookie, let me get you a ride."

"I don't need no damn ride!"

Lee said, "Cookie, I'll take you home, I still want to ask you a couple…"

Cookie stopped, turned. He seemed about to explode, but suddenly deflated, becoming almost apologetic of an instant. He said, "Boy. *Lee.* I know you, always kind of liked you. I remember when you was the quarterback. Best damn one St. Thomas ever had. I knew your folks died, way back when, and how Buck helped take care o' you. You ain't had it easy, even if it's true that you got all that money. So I'm gonna say this one time. Live your life. Be happy. Forget about what you heard. Looking for dead people around here ain't gonna accomplish anything."

"But wait, how do you know she's dead?"

"She is, and we'll all be soon enough, son. Best you don't rush it. Forget about Camellia." He turned, and was gone.

Zack Ellis left the Cronus Casino shaking his head, incredulous. He and a crowd of at least fifty tourists had watched the little cowboy for the last hour or so, and what they had witnessed further galvanized his utter contempt for casino gambling. The drunken little fool had amassed an incredible

amount of chips, tens of thousands of dollars; he was playing
all six positions on the blackjack table, betting wildly, winning
everything. Then, his luck changed.

The change was not subtle, or slow. One moment, he
couldn't lose; the next moment, he couldn't win. And even
though the crowd urged him to quit, he kept playing. If the dealer
needed a three, he got it. If the cowboy got a blackjack, so did
the dealer. His descent was short and merciless. He lost it all,
including whatever was left in his rubber band. Ellis climbed into
his car in the parking garage, and left.

Upstairs, the security manager got his report. The young
stranger had not shown up on any "banned" lists, or in the casino's
face-recognition computer files. He turned up in the police files:
Special Agent Zachary Ellis, late of Washington, D.C., relatively
new in the coast office, in Gulfport. The security manager
frowned. Just what he needed, a new fucking F.B.I. guy floating
around, checking the place out.

But what did he have to worry about? The bosses in New
Orleans were as happy as they had ever been; the new guy, Nick
Bonacelli, was doing his job, which consisted mainly of staying the
fuck out of the way. And, except for an occasional flare-up from
some old fool using this new Destiny drug, and freaking out in one
of the cheap suites, things were smooth.

He decided not to tell the Bardinos about the new FBI guy,
and he damn sure wasn't reporting to this Bonacelli, or Bonehead,
as the Bardinos called him. And how about this little fool in the
cowboy costume, just now leaving the casino. He'd spent the last
several minutes puking in the main men's room, under the watch
of undercover floor security. The security manager turned to
the bank of technicians, said, "How far did we go into that little
bastard?"

"Seventy-two grand," said one of them.

"How much did he lay?"

"Ten-ish."

"How much did he give away?"

"Fifty-two hundred to the crowd, four thousand to the waitresses."

"Stupid fucker. Get two grand of it back from the girls. And get Roy Rogers a limo home."

Lee was driving home from the Long Gravy, thinking about what the old fool Cookie had said. Or rather, what he didn't say. Obviously, a Camellia had once existed. So Mama Thea had at least told him the truth about that. But she had said herself she was senile. The story was just unbelievable. Still, if a Camellia did hang around back then, she had been killed. So she could not be the same one. Lee had a sudden sick feeling at the realization that Mama Thea was actually *dying*. His only real family was dying.

His cell phone rang. It was Meat, at the Blue Stone. Bonehead was in the bar, snooping around. And on Lee's night off. Lee stopped at his house in Azalea, hoping to catch Diana there. She was not home, had left no message. Lee fed Iris, jumped in the car, and headed to Biloxi. Pulling out of his driveway onto highway 90 East, he nearly got broadsided by a truck with only one headlight, speeding west. *Idiot*, thought Lee, *get your headlights fixed, and slow down*.

Speeding west on highway 90, Ed Ford was disgusted. He wished he would run into some damn fool, like the one that just pulled out in front of him, and kill himself. He didn't, though, so he laid on his horn and shot the maniac the bird, even though he couldn't get his damn window down fast enough for the fool to see it. He couldn't believe it. He had had those arrogant, greasy

casino thieves right where he expected - was winning everything
he played, was the star of the show.

Big Ed - the crowd was actually *shouting his name*! Then, the
bastards had started cheating. Somehow, they dealt him bad cards,
anticipated his strategy. They always seemed to get what they
wanted: five here, six there. Face cards. Blackjacks. They had
cheated! Deprived him of his *glory*! If all that wasn't bad enough,
he got sick from all whiskey sours they kept pushing on him.
He - a deacon in his church - a known, righteous teetotaler from
Picayune, had actually barfed all the way to the bathroom. Some
of the same people he had been tossing money to earlier were
laughing at him in his misery.

But he had refused their damned limousine. Sure, he was a
little drunk, but he could drive, dammit. Besides, he couldn't pull
up to the house in a limo, his wife would want to know where he
had been. And he had skipped work today, so he needed to have
his truck, to be in early tomorrow. Hopefully the co-op wouldn't
fire him. Maybe he would not get pulled over for having just one
headlight. Stupid old Chevy.

Lee entered the Stone through the front, the old movie
theater foyer. The club was blaring, packed, and a few patrons
mingled around the huge sapphire on display. Lee overheard one
say that he knew it wasn't real. Maybe not, Lee thought, who
knows?

He entered the front of the cavernous band area. A local
band, Johnny Rock, was playing a rock and roll song, and the
place was teeming. Johnny Rock had turned into a big draw at the
Stone. The singer was a young lady in her early twenties whom
Lee had known for some time. She was from somewhere down
in south Louisiana, close to New Iberia, had grown up among
family whose first language was French. Lee didn't know her

real name, which was also French, but only knew that it ended with Melancon, or something similar. He just called her Tam, like everybody else.

Lee marveled at her. In addition to being beautiful and having a fantastic rock and roll voice, she had an impossibly perfect body, which she did not mind showing. As she prowled and leaped around the stage, her blue black, waist length hair swung around her upper body, clad only in a tiny black leather bikini top. Her matching leather pants were so low on her hips, Lee wondered how they stayed on. She noticed him in the back, and screamed his name over her microphone. Embarrassed, he slipped back out into the foyer, intent upon going around to the back entrance, and finding Meat. Before he could make it to the front door, however, someone called him. He turned, and saw that it was Bonehead. He strolled across, meeting Bonacelli next to the Sapphire case.

"I've been trying to get in touch, Mr. Farrell," said Bonacelli.

Lee expected trouble, but could not immediately rate Bonacelli's temperament, though he did not seem hostile. Maybe a little drunk.

"I'm not hard to find, Nick. If you want to chat you should come over yourself, not send Flounder."

"Who?"

"Flounder, your driver."

"Flounder. Hmmmm...interesting nickname. You'll have to tell me more about that later."

"Well, Nick I'm just dying to. What, are we chums now?"

"Maybe. Maybe." said Bonacelli. "Want to see something?"

Bonacelli spun, without waiting for a response, went behind the sapphire display case, which sat in the middle of the huge foyer. On the back of the case, about waist level, was a small keypad. Bonacelli punched some numbers, and the keypad flipped open. A second keypad electronically emerged from behind the first.

Bonacelli punched several more numbers into it, causing a latch to release, and the back of the case to open. Bonacelli reached inside the case, and took the big sapphire.

"Dude, what are you doing?," said a guy who had been looking at the stone.

"Here, catch," said Bonacelli, tossing it to the guy. He caught it.

"Here, dude," said the stranger, handing the stone back to Bonacelli, "I ain't getting involved in whatever you're up to." He rapidly went out the front door.

Bonacelli chuckled, wiped off the stone on his shirt, replaced it, closed the case.

"Why don't we go up," Bonacelli indicated the office, upstairs, "and talk?"

Lee said, "Listen, Bonacelli..."

"Please, Nick."

"OK, Nick. I'm a little confused. I thought you and me were fighting last time we saw each other, in fact the *only* time we saw each other, so I don't see what we have to talk about."

"Good point. If you give me a few minutes, I promise it will all become clear."

"Well, I'm here, so let's go."

Buck Carter hung up the phone, plopped on his couch and lit a cigarette. He got up and poured an Irish whiskey, downed it. That drunk old fool Cookie had just called him, blathering about ghosts and curses and dead people. And Lee Farrell. Buck couldn't make sense of it. But he knew nothing good could come from Cookie yapping about the past. No telling what ghost he was upset over, there were so many.

Nick Bonacelli took a stool at the small bar in Lee's office; Lee went behind it. "You drinking?," said Lee.

"Whatever you're having," said Bonacelli.

Lee poured two highball glasses half full of twelve year old scotch, neat. He slid one to Bonehead. "Now what's this about?," Lee said.

Bonacelli picked up his glass, strolled across to the one-way glass, looked down in the club. "Fascinating," he said.

Lee eyed Bonehead's back. He stayed behind the bar. "Yeah, a real study in human alcohol consumption. So?"

"You know why they're here?," said Bonacelli.

"Cold beer, loud music, and the remote chance of getting laid. Because everyone else does."

"Exactly," said Bonacelli. "Exactly. People come here, because everyone else does. They think they *have* to, to fit in. Even though most of those losers down there - the lawyers, the bankers, the ice heads, the fashion freaks - they all fail *most* of the time."

"Like casino patrons?"

"Like casino patrons," said Bonacelli, returning to the bar stool. "Just like the sheep across the street. Why do they do it?"

"Interesting philosophical questions, Nick, but I'm not really in the mood for dialectics, right now. Can you get to the point?"

"Dialectics. Good one. You pick that up in law school?"

Lee started to say something, stopped.

"You did flunk out of law school, didn't you, Lee?"

"Look, Bonacelli, I don't know what you're getting at, or how you know I went to law school. As a point of fact, I quit, I did not flunk out. What the hell are you doing asking me about my business? About my past?"

"Oh, I know plenty about your past, Lee. Just indulge me for a few minutes, OK?"

Lee stared.

Bonacelli said, "I'll give you the answer to my previous question. People do these things because they are stupid, plain and simple. Lack of intellectual curiosity. Fear of standing out, of being judged. Peer pressure to be average. They can't handle being rejected for their hair, their clothes, their...weaknesses. They are afraid to go it alone. The best they can hope for is to die within the terms of their life insurance policies, so their pitiful children can pay off their student loans. All the powers have to do is make sure the masses have their whiskey, and their religion. Machiavelli and Napoleon, at work before your eyes. Yet, those same people have the gall to judge other people, people who do not follow their timid ways."

"OK, so what does…"

"Like background, for instance. Do you realize that people still presume to know what a person is like because of their parents, their race, or heritage? Their *name*?"

"Yeah, I'm from Mississippi. I get a dose of that kind of superior crap every time I leave the state."

"I bet you do. In that respect, my friend, we are just alike. Ever wonder how the Italians lost the world?"

"No."

"Well, I'll tell you anyway. Think about it. When most of Europe were fighting each other with clubs, Romans were building the Coliseum."

"Which now is in ruins."

"Volumes have been written on that subject. I did a paper on the economics of it myself in school."

"Impressive. Remind me not to play you in Trivial Pursuit. So how did they screw it all up?"

"The simple answer is, they drank it away." He walked back to the window. "Just what's happening here. These fools are all out there whooping it up, while their empire dies around them."

"Heavy. Now, if you don't mind, I'd like to go down there, and mingle with the doomed."

"Let me buy you a drink here. We've got business to discuss."

"You're mistaken. Look, Nick. I hate we got off to a rusty start, but that was not my fault. I know who you are, who your bosses are. I don't want any trouble, just to do my job, as I have done since we opened. I understand my role. If you are here to check on that, you can relax. You'll get no trouble from me."

"That's not why I'm here. I assure you, I know you are smarter than to make trouble. What I'm here about is not my troubles, but yours."

"Hey, I didn't bring on the fall of Rome, sport, and I don't have any trouble with the empire." Lee headed for the door.

" Let's talk *now,* Sergeant Farrell."

Lee froze. Fear rose up his legs, washed through his chest like ice water. It immediately receded, leaving nothing but anger. He turned on Bonehead in a flash of rage. Nick Bonacelli was shocked at the quickness and ease with which Lee Farrell had crossed the room, snatched him off the stool. Now laying on the floor, on his on his back, he gaped at Farrell, astride him with his fist cocked, and his upper lip twitching.

Lee said, "This is the last time I'm going to warn you about fucking with me. *Understand?*"

"Farrell…"

"*Yes* or *no*, asshole."

"I know what happened at Cat Island, Farrell. Now get off." He pushed Lee aside, stood up.

Lee, slowly rising, said, "How…, uh, what do you mean?"

"You know what I mean." He straightened his shirt, dusted off.

"Listen, Bonacelli, I've lived here most of my life, and done a lot of shit at Cat Island. Now why don't you get to the point?"

"Please, Mr. Farrell. Why don't *you* get to the point? How many times have you gotten two police officers killed?"

Lee stopped. "Fine. What do you intend to do with whatever it is you think you know?"

"Sit down, Lee. Let's make *sure* you understand the big picture." Nick strode around the back of the bar, now completely composed. Lee sat on the couch.

"Want another drink?," asked Nick.

"Yes," said Lee, staring to his right, down toward the wild crowd around the stage. Tam was creeping across the stage on her hands and knees, screeching a song by Joan Jett. Nick arrived at the couch with two shots of vodka, chilled. He sat. Johnny Rock's heavy rhythms vibrated soundproof glass. A couple sat right outside the window, obliviously smoking a small wooden pipe.

Lee downed his shot of vodka.

Bonacelli said, "Like it or not, you and I are just alike, Farrell. We're both severely underestimated."

"There's one big difference, Nick. You think you're a bigshot. I *know* I'm just a redneck."

"And apparently incapable of grasping the big picture."

"Unwilling, maybe."

"Fine. Well, like it or not, there's a new arrangement. I know about the Army, the drug deal, the killings at Cat Island. You went to law school long enough to remember the concept of felony murder? Well, let me remind you. Let's say, for instance, a group of guys conspire to commit a *bunch* of drug dealing felonies, and some sheriff's deputies get killed in the process. No matter who does the actual killing, in the eyes of the law, *all* the bad guys are murderers. And in Mississippi, that means the death penalty. Did I mention there's no statute of limitations on murder here?"

"Who else have you told this to?"

"Don't worry about that. After all, you can't help me from death row, can you?"

"So, how do you know I won't just go the FBI about you and your little adopted family?"

"That's a risk I just have to take, Lee. Most of what I know about the so-called 'Family' I learned off the History channel. You willing to fight a murder rap while I'm fighting a bullshit RICO charge?"

Lee stood up. "No," he said. "I'm not. Now what do you want?"

"Good. I'm working out a transaction that I want your assistance with. I'll let you know the details later. I'll kick back to you appropriately. Your cut might rise over time, if you're a good partner."

"I'm not your partner."

"Yes, you are, Lee, so you might as well get on the team voluntarily. The alternatives for you and Diana are not advantageous."

"You leave Diana alone," Lee snapped.

Nick stood up, headed toward the door, where he stopped. "Temper, temper. Lee, the state of Mississippi is, as I understand, very proficient at executing cop killers."

"I never killed anyone."

"So *you* say. In any case, I hope you are not under the impression that I rely on the state, so to speak. You cross me, and you die. Either way. And I suggest you do not share this conversation with your wife. She and Sarah are together quite a bit, and I don't want that crazy woman knowing my business. One word to Diana, and the deal's off." He checked his gold watch. "It's getting late. Any questions?"

Lee sat silent.

"Good. You can expect my call, soon." He turned.

"One more thing," said Lee, "How did you find out about Cat Island?"

Nick turned slowly, savoring the question, smiling. "Let's just say I've got some college buddies in government that owe me."

"You mean a bunch of government hacks know about this, too?

Nick laughed. "Come on, Lee, they're in a secret government spying program. You trust your government, don't you?" He laughed again, opened the door. Meat was standing there.

Meat eyed Bonacelli suspiciously, then said to Lee, "Everything OK, chief?"

"Yeah, Meat, just me and - ah - Mr. Bonacelli having a few laughs. That's all for now."

Meat and Bonacelli went out the door. Lee walked up to the glass, watched Tam sweating across the stage. He rubbed his brow, noticing that it was damp, too.

As Big Ed Ford finally made his way into the edge of Picayune, he started sobering up, realizing what a fool he'd been. What the preacher always said about gambling. How he'd taken up with the devil, gotten his just reward. He looked in the rearview mirror at himself. He had been prepared to leave his wife, the woman he loved, for *money*. "Big Ed," he said, and snorted. He took the hat off, flung it out his window. He pulled up in his driveway, noticed his wife had left the front light on for him. "Dang," he said to himself, " I hope the meat loaf's good tonight."

Chapter 5 - New Orleans

Boot had not been running many charters; he had cooked up a new scheme, and was cashing in while it lasted. He had marshaled a group of women to go to rest areas along the coast highways, and sell fake maps of coast casino slot machine areas. The girls told tourists they were connected with someone in casino management, and knew where the daily "loose" slot machines were. With so many casinos and so many tourists, business had exploded, and Boot almost didn't have time to fish.

But Lee had gotten him to go out two weekends in a row, just the two of them, limiting on specks and redfish down around the Chandelier Islands, thirty-five or forty miles off Azalea.

"You're going to get arrested eventually, you realize," Lee said, when Boot told him about the scheme.

Boot shrugged. "Ain't been popped in a year or more, boss. I ain't on paper, got no warrants." To Boot, getting arrested was a normal part of everyday life; time in jail was useful for picking up tidbits of information, as long as it was the county jail, and the stay was not overly long.

Lee had not heard from Bonacelli. After he had time to think about it, he figured Bonacelli was just repeating rumors he'd heard. Lee and Boot were steadily catching fish when a true gulf squall popped up and rolled right over them, almost instantaneously. Lee wasn't scared of the rain, but he was of the lightning. They powered the big fishing boat toward shore, and were a couple of hours toward home, nearly at the Azalea harbor before the rain let up. They decided to run down to the Long Gravy, since the fishing day had been cut short. Plus, Lee wanted to have a beer, shoot some pool.

The Gravy was busy, for a Sunday. Local bikers, many of
whom were professionals riding machines they could barely
afford, were in the bar whooping it up. Buck had evidently
delivered a big pot of gumbo and left. Lee and Boot luckily got
an open pool table, and were four games into it when Lee noticed
old Cookie ensconced in his spot at the bar. Boot made a called,
banked shot on the eight ball, sending Lee to the bar for a new set
of beers. Cookie nodded at him, waived him down. The juke box
was up loud. Lee leaned in close to hear the old man's gruff voice.

"Need to talk to you," he said, then exploded in a coughing fit
that caught the attention of the two dozen or so patrons milling
around. When he recovered, he said, "got to clear something up.
When you get a chance."

The next couple of games were routs, and Boot was declared
world champion. This was apparently overheard at the next table,
where two young players, construction workers from out west,
they said, were ready to contest the title. Boot quickly made
friends with the two, happy they were from out of town, and
unfamiliar with his game. He was busy getting all the bets straight
when Lee meandered to the bar. The jukebox had played out for
the moment. Still, he and Cookie moved the far, vacant end of the
bar, for privacy.

Cookie said, "That talk we had a while back. You been asking
around, any more questions about this," he looked around, all sides,
to make sure no one was watching, "this Camellia you heard about?"

"No, Cookie, I haven't. But it's real important to me. It looks
like we may be talking about two different people, but I want to
know for sure. I don't intend to let it go, if that's what you're
asking."

"That's exactly what I'm asking. What I'm *saying*. You got to
leave this alone."

"I'm looking for somebody, and I'm not planning on stopping. It's something I feel like I have to do. If that hurts feelings, frankly, I don't give a damn."

"Son, the past is dangerous here. You can get hurt."

"Well, if that's what you want to tell me, you can forget it. I'm not scared. Have a good day." He got off the stool, started back toward the pool tables.

"Wait a second. I'll - tell you what you want to know, if you'll promise me you'll quit stirring up shit around here."

"To be honest, Cookie, I did not realize I had done that."

"You kidding me? Buck damn near had a stroke when he found out."

"How did he happen to find out?"

"Well, I let it slip, I guess."

"You going to run tell him about this conversation?"

"Hell, no. He'll shoot me and you both, in a second."

"Buck? He's practically my dad, Cookie, he's not going to do anything to me. And you're his best friend, aren't you?"

"Yeah, but mainly 'cause he knows I know too much. Plus, I can't get around very good with my damn leg; he drives me around, for the company."

"How long have you and Buck been hanging out together?"

"Shit. Forty something years?

"You mind me asking, what happened to your leg?"

"Yeah, I mind. What did you hear?"

"Oh, different things. Wars, car wrecks. Lots of things."

Cookie said nothing.

Lee said, "Alright, what do you know about a Camellia?"

"Son, if I tell you this, and you repeat it, we'll both be dead. I just want you to shut up with the questions, and that's the only reason we're talkin' about it. Deal?"

"Deal." Lee crossed his fingers behind his back, a silly gesture that he had not made since childhood. He stayed serious, though, because Cookie was so earnest.

"Camellia, the one I knew, is dead."

"That's what you sort of said, before."

"Because she is."

"When, where?"

"Buck conked her on the head, loaded her up in the skiff, and dumped her in the gulf. She sunk pretty quick, 'cause he had two big old cinder blocks tied to her."

"What the hell for?"

"Well, so she would *sink*, son."

"That's not what I mean. Why did he kill her?"

"I can't see how that helps you out. That's all you need to know. The Camellia we all knew around here, she's dead."

"How old was she? "

"Young."

"What did she look like?"

"Little, skinny, normally, except she was pregnant at the time."

"Jesus."

"You understand who we're dealing with, now?"

"Well, it can't be the same person, because this other Camellia, well, she didn't die like that."

"Good," said Cookie. "Then this is settled?"

"Yes, I guess."

"Like I said, this conversation ain't happened."

"One more thing," said Lee.

"What now, goddammit?"

"You were there, right?"

Cookie looked around again, said, "Yeah."

"When was this?"

"The year that hurricane hit. Camille. 1969."

All the way home, Lee thought about that. 1969. The year his adoptive birth certificate said he was born. But the only Camellia he had located had died in the cruelest way, that same year. And Buck Carter wasn't just a mean old drunk, he was a murderer.

Several days later, Lee walked down the middle of Bourbon Street, which smelled like a combination of rotting garbage and urine. Which it was, in more than just literal ways. He stopped to look at the pictures posted outside one of the many "gentlemen's clubs" that had germinated along the street during the Hurricane Katrina occupation; the federally funded influx of out-of-town police and military personnel affected burlesque and prostitution in the French Quarter like no other era since the feds shut down Storyville. Katrina relief efforts had touched off a titty bar and hooker renaissance.

He noticed a group of tourists negotiating the uneven brick sidewalk of the ancient street, trying to stay under balconies, out of the afternoon swelter. They were so concerned with keeping their footing, they never noticed the steady drip they were approaching, something that had come from one of the apartments above, where a gay couple were out watering their ferns, and cleaning the balcony with brushes and a bucket. As the tourists passed, one of the guys dumped the rest of the bucket's contents on the balcony, which cascaded upon the group below. The tourists scattered, Lee smiled. The guys on the balcony never noticed.

Several years earlier, when Lee had gotten a loan against his trust money, and had bought an apartment in an old building on Chartres Street that was being renovated into condominiums. His friends thought he was nuts to buy anything in the dilapidated east end of the French Quarter, and his lawyer had practically cried. But he bought it anyway, had contractors strip out garish carpet and layers of old wallpaper, restoring it to the original nineteenth century hardwood and plaster townhouse of its birth.

He and Diana used to sit out on the balcony in the mornings, drinking thick coffee, reading the Times Picayune and listening to mule drawn carriages, which were kept around the corner somewhere, clopping toward the French Quarter. Their drivers would spend the rest of the day hauling tourists around at fifty dollars a pop, telling them outrageous lies about the city's landmarks and history. Lee and Diana's greatest nights had been spent making love under the old building's nine foot plaster ceilings as locals streamed below, dodging French Quarter tourists, shouting, singing, or arguing their way toward the cooler clubs of the Faubourg Marigny, just across Esplanade.

As Lee sweated on Bourbon Street, he wished she had come along. She was busy, she said. Lee wondered what business a career unemployed person would have, but now he was glad she didn't come. Now that Bonehead might have him cornered, and he seemed to have stumbled upon an old coast murder, he just needed some think space. So he had come in to the city late the night before, having left a recorded message with the Blue Stone's mysterious accountant that he would be gone a couple of days. Family business. Lee chuckled at the irony.

He had stayed in last night, gotten up early, gone around the corner to the French Market to pick up some coffee and something to eat. The early morning French Market was, for Lee, one of the greatest, most humorous sights on earth. Dozens of vendors scrambled around, setting up their tents and their booths inside and outside the protection of the main open air pavilion. Under it, the older vendors, or at least the ones with the oldest spots, shouted relentlessly at their suppliers, who were themselves scrambling to unload trucks and get out of the madness of the of the lower Quarter traffic jam they caused. Across the street, produce suppliers and shop owners swept and hosed the sidewalk, beating sleeping drunks with their brooms.

Everywhere, shouts in English, Italian, and Spanish shot through the rapidly heating air, as early tourists slowly emerged from coffee houses down Decatur, covered in powdered beignet sugar. Lee patiently waited to purchase some bananas at a fruit stand, where two young boys, no more than eleven or twelve, were busily ringing up purchases; periodically, one would dart from behind the old wooden, elevated stand and demand five dollars from a tourist who had taken his picture, or any picture in their general area, claiming their images were "registered." The startled tourist always paid. It was one of the oldest scams in the Quarter, and had worked for generations.

As he waited, Lee remembered reading that John James Audubon, the famous traveling naturalist, had visited New Orleans and this same market nearly two centuries earlier. He had lost his wallet to a pickpocket, observed brutal street crime, and been shocked by the uncanny accuracy of local hunters who killed migrating birds by the thousands. Audubon thought New Orleans was the most depraved place he had ever visited. The city had nevertheless eventually named its greatest public park after him.

After breakfast, Lee went uptown to Tulane University, where an old friend from St. Thomas was now a professor of antiquities. Lee wanted his friend's opinion of the amulet Mama Thea gave him. He was still skeptical of Mama Thea's voodoo talk, but knew better than to shrug off anything in this nutty city. Besides, he could use some good luck.

His buddy looked at the amulet with some amazement. He wanted to keep it over night, and asked Lee to come back in the

morning. So, rather than waste the day, he decided to head back
to the Quarter and get drunk.

Nick Bonacelli parked out on the street in front of his house,
under the pretense of checking his mail, in case anyone cared. He
went to the front door and let himself in, knowing that Sarah and
Diana were probably out by the pool. He left his uncomfortable
black leather dress shoes in the mercifully cool foyer, slid through
the hardwood den and kitchen to his new favorite window,
overlooking his damned expensive teak pool chairs. It was what
the chairs contained that he was interested in.

Lunch at home alone had been his periodic habit since he
accidentally discovered his wife and Mrs. Diana Farrell working on
their total body tans several weeks earlier. To his knowledge, neither
one had ever been aware of his dozen or so private lunches since.

Nick was not a hasty man, not prone to drastic decisions. He
was aware of this trait in himself, had nurtured it. Before Nick
had run away from home the old man who adopted him had tried
to teach him some lessons. He said to always stay back, see what
others do first. Never take a position, physical or in rhetoric, that
afforded no retreat.

Like his new favorite window, at the house. It was in the breakfast
area, overlooking the pool. And it was easy to abandon, affording
retreat without commotion, if necessary. He grabbed a sandwich
and diet soda, took his seat. Sarah and Ms. Farrell were reliably naked,
and apparently halfway through a joint of his best weed.

The old man had also said to avoid being too careful. Brains
are good, he said, necessary. But balls count as much, maybe
more. *Brains and balls*, thought Nick, laughing at himself. *This is
what they get you. You sneak home every few days to stalk your wife and
her - what? Friend? Lover?* He'd never seen it, but he knew Sarah
had her little female flings, especially in East Village. The thought

made his throat constrict. *What a whore*, he thought. *She does it with women all over the goddamn place, and tries to make me beg.*

Diana Farrell, on the other hand, did not appear to Nicolas Brains and Balls Bonacelli to be the kind Sarah was, and usually gravitated toward. Shit, she had to be what? Ten, twelve years older than Sarah? But she looked just as good, and had a hell of a lot more class. How could the ambitionless Lee Farrell ever have landed such a beauty?

Nick had Lee Farrell thoroughly investigated before their talk at the Blue Stone. Nick knew from his spies that Farrell has been a big shot quarterback in high school, but that couldn't explain Diana. She was just on a plane above him. He was a bar manager. He'd pissed away every opportunity he had. He'd quit his football scholarship at Mississippi State, gone into the military, then finished college down in New Orleans, where he met Diana, at Tulane. She married the bastard; her old man, the lawyer, apparently helped get him in law school at Ole Miss, and the fool had quit after two years. Who quits law school after two years? Loser. Nick Bonacelli made an uncharacteristically hasty decision. When he killed Lee Farrell, he'd kill Sarah, too. Then he and Ms. Farrell would get out of this horrible shithole to somewhere civilized.

This business with Farrell had him thinking about the past, and interfered with his current lecheries. As a teenager he had run away, taken Bonacelli as his new name. He was smart and fearless, and had been more or less adopted by a street crew in Chicago. He had kept his mouth shut, and learned as much as he could. They eventually realized how smart he was, and that he was utterly ruthless. The Chicago mob boss at the time, Johnny Toria, took Nick into his own home, practically adopting him, as Roman emperors had traditionally adopted their successors. Bonacelli was being groomed. Toria was fascinated by Roman history.

Toria and the Chicago mob eventually paid for Nick's college and grad school. In mob circles, he was part of a modern phenomenon; a business executive who had been grown for the specific purpose of serving the interests of the modern American La Cosa Nostra. He finished his sandwich, took a last look at his old and maybe new wives, and left, slamming the door. He did not care if they heard.

On the drive back to the casino, Nick felt ebullient. Having made the decision to remove Sarah, he had collaterally solved a number of issues related to his developing long term plans. When he had taken over the Cronus, which he viewed as a temporary thing until he could decide what to do, he worried that Sarah just would never fit into the circles he was headed for. She was, after all, a goddamn art student at NYU titty dancing for tuition when he met her. He had been on a business trip to New York City, and she hit the fucking lottery when he walked in.

Diana, on the other hand, would be perfect. It was simple, brilliant even. Of course, everything had to line up right. After he was bankrolled, and Farrell and the bitch Sarah were gone, he'd decide what to do next. He figured he could clear eight or ten million dollars off the deal he was arranging, and it was time bring Farrell fully into the loop. Temporarily. Too bad he had to kill Farrell to make it work; disposal was always the biggest problem with dead people.

For the rest of the drive, he mused about getting rid of the bodies. As much as he would like to kill Farrell himself, he needed someone else, for obvious reasons. Someone ruthless, but competent enough to get them both. And expendable, since he would have to be clipped, too. Somebody just like the fool Flounder. He looked like he would do anything to get a real Rolex. Gazing out at the gulf, he realized why the Bardinos never got popped for murder. These local fools never even found all the bodies after Hurricane Katrina. There had to be a million swampy places to dump around here that no human ever saw. No normal human, anyway.

The thought of killing two or three human beings did not bother him. Nick had pondered these things when he was younger, and still bothered by a conscious. At some point, he concluded that *everyone* was dirty, not just mobsters, and had therefore given tacit consent to being whacked. Justice and fairness, and God himself, Nick had long since realized, were concepts invented and continually validated by the weak, penitent minds of humans driven mad by the knowledge of impending death. Yet those same people had yet not matured philosophically beyond violence and self destruction. These faithless creatures were afraid of death, yet more than willing to tolerate it inflicted it upon others. Hypocrites, they all deserved to die.

Nick did not believe in God, had evolved beyond such trivialities. Faith was for fools. God had done no favors for his children, only established a set of standards so unobtainable that they merely assured eternal damnation. If Jesus actually practiced true tolerance and forgiveness then he was unique among the race his Father had created; the rest were busily distracted from their fate by whips, bullets, or the eternal, fruitless pursuit of gold. Murder was historically not a matter of faith, or morality, or even justice. It was pure business.

These realizations had been, for Nick, a panacea. The perfect solution to a long term problem with potential serious detriment to clear thought. He may be called upon at any time to kill a friend. A successful man must not be distracted. As Johnny Toria always said, friends are friends, business is business.

Lee's whole body resonated with the pounding of the terrible dance music inside a dark titty bar. Dahlia was not around; some

dancer had pegged him as a good tipper, and had insinuated herself
at his table in the small VIP area where he sat. She had managed
to run off all the other girls. Lee had passively ordered her and
the waitress several shots of some green stuff they liked, and he
had given the dancer a wad of money during her occupation. He
wasn't sure exactly what she looked like, but did not particularly
care.

He had been watching a guy down by the front of the stage,
who was wearing a black eye patch, the kind that ties around the
head. Underneath, he had a surgical dressing, attached to his face
and head by reams of wide white tape, had obviously recently had
a surgical procedure, or some kind of injury. Lee wondered what
the patch was for, since the fellow could not have possibly detected
any light through the white bandage. Style, he figured. Between
the baseball game on a large screen near him, the steady stream of
clueless patrons and the eyepatch man, Lee was busily not paying
attention to his girl. Which was fine with him, but not her.

"Listen, honey," she shout-whispered to Lee, "I'm getting off
pretty soon, and, well, I was hoping to make more money today."
She sat back, pointing at the fives and tens he had periodically
poked in her sequined garter belt, looking at Lee expectantly.
He glanced at her vaguely, not sure what she had said in the din
of music. Just then, Eyepatch tried to light a cigarette; being
handicapped by his recently acquired lack of depth of perception,
he missed the end of the cigarette. Trying again, he hunched
over the lighter, then jerked his head back, yelping, swatting at a
smoking eyebrow. Lee laughed, reached for his beer, knocked it
over in the lap of his increasingly irritated personal titty dancer.

She cursed, jumped up, dramatically swiping beer off her
thigh, the one without the garter belt. By the time she got back
from the bar with a towel, Lee had ordered another beer, and the
bar DJ was repeatedly blaring for "Crystal" to report to the main

stage. Lee's annoyed tablemate popped up again, saying. "Well , I've got to go to the fucking stage. When I get back, we're gonna go upstairs, right?"

Lee was unsure whether she wanted a response, though he was mildly relieved that he now knew her name. He was not about to commit to the "upstairs" money trap, at least not with Crystal. It was a "private lounge" full of attentive bouncers, whose main function was to make sure that any tourist stupid enough to go there expecting sex was disappointed. And, they made sure the sucker paid for the fabulous bottle of Champaign that went along with the deal: a hundred dollars for something that high school kids would buy for their first drinking party. Lee decided not to respond, and Crystal stomped off to the stage.

Lee found the waitress again, asked for his tab. Crystal stalked around on the stage, and Lee got his first full look at her. She was not bad, he decided, for a titty dancer obviously late in her career. But no Dahlia. The door out to Bourbon street opened across the club, and a sole patron entered. Even in the dark, smoky din of the club he recognized the Mafia figure, a ghastly old man known in the New Orleans press as The Raven. He was by himself, and walked around the tables directly toward Lee. The small table next to Lee was open; one of the floor managers admitted the mobster to the pitifully small VIP area, which only had four tables to begin with. The Raven took the open table. Lee could not help but stare.

The old man surveyed the crowd. He was not interested in the dirty whores on stage or the ones offering their nasty bodies for lap dances. He was there to check on business, and if he managed to meet some nice young man, it was pure lagniappe. He was a great uncle of the current boss of the Bardinos, Petrino Mallini, who had given him his grotesque nickname, a betrayal the old man had not forgotten. His real name was Francis, but it might has well have been anything. Once you get a tag like "Raven," it sticks.

He was the family representative on Bourbon Street, in charge of collections from Quarter merchants, restaurants, bars and adult joints. His periodic presence was designed to keep the management uncomfortable. He ordered a drink, a tall glass of club soda with lemon, no ice. None of the girls were coming by, but the floor manager paid his respects. Nobody charged him, and he did not offer.

The Raven's father, a non-mob connected first generation Sicilian - American immigrant, had been drafted into the Navy, and killed in the Pacific during World War 2. The young Francis was very religious, and initially accepted the irony that God had allowed his father to escape Mussolini for America, only to be killed by another group of fanatics in another part of the world. It was God's will, and not to be questioned. Francis had been raised by this mother in New Orleans, who was determined to keep him away from the other Italian immigrants, whom were too often involved in crime. He went to Catholic school, and was an altar boy. Life revolved around the church. He was devoutly Christian, believed God had a plan for everything.

One day in junior high school, a good friend of his who also had no father was molested by one of the priests. He was a small boy, unable to defend himself, and horrified to tell his mother. The boy killed himself the next weekend. Francis was so enraged, he decided to take revenge. He asked the priest to meet him after school, at the small football practice field, on the edge of a large wooded area. Francis asked the priest to teach him about sex, and the wretch had eagerly agreed. They went out in the woods. When the priest exposed himself, the Francis pulled out a knife and emasculated him. The boy left the priest in the woods to bleed to death. The police never solved the case, and the church helped cover up the incident. No one was arrested.

Francis lost his youthful faith, and like many of his contemporaries, quit school for work. He picked up with the Bardinos in New Orleans. He liked the sense of family, particularly of retribution. No wrongs went unpunished. He came to feel that he was an avenger, on a mission to punish those who needed it. He became a prolific, artful killer, taking care that his victims were always completely unaware of their fate, if possible. When he finally became an adult, he was aware that the rest of the Bardino family, whom had initiated him on his eighteenth birthday, regarded him as utterly insane.

He married a pious young Catholic girl, had a family. His three children were all smart and good looking. One night in 1965, the drunken son of a man Francis had killed firebombed his house, killing Francis' wife and all his children. Francis spent some time in a mental hospital, and emerged believing that Satan was the only true god, and had been deliberately slandered in the Bible. He became as devout in his loyalty to the devil as he once had been in his loyalty to the God of the Catholics. Eventually, he became homosexual, and came to look upon all women as hateful, evil. He was semiretired from active duty for the Bardinos, who basically now paid him to stay away. Bourbon Street was his only remaining responsibility, and the only place his stark countenance fit in.

By the time Lee saw him, the Raven had become an extra-human creature. Too much plastic surgery had made his face too small for his head. His hair was died black, slicked straight back. His clothes were invariably black; his total appearance was Draculian. After a few minutes, he left. Lee had an odd feeling of relief, like everyone else in the place.

Crystal was finishing her stage tour as her potential sponsor was getting his check. She had wasted at least a couple of hours on the fish, and had only squeezed two hundred out of him so far. She had figured him for an easy thousand. Snatching up the crappy twelve bucks she'd made on stage, all ones, she darted through the backstage curtain, and redressed while scooting through the tiny dancer dressing room, managing to dodge the four girls who were hunched around a dressing table, snorting crystal meth. As she emerged on the main floor, seconds later, she was completely dressed, composed. But not about to let this guy get away that easy. She was *owed*, dammit.

Lee was relieved the waitress had brought the bill before his stalking friend Crystal made it back to the table. Unfortunately, she reappeared. Crystal plopped down in her former chair, said, "You're not leaving are you, Lee? It's Lee isn't it? Because, you know, if you're *out of money*, you can get some, well, we call it "funny money," but it works just like real money, and I could take you upstairs…"

Lee knew how the funny money routine worked too, having blown wads of it in titty bars up and down Bourbon Street in the past. Basically, they gave you fake money on your credit card, which can only be spent in that club, on that day. And, they charged ten percent for the service. He chuckled at Crystal's audacity, said, "Well, I've already paid the tab, and, like you say, I guess I'm out of money, so…"

"But that's not fair!," Crystal snapped, hopping up, "I sat over here with you for three or four hours, and all I got was a lousy *hundred bucks*!"

Glancing at his watch, Lee said, "Miss, I've only been here two hours. I didn't invite you to sit here, and I've given you more than that." He wasn't sure how much.

"Well I just think it's bullshit," she said, plopping back down. "One of the bartenders said you were some kind of big spender. Yeah, right. I bet that Rolex is fake, too." She was still pissed, but she knew she was pushing her luck with the floor manager.

Lee said, "Look, you seem like a nice girl. Let's reason this out."

Crystal stared at him, not sure whatever the fuck he was getting at, but titty-dancer-aware of the appearance of a new chance.

Lee said, "Say you sat here for a couple hours, and made a couple of hundred bucks."

"One hundred."

"Well, we both know that isn't true, but let's say you got, by your numbers, fifty bucks an hour. She started to say something, but he continued. "But you were expecting to make more. What, three or four hundred? That would be a hundred fifty, or two hundred an hour, just for sitting here and talking to me. Right?"

Crystal didn't like the way this was going, but she decided to be quiet.

"Either way, you're getting a good rate, in my opinion. More than most professionals, people who spent years in college. Are you in college, any kids?"

"I've been doing this shit for twelve years. Who's got time?"

"Got a house note?"

"I live with my boyfriend. Look, are you going upstairs with me, or what?"

Lee sat silent for a moment, amazed. "I'll tell you what," he said, "call the waitress back over here."

Crystal literally ran after the waitress, poked her back across the floor to Lee.

Lee asked the waitress, "You making any money today?"

"Only what you tipped me earlier, Mr. Farrell, but it's early."

"Call me Lee." He pulled a little leather covered money clip out of his front pants pocket, unfolded several hundred dollar bills. Crystal actually started to reach for the money, but Lee pulled it away. Lee said, "Well, Crystal here has been explaining the ropes to me, so I wanted to set everything straight. You married, got any kids?"

The waitress nodded. "Two little girls," she said, "Three and six. And a jerk ex. Want to see my kids' pictures?"

"No, thanks," said Lee. He peeled off five hundreds, about half his stack, handed it to the waitress. "Promise me you'll buy them something nice?" Lee stood, started to walk away.

"Thanks!," said the waitress, hugging him.

"Wait a minute!," shouted Crystal, as Lee walked away. "What about *me?*"

As Lee passed through the front door, he could hear Crystal screaming "Asshole!" until the door closed. Heading back down Bourbon, he realized the allure of the titty clubs was wearing off. The whole scene was just getting sad. Plus, he was tired of disappointing Diana, and everyone else. He wanted to get back and see her, as soon as he finished up with the professor.

Diana Farrell walked into her home, put her purse and bags in the bedroom. She let Iris out the back door, noticed the cover on the hot tub had been blown off again, by the wind. She turned on the television, just in time to catch the local on-the hour news update. She turned the television up, passively listening as she went to the kitchen to make a sandwich. She wondered where Lee was. The newscaster talked about burglaries, car wrecks and some retiree from Hernando Beach, Florida who had just hit a four million dollar jackpot on a quarter slot machine, passed out, and was in a Biloxi hospital, his condition unknown.

Lee had perched on a barstool in an airy little joint on Bourbon Street. Music blared into the street, the three same three Zydeco songs in repetition, enticing tourists by twos and threes in to try the dollar jello shots described on a lime green sign outside. Tipsy housewives, daring college kids, and sunburned conventioneers streamed in and out as the bartender set up dozens of little white ketchup containers full of something gelatinous, which he topped with individual squirts of canned whipped cream. When asked, he said the alcohol element of the shot was "PGA", by which he meant "pure grain alcohol." What he always failed to mention was that the bar owner's cousin in Chalmette made the PGA fresh, every weekend.

A few beers into a hot New Orleans afternoon, Lee was having a hard time catching a relaxing buzz. He was preoccupied by the business with Bonehead, and wondering how he was going to get out of it. The continuous side show of goofy tourist attempts at Cajun dancing was amusing, however. One fool played air washboard for two whole songs.

He focused on the pictures all over the wall, some new, some signed by football players who died forty years ago. He had seen dozens, maybe hundreds of pictures just like these in joints all over the Quarter: jocks from the fifties or sixties posing with drinks and big breasted women. Dead guys forever congratulating each other in the good old days on walls next to practically naked women in new beer posters.

But bar pictures and garish neon signs, posters of perfect models wearing tiny bikinis, goofy moonshine addled tourists, and all the beer in Louisiana, he knew, would not alter the fact that he was in what a master sergeant he once knew always called a "flawlessly fucked up situation." Even as he stared into the eyes of the beauty on the wall right beside him, he could not escape the memory of that damned night at Cat Island.

In the first place, nobody counted on it raining like hell. Lee and Kiger were easing the rented Hatteras up to the southwest side of Cat Island, to Smuggler's Cove, no less, and visibility was pitiful. Their third partner had proved to be a worthless deck hand, and was in the head, puking.

Lee knew the keys, shoals and holes around the island as well as anyone could. But he could barely see the channel markers off the island, and radar would have been useless, even if he had it. The Gulf of Mexico had churned up one of its famous tropical systems, had popped it on top of them in a few hours; parts of the same system dogged them with wind, waves and heavy rain the last half of the trip.

Still, there was no choice but to proceed; the boat had to be back the next day, and the well worn salon below was stacked to the ceiling with something like a half ton of Panama Red marijuana. Forty suitcase sized bails of it, double wrapped with good, government issued tarpaulin, and taped up to keep out water. All he had to do was get close to the island, drop in the skiff, and make a few short trips to the beach. And hope that no nosy island campers or water cops were around.

He had managed to get within a hundred yards of the beach, and was getting tossed around. He could not see the lights of Azalea, which normally lined the horizon. He told Kiger to deploy the anchor, and was busily figuring the logistics of the offload, when the lights came on.

He had somehow let a sheriff's marine patrol get right off his port side, blocking his exit from the natural hole he was trying to anchor in. Traveling without running lights, he knew, was enough of a violation to allow the cops to board and do a safety check, and hiding the weed was just impossible. The only other way out was a mad dash east through the rain, and miraculous luck to avoid the constantly changing underwater sand off the shallow island. He didn't even try.

Lee was already imagining what he was going to say to Sheriff Buck Carter, who was practically his stepfather. He thought of his best friend Jake, Buck Carter's son, in school up at State. Then, the wet night exploded.

He first thought that lightning had struck, but he quickly realized the sheriff's boat was taking heavy automatic weapons fire from somewhere.

Lee and Kiger's third partner was panicking, had just tripped trying to run up the exterior bridge ladder, was flopping around, cursing, and holding his knee, which was spurting blood. Lee was strangely calm, almost in a dream, as he reflexively engaged the boat's two big diesels, and brought her bow around, away from the sheriff's burning craft. He slammed both throttles forward, and she bellowed a huge black cloud, made visible through the rain by the burning ship behind.

As Lee jerked the boat on heading, he thought he might have caught a glimpse of another boat, off the starboard bow, tearing through the waves of the dissipating storm, with no running lights. He set the autopilot, and he and his buddies spent the next frantic minutes throwing bales of pot into the dark gulf waters. By the time they got back to Panama, they had cleaned up all the blood, and thrown their empty extra fuel cans overboard.

And that was it. Of course, the idiot with the cut knee eventually spilled the beans about the whole thing, and Lee was prepared to spend his prime years in a military stockade somewhere. Instead, he was offered early discharge from the Army, and took it. He never saw the one with the bad bloody knee, after that. The other one, Kiger, was his head bartender at the Blue Stone. The whole thing would have become a distant, crazy memory, if it had not been all over the news that two sheriff's deputies had gotten killed busting up a "major drug ring". One of them had graduated from St. Thomas with Lee. Buck Carter had not been on the boat, which was a relief. Lee never knew who had fired at the deputies, or why.

None of the tourists staggering out of the Bourbon Street bar were concerned with these things, and Lee suddenly felt like moving. He forgot the step down to the sidewalk, and lurched across it into the edge of the street. He did not feel drunk or sober, but only an intense conflict between the need to go home, grab Diana and haul ass, or to try to stay calm, hang around for a day or two, and make a sober decision. He burst out in maniacal laughter at the absurdity of literally standing in the middle of Bourbon Street at a crossroad in his life, where either decision could easily lead to his own death.

He temporarily saved from the fateful decision by the sight of an old lady across the street, taking down a rickety wooden table, about to load it and a hand painted wooden sign on a contraption that looked like it once was a shopping cart. It had been upgraded with bicycle tires. The sign read "Fortune," and something, but she was blocking the rest with her enormous girth. The fortune teller was black, and her general resemblance to Mama Thea made his heart fall. He suddenly became overwhelmed by what he knew was a completely irrational urge to find out if this old lady had ever heard of Mama Thea's Camellia. "Irrational," Lee said to no one as he walked across the street, "compared to what?"

The old lady had just finished loading her table when she noticed Lee. "I'm done today, mister," she said, "Plus, I don't mix with drunk people."

Lee said, "Are you kidding me? Listen, lady, in the first place, I'm not drunk. In the second place, even if I was, this is Bourbon Street, for God's sake, and you don't talk to drunks?"

"God ain't got no part in this, young man, except to take offense at your language." She turned back to her packing. "And you got a fast mouth for a young man, telling an old lady about her business. You might not be drunk yet, but I can't help you today, anyway. My permit says I'm open until five, and it's five after now. I don't have any problems with the police, and I don't want any. In fact," she stopped, glanced at him, then picked up her last sign, "as far as I know, you *are* the police."

"Come on, lady, do I look like a cop to you? No, look, I don't want my fortune told. You just looked like somebody who had been around here an, ah… long time, and I just wanted to ask you if you might know somebody who used to live here."

She said, "Son, you ain't got no artful way of telling a lady she's old." She started pushing her cart down the sidewalk, and Lee followed. "Besides, I've already talked you more than I do to most people that give me, oh, twenty dollars."

Lee stuck a hundred in front of her face, and she stopped. "All right," she said. "You're either serious or just plain crazy. Ask me what you want, but I'm not promising anything, and I ain't going to lie."

"How long have you lived around here?"

"I was born five blocks from here, during World War 2."

"Good."

"That's your opinion."

"Yes, ma'am. Back in the sixties - late sixties - there was a lady around here, she was a, well, a prostitute and also…"

"Well I can tell you right now, I don't know any prostitutes, don't mix with *them*, either. No drunks and no prostitutes. Sorry I couldn't help you."

"But you haven't heard the rest of …"

"Don't need to. I told you, son, I don't hold with no prostitutes. Don't mix with 'em. Them, or drunks."

"But she was also supposedly a *Mamissa*, which is some kind of…"

"Hoodoo witch." The old fortune teller said. She stopped, looked at Lee. "Don't mix with them either. No drunks, no prostitutes, and *especially* no hoodoo witches. Lord, especially no hoodoo witches. And you best leave all them people alone, too."

"Well, I can't," Lee said, disappointed. "It's someone I need to find out about. I guess you can't help. Have a good day." He walked away.

"Stop, boy," said Miss Tracy, which Lee could now see on her sign. "Wait one minute."

She left her cart, suddenly spry as she strode to Lee, reached, and grabbed his right hand. She pulled out a taped up pair of reading glasses, perused his palm, said, "You've been on a terrible journey. Have a long way to go. You're…torn between what you think is good, and what you think is…evil. You're torn. This is the hand of a man who wants to do good, but he almost always falls short, at least in his own opinion." She looked up at him, right in his face, and said, "You ever hear that song, the old one that says 'you can't always get what you want'? That's right. Them boys got that right. But the next part, that's wrong. You see, son, you ain't *ever* going to find out what you really did need, until it's too late. That's God's privilege."

"Well, alright," Lee said, "I'm sorry I bothered you." He tried to release, but she held his hand firm.

"Son, you seem like a decent man. Decent folks don't mix with drunks, and prostitutes, and hoodoo witches." She stopped, half expectantly.

"But you're not going to quit looking for this Mamissa, are you? Well I ain't saying you aren't a decent man. Just confused. You go up to Rampart Street, in the last block, down by Esplanade. You are looking for an old brick house, two stories, with a rooftop deck."

Rooftop decks, Lee knew, were not a normal feature in that part of the Quarter. "Who am I looking for?," he asked.

"There's a lady, she knows all about that kind of business. All them businesses."

What's her name?"

They call her Miss Ruby. You'll find her, I reckon." She
turned, walked away. Lee looked down at his open palm, where
the hundred he'd given her lay. He started to say something, but
changed his mind and turned away. As he walked, he heard her start
singing, in the distance: "You can't always get what you want…".

Lee was hungry, and stopped in a place off Bourbon, on Saint
Peter, that made Greek food to go. It was no bigger than his living
room, and did not have space for more than eight or ten people,
but the food was perfect. Lee spent some time munching baklava
and talking to the owner, who was happy for the business.

Passing into the north Quarter, he pulled his watch off, and
stuck it in his back pocket. The walk was not long, but he was
wary, and stayed in the middle of the street, where he could.
Armstrong Park was across Rampart, appropriately fixed in the
old Storyville district, where young Louis had gotten his start
playing. He arrived at the only house on the street that fit the
description. It was very well kept, and had little landscaped
shrubs up to the sidewalk, where an ancient magnolia tree gnarled
up out of the concrete. He knocked; the interior door swung
open almost immediately, startling him. The house, or what he
could glimpse of it through the heavy wooden screen door, was
barely lit, and full of lamps, figurines, and antique furniture.

"Do you have an appointment?," demanded the voice of a
young lady hidden by the door.

"Well, no, actually, I…"

The door slammed. Lee started to leave, but he stopped
under the cool canopy of the magnolia. Here was a chance,
maybe, to find out about his real mother. He went back, knocked
again.

"I've got a gun!," the girl inside screamed.

Lee instinctively stepped to the side of the door, shielding his
body with the wall. "I need to speak with Miss Ruby," he said.

No response.

"I'm not leaving," Lee said.

The door crept open, just wide enough to speak through. "Are you an officer?," she asked, "because if you are, you have to tell me."

Lee laughed to himself about all the people now in jail because they believed that street-law myth. "No," he said, "I'm not a cop. I'm a …reporter. I want to interview Miss Ruby for a story."

"Wait." The door closed again.

Lee acted casually, while carefully surveying his area. Miss Ruby obviously had a taste for order and beauty, tastes not widely shared by her neighbors, or the squads of youthful drug dealers fanned out along the wide Rampart. Lee knew that he was a perfect target for the Quarter's infamous bicycle squads: a bicycle, two kids and a popper - .25 automatic, or the like - had for sometime been the robbery mechanism of choice for the gangs in the area. So far, Lee saw no bike.

The door creaked open again, and the young lady did not speak. Lee opened the red screen door, painted to match the shutters of the clapboard house, and entered. The contrast of the cool, dark interior to the swelter outside made Lee realized he was sweating heavily. When his eyes adjusted, he gaped at the beauty before him: a young lady, maybe eighteen or nineteen years old, tall, with huge brown eyes, over high cheeks and perfect lips. Her skin was as dark as the mahogany furniture that formed sitting areas in the large room. She directed him toward an antique settee with a simple, elegant gesture. When he was seated, she asked, "would you like iced tea, or a drink?"

"Yes, tea," he said, and she glided out of the room.

Lee looked around the old parlor; heart pine floors aged dark were covered with elaborate Persian rugs, and each area of floor space had some piece of antique furniture.

The surfaces were polished and mostly covered with embroidered linen doilies. The whole place was permeated with a faint scent of…something he couldn't identify, but it was sweet, and he liked it.

The young lady returned , and presented him with a large sweating glass of sweet tea, which he gulped.

"I don't believe you're any reporter, mister, but Miss Ruby has agreed to see you." She fixed him with her perfect stare.

"Well, I am a reporter, just moved here, as a matter of fact, and I appreciate you letting me in. Now, if I can see her?" He started to stand up.

"Just sit, Mr. Reporter," she said. Miss Ruby will see you when *she's* ready." She started to leave.

Lee said, "Wait, can't you sit with me, until she's ready to talk?"

The young lady laughed. "No, sir," she said, "my time's not free. Now, if you care to talk business some other time…then we'll talk."

"What's your name?"

"Sorry, mister, that's off the record." She smiled, and left.

Lee nearly dozed sitting on the comfortable settee, its pattern of roses well worn with use. The young goddess finally showed up and led him up to the third floor deck, which was as elaborately decorated as the rest of the house. He admired the near twilight view of the northern part of the quarter. Scrolled, black iron railing surrounded the deck, which was equipped with iron furniture, covered with padded cloth cushions. Miss Ruby herself was reclining on an elaborate chaise lounge. She had a woven Afghan wrapped around her short legs, even in the heat. Her long gray hair pulled back, she was wearing what looked to Lee like a long Oriental white robe, no shoes, and prescription glasses, with a sunglass attachment. Her face was nearly inscrutable, but she was extremely wrinkled.

"Please, sit," Miss Ruby said. "I understand you are some kind of newspaper man."

"Yes ma'am, I'm doing a story on…"

"Excuse, me, young man, but we weren't properly introduced. I am Ruby. 'Miss Ruby' to my, ah, friends." She presented her hand. Not knowing what to do, Lee stood up, clutched, and awkwardly kissed it.

"My name's Ralph Elkington. I'm doing a story on some people who used to live around here. I was hoping you might help me."

"Interesting," said Miss Ruby, "who is your editor? And what could an old lady like me have to say that could possibly help?"

Lee's reporter ruse was suddenly more of annoyance than it was useful, but he could not see a clean way around it. "My editor? Let's see, it's Bob, uh, Bob something. Like I said , I'm new." He started to laugh, but stopped it, and only emitted one small high pitched chirp, like a bird.

"Are you OK? Can I get you some more tea?"

"No ma'am," Lee said, regrouping. He decided he'd better get to the point, before she kicked him out. He said, "Miss Ruby, I'm working on a story about the old days, around here, thirty, forty, fifty years ago, and I was told you might be able to help me. I'm particularly looking for a lady who supposedly lived around here…"

"Oh, we're not in an hurry, are we, Mr., oh, what was it?"

Lee couldn't immediately remember what he said his damn name was. He thought he'd for some reason said "Ralph," and wondered where that came from. "Well, anyway, I don't want to take up your time," he said, ignoring her question. "If you can give me a minute."

"What, no writing pad, or tape recorder? Where indeed did you go to journalism school? And forgive me for saying, but you seem older than a new reporter. Where did you work before coming here?"

"Well, I don't really like to talk about me, Miss Ruby…".

She cut him off by slowly standing, said, "Excuse me, handsome, but I've got to tell Gloria what to put on for dinner. I'll be back in a few minutes, with fresh tea," she said, and she retrieved his glass. Turning, just before she went down, she said, "You never answered me, Ralph, or Bob, or Ted, or whatever your name is. While I'm gone, why don't you think about who you really are, and what you want." She moved away slowly, and appeared to Lee to be much older than her sharp mind would indicate.

Lee spent the next few minutes under the pink and yellow twilight trying to figure what to tell her, what to ask her, and how to get out of this house and back to the bar district without getting shot. He solemnly resolved not to make any more dangerous decisions while he was drinking. Miss Ruby returned. "I'm sure I've offended you by not asking your company for dinner, but I believe you'll forgive me under the circumstances." She handed him tea. "Now why don't you tell me what you really want."

"Look, lady, I'm sorry I lied. I just didn't think…well, I didn't know what to expect."

"So who are you?"

"My name's Lee. I live on the coast, in Azalea."

"Oh, child, that terrible storm."

"Yes, Ma'am. It destroyed everything."

"The spirits have been very, very angry."

"Pardon me? You said, 'the spirits?'"

"Oh, that's nothing, son. Just an old lady running on."

" My, um, my mom used to know a lady in the French Quarter back in the sixties - the late sixties, who was in the, well, your business. But the lady moved away, somewhere up north. She might have died, but there is a possibility she didn't. Either way, mom wants to find out, you know, whatever she can."

"Why doesn't your mother find her friend? Did she send you?""

"Mom's sick. I'm - we're just right up the road, so I thought I'd take a shot in the dark, and ask around. I was in the neighborhood, and was told that you might know who I'm talking about. Her name…"

"Many people in this city are here because they do not want to be found. Have you considered this?"

"Yes, ma'am, I have. This is really sort of crazy, but it is very important. At least to my mom."

"As you might expect, Lee, ladies in my profession are expected to keep secrets, not reveal them to strangers. Before you go further, let me ask you. Why me? There are hundreds of New Orleans ladies in, as you say, my business."

"A palm reader down on Bourbon Street told me about you."

"You'd do well to avoid relying on palm readers for good advice."

She's not fond of your avocations, either, Lee thought, but he said, "It was good enough to get me sent here," almost blushing. "I hope you don't mind me saying, but your…assistant is a very pretty lady."

"And you are a handsome young man. And respectful to your elders. Now, I really must be going. As you have deduced, or been told, I have business to conduct. Evening hours are, so to speak, office hours. And I can't promise you I will help you, even if I could. Now, what is the name of this friend of your mother's?"

"Miss Ruby!" Someone was calling from downstairs. "Gloria needs you in the kitchen! She says she's damn near about to burn the house down!"

Miss Ruby said, in a surprising tone, "Tell her I'll be there in a minute. Now leave me alone!" To Lee, she conversationally added, "Excuse the interruption. Gloria's lazy, so she's probably lying. Thing is, she might not be." She stood, started walking away. "I'm afraid I have leave you, Lee. What's your mother's friend's name?"

"Camellia."

Miss Ruby paused, but didn't turn. "Did you say *Camellia?*"

"Yes ma'am."

"No one here goes by that name that I know of, Lee. I'm sorry I couldn't help you," she said, and she was gone.

Lee awakened the next day sitting on his couch at the condo, his feet propped on a coffee table, the television on a sports channel, no sound. The stereo was on, but no music was playing. On the bathroom counter was a square of toilet paper with a message: "Had to run - sweet dreams, Sleepyhead." It was signed "Dahlia" with a flourish at the end of the "a" that had torn the paper. Lee guessed the brownish writing was from a makeup pencil.

Sifting through the previous evening over coffee on his balcony, he was clear all the way to the point of entering the condo. After wasting his time with the old hooker on Rampart Street, he had disregarded his temporary disgust with titty bars, and hit them all until he found Dahlia. He lavished her with money, and decided he was, for once and all, in love with her. He had been stunned that Dahlia agreed to go home with him, and had celebrated by doing shots of vodka, and getting shitty drunk with one of the assistant managers while he waited on her.

Dahlia did not get off until 3:00 a.m., and no threats, cajoling or, incredibly, money would get her out earlier. His manager pal had explained the club's short staffing issues to him when he griped about it. The last thing Lee clearly remembered was sitting on his couch while Dahlia used the shower, thinking of Diana, and feeling stupid. He had apparently slept where he sat.

After getting dressed, Lee called his friend at Tulane, and headed to meet him at his office. The Tulane campus was lush with tropical greenery after a full summer of rain; Lee paused in the parking area to take in the smell cut grass. It made his head feel better.

His friend's office was a small, but in a corner of a midcentury dark red brick building, under a canopy of Live Oaks that had been fully grown before Tulane was even founded. "Derek Bissell, Ph. D." was lettered on the door and etched in a plaque on his desk.

"So what do we have here, professor?," asked Lee

"Lee, I've got to say, this is something exciting. Where did you get this thing? Well, it doesn't matter. To *me* that is, but I wouldn't go running around showing this to any federal agents, because it might, in all honesty, be in violation of federal law, which makes it illegal to…"

"Hold on a second, sport," interjected Lee, "let's not get carried away. No one knows about this, but me and you. I assume we can keep it that way?"

Derek nodded yes.

"Besides," said Lee, "that thing was an heirloom, something I got a long time ago. It's been lost and my - a member of my family recently found it. So let's forget about violation of any laws."

"Well, how you obtained it is not…,anyway, this thing belongs in a museum."

"Really. What is it? What does it mean?"

"First, *what* it is." He held it up to a lamp on his desk, they both leaned close. "Of course we could have it tested."

"But we're not going to, old bean, so what's your best guess?"

"It's a talisman called a 'hand,' or 'gris gris,' made by devotees of voodoo, or hoodoo, or in some places, Houdon. It's meant to cast a spell, or prevent a spell, I'm not really sure." He stopped and bent toward the thing, scratching his chin in an unintended parody of college professorship. Realizing Lee was smirking at him, he said, "But let's go on. It is old, I'd say at least a hundred years, maybe quite a bit older. Probably first crafted in the Caribbean islands, from African materials."

"Why do you say African?"

"That wood is not from this hemisphere. The materials were assembled in the Dominican Republic, most likely, or Haiti. Maybe even here, in New Orleans. And these inserts? Some of them are seed, some rocks, and these four attached to the points of the cross? They're teeth. Human teeth." He took a quick sip from a cup of black coffee, winced when he swallowed. "The cross is a symbol of a voodoo god, or demigod, Legba. He was, well is, to those who believe in these things, a *very* powerful figure. He serves as a liaison to the spirits, a sort of gatekeeper, and is, well, sneaky by nature. I don't understand all of it, but this is the guy you would go to if you really needed something done. If I had to guess, I'd say the entire gris gris is meant to protect the bearer against something. It also suggests to the bearer, that's you, that the spirits demand payment in full for their services."

"These are all probabilities and guesses?"

"Most of my kind of science is, my friend."

"Payment in full? What the hell does that mean?"

"In modern terms, *quid pro quo*. Something for something."

"So I owe some African or Caribbean god something for the protection I receive from this thing?"

"Something like that." He looked sheepish.

"And you believe this?"

"I didn't say that. I'm interested in the historical and academic value of it as a relic. Voodoo is, after all, as part of Americana as God and apple pie."

Lee said, "Yeah, well, I wouldn't say that outside academic circles, professor."

Lee took the amulet, against the relatively animated protestations of his normally docile friend, and left. When he got back to the condo, there was a folded piece of paper stabbed to his front door with a cheap switchblade knife, of the type commonly found among the thousands of trinkets in the French Market. He looked around, took the note, and went upstairs. He opened it on the balcony, while sipping coffee. The note was short and clear:

> In case you think our lack of communication means the deal is off, forget it. Here is a reminder: While you were all in the Army, stationed in Panama, you, your buddy Kiger, and another fool decide to take a load of weed up to the coast from Panama while you were supposed to be on leave fishing. Turns out, two sheriff's deputies get killed. You know the rest. I am finalizing our plans, and will contact you soon.

Lee wadded the damned thing up, and threw it away. So Bonehead knew. But not the whole story. Not the fact that Lee hadn't shot those cops. Somebody else did. But who would ever believe that? Lee knew he was about to have to make the toughest decision of his life. When he finished his coffee, his first inclination was to run and get Diana and leave. But he knew that would only put their lives in danger. He had to be methodical. And before anything else, he had to go back to the Delta, to take care of some business.

Chapter 6 - The Delta

Special Agent Zachary Ellis leaned his business class seat back as the midsized jet rose from Reagan National Airport in Washington, D.C. He had, for the first time, paid the extra fifty bucks to upgrade his government discount coach seat; having just stumbled upon a gold mine, he believed he could afford it. Soon, anyway.

Ellis was dizzy. He had just spent hundreds of hours over the last couple of weeks immersed in classified CIA, FBI and National Security Agency files, still-secret documents and testimony gathered by subpoena and kept under seal during Congress' spectacularly ineffective investigation of the 1980s Iran-Contra affair, and gigs of data accumulated by the Homeland Security Department about, well, everything.

He had gone to D.C. to put together a RICO case against the Bardino Mafia family of New Orleans. That simple plan was distant to him now, puny. He had just read more than since his panicky first semester in law school; what he had learned was worth more to him than a thousand law degrees. He always intended to work his way into politics. Politics requires publicity. Publicity prefers scandal. His chances, he believed, just got better.

As Lee Farrell made the swampy drive out of New Orleans, across Lake Pontchartrain, he had the dreamy feeling that he may be leaving home soon, for good. He called Jake, who said, "Where the hell have you been? I dropped by the Stone yesterday, and Meat said you took a few days off."

Lee said, "Well, now that you mention it, I haven't seen much of you lately, either."

"It's work. Your reporter buddy Roark at the paper has been hounding the shit out of us -well, *me* - about so-called corruption in the coast casinos. He thinks we aren't aggressive, and it's starting to catch on with the usual parrots."

"Yeah, I read all that stuff. He run across anything significant?"

"You know the rumors. I don't know, and don't need to know. Anyway, we've had to push up some murder trials. Get the public attention steered in another direction."

"So you're trying cases now?

"Me? Hell, no. You know I hate trials. But I've had to hang around more. Appearances."

"You politicians. Besides, you're actually good at trials, aren't you? Didn't you get written up in the Sound a few years ago, as one of the great young criminal trial attorneys on the coast? Come to think of it, wasn't that Roark who wrote about you?"

"Yeah, ironic, huh? That's what got Pops thinking about me running for D.A. You know I never would've done it without him pushing."

"Still afraid to disappoint the old man. Tsk, tsk."

"Screw you, Lee. You're scared of him, just like I am."

"True. Who isn't? Speaking of which - I was talking to old Cookie the other day. I asked him about this character Camellia, the one Mama Thea mentioned. I told you about it."

"Your supposed birth mother," said Jake.

"Yes. 'Birth mother.' Sounds sort of clinical, doesn't it?"

"I'm sorry, brother, I know that's a weird subject."

"It's probably all bull. But I am curious. I asked him if he ever knew anybody named Camellia, and he damn near popped a scotch leak. Told me she was dead, and, get this, your old man killed her. I got the impression he definitely knew who I was talking about, and that she was dead."

"I wouldn't lay heavily on what that old drunk says. But who knows?"

"You think Buck and Cookie really used to kill people?"

"Lee, you know Pops about as well as I do. After my mother died, he raised me. Well, actually, about two dozen of his nannies and girlfriends raised me. He was around, but not, you know, *engaged*. He always seemed like more like a grandfather than my dad. You remember how he was."

"Yeah, not too many backyard games of catch. I'm sorry, I had forgotten about your mom."

"I was only three. I don't really remember her. Anyway, Buck was always out, in the middle of something. And believe me, there was plenty of *something*. The kind of stories they tell around here about him now…I don't know what to think."

"So should I ask him about this Camellia?"

"If there's any truth to what Mama Thea said, he would know. The thing is, if Cookie said she's dead, she's probably dead. You might have noticed that Pops ain't too sentimental, and I decided a long time ago that I don't want to know what all he does. Or did. Maybe you ought to do the same."

"But if she was on the coast, how else could we find out?"

"Look, I hate to play lawyer with you, but didn't Mama Thea tell you that your Camellia died up north? In Chicago, right?"

"Yes."

"And Cookie said that a Camellia he knew was dead, too? Killed on the coast? And Cookie had something to do with it?"

"That's the hang of it."

"Alright, so don't you think that sounds like we're talking about two different dead people?"

"It has occurred to me."

"So, why take a chance on scraping it off the bottom of the pot with Pops if it's likely, hell, *probable* that your Camellia and this other one aren't even the same person?"

"Yeah…I guess you're right. But wouldn't you like to know what Buck and Cookie were up to back in the fifties and sixties? I've heard some amazing things - gambling, prostitution, killings. The governor, the mob, your dad, they were all supposed to be in on all these…"

"Lee. Sorry to interrupt, but let me give you some sage, brotherly advice. Your Mama Thea used to have all these sayings, right?"

"Yes. So?"

Well, my favorite one was, "Don't start nothin,' won't *be* nothin.' That seems appropriate here."

"I'll remember that, brother. Listen, I might be in some trouble."

"What kind…"

"Just listen. Something I did, something stupid, *really* stupid, a long time ago, has sort of popped back up. I might have to go somewhere for a while, and if you hear about anything that I've done, well…I'll contact you later, and straighten it all out."

"Jesus, Lee, could you be a little more vague? Does this have anything to do with whatever happened to you in the Army?"

"That's all I want to say right now, brother."

"You're going somewhere? What about your job?"

"Well, I'm not leaving yet, if at all. I'll be back in a couple of days. We'll talk then. Besides, I've decided to quit the Stone. I haven't told anybody yet."

"Look, Lee, I obviously don't know what's going on, but quitting your job seems a little drastic. You're not talking about doing anything illegal are you?"

"I would never ask you to do anything that would get you in trouble."

"Good. Because that would be stupid. And I like doing stuff that's smart."

"So how are you going to handle the prick Roark?"

"What can I do? You went to law school. It has something to do with the First Amendment. You remember…freedom of the press, and such."

"I thought the feds had already gotten rid of that one."

"No, that was the Fourth Amendment. Unreasonable searches. You know, pesky warrants and such."

"Everything qualifies as a reasonable search now, right? Terrorists."

"Right. Terrorists. Listen…are you and Diana OK?"

"You mean sick?"

"No, I mean OK. Like, getting along."

"Hell, yes, as far as I know. She's usually gone when I get up, and tells me she spends all her time with Sarah Bonacelli, so I don't see her a lot. Why?"

"Nothing. I'll talk to you when you get back."

Zack Ellis' plane arced over the eastern seaboard, en route to Atlanta and eventually the Gulfport-Biloxi International Airport on the Mississippi Gulf Coast. He studied his notes, and for the first real time let the entire story congeal in his mind.

When he had gone to D.C., he knew he needed more security clearance than he possessed. So he got Senator Ford to obtain a temporary extreme clearance, subject to an administrative finding and authorization, pursuant to a standing Presidential Order, which allowed him basically unfettered access to whatever the federal government knew. With two caveats: he couldn't look at any classified files from within the past five years, and he could not look at any U.S. Department of Treasury's information.

Zack mulled the cavalier way the senator had obtained such clearance. The senator, who was no longer in the majority party, had apparently sent memos to the bosses at FBI, and to the White

House. Ellis' clearance had been ready in two hours. Seniority. What a concept. He wondered what the memos said. As far as Ellis knew, the senator had to allege an emergency on the level of an imminent terrorist threat to allow such a classified record search without a warrant or court order. He had not asked, and Senator Ford did not say.

Zack wanted to find a money trail connecting the Bardinos and the Cronus Casino, or any number of the money laundering operations they apparently operated in New Orleans and along the Mississippi coast. Early in his search, he was stunned by the huge number of references to the Bardinos he found in the recently consolidated files of the low profile National Security Service.

Apparently, the Bardinos had for years been in partnership with the intelligence wing of the U.S. government, providing money, muscle and cover for classified tactical actions in and around the Gulf of Mexico. In return, they had enjoyed repeated, generational protection from federal prosecution. From the 1961 Bay of Pigs invasion of Cuba through the 1980's guns for hostages scheme that originated in Nicaragua, and became known as the Iran-Contra Affair, the Bardinos had been a convenient, willing, and efficient tool for assistance in seeking to accomplish the United States' unofficial Latin American objectives.

Ellis had come to think of New Orleans, his hometown, in different terms. Less as an isolated entity, home of the Saints, and Mardi Gras. More like a the capital of a region. The central gulf coast, Mississippi, Alabama, and part of the Florida Panhandle, starting somewhere around Panama City and ending in New Orleans, the 'Redneck Riviera' to locals, were so culturally different from the rest of their respective states, they more or less formed a *de facto* coastal state that transcended by social, cultural, and economic similarities what arbitrary state boundaries belied.

Which Ellis knew made sense in historical terms, since the same area had been traded back and forth between the local Native American Indian populations, the French and the Spanish for generations before it became part of the United States. Each culture left its food, music, buildings and descendants, and perceptibly separated the people of the area from their inland neighbors.

They were also hurricane aware, and naturally inclined to pay more attention to the southern horizon than the northern one. This culture, Ellis' own extended neighbors, were part of a uniquely durable and nutty brand of Americans that populate the northern edge of the Gulf of Mexico, who live off seafood, dodge hurricanes, and listen to Jimmy Buffet, who Ellis secretly liked, too.

So he did not resist the easy extrapolation that New Orleans' organized crime could be just as different from the rest of the country as its civilians were. Why not? Anybody who could survive the local politics alone, and still make money, had to be eminently malleable.

The Bardino family's usefulness to CIA, in particular, was enhanced by the geographic location of New Orleans, which offered not only easy, fast and secret access to and from Latin America, but was also of remote interest to television news media centers of New York, Chicago, Atlanta, and the West Coast. Some of the career FBI agents in Ellis' office in Gulfport assumed that after massive federal prosecutions of the eighties, the Mafia there no longer effectively existed. In fact, the Justice Department had been instructed by the CIA, through channels, to leave New Orleans alone.

Even though the Central Intelligence Agency had no legal jurisdiction to instruct the United States Justice Department to do anything, the bosses at Justice understood the maxim: if the

old rules do not work, change them. So the Bardinos had gotten a
pass because of their historic ties to CIA.

For the Bay of Pigs Cuban invasion, CIA had gathered a group
of businessmen, mostly rich Cubans living in Miami, whom
would take control of the island after the shooting stopped.
They recruited the Bardinos to provide transportation for the
businessmen. Thus, the ostensible future political leaders of
counter-revolutionary, post-communist Cuba were smuggled
to the island during the doomed invasion aboard trawlers the
Bardinos used to run marijuana and rum out of Panama, Jamaica,
Haiti, and Cuba. The Bardinos' passengers were delivered to an
area east of Havana, and disappeared into history.

The Bay of Pigs disaster did nothing to adversely affect
Bardino family business. President Kennedy publicly accepted
responsibility without disclosing, perhaps unluckily for him,
the involvement of the Mafia. The Bardinos, whom still relied
heavily on the street sale of cheap, tax-free, illegal rum imports,
kept right on with their ancient rum-running operation. And the
Cubans whom had sold their rum to the gringos since the days of
Prohibition were happy to continue the business, no matter who
was running things over in Havana.

Special Agent Ellis also noted that many sources, and not a few
United States Congressmen believed that the Bardinos were acting
on a request from the Mafia Commission, or the CIA, or someone
else to hire the hapless Castro supporter and part time New
Orleanian Lee Harvey Oswald to take a shot at President Kennedy.
Oswald had an office on Camp Street in downtown New Orleans,
and was regularly arrested for disturbances caused by his vocal, if
inane, demonstrations in support of the communist Castro.

In fact, the Bardinos apparently had not expected the little
fool to actually kill him. Ellis found a permanently classified FBI
memo that quotes an anonymous Bardino family insider saying

they had retained Oswald to 'scare the shit out of' Kennedy. They figured that Oswald would get killed in the process, and that Kennedy would get the message to stay the hell out of Caribbean politics and business, and tell his brother Bobby to quit fucking with the Mafia.

Lee Harvey Oswald fit the perfect profile of a lone, crazed killer, motivated by his love for Cuba and all things communist. He was slight, stupid, and had a military background. When the Bardinos hired him, they neither knew nor wanted to know where Oswald would make his attempt. Neither did they believe Oswald could get an easy enough shot to kill him. Plus, he was already being tracked by the Secret Service, so he could not possibly survive the attempt.

The surprising death of John F. Kennedy had the desired effect. Though Oswald had to be eliminated, causing much unwanted scrutiny, the United States Justice Department was delayed for twenty years in its institutional mission of attempting a full scale, national eradication of the Mafia.

The Bardinos' involvement in the Iran-Contra scandal was much more complex. Congress, using its tattered war making powers, had outlawed official U.S. intervention in the civil war in Nicaragua in the 1980's. But the Reagan administration wanted the Cuban backed Sandinistas out, and the Contras in. So, the CIA had once again turned to the Bardinos.

Getting weapons to the Contras, primarily based in Honduras, required lots of secret transportation. Fortunately, the Bardinos had an elaborate cocaine trade arrangement with Columbian suppliers which moved the product with planes and boats from South America, through Central America to New Orleans.

Their arrangement was a natural coupling of the CIA's need for an unofficial air and sea armada, and the U.S. cocaine importing business, which had one. The Columbians and Bardinos needed an unimpeded supply route to the United States; CIA needed unregistered, undetected shipments of the hardware of war to the Contra forces fighting Nicaragua's revolutionary neo-communist government, the Sandinistas. The Columbians were familiar with the terrain; they had made fortunes from Cuba/Russia running guns and supplies to the Sandinistas when *they* were Nicaraguan guerillas, a couple of years earlier.

The CIA did not directly participate in the trade of cocaine; they never bought or sold drugs. They simply made sure that the United States Coast Guard, the United States Drug Enforcement Administration, and myriad factions of the United States military did not blunder upon the steady flow of planes and, to a smaller extent, boats moving equipment, money and other supplies from Panama, New Orleans and Miami to an evolving array of Contra paramilitary bases in Honduras and Costa Rica. Unmarked aircraft leaving Columbia loaded with coke stopped over at the United States' Howard Air Force Base in what was left of the Panama Canal Zone; military supplies were loaded and flown by Columbian and Panamanian pilots to Contra forces in Costa Rica and southern Nicaragua, as well as in Honduras.

Cocaine aboard the planes was officially ignored. Once the military supplies were delivered, the planes were refueled, and most were flown to airstrips carved out of the cane on rare dry land south of New Orleans. The Bardinos picked it up, sent it upriver to the city. From there, it went everywhere else. The planes, pilots, crews, and fuel were supplied by the Columbians, whom were also required to make large cash contributions to the Contras and the CIA itself.

The scheme worked for a few years before the inevitable happened. In 1985, a plane with a clogged fuel filter and five hundred kilos of cocaine crashed in Costa Rica; when the coke was scavenged by locals, the Columbians came looking for the

Panamanian pilot, who had unfortunately survived. Knowing his chances for further survival were rapidly diminishing, he fled to Miami. There, he sought the protection of the FBI, whom did not know of their government's Contra policies. The news media got wind of the story.

CIA immediately withdrew its support of the cocaine shipments, and shifted the focus of its Contra fund-raising efforts to arms sales. So, the Bardinos' halcyon era of government-endorsed drug trade was prematurely ended by a clogged fuel filter.

Congress' slow subsequent investigation practically ignored the drug scheme, and a dozen other related actions which never surfaced. How the whole new operation was paid for, and the involvement of the White House based National Security Agency, had been fleshed out in the news media at the time, and was of no further interest to Ellis.

With Congressional and media attention focused on Nicaragua, the Bardinos apparently decided it was a good time to get out of the cocaine importing business altogether. The family had never been richer, but to keep everyone busy, they were reduced to shaking down video poker houses, titty bars and late night daiquiri shops on Bourbon Street, to supplying crack and crank - methamphetamine - to French Quarter street hustlers, to running whorehouses, brokering call girls, and running the sports book in the city and along the Mississippi Gulf Coast.

As the eighties ended, Bardino influence on the Mississippi River port docks and among the banks, Mardi Gras Crewes and private, secret bankers' clubs that had always run New Orleans had diminished along with the city's national economic importance. The city of New Orleans, through mismanagement, bad luck, and corruption, had lost all its large companies, had become little more than a Mecca for rude tourists.

None of the Bardinos were implicated as a result of Congress'
amateurish investigation of Iran-Contra, partially because the
national news media focused almost exclusively upon its latter
stages, which involved selling weapons to Iran. Many of the New
Orleans' old mobsters, devout Catholics, regarded their latest
bye from federal prosecution as a sign from God to get out of the
business, into something legitimate. Regardless of New Orleans'
sorry fiscal shape, the flow of drunken tourists in the French
Quarter had actually increased, along with the opportunity to
legally gouge them in restaurants, hotels, and taxis. So many of
the old mobsters simply retired into new professions.

While the old guys heeded God's warnings, the young guys
in the family recognized legalized gambling in Mississippi as
Godsend. New Orleans itself had legal casinos, but after city,
parish and state governments were satiated through bribery and
taxation, profits were off. Mississippi, conversely, had the lowest
casino taxation rate in the country, and absolutely no banks with
capital assets sufficient to enter a competitive nationwide gambling
market.

Petrino Mallini had become the head of the Bardino family
at age 33, in 1986, after Two Steps made his RICO deal. "Pete"
Mallini was representative of a different generation of La Cosa
Nostra. He had worked in New Orleans through high school in
family owned restaurants on St. Charles Avenue, and on Bourbon
Street. He had gone to college, then gotten an MBA from Tulane.
He was a rich businessman, having filtered the family's cocaine
fortune through shell corporations primarily in Canada, and
invested much of it in the Japanese stock market, and in Las Vegas.

Pete Mallini had perfected the imperative of filtering large
amounts of illicit cash through various legitimate businesses -
restaurants, pawn shops, used car dealerships, others - a little
at a time, while under the watchful eyes of federal agents. He

had learned much from marshaling the family through the cocaine smuggling days and subsequent criminal investigations: Congressional, special counsel, local.

Most of all he had learned to outsmart his enemies, rather than kill them. Not that he was above killing; when Two Steps made his deal with the feds, he arranged for his own nephew to take over, which would have restored the Bardino line of bosses to a direct descendant of Nofio himself; but Pete and the smarter end of the family recognized this as a bad idea, likely to draw too much media and prosecutorial attention. Pete arranged for the apparent Bardino heir to take a one-way blue water fishing trip. Two Steps, offended, spent the next two years safely ensconced in federal prison. When he emerged, he had come to appreciate, in a financial way, the wisdom of making Pete the Boss.

The Mississippi Gulf Coast, always in the shadow of New Orleans, and forever under its cultural sway, got casinos. Petrino saw it as his obligation to the family to get in - to maintain control in the family's home territory, to avoid the risk of irrelevance, to expand or die. Casino gambling was a potential expansion of Bardino operations on a exponential scale. He had to make sure other criminals did not beat him to the pot of gold, and the power brokers, political and otherwise, that pot would attract like gadflies.

Mallini was truly a financial player. He had reinvested the family's laundered money in traditional, conservative securities: T-bills, government bonds, utilities. He then loaned those securities to investment banking companies, who used them to guarantee development loans to new casino operations all over the world. The investment bankers paid Mallini greater loan interest than he could ever receive conventionally.

The investment bankers usually took a piece of the equity in the casinos they financed as part of the deal. What the borrowers did not know was that the Bardinos owned the investment banker companies, too. This way, they double dipped the loan interest, and gained a piece of the ownership of each of the gambling deals they underwrote.

Mallini had invested the family's money in the casino business, but prudently decided not to make a move into outright casino ownership. Then came Hurricane Katrina, which wiped clean the slate. The state of Mississippi had become addicted to the annual flow of tax capital from the casino industry. Faced with the possibility of losing its base, the Mississippi legislature and Gaming Board essentially opened its doors to new operations, with more regard for profit that its previously sanctimonious attention to character.

All funding for construction of casinos and their hotels along the Mississippi Gulf Coast had to come from outside the state. Since no out-of state banks were willing to risk huge loans in Mississippi, especially after Katrina, prospective casino operators were reduced to two groups: those currently in the casino business, and those who could come up with the money through unconventional means. The Bardinos' seamless entry into the post - Katrina gambling market in Mississippi was a simple matter of corporations and cash.

Ellis leaned back in his seat, closed his eyes. As interesting as all that information was, and as new as it was to Zack Ellis, he knew that none of it - not even the Kennedy story or Iran-Contra were new. People already believed that the President had been murdered as a result of a conspiracy; the mundane facts of its execution, the blundering approach of its participants, and the fact of Oswald's presumptive incompetence *would* make a good story, but an unprovable one. He would lose his job, and his aspirations if he told it. What had him happy at the moment was what happened *after* Iran-Contra shut down.

Zack had to connect the dots on some of the details, but it appeared that Panama's de facto dictator was not willing to shut down the Contra gun running operation just because the U.S. had gotten cold feet. His end of the deal had been essentially security - he made sure the drug runners out of Columbia did not get hassled by Panama. In return, he was paid a virtual ransom equivalent to ten percent of the total value of all shipments which passed through his country, a staggering sum in the tens of millions of U.S. dollars, which was the only currency he would accept. He squeezed another couple of million dollars a year out of the CIA, just to keep his mouth shut. So he was not at all interested in seeing the party end, just because some *estupido* forgot to change a fuel filter.

The United States government was being held hostage by drug dealers and one incredibly bombastic third world dictator, and could not possibly shut the whole lot of them up. By 1989 they'd had enough, gotten tired of being blackmailed. So the dictator got "arrested," and stuck in a U.S. federal prison, convicted of drug running.

That Lee Farrell was in the Army stationed in Panama in 1989 was, to Ellis, merely an interesting coincidence. Then he ran across a newspaper article, a blurb really, attached to one of the endless files that had been scanned and digitized. The article was actually on the same page of a Washington newspaper story on the capture of the dictator, and mentioned a deadly drug deal on the Mississippi coast. Ellis went back and found the article. The incident had happened at a spot on the map called Cat Island, offshore of Azalea, Mississippi, Lee Farrell's home.

Ellis had dug up Farrell's military records. It was all the expected blather, no misconduct or commendations, though he did advance promotions rapidly. Then, he was suddenly discharged, honorably, having served less than his full enlistment.

Addendums to Farrell's records, which had been prepared by the U.S. Army CID unit, the Army's criminal investigation wing, had been completely deleted. The documents had been physically blacked out, apparently by a dark marker, before being scanned.

Ellis located an ex-CID officer who had been in Panama at the time. He had retired to Maryland as a full bird colonel. At first, the colonel was not at all interested in talking to the young FBI agent, and did not recall any case involving Mr. Farrell. He had tried to get Ellis to agree to have a beer, maybe a round of golf. But Ellis had simply declined and started to leave, suggesting that the colonel could expect federal grand jury subpoena soon. The prospect of federal testimony jostled his memory.

According to the colonel, Farrell and his two buddies apparently knew what was going on with Noriega and the drug shipments. In fact, knowledge of the ongoing affair was common among the U.S. military stationed in Panama in 1989, because of their constant intercourse with the Panamanian army, in which secrecy was a laughable concept. And acquiring volumes of cheap marijuana in Panama was as easy as a short trip downtown to Chorrillos. Thus, the colonel gauged, general attitude among troops at that place and time was: if the government can ignore the law, why not everyone else?

Farrell's little gang had arranged an amateurish marijuana delivery to Mississippi, using a rented cabin cruiser, under the guise of being on a fishing trip. Farrell's choice of dates had no connection with the surprise U.S. operation against the Panamanian dictator, other than bad timing. Army command in Panama did not want to cancel leaves for fear of tipping off the numerous spies.

The colonel had practically begged Ellis to guarantee him anonymity for the final part of the story. His CID unit had been notified by Farrell's commanding officer that Farrell had been a day late returning from his leave, and was consequently suspected of being an agent for the Panamanians in the ongoing military action against the Panamanian dictator. The colonel had been assigned the case.

Turns out, one of Farrell's gang, a yokel from New Orleans whose name the colonel could not remember, had blathered about the trip beforehand around some MPs at an NCO club. When he closely questioned Farrell and his compatriots, all of whom had been together on leave, and all of whom were late returning to duty, the story of the drug deal gradually emerged. The miscreants were resigned to terrible destinies, and were stunned to eventually learn that they would not be prosecuted.

The colonel found out that Farrell's boat trip had been discovered and tracked by an armed CIA vessel. The CIA was not about to chance letting freelance drug runners get caught and potentially draw too much attention to their ongoing operations. They had chased Farrell around the edge of the Gulf of Mexico, intending to sink him, but had been stymied by bad weather. They finally caught up to him in the storm right off Cat Island and, surprised by the presence of the local police, had killed the deputies and sunk their boat. Killing the cops was necessary, since they could not be reliably controlled. And letting Farrell go was necessary, since two blasted boats would imply the presence of a third. Any minimally competent investigation might attract the news media's attention, and the whole covert Central America can of worms might be permanently opened. The two dead cops were ultimately saluted as fallen heroes in the "War on Drugs."

So somebody in the U.S. covert community had murdered two of Sheriff Buck Carter's deputies. But the real nugget came from the colonel in an offhanded fashion. He had said, "In the end, if it were not for the intervention of Senator Griffin Ford in the Iran-Contra investigation, we would probably all be in jail, or dead." So Zack had gone back to see Senator Ford.

Ellis ordered a beer, something that he did not normally do while working, even on a plane. He almost took his wallet out before he remembered that business class drank free. He was heading to the coast for one reason: to protect his territory. If anybody else in the bureau found out about all this, they would surely blow it for him. The Bardino investigation had, for Agent Zachary Ellis, just transformed from a potential career booster to a blank invitation to the halls of power in Washington. That is, if he did not manage to screw it up, somehow.

Nick Bonacelli was getting irritated with his golfing group. A high roller just shanked another one about fifty yards dead right off the tee, a football field short of the green. "Goddamn grips!," the old man barked, accidentally spitting out half a Cuban cigar, which made him madder. He blared a guttural "FUCK!," swung at and missed the smoking cigar butt. Losing his balance, he gamely tried to long step his way back vertical, then did a belly flop right in the middle of the plush Bermuda grass tee base.

Nick was immediately cheered up, though none of the five man group said anything for a second or two. Finally, the old man's cart mate, probably his cousin, or a vice president at his bank, hopped out, ran over and started blaming everything from Adam and Eve to now for how his benefactor had just made himself look like a redneck pine tree farmer, which he used to be, instead of a retired majority stockholder of a bank, which he was. Nick couldn't hold it any longer, and him laughing made everybody else laugh, too.

But his good nature was gone several shanks later, in the middle of the next hole. These fools were guests at the casino, not "whales," like in Vegas, but bigshots from local communities that would lose fifty or a hundred grand on a good weekend, as long as their asses were sufficiently kissed. Nick's only real duties at the casino included entertaining these types. Fortunately, the pine tree farmer started getting overheated, and had to quit early. Nick declined to join the boys for a beer at the club house, got in his car, and headed back toward the beach. He was anxious about the deal with Farrell. The idiot Flounder had left the note for Farrell in New Orleans, then gone off and gotten drunk. Nick was ready to move. His partner in Saudi Arabia could not wait.

And there was the looming fact of his betrayal of the family. Pete Mallini had made it clear the only time the two had ever spoken, on the phone. "Don't fuck up," he had said. "We all know you're a smart guy. Hell, most of us even overlook your questionable origins. We let you in. Do *not* fuck up." That was it. The arrogant bastard never called, or visited. Never. *Fuck him. Fuck them all*, Nick thought.

Jake Carter did not like the feeling he had about Diana. He also needed to do something about Bonacelli, just to cover his ass in case Roark and the paper found out anything damaging. Maybe a quiet search of his home was in order. A "sneak and peek" search warrant that no one else would know about. He pictured the verbal exchange with the judge:

"Let's get this straight, son. You want to search the home of the boss of the biggest casino in the state, and you can't state to me with any particularity what you're looking for? Or that the man has committed any specific criminal acts?"

"Judge, you know as well as I do that the court issues search warrants every day without any particular basis, on the word of my office, or the police."

"Are you suggesting, Mr. Carter, that I am in the normal habit of violating the Constitution?"

" Of course, not, sir..."

It wouldn't work. Besides, some clerk or court reporter would inevitably find out, and that bastard Roark would have it all over the news. Still, he needed to get in Bonacelli's house, find out what was going on with Diana, whether the young FBI shit Zack Ellis was telling the truth. He knew better than to take those guys at their word. *There's no problem getting in the house,* Jake thought. *If she's up to something, she'll be going over there while Lee's out of town. The problem is, if I get caught without a warrant, what do I say?*

So Jake Carter drove out to Bonacelli's house. Diana's car was there, and he let himself in the unlocked front door. Creeping, he checked the kitchen and pool, skipping the dark formal dining room and huge den. He could hear chatter coming from back in the house, the master bedroom.

Entering, his heart pounding, he ducked behind the open door, just as Diana walked through. Sarah followed, stopping to pull at her hair once, looking in a huge floor mirror. She walked out of the room.

Jake waited a couple of minutes, after he thought he heard the two going out the back door of the house. He eased through the kitchen, where he could see through the small breakfast nook window. There stood Diana and Sarah Bonacelli, kissing by the pool. They turned and got into the swimming pool, and he left.

Driving through south Mississippi piney woods, Lee called Kiger and Meat to make sure the club was OK. Then he called Boot, told him to get the boat fueled up, and check the engines good. Just in case.

Even if Bonehead was looking for him, no mob goon would chase him into the heart of the Mississippi Delta, one of the greatest primordial swamps in the world, whose ancient population of deer and bear had given rise to legions of expert shooters. A couple of hours later, he turned west in Jackson, drove the forty miles or so to Vicksburg, and got off at Washington Street, the last exit before Interstate 20 crosses the great Mississippi River. He drove up to a river overlook, which was a Civil War fort site, currently part of the federal government's extensive park holdings. He climbed chipped concrete steps to the top of the tall hill; all battlements or signs of soldier occupation had long since rotted, worn away or been dug up by collectors.

Lee thought about the crude fighting that had gone on here. In 1863, Vicksburg was surrounded by the federal army of General U.S. Grant. Its citizens and army had dug into hillsides, ate their livestock, then their dogs, then their horses, then their shoes. After several weeks, they were sick and starved, firing nails at the yankees; Grant finally won by famine and disease what he could not by force. The city fell on July 4, 1863; its citizens so resented the Independence Day correlation that the national holiday was not locally recognized for a century after.

Lee climbed atop a huge cannon sitting on the hill, straddling it like a horse, watching the awesome river below. The sun was just setting over the flat land of northern Louisiana, and the two bridges below. The oldest bridge was closed to everything but trains, which labored over it several times a day.

Lee knew parts of the river as much as it would allow; its meanderings from the mouth at South Pass below New Orleans to where he now sat only covered maybe 250 miles in a straight line, but greatly exceeded that number along its crooked path. He had spent a lot of time on the river with his father, and Keep Marlin, the Farrell Farms foreman. The river was as majestic and terrible as it was when he was young. It represented a kind of wild freedom, always moving, never the same shape, or depth, or color.

It also represented his deepest fears; his occasional nightmares often involved its enormous eddies. He had once seen an entire grown oak tree, roots and all, pop up in the middle of the river, having been held under by its natural undertow from some unknown place north. That scene galvanized in his mind the eternal power and mystery of the water, which had mesmerized men for ages.

Now a couple of cars pulled around the circle and stopped, just in time for the last burning fringe of the sun to disappear below the horizon. Lee thought about his choices, the most momentous decision of his life. Sitting on a cannon in a park by the river. He could not help but laugh.

The disappearing sunlight across the river refracted on the swirling surface into millions of crystalline colors. The river was beautiful. Suddenly Lee remembered sitting on the same cannon years earlier, a summer when he was fifteen or sixteen, just old enough to drive. He had taken his dad's Chrysler down to Vicksburg, across the old bridge, and down to the levee, to a huge roadhouse called Peacock's, that made its living being the closest place in Louisiana where Mississippians could buy cheap liquor.

Peacock's had originally been just a liquor store, but had developed into a sprawling pool hall, with country rock bands, semis and Harleys in the parking lot, and a steady population of the peculiarly beautiful young women who yearly come of age and emerge from the hills of Vicksburg, the flatlands of the Delta, and farm villages punctuating the regal cypress wetlands of northern Louisiana.

Lee had gone with his girl across the bridge that afternoon, gotten a cheap bottle of berry flavored wine, come back and sat with her on this same cannon, watching the same sunset. Lee had been worried to death about getting caught; he knew his father wouldn't say anything, would only take his car keys away for a few days. Her father, however, would probably kill him.

Lee felt a surge of sadness as he remembered. At the time, when he was a teenager, he believed his life was charmed. He was smart, good looking, and from one of the oldest, most respected families in the Mississippi Delta. What were his worries?

He'd wound up getting sick on the wine that day, and had to throw up on the side of Mississippi 61 as they headed back to the Delta. He got her home, nobody got caught. She had given him his first real kiss, and the day had fossilized in his young conscience as the perfect day. Now, he could not remember her name.

He *had* been charmed. As the last of the sunset gave way to the stars, the two other cars at the circle cranked up and pulled away. How had he gotten here? Hassled by the Mafia. His wife's life in danger. Pure stupidity. He did not know yet what he was going to do, only that he had to be prepared to leave, if necessary. Forever.

Back home, Ellis propped his feet up, flipped on the TV. When he had gone back to see Senator Ford, he was halfway expecting some sort of Perry Mason moment, the senator realizing the jig was up, that he had been caught by the young legal sharp. But it didn't happen that way. The senator, when confronted with the political death sentence of his own participation in the cover-up of U.S. forces murdering domestic police officers, he said, "Very good, Zack. I was hoping you would find that. Actually, I'm surprised the information still exists."

Zack said, "But, Senator Ford, this information is crucial, I would even say, *material* to the investigation I am conducting. Do you know what this means?"

"I do, Zack," the senator said, "I was a young attorney once, just like you. In love with the law, you may say, though I am sure the atmosphere was much different then.

Zack said, "But if these things...if I have to reveal what I know, which is my *duty*, you'll be ruined, politically. You may be indicted for obstructing a murder investigation."

"I had considered the possibility," said the Senator Ford, with a wink. He rose from his wide, worn leather chair, moved slowly across the office. He pulled a book from its spot on a shelf, leaving a dust outline. Handing the book to Zack, he sat on the edge of his desk. "It's Jefferson," he said. "Complete writings, including all his published drafts and notes. Remarkable, really. The man was an amazing keeper of records, very aware of his place in history. He knew that he and Adams, Washington, Franklin, and all the rest were on a course that could only end in two ways: the start of a miraculous country, or death, most likely by hanging."

"Sir, I've read most of..."

"Please, son. Indulge an old man. I will make a point presently."

"Yes, sir."

"You see, in the eighteenth century, the idea of a republic, a democracy that would not destroy itself by infighting, or allow its military to dominate its politics as the Greeks and Romans did was, well, absurd."

"But they managed to do it."

"They managed to get it *started*. Surely, those four gentlemen disagreed on how to go about it. There were many others, of course. Madison, Hamilton, Hancock, Henry, Samuel Adams, the Lees...they all had their own ideas. The fact that the new country did not dissolve in the midst of their arguments is evidence of the hand of God. Yet, regardless of their major differences, they eventually constructed a union under a Constitution that has managed to endure for over two centuries. Do you know why they were able to accomplish this?"

"God, sir?"

"Well, maybe. But these men, these revolutionaries, whom had thrown off the chains of monarchy at the peril of their lives, ultimately could agree on one thing: that the experiment, the impossible idea, the *country* they had bet their lives upon was *more important* than their political differences. They agreed to compromise even their greatest personal desires in deference to the preservation of that idea. This is where mankind first truly realized a government of laws, and not men, choosing to live under a system of rule by compromise, in a democratic republic. Think of it. It is nothing less than a miracle. A series of them."

Agent Ellis fidgeted, embarrassed at the old man's gushing.

Senator Ford continued, "The Constitution itself merely memorialized the greater understanding that men would no longer owe liberty to the whims of a despot, or even to a despotic majority. That the rule of law would always supersede their own fickle desires. And the only way to accomplish this miracle of government would be to divide the powers of the people among *branches* of government. It's unbelievable really, rich men agreeing to relinquish their own political powers. Heady, heady stuff. Read that book when you get a chance."

"I will."

The old senator returned to his seat, grimacing. He smiled, wryly. "You see, Zack, those men gave us an idea, that the law, the *country*, is greater than the fates of individual people. However, from that time until now, there have been those who come here, to Washington, and think they are better than the law. That they know better than Jefferson, and Adams. And Washington. These people are our real enemies."

"Who are we talking about, sir, specifically?"

"Anyone who decides that politics is greater than the law. Because then it becomes greater than the country."

"Why are you telling me this?"

"Because I failed. I helped people do damage to the Constitution, and the memory of our founders. Even though I believed at the time that what we were doing was right. See, it did not occur to me until later in my life that the real reason for having the Constitution is to tell our government what to do in bad times. In good times, people generally do the right thing, and don't need to be told. We forgot that. It's up to your generation to fix this mess we've made, or start over."

"But, sir, what can I do? I'm a low level FBI agent."

"Just do your job, son."

"But doing my job will hurt you, sir."

Senator Ford laughed, and it was genuine. "I'm not worried about me, son. I'm just looking forward to one last big fireworks show."

Ellis flipped off the TV, headed for bed. He decided his first move would be to corner and flip Lee Farrell. Farrell was probably not even in on anything the Bardinos were doing, but he could be leveraged, and Ellis needed an insider.

And the best way to get to Farrell was through his wife. Seeing Diana Farrell was a good thing no matter what the underlying motive. He would visit her right away.

Descending the last slopes of Vicksburg, heading north up Highway 61, Lee entered the heavy Delta air after dark. Mosquitoes made him use his windshield washer, and dimmed the glow of his headlights. Nothing else came out to greet him as he crossed the high, narrow old bridge over the Yazoo River, which was the frontier between the Delta and the normal world. Rather than drive all the way up to Farrell County, he decide to turn west toward the oxbow lakes, Eagle, Chotard, Albemarle, Airplane, and a few others formed by the Mississippi River's ancient visitations. He figured his old buddy Keep would be at his favorite bar at Lake Chotard, across the Mississippi River levee.

Keep was sitting at the bar, like Lee knew he would be, leaning into a good sip of Jim Beam. He was dressed just like Lee's dad Mr. Hayes always was, except Keep was dirtier.

Lee said, "What's the cotton look like?"

Keep said, "I know you didn't drive all the way up here to talk about cotton." He stood up, grabbed Lee around the shoulders, hugged him. "You want a drink?"

Lee said yeah, did not specify what type, since he knew it would be Beam on the rocks, same as Keep. Keep waived at one of the bartenders, signaled "two," like a peace sign. Lee watched a pool game on one of the crooked tables; a bored girl was watching, too, sitting on the next table. She caught Lee's glance, and he looked away, self-conscience.

Lee said, "You're getting the farm."

If the news shocked or surprised Keep, he hid it. He took a long sip of whiskey, stubbed out a Marlboro, lit another, and said, "What the hell are you talking about, Lee?"

"You're getting the farm, and I'm going working it out where you don't have to go in-pocket. We've got to go to Bob Abbott's office, tomorrow."

"Lee, you can't just..."

"I'm not talking about it anymore tonight, Keep. And this isn't something I just thought of. I'm tired, and I'm going to the hunting camp. See you tomorrow."

"Or tonight. I'm prob'ly staying over there, too."

"You won't see me, pal," Lee said, picking up the plastic cup, draining it, throwing it across the bar into a trash can. "I'll be asleep." He slowly walked to his GTO, tired. A couple of college aged kids, professional catfishers from the river, were squatted in their white boots, checking out the car. Lee jumped in and took off. Kids. What they don't know yet.

He went across the levee, where his headlights showed a couple of deer munching on the edge of a soybean field. They ignored his car. A few minutes later, in his bed at the camp, he thought again about childhood. And that tomorrow was his fortieth birthday.

Nick Bonacelli sat in his airy office atop Cronus Casino. Through plate glass windows, the rising sun shot streaks of red, yellow and orange like a Roman candle across the horizon. The view across the gulf would be enough to make him thank God, if he believed in one.

He was waiting for a phone call from Saudi Arabia. His friend from Harvard grad school, Fuad, was to give him the particulars of their new venture. Fuad was one of the endless uncles or cousins of the Saudi royal family, and therefore entitled to practically unlimited money. He first explained his scheme to Nick a couple of months earlier, when Nick had to take his wife on a shopping trip to New York.

They sat in a cigar bar on the upper east side that had old tooled leather ceilings, mahogany fixtures, and private cigar lockers for its regulars. Fuad was an inveterate cigar smoker, and kept a succession of double corona Montecristos lit during their visit. He typically only smoked a third of one before he lit the next.

Fuad said, "These bombs you see on CNN, in Lebanon, in Iraq, in Afghanistan, many times they are terrorist attacks. Attacks between Sunni factions, attacks between Shiite and Sunni militias, al Qaeda attacking everyone, attacks on America, Israeli, European interests. But many times, they are just messages."

"To who?," Nick asked.

"To my family."

"I don't get it."

You see, my country is primarily Sunni. Sunnis have run the Arab and Moslem worlds for many centuries, since the Ottoman world, which was broken up by the allies after World War I." He paused, took a drag from his cigar, blew it out, took a sip of

Macallan scotch. "Your country has always maintained ties to mine, in combination with Israel, to effect a balance against Iran and Syria, and ultimately their backers in Russia. This is for the secure flow of oil."

"I've read the theories."

"The thing is, the militias, the terrorists, they can stop the flow of oil whenever they want. In order to prevent this, we essentially pay them ransom."

"But why you? Why not anyone else?"

"My country, my family, we exist on oil revenues. We have no other economy. Our next biggest export, after oil, is rugs. The terrorists know this, that we cannot survive without oil trade with the West. Also, these people -jihadists - they are extremely religious. They do not drink, or smoke, and do not miss their prayers. They think of themselves as pure, and do not approve of our habits." He held up the cigar for emphasis.

"They don't seem to regard murder as a particularly reprehensible vice."

"They do not consider their actions to be murder, but necessary in the performance of their duty of jihad."

"Jihad, war, business, murder. Everybody's got a different name for it. All right, so your family pays ransom, for protection. What's the catch?"

"The catch is...and Nick, you must swear to me you will never, ever repeat this."

"I swear, Fuad. You know me."

Fuad looked around, made sure none of the other dozen or so patrons could hear. "The thing is, it is my job in the family to get the money to these...these groups. Cash. Huge amounts of it."

"Why not just wire it?"

"Are you kidding me? Your government watches everything, and I mean *everything* that happens electronically worldwide. We can't even set up new accounts without their knowledge."

"You gave consent for this?"

"Of course not. They did not ask. And you don't ask how I know."

"Don't want to. So you've got all this cash, and?"

"Right. So, I found out that some of the money was being used to purchase raw stones, diamonds, emeralds, like that. The stones are sold on the black market, and the jihadists make many, many times return. This is one of the ways they have become so well funded. Believe me, we do not want them rich."

"Sounds, I don't know, sophisticated for a bunch of religious freaks."

"No, no, my friend, these people are very smart. Very well educated. They have mastered the internet. Some people in my country even believe they were the source of much of the faulty intelligence the U.S. received to justify its invasion of Iraq. The jihadists wanted to precipitate a regional civil war. They think it is their duty to God."

"All right, so you got something to tell me?"

"So impatient, Nick. Yes. I have something to propose. You see, I found out how the gemstone thing works. These stones are bought mainly in Madagascar. They are sold to gem dealers, who cut them, and sell them in your jewelry stores. The thing is, the stones are illegal, since they have been illegally taken from Africa. The price is better for the stone buyers, but the risk is greater. So they will only trade outside the U.S. In this hemisphere, many are located in the Republic of Panama."

"So you figured to get in on the action?"

"Why should they make the cream? My life is in danger as well. You would not believe some of the places I have been, to take these people their money."

"You have my attention. Only, I hope this doesn't have anything to do with the casino I run, because I'm not about to…"

"No. Nothing like that. I decided to divert some of the cash I was supposed to be giving to the jihadists into our new investment. With the profits, I will replace the money. My problem is, I cannot be running to Panama, nor can I do business on my side of the Atlantic."

"Because if your family finds out…"

"I have six or seven uncles who would kill me just for telling you about the ransom, much less withholding the payments."

"So you need my help."

"Yes, and fast. The first batch will net several million."

"Dollars?"

"Dollars. U.S."

"No *shit*."

That's how Nick had gotten in the black market jewelry business. Of course, figuring out how to screw Fuad out of his share of the first shipment was easy, and natural. Finding Farrell, and finding out about his little drug dealing escapade, was so perfect, it almost made him reconsider his position on God. His office door slid open, and his assistant told him Fuad was on the phone.

Ten hours ahead, Fuad sat in an open air café. Nick picked up, and Fuad said, "Nick! My cousin is in town, and would like to see you."

Nick said, "Fine. When?"

Fuad said, "Right now. Give him a call." He hung up.

Nick slowly hung up the receiver. The fucking deal was on, and his patsy Farrell had gone off-grid. He picked up the phone and called Flounder.

The next morning, Keep was already up and gone when Lee headed toward his lawyer's office. He called Keep on the way, telling him when to meet. He passed Farrell lands for several miles into the little town of Farrell, where the bank, the post office, two churches, the school and the courthouse were. A few houses still had families in them.

The modern land holdings of Farrell Farms, Inc. was not a proper, identifiable tract of land that had a central location, and definite parameters. Farrell Farms was a modern concern, a conglomerate which encompassed approximately fifty thousand acres, spread across the county. Most of it was owned outright by the company. Some of it was in various stages of mortgage life, or liened against seed, fertilizer, diesel.

A good, healthy cotton growth's height will hide a standing man. That's why being in high cotton has always been understood in the Delta, and around the South, as being a good thing. Lee saw the cotton was indeed going to be high this year. His buddy Keep Marlin had been running the farm for several years. He was the Farrells' foreman; the Farrells had been, in a way, Keep's surrogate family. Lee thought about that. How many friends did he have with intact families? None? Was that a commentary on families, or was the country unraveling, family by family?

Hayes Fike Farrell, Lee's dad, was called "Mr. Hayes" by everyone. Mr. Hayes, who was in his late forties in Lee's earliest awareness, had been in and around these fields all of Lee's childhood. He was a typical Mississippi Delta farmer in many ways. He seemed to require little sleep, or food. He was skinny, but tough as a creosote post.

Other than Sundays, Lee had only seen him once without Wranglers and roping boots on; the family had gone to the coast one year, like they did every year after the cotton was cut; they had stayed in the cottage in Azalea. He went to the beach where Lee and a group of other kids were gathering driftwood and trash for a later bonfire. Mr. Hayes was wearing shorts, and the tanned coast kids had ragged him about his white legs.

He had taken it with great humor, even gotten out his chainsaw and cut some good wood for the fire, off a huge pecan tree that had fallen during a recent tropical storm in one of the neighbors' yards. He and Lee's mom Jenny had gotten out and danced around the fire that evening. Lee was about nine or ten at the time, and it was a good weekend to remember.

Mr. Hayes had broken his leg on a big combine tractor when Lee was in his first tour of college, at Mississippi State. It was a bad break, above the knee. He spent some time in the University Medical Center in Jackson, had some blood complications which prolonged his recovery. He had been forced to consider selling, since an operation the size of Farrell Farms had too many employees, too much equipment, and too much revolving debt to be out of service even a year. In the end, he settled on a hierarchy of assistants, with Keep at the top running things, which formed the groundwork for how the farm was run today.

Mr. Hayes never recovered from the leg injury, he died before he could. Lee had gotten a full football scholarship at Mississippi State, and was widely hailed as the future star quarterback in a school that had long been deficient at the position. He redshirted a year, and was probably going to be the starter the next year, a huge responsibility for a young man in the brutal, fast Southeastern Conference. But during the summer between Lee's freshman and sophomore years, the Farrells died. It was the seminal event in his life; the one that had set him inevitably on his current course. Whether that was good, or bad.

The death of the Farrells had been bizarre. Mr. Hayes had missed the spring plant, the first of his adult life. It was terrible. Not for the farm, but for him. He had never actually seen a daytime television show. He was physically unable to work, according to the doctors.

Mr. Hayes believed the doctors were taking their orders from insurance companies, and made sure everyone heard about it. He was effectively confined to his house, with a few short rides around the farm weekly. His leg, exacerbated by his age, was too delicate for any kind of serious strain. He was, by any practical notion, retired.

But he couldn't stand it. For the first time, he had to trust someone else to handle the farm, even if it was his protégée Keep, who did everything just like him. When he drove by a field, noticing that they had planted it in the wrong direction for the drainage, or that the crews were spread too far for the fuel supplies to get to them effectively, or any number of things he had always just done without telling anyone how, he railed on the radio at Keep. He'd rather have done things himself, but he just couldn't.

It got so bad, he had taken the unbelievable step of going to a therapist. And a woman, too. She told him that retirement did not mean he had to do nothing, just something different for a while. He didn't need any more money; she told him to find something he liked to do, to learn how to relax. So he took up adding on to his house.

The only things he ever built before were barns, outbuildings, and such. He had this idea about a big cypress room; he was going to use some timber the Army Corps of Engineers had found at the bottom of the Sunflower River, which loggers had lost a century earlier. But Mr. Hayes never could get it framed up right; he kept tearing it down, rebuilding, tearing down, rebuilding. He wouldn't ask anybody to help, hobbling around. Worse, all the coffee cup farmers down at the local grill started ribbing him about it.

For some reason no one ever understood, he was on a ladder with a lit blowtorch, the little kind you solder with. He fell, got knocked out, and the blowtorch rolled up against a pile of two-by-fours, and caught them on fire. Mrs. Farrell was upstairs taking a nap. She never moved, was dead from the fumes in her sleep before the fire ever got to her, the coroner said. The whole thing was ruled a tragic, horrible accident, and even the insurance company didn't fight it when the Farrells' lawyer, old Bob Abbott, filed a claim for the full coverage.

After the funeral, the preacher cracked, "Poor old Hayes, he done himself in trying to learn how to relax." It was true, and everybody laughed uncomfortably, like people do at funerals. There were no other family, only Lee. All the uncles and cousins had long since either died, moved away, or become jealous of Hayes' success, and faded away from kinship. Lee remembered for the first time feeling that everyone in Farrell County knew by now that he was just an adopted son, and not a real Farrell. Things like that mattered more in the Delta than they did anywhere else, even in the rest of the South, because of blood ties to the land itself.

Within two weeks, Lee had withdrawn from school without talking to anybody, not even Jake, who was a favorite on frat row, and was being coaxed by the college Republicans to run for student body president. Lee had heard all his life about Farrells serving their country in the armed forces, so he went off, joined the Army, and they eventually sent him to Panama.

Lee pulled up to lawyer Bob Abbott's office, which was originally a house, probably built around World War II. It was painted white, with black shutters, long overhanging eaves, and a huge screened front porch. There was a contoured wooden blue porch swing that could hold four people, but only contained Keep, swinging.

Lee and Keep went in. The porcelain knob of the old door rattled cold in Lee's hand. Keep accidentally let the wooden screen door slam. It had ornamental metal scroll work that clanged and clamored, causing Abbott's old gray snouted English Pointer to open one eye, then roll over on the sitting room rug, napping.

"That old door," said Miss Jeanie, Abbott's secretary. "Y'all go on back, Lee. He's pretty light, today."

Lee led Keep clomping down the short pinewood hall, into Abbott's office. Abbott said, "Pardon me, gentlemen, if I don't get up. The back's flaring up again."

Lee and Keep shook hands with the lawyer, settled across from him in heavy oak chairs.

Abbott said, "Lee, I've had these matters prepared for some time, as you know, since you requested me to do so a couple of years back."

Abbott said, "So, if you gentlemen will sign where Jeanie has marked, Lee, we'll get your check, and you two can get on your way. Of course, Keep, you can take that to another attorney, if you like. I'm required to tell you that. But since you're getting everything, presumably that includes me."

"I ain't interested in talking to any other lawyers, Mr. Bob. What you say is good with me."

Lee said, "Mr. Abbott,…"

Abbott said, "Please, Lee, pardon me for interrupting, but folks of a certain age, as they say, are traditionally afforded deference, you know. I used to think that was because of approaching senility, or even out of respect. But now I know it's just worn out manners. Anyhow, call me Bob. I know I'm older than wood, but give me some hope."

"Yes, sir. I was hoping you could explain the deal, the basics, to Keep. I've actually never told him much before now."

"Really. Well, you, my boy, are a fantastic keeper of secrets. And you, Mr. Keep Marlin, are now a very wealthy man."

Keep signed the last spot and pushed the stack of paper across the attorney's wide desk, which was entirely covered with a polished leather desk pad, and said, "What just happened, exactly?"

Abbott said, "Well, the nut of it, Keep, is you just bought the farm, so to speak, at terms only a fool would decline. I am happy to see that you are no fool."

Keep said to Lee, "I don't really know what to say, little brother…"

"Don't start crying, Keep. It wouldn't sound good at the hunting camp."

"Believe me, brother, if I was a crier, I'd being squalling. But really. Thanks."

Lee and Keep traded nods.

Abbott said, "Keep, all of Farrell Farms, Inc.'s holdings, land buildings, equipment, debt and equities, contracts, everything went into a trust when the Farrells, God bless them, passed away. It has been administered through the trust in Lee's favor since. When Lee reached the age of twenty-five, the trust fully inured to his benefit. He chose to leave the assets in place. My office administers the trust, pays Lee a yearly dividend, which allows he and his wife to live comfortably, and is advantageous tax wise. That arrangement will continue for Lee and his wife, as long as the farm remains viable. You will now receive a yearly dividend as well, astronomically more than you make now. Profits from the farm will pay the transaction taxes. Of course, you are now the owner, and can alter the arrangement at any time."

"I won't be changing the deal. There is one thing, though, that I'd like to ask."

"What is it?"

"This is more directed at Lee. You know Mr. Hayes was like my own daddy, in a lot of ways. He took me in, like he did you,

Lee, and getting to carry on the farm, well, is just real special.
Mr. Abbott, Lee knows this, but you don't. My first wife, we were
married more than twenty years…"

"I know her, Keep, she owns that little hair shop out on the
highway, doesn't she?"

"She does. Anyway, me and her, we split up. It wasn't
anything horrible, no fighting, or nothing. After the kids left- I got
three grown girls - she just got bored, I guess. She got up one day,
and decided she was ready for something different. I helped her
get that little shop started, and, well, she just wanted to be alone.
So we got divorced. I got married again, a couple of years ago,
and I got twin baby boys, now. What it is, I was wondering…Lee,
would you mind if I changed their last name to Farrell?"

"Of course not, Keep. Hell, I've got no more of a claim to the
Farrell name than anybody else."

Abbott said, "Lee, if I might interject, that's not exactly
true."

"I know the legal status of adopted people, Bob, but I'm
talking about real life. Keep, I think that would be perfect. Not
only would it honor mom and pop, but it would make it possible
for the farm to stay in Farrell hands from now on."

"Interesting," said Abbott, standing, waddling across the
room. He took a heavy history volume off one of numerous
laden shelves, flipped it open. "Very reminiscent of Rome, in the
age of, I believe," he poked around in the book for a second, "Oh
yes, in the age if the Antonines." He closed the book, returned
it to the shelf, waddled back to his desk. "Very similar. Farrell
Farms is indeed an empire. Mr. Farrell picked you, Lee, and
Lee has picked you, Keep. You've been entrusted with the result
of many generations of toiling, even before most of the Delta
was inhabitable. Your father would approve, Lee. He was very
interested in history, and the history of the Farrell family. He
would be happy to know that the farm stays intact."

"I used to hate hearing him go on, but I read a lot of history myself, now. I wish I had him to talk to."

"We all miss our parents when we get older. Yours were taken far too soon."

Lee and Keep left, dropped Keep's truck off at one of their barn sheds. Driving, Lee said, "Old man Abbott is a good one. I'd keep him, if I were you."

"I will. You sure it's okay about the name change?"

"Of course, Keep. Dad should have adopted you, anyway. This sort of wraps up that loose end. But I'm wondering, don't you want the Marlin name to carry on?"

"I'd change my own damn name, if it wouldn't be such a pain. My old man was a real winner. The only reason I remember him at all was the way my mama used to cry and scream and carry on when he was drunk and whipping her ass. I'd like to know where the sumbitch is right now."

"What happened to him?"

"Don't know. He cut out when I was real little. Then, Mama got so sick right about time I went to high school, she had to go live with her sister. I figured I was big enough to take off, and I went to work for your daddy. Ain't never left."

"And now you own it. God bless America, huh?"

"Land of the free, little brother. Home of the brave."

Lee and Keep drove up the highway a piece, to check on Mama Thea's house. She was in the hospital in Greenville; they said she was in and out of consciousness, and couldn't recognize anybody. She had instructed the doctors not to let anyone, especially Lee, see her in that condition; under the law, they had to do it. So Lee was effectively banned from the hospital. *Typical of that old Mississippi possum*, thought Lee.

Keep waited in the car as Lee went in the house. The front door was unlocked, like he knew it would be. The air conditioner had been turned up since she was gone, so it was warm inside. The whole place smelled like gardenias. She had photos of Lee all over the place. He thought for a moment about how that old lady, his real mom no matter what his crazy history might be, had more or less devoted herself to making sure that he was at least started in the right direction.

He physically winced at the recurring idea, accusation really, that he had let her down. How could she be proud? He'd quit everything that mattered. He'd gotten lazy. He had a cushy life, and took advantage of it. And he was a fucking criminal, had been involved when he was young in an idiotic scheme to make money off weed, that had gotten people *killed*. And he was about to do something illegal again. What would she think? Sadly, he knew what she would think, and he quietly walked out.

Lee and Keep drove a couple of miles to a cemetery where Mama Thea had already declared she was to be buried. The old part of the cemetery had been forgotten during the Depression, and been part of a farmer's corn field. In the seventies, it was rediscovered by anthropologists from Mississippi State looking for Indian artifacts. It was mapped and restored, then turned over to Mama Thea's church. The church maintained it in perpetuity, and Mr. Hayes had bought her plot years ago.

Her gravesite was in the shade of a big sycamore tree. Keep strolled through the markers, smoking. Lee sat on a cool concrete bench, remembering all her little advices, and nuances. She had approved of this spot; she no doubt had visited it on a few occasions, preparing for death as she had always prepared herself and everyone around her for life. She was, Lee realized, the only person he ever knew who seemed completely unaffected by the unknown. He looked around the grounds. All the close graves were of the twentieth and twenty-first centuries; some in the oldest part of the cemetery were second and third generation slaves, captives who had died in a foreign land, who had no more say over their burial than they did over their own lives. Lee scanned the flat Delta horizon, wondering if those slaves would notice much change. In the Delta, the difference between past and present is unclear; persistent sameness erases the passage of time.

Lee could tell Keep was getting anxious about getting back to the farm, but he wanted to see one more thing, the old Craft antebellum home. Besides, it was on the way back to Keep's truck. It was a towering, three story antebellum mansion that was always in some stage of rehabilitation. No one had ever seemed to live there long. It was built right on top of the biggest Indian mound in Farrell County, and was justifiably believed by the locals to be haunted, especially in the cellar. Competing federal laws both outlawing its presence on the burial ground, and its destruction, because it was a registered historic site, kept it in a perpetual state of legal limbo.

The house was locked. Lee had wanted to go up on the widow's walk, where you could see forever. He had to settle for the good view from the top of the mound, which he had just climbed in his car, up the steep spiral driveway. The vast, panoramic view included much of the Farrell holdings. The green cotton and soybean fields shimmered in the heat. A dust devil as big as a small tornado crossed a tree line a mile away, and broke up.

Keep said, "Your mama would lay a wood duck if she knew you were up here in the Delta like this, without your wife."

"Well, mom always had her concerns about appearances. I never could figure out how she felt about anything else."

"Well, I don't know what y'all's private business was like, but she sure did talk about you like she was proud. Same for Mr. Hayes."

"Really? They never said so. Not much."

"Mr. Hayes wasn't the kind of man that thought things needed saying more than once."

"That would be true, if everything was equally important."

"Well it ain't none of my business, but there was a lot of friction between Miss Jenny and Mr. Hayes by the time you came along. Getting you didn't make it any better between them, maybe worse, but they both always carried on like you was the best thing alive."

"Yeah, I remember sometimes thinking that they were competing over me."

"They were. And it was all based on the idea Miss Jenny had that Mr. Hayes was - you know - sterile. "

Lee laughed. "Yeah. I heard the discussions."

"You, and everybody else in Farrell County. Your mama, I hope you don't mind me saying, was a strong woman, vocally."

Lee nodded. A few crows landed in one of the fat pecan trees along the edge of the mound, squawking.

"Shit, Lee, what are you going to do next? You're still the smartest sumbitch I ever met."

"That doesn't say much for your company."

"Which I notice you got the hell away from."

"Sometimes I wish I hadn't. It's just…I don't know. There's some kind of attraction for me on the water. Like I need to be there." He thought for a moment. "So, what was the friction between mom and dad really about? Just the sterility thing, or was there something else?"

"Something else? There couldn't be anything else bigger. Shit, think about it. Here's Miss Jenny, she's a blue blood, you know, kin to the Percys and everything. She was the homecoming queen at Ole Miss, back when that *really* meant something. She was high dollar stock, if you'll pardon the expression."

"You know better than to worry about saying anything to me, Keep. You're as close to a big brother as I ever had."

"Yeah, I been thinking about that, too. You riding around with me after work, checking the fields, me drinking beer, and smoking. Cussing like a drunk fool, which I was, sometimes. That wasn't no way to carry on around a little kid. I should've known better."

"Shit, Keep," Lee threw a fake punch, which Keep pretended to dodge. "Those are the best memories I have. This whole place…it's like a dream. Like the Wizard of Oz."

"OK, who am I? The candy-ass lion, or the rusty one. Was there another one?"

"Funny. You know what I mean. So, tell me the rest. What was the big deal with mom and dad?"

"Let me tell you, Lee, when those two got married, they said, the governor came. It was Miss Beauty Queen and the last Farrell standing. It was a big deal."

"Sounds good, so far."

"And it was, for a while. Keep in mind, this was all told to me, mainly by Mama Thea."

"Mama Thea was the hub."

"She was. And sneaky, too."

"Mama Thea? You're kidding."

"Oh, no. Mama Thea, she was a card. Miss Jenny used to catch her all the time, hanging out around the corner, pretending she was dusting, or something, but listening."

"What was she up to?"

"Not a damn thing. It just kept her up front in the gossip yard every Sunday after church. You notice who all them dinner guests would always wind up flocking around? That old lady could tell a story as good as any bobcat hunter I ever heard."

"Was she really as religious as I remember?"

"Oh, she had her times. They said she used to get wound up on homemade muscadine wine, ever once in a while, and head off to Cleveland, or Memphis. There were some damn good blues joints back in those days."

"Mama Thea in road houses? Come on!"

"Shoot, son, they said she was something, and could shake it like Big Mama Thornton. And, she was from way off down there in New Orleans. Made her special."

"I'll be damned. It's just hard to picture."

"Ain't no harm in young people having fun. Anyway, about your folks. Think about it. Mr. Hayes was the last Farrell out of that whole line, and he couldn't have his own kids. It tore him up when he was younger. They did everything they could, that was available in them days, to have a baby. But it didn't work. Your daddy - you know how he was about family, especially about history..."

"Yeah, I heard about it all the time, believe me."

"Well, that stuff really meant a lot to him. It meant a lot to him when Mama Thea brought you along. Shit, you came down that road right there, in the back of a Ford pickup, in a paste board box full of you and bananas."

"Bananas! Where did *they* come from?"

"Hell if I know. Come to think of it, that was an unusual sight around here in those days. Your daddy, he hired me two or three years before that. Mr. Hayes took me in, like a stray." He stared off at the horizon for a minute. Mr. Hayes, Miss Jenny, they took us both in."

"Well, I know daddy always thought of you as his son, too. That's why I wanted to make sure you got the farm. Now. By the way, did he ever say for sure where I came from?"

"Memphis. But I never heard your daddy say that, only Mama Thea, at one of them Sunday dinners."

Lee smiled as he remembered that in Farrell County, the noontime meal is "dinner."

Keep said, "I heard her say it a bunch."

Lee pictured what seemed like hundreds of gatherings from his childhood; Mama Thea cooked, and there was an open invitation to practically everyone in the county to come over. It was not unusual for three or four dozen people to show; Miss Jenny was always at her best then, entertaining, making sure everyone was fed, had tea, was involved in a conversation. She and Diana were so much alike in that way. He wondered if that was what has initially attracted him to Diana. He missed her.

Lee was grown, and Miss Jenny was dead before he ever could appreciate the social aptitude she possessed; she could carry on several conversations at once, as she flitted through the house, the veranda, grabbing empty glasses, promoting Mama Thea's pecan pie. How she could bolster the ego of men whom were her intellectual inferiors. How she could gracefully usher away the priest, and a few Ladies Auxiliary members, who always sat together, in case any new social business happened to pop up.

The drinkers, or at least the ones that would drink in front of each other, would stay around; the women would go in the dining room with their wine and play cards, or just talk. The men would start out on the big front porch, or "veranda" as Miss Jenny called it, with whiskey, and would usually wind up in the den shooting pool. Those were some of the few times Lee ever saw his father seem happy. All the rest was worry. Lee said, "So go on about the Farrells."

"Well, two or three years went by, they said, and all Miss Jenny's aunts and uncles and granddads - your great granddaddy was still living, then - they were all about ready to blow a flap over them two having kids. Well, they never did. Soon enough, Miss Jenny let it out at church, or over at the tennis club, the country club, whatever, that Mr. Hayes' systems wasn't in order. When he finds out, he *does* blow a flap. He never did get over being pissed off about that, and she always blamed the whole hullabaloo on martinis. That got him even hotter. They squabbled about that all those years, until the day they both died."

"Did he ever say anything to you about it?"

"Damn sure did. He made sure that every time the guys got together, you know, hunting or fishing, that he let out that it was his poor wife's condition that she couldn't have children."

"Which one was true?"

"Well, how the hell would I know?"

"Bullshit, Keep. You knew my dad better than anyone else. I know you have some idea."

"Well, your daddy damn sure thought his pecker was working fine. He told me one time that he thought he might've had another kid out there somewhere. To tell you the truth, I always sort of figured that you were really his, and that he and Mama Thea cooked up all that other stuff."

"*Wow*. That's new. He let out an unwelcome breath. So dad screwed around? What an asshole."

"Be careful. Mama Thea always said, 'don't hold other people to a higher standard than you hold yourself to.' "

"Yeah, committing adultery in your heart, and all that stuff. Still, there's a difference when you actually do it." Which he knew made him an asshole, because he had every intention of screwing Dahlia, but he got too drunk.

Keep said, "True. And that part about Mr. Hayes being your real dad? Don't get the idea that anybody told me that. That was strictly my idea."

"Well, apparently everybody's got a different theory about my mysterious origins. I guess I'll never know. Did he…ever talk about God, stuff like that?"

"Your daddy didn't say much about anything like that. But I do remember once, he said, 'If there *is* such a thing as hell, none of us ever had a chance to begin with.' "

The top of the old Indian mound was silent. Lee started to say something, but decided not to. Finally, he said, "I may not be back around, Keep."

"Until when?"

"Ever."

Keep dug around in his shirt pocket, then lit a cigarette, cut a glance at Lee. "Mind saying why?"

"I can't." He looked around, trying to ignore his constricting throat. "This place," - he waived around - "I'm happy for the Farrell family, for mom and dad, that you got it."

"You're up to something, Lee. I hope I ain't asking your business, but in a way, you and me, we're family. I want to make sure that you know, anything I can do, well, you know."

"Yeah," said Lee.

Keep's truck radio blared, "Keep, you there?"

Keep walked around the driver's side, glad for the break in the conversation, so he could covertly wipe the tears from his eyes, under his sunglasses. Keying the radio mike, he said, "Go ahead."

"I'm northwest, in that sixty we just planted the first time this year."

"Yeah, I know where it is. I'm in a meeting. What's up?"

"A *meeting*? Where the hell are you, the VFW?"

"That's incredibly funny, tater. What do you want?"

"I picked up another fuckin' shed. I can't believe the luck. Now, I can't see a *horn* in the woods, but let me get in a fuckin' combine. That's two already this week. I called the truck."

Lee had seen what a big whitetail buck's discarded horns could do to a tractor tire.

Keep said, "Sounds like you got it handled, huh, hotshot?"

"I didn't want you sneaking up on me and thinking I was fuckin' off."

"How about a little less cussin' on the radio, sport?"

"Uh, OK boss. Out."

Keep said, "Look, I need to go look in on knucklehead over there. I ain't looked at that field since we planted it. Want to ride with me?"

Lee said, "No, I really have to go. I'll check in with you, every once in a while."

Lee shook Keep's hand, then hugged him, and was glad to get in the car. As he started to long drive toward the coast, he passed over the Sunflower River, where he had learned to swim. And for the first time since those days, a tear drifted down his cheek.

Chapter 7 - Best Laid Plans

Diana sat on her front porch, gazing at the slight surf two hundred yards south. She sipped tea, in the breeze. The normal tropical smell of the gulf had temporarily been replaced by the smell of the great pine woods and red clay of south Mississippi.

She had just finished reading an article in the New Orleans newspaper, which was her favorite, about the multicultural makeup of her hometown. She was at heart a southern girl, but she was foremost a New Orleanian. The article talked about how New Orleans is unique among southern cities, all American cities really, in its adherence to the international culture it inherited. French, Spanish, Italian, Native American, African, and European, its founding influences are many, and the city continues to be a haven of tolerance by design, and of necessity. Diana thought in many ways that New Orleans was the last free part of the country, where people can do, within reason, whatever they wanted, as long as they didn't hurt others.

She missed home. She and Lee had drifted into a pattern of equilibrium ever since Hurricane Katrina. Not that Katrina was the all-encompassing solution for everyone's ills in the gulf south. Plenty of people had worn that excuse out, for everything from chronic drinking to unemployment to the thousands of criminal acts of fraud committed by carpetbagging vultures after the storm. So many heroic acts of assistance, and self depravation, acts of pure, unrewarded bravery by the legion of military people, volunteer relief workers, police officers and legitimate construction firms had been sullied over the last couple of years, as the feds had rooted out scam after scam.

No, it was not the hurricane that had caused a malaise to settle around she and Lee. The general affliction had been there long before. She was still mystified about Lee's actions in law school. Lee had busted his ass to complete his undergrad degree at Tulane. He wanted to go to law school, he said, he had to redeem himself. Before Lee's second stab at college, he'd gotten out of the Army, bought a new Harley Davidson, and ridden all over the country. Then he went to Tulane, they'd re-met, and gotten married.

She had listened to his stories, and was enamored with him from the beginning. She had broken up with her boyfriend, hopped a plane with Lee to Vegas. They got married that night, with a drunken eighteen year-old couple from Cleveland, who were both wearing Guns-n -Roses T-shirts, giggling in line behind them. Lee was magnificent, beautiful. He had an entire seven course meal served in their suite that night at 3 a.m.

It was not his money that attracted her. Money bored her, because people who had it, including her own parents, felt the need to constantly talk about it, as if it was some great portrait that somehow needed illumination for the guests. She had never been without money, and somehow felt sorry for that fact. Not that she wanted to be poor, but she understood that there were huge swaths of human experience which she did not share and could not understand.

Lee was the same way. He had never known the annoyances his college peers, most of whom were younger undergrads than him, had to deal with on a constant basis. No odd jobs at the grills or bars that dotted the neighborhood around the campus. It was a blessing for both of them, she knew, and neither one had so much that they could retire directly into a life of fishing, golf, and functional alcoholism like so many of their other classmates, the ones whose grandfathers had purchased offshore oil leases for pennies. Those people were bulletproof, and made sure everyone else knew.

Yet she and Lee knew a pressure that the others did not. They were expected to be successful, to carry on being successful. Even the oil rich kids did not feel it; they could not possibly destroy the financial inertia of their forebears. Yet Diana knew she had not made a serious attempt to further her own career, or calling, or whatever her standard was. And Lee had simply walked away from the pressure of other people's expectations. Twice.

She and Lee had been in love since their first long walk through Audubon park. She had met him in the spring semester, which was his first back to college since the Army, and the irises and other flowers were in full bloom. Later on, he'd gotten his Australian Shepherd puppy and named her Iris in memory of that day.

Diana never doubted her love for Lee, not even when he inexplicably quit law school. She could not remember her exact feelings at the time, but he was supremely miserable at the thought of actually being an attorney, said he wanted to be a writer. Plus, they had the money, as far as she knew. She had never really gotten into the arrangement with the Farrell estate, but she knew he was the only heir.

When he had been in law school, she loved the little community of Oxford, Mississippi, with its writers' conventions and restaurants, bookstores, lively college bars and football games. It was a idyllic existence for her; she walked every day, went to Memphis to shop. She had her degree, and considered many ways, in those days, how she might use it in her own employment.

She was not necessarily ashamed of Lee's actions; she had understood the pressure law students are under. But she did not believe Lee quit because he could not handle the work, or because he only wanted to write. He had quit because of something darker, deeper. And he had written faithfully during his spare time, never sharing the results with anyone, until Katrina. Katrina had not only washed away most of their possessions, but had seemed to sap the heart out of Lee. Since then he never talked about writing, or anything else, really. He had seemed to settle into the life of a trust baby, with no ambition other than to keep that silly bar running, and his occasional golf games.

Diana finished her tea, studied her toenails, which needed painting, she thought. Iris whined, opened her mouth, like she was trying to talk. She wagged her stump of a clipped tail so fast she was rocking back and forth as she crawled up into Diana's lap in the wicker couch. Iris had rarely done that before, not to Diana. Iris was such a symbol of her marriage: efficient, resilient, prepared. But not ever crossing the threshold to what she considered real love. That kind of feeling was defined in her mind by an old tintype picture she'd seen in New Orleans years ago; a lady and her soldier beau embraced as he returned from some terrible field of war.

Not that she was incapable of that feeling. In her secret dreams she was still greeting her soldier, and was overwhelmed with devotion. But in her real life, she had reserved that feeling. It was the last purely private part of herself, and the thought of sharing it, of being that exposed with a man always made her, well, afraid. Maybe that's why she saved it for dreams. Iris looked at her, and back at the road. Diana realized that Iris was worried about Lee. Could she somehow know it was his birthday?

Lee had been gone for a couple of days, and had just left her a short message on the house answering machine. *Be home today. Be there.* Iris' concern for Lee made Diana weepy. Suddenly, she hated the fact that she had left him out of her secret life. Could he tell that she held her deepest feelings in reserve? Had she cheated him? She missed Lee more than she ever had. That instant, she felt she could grasp him like he had just gotten back from war, and had not been shot, or dismembered, or wasted in some crazy charge across a battlefield, but had fought and prevailed, survived and returned to her, sustained only by their bond. Could such a thing be possible?

She then realized with crystal clarity that the woman in the tintype picture was not in love with an *idea*, she loved the *man*. Her marriage and their lives were not pure, or perfect. They could not be in real life, only in a picture. It was the picture that Diana had mistakenly aspired to emulate, not the people in it. She had always been in love with an idea. An unobtainable one. And she wished she had Lee in her arms right then.

Had she ever really considered that they would not be together? Many times, she had imagined herself with a nameless, faceless man, not Lee. She could not see it. She had actively tried to picture them apart over the last several months, in a way to prepare herself for the possibility that, because of the distance between them, he would leave her. But he hadn't, and except for his infuriating occasional habit of hanging out with that fool Jake at titty bars, and his obvious infatuation with the titty dancer Dahlia, or Elizabeth, or whatever her name was, he had stayed faithful as far as she knew.

In a way, she had not cared, after the hurricane, whether he was faithful or not. She did not care about anything in those days, and had allowed herself to believe that the loss of all their possessions was somehow his fault. She pondered for months why she had agreed to live in this tiny cottage on the very edge of the gulf, with no protection from the weather. But eventually she came to love the water again, and she processed the calamity into a moment of unreality; a mythical visitation of destruction that simply could not be explained, or understood. She had even forgiven Lee, who never knew he was blamed in the first place.

And then there was the problem of her sexual life. Before Sarah, Diana had been something of a dutiful, though not uninterested, participant in sex. She had slept with a couple of boys before Lee, but had never had a memorable experience. She had advanced her experiences considerably with Lee, even developed a relaxation that occasionally allowed her to enjoy it. Yet, there had always been a reservation to expose herself emotionally that was a frustrating impediment to both of them.

The ongoing fact of their lack of children was a social problem for Diana. She was compelled by southern tradition to bear numerous sons and daughters; but she hadn't, and in some way it dulled her desire. She and Lee had been tested sufficiently to establish that the problem, if there was one, was not physical. It was the genesis of a tiny doubt about her marriage that she had allowed to seep into her subconscious. The doubt had never really grown, but its presence had gradually faded her desire.

All that had started changing over the past summer. Her relationship with Sarah, and the sheer mechanics of sex between women, had finally given her the chance to focus on her own body and pleasures. She had come to realize that she was always so concerned about Lee during sex, she rarely paid enough attention to herself to make it interesting. Some of it was Sarah herself. If ever a person was the living example of how to engage in self indulgence, it was Sarah. She could have a string of orgasms that went on until she was exhausted. She had taught Diana by example how to relax.

Diana's new interest in sex had recently revived her feelings for Lee and their old love affair. When they had dated at Tulane, they used to talk about being the starting quarterback and head cheerleader, how utterly stupid those institutions caused people to react. Lee knew intuitively, as she did, that most quarterbacks and cheerleaders peak somewhere around homecoming, senior year of high school, then shuffle offstage as next year's crop steps up. Schools, communities, newspapers need fresh heroes, no matter how inconsequential or provincial, to compensate for their own failed expectations; she and Lee laughed about those things their first conversation. And they had done so recently. Right then, she wanted to see Lee worse than she had in her life.

He had been extremely vague about why he wanted her to be at home; she was hoping it was a good surprise, but afraid it wasn't. A car turned into the driveway, Iris went berserk, flew off the porch, tore across the lawn, down the short drive, started biting the car's tires as they stopped rolling. It was not Lee, but the guy from the FBI. She could not remember his name. Her breath caught as she thought that something may have happened to Lee. But she immediately reasoned that the local or state cops would come by then, not the feds.

Diana yelled a few times at Iris before she gave up on the tire and came trotting back to the porch, puffed up. Diana put her inside, stood on the porch, not sure what to do.

Zack Ellis hopped out of the car, then mentally scolded himself for moving too fast, too eagerly. Walking toward the porch, he said, "Ms. Farrell! Diana, isn't it? How are you? Special Agent Zack Ellis. We met at the Mardi Gras parade, this year."

"Yes, Agent Ellis. Are all you guys this friendly? You seem so dour in the movies."

He wasn't sure if she was being sarcastic, or not. "Yes, well, sometimes you have to be, others, you don't."

"Can I get you a glass of tea?"

"Actually no, Ms. Farrell, I was hoping, ah - wanting to speak to you. Do you have a moment?"

"You mean right now? I was just about to start cutting back my azaleas."

Ellis was not sure what to say. People were supposed to be scared of the FBI, and agree to whatever they say. That's the way it had been so far, anyway. He said, "yes, ma'am, now would be my recommendation."

"Recommendation? Well, I was just joking, officer Ellis, but now you're starting to sound official."

"*Special Agent* Ellis. Yes, Ma'am. This is, in fact, official. Please, can we take a ride?"

"No, we can't, Mr. Ellis. I'm waiting on my husband."

"Is he here? Here in town, I mean?"

Diana thought that was definitely too eager. "No, you didn't let me finish. I'm waiting on him to call," she lied.

"Where is he?"

"I don't know." That was true. "Why do you want to know? Is he in trouble?"

"Let's just get out of here for a minute,"

"I like it here, Mr. Ellis, and I'm not leaving voluntarily."

"I'm going to have to insist that you get in the car."

Six months earlier, Diana would have tried to dissolve the situation with charm. Now, she was pissed. She liked the change. She said, "Are you serious? Are you telling me I am under arrest?" She snatched her cell phone off the seat of the porch swing. "Because if you are, I want you to know that I am on the phone *right now* to my father, who is a prominent attorney in New Orleans, and I want you to personally explain…"

"Ms. Farrell, please, lower your voice. Let's not stir up the neighbors. You are not under arrest. I just need to talk to you about…something important."

"Important to me, or you?"

"Well, both. Now, please."

"I'm not leaving. Say what you have come to say, and go."

"You can't leave a message? Say you went to the store, and will be right back?"

"Thanks, Zack, but I can handle the little domestic white lies without help from the FBI. Now, if you insist on talking, you can have a seat, and I'll get us some tea."

Ellis started to protest, but she was in the door and gone too soon. He lowered himself gently in the swing, testing it. He looked around, making sure no one could see or hear. Other than the traffic, they were alone. Still, this was not going as he envisioned it. He was determined to change the tone. She came back, with the tea.

"Ms. Farrell, I..."

"It's *Mrs.* Farrell, but you can call me Diana, Agent Ellis,."

"Yes. Well, Diana, you may call me Zack. I am sorry for my, for the way I spoke to you earlier. I was perhaps overly concerned about being overheard. But I see we can speak privately, here."

Diana's heart raced, though she hid it. "Well, I suppose on occasions I can be injudicious, Zack. Pun intended."

Ellis tried not to frown, since he still couldn't tell if she was being a smartass. So far, she was neither the charming beauty he'd met at the Mardi Gras parade, or the wanton vixen he'd seen engaging in apocryphal sex with Sarah Bonacelli in something like five edited hours of quality FBI surveillance. She was just plain, well, bitchy, and he was now fighting a significant urge to bolt. Still, she was so beautiful. He said, "Diana, you may be in danger." She started to speak, but he waived her off. "Listen to me, please. We have reason to believe that your husband is involved in a broad scheme to, ah, legitimize illegal cash through the Blue Stone, and other businesses."

"Lee's laundering money at the bar? For who?"

"I wasn't sure if you were familiar with the term 'laundering.'"

"Come on, Zack," Diana said, with less enthusiastic irony, "we southern gals aren't just tits, ass, and legs. Most of us can read, now, and we even have cable television."

"I didn't mean...well, no matter. Look, you seem like a nice lady. I was, well, impressed with your charm and, well, *beauty* when we met at the Mardi Gras..."

"Nice. So what is Lee accused of?"

"Well, he hasn't actually been accused of anything, only observed in regular operation of the business."

"Running the night club he was hired to run."

"Which we think launders money for the Mafia."

"That's what The Mississippi Sound recently rumored. I wouldn't place much weight on anything those clowns write. However, if any of it is true, I assure you Lee has nothing to do with it."

"Please, Diana, do you really think he doesn't know where the money goes?"

"I *know* he doesn't. He doesn't even count the receipts. He or Meat - that's the head bouncer - one of them bags up the cash and credit card charges, and drops it in a night box around the corner. Somebody else handles all the money. Lee's checks come in the mail, and he has *never* seen his boss."

"Doesn't that strike you as odd?"

"No. Have you ever met the United States Attorney General?"

"No, but that's not quite the same…"

"*Sure* it is. He's your boss. You work for a big company, and he's your boss, and you don't see him. Besides, don't a bunch of corporations own the Blue Stone?"

"Yes. Backed by the Bardino crime family of New Orleans, which use it and a number of pawn shops, title loan outfits, used car lots, even bogus Laundromats to legitimize illegal money."

"Have you ever tried to start a business?"

"A business? No, but I don't see how that is relevant…"

"Let me make it clear for you. I wanted to start a boutique after the storm."

"Hurricane Katrina?"

"Yes, Agent Ellis. Katrina. *The* storm. It put thirty-five feet of water where you are now sitting. Jeez. Anyway, after licensing, inspections, sales tax bonds, utilities, inventory, furnishings, ADA compliance, salaries, health insurance, which you have to offer to your employees, by the way, and they can't afford it, so you have to give them a raise to be able to deduct it from their checks. Now I haven't even gone into liability, fire, flood, and wind coverage. Let's see, what else? Oh yes, operating capital. If you have a hundred thousand dollars, for example, you can probably find a bank that will be glad to hold it for you against a hundred thousand dollar loan, at prime plus two, with a cosigner. That's for loaning *your* money to you."

"OK, I'll play along. So why not spend the hundred thousand on the business, and circumvent the banks?"

"Good question. Because that little bit of money, if you have it to start with, won't get you open. You need credit. Lots of it. Here in Mississippi, after the storm, you can't even get suppliers to deal with you on a invoice basis without a commercial, verifiable line of credit."

"What happened to all the aid that was going to businesses after Katrina?"

"Another good question. One I'd like to see the FBI look into more thoroughly. The big guys, the casinos, they started back with insurance and venture capital money. You saw what they built, and are still building. Somehow, they came out eons ahead of where they were. It's the regular people who got screwed. Find out what happened to all that money. There are your real criminals."

"I'll stick to the Bardinos, for now. I must admit your intellect is quite…"

"Off-putting?"

"No, not at all. In fact, I find it *very* attractive. You have such a rare gift, beauty and brains. But, please, I have to go. Finish your story, so I can finish mine."

"Agent Ellis. Zack. I never started the boutique, because I couldn't afford it. Look around you. We live on the beach. I drive a Mercedes. Hell, I've never driven anything but a

Mercedes, since I was in high school. Lee's mom and dad were some of the biggest farmers in Mississippi, before they died. Lee's got a trust fund that's probably worth millions, but it's all tied up." She stopped, realized she was talking too fast, took a breath. "It's like this, Zack. We are, for all intents and purposes, *rich*. Yet, we can't afford, under the layers of regulations small businessmen have to live by, to get started. If we can't, who can? *Nobody*, that's who. Nobody but the mega rich. The days of mom and pop businesses are over. That's why places like the Blue Stone, or the casinos, or chain stores, or restaurant franchises are the only places to work, because the hyper rich own them, and can afford all the fucking headache. Excuse my language."

"So Lee is somehow an innocent victim of this system?"

"Yes. If he wants to work, he has no choice. Neither do you. It's bullshit. Again, pardon the expression.

"You don't have to keep excusing yourself. I think it's - cute. But I still don't see your theory, as it relates to Lee."

"He works at the Stone, because he has to. People work at casinos, or retail boxes, or fast food joints because they *have* to. Because of laws, and banks, and insurance companies, nobody can afford to go it alone, anymore, so they have to work for these big companies. And according to you, the Bardinos own all these businesses which are really illegal operations. So, are all those employees guilty too, or just Lee?"

"Diana, I believe you have been listening to your father the lawyer too much, because you make a strong argument. Unfortunately, there's a federal law, a group of laws, really, called RICO, which you may have heard of..."

"Racketeer Influenced Corrupt Organizations, if I'm not mistaken. I'm familiar with it. I'm around the D.A. a lot too, you know."

"Yes. The D.A. He's another subject, for another day. Anyway, under RICO, there is no question in my mind that a reasonably competent prosecutor could easily prove a case against Lee, regardless of whether he actually handled any money."

"But it'd be up to the FBI to seek indictments, right?"

"Well, the U.S. Attorney, actually, with our recommendation."

"And it's your case?"

"Right."

"And any minimally competent FBI agent can see to it that damn near anybody gets indicted, if he wants?"

"Within reason."

"So, are you in the habit of tipping off the spouses of your investigation targets prior to indictment, during the investigation?"

"Hardly. This is my first real…, I mean, this is a special case. *You* are a special case, in my view."

"Agent Ellis, so far you've referred to my charms in a variety of ways. Am I to assume you are here for something other than furthering your investigation?"

"Well, it seems clear to me that there will be charges. Lee will undoubtedly have to work for us to avoid prison. After that, he will have to go into the witness protection program, and give all this up. You, too. That is, if you stay around."

"And now, we finally reach the point. You thought it might appeal to me to get off the ship before everyone knows it is sinking."

"So to speak."

"And you're here to offer personal assistance?"

"If you…were *interested*, or in need of a place to go, I would… well, I could help you out."

"Meaning I could stay with you?"

"Oh, not now, of course, but in time, I'm sure, I mean, if that's what you…need."

Diana's cell phone rang. She was fixed in a mini staring contest with Ellis. She picked up the phone, stepped inside the front door, saw Lee's number on the phone's display, and answered it, saying, "Hi, mom. Can you put off dropping by the house for a while? I'll call you back." Diana reemerged, a scent of chamomile wafting with her. Ellis looked up expectantly.

Diana was smirking herself, almost guiltily savoring the moment. She eased into a wicker rocker across from the swing. Ellis tried not to look disappointed that she had not sat down in the swing.

"Sorry for the interruption," said Diana.

"Your husband?"

"No. Now, let me say, I'm flattered that a good looking, nice young man like yourself would take interest in an older woman, like me. And your concern for my safety is, if I may say, gallant. Worthy of a true southern gentleman."

"I appreciate the compliment."

"You are welcome. But I'm curious. Did you really think you were going to drop by, flash your little badge and scare one of the local gals into giving you a piece of ass? Are you fucking crazy?"

"But, I thought…"

"What? That I don't read newspapers? Or hear bathroom gossip like you do?"

Ellis popped up, suddenly official again. "It's because I'm black, right?"

"Are you *totally* insane, Special Agent Ellis? It's because *I'm married.* I don't care if you are black, white, purple or pinstriped."

Ellis stomped off toward the car. He stopped, militarily stiff, spun around, said, "Mrs. Farrell, you have obviously misconstrued our conversation. I would remind you that conversations with a federal agent during an ongoing investigation are confidential, and therefore…"

Diana laughed out loud. "You *are* pathetic Zachariah, or whatever your name is. When you leave here, I'm going to call my daddy, who's going to call your boss, the United States Attorney General, who is my daddy's friend. They play golf whenever his honor is in New Orleans. You want to bet on whether there's a job waiting for you when you get back to Gulfport?"

Ellis started to speak, but couldn't think of anything sharp.

"That's right, Mr. Ellis, we New Orleans girls still rely on our daddies like that. I believe you call it the good ol' boy network?"

"Mrs. Farrell, I…you obviously misconstrued my intentions. Please accept my apology. And please do not have your father contact the A.G. I would lose my job. Or worse."

"Damn right you would. Now get the hell out of here, and if my husband even gets a ugly look from an FBI agent, I'm making the call."

Nicholas Bonacelli stood before an enormous floor mirror in his bedroom, naked, assessing himself. Not merely appraising the condition of his body, which, at forty-five, was good. Or his dick, which was plenty adequate. Not porn star big, but big enough, and damned effective, especially lately. He had screwed his way through about half the wait staff at the casino, and by his estimate, eighty percent of the good looking ones. He noticed Human Resources had quit hiring the really hot ones he liked; he'd have to get rid of the bitch that ran that department as soon as possible.

Nick thought of himself as an American dream. Poor Italian kid from the streets. The perfect blend of intelligence, ruthlessness, and durability. The ignorant Bardinos would soon discover that they had underestimated him for too long. Satisfied with his image, he prepared for his destiny. This would be the beginning.

Farrell had left a message that he wanted to meet. Today, at The Blue Stone.

Driving home, Lee had time to think. He had underestimated Bonehead's tenacity, particularly since anything that got Lee in trouble would surely end in disaster for Bonacelli himself. If Bonehead ratted Lee out, then Lee would rat Bonehead out. It was simple personal mutually assured destruction that required brinkmanship on both sides. Or he could run. But it wasn't that easy; Diana was utterly innocent, a potential victim of his stupidity from years earlier. She was the only reason to go back. He could simply cash out and haul ass, otherwise.

Then, there was the problem of Bonehead's scheme, whatever it was. That crazy bastard might have something in mind that was impossible to accomplish, without getting caught. And what about the people around him? Lee could be dispensable for Bonehead and a whole group of sociopathic criminals. And he had to consider plain old right and wrong. His one felony experience had been decidedly different from what he anticipated, and he certainly was not interested in repeating it. He obviously had no objection to crime at that time. But that was a long time ago. He was young, in shock from the deaths of his parents. Was it that? Did he do something then that he would never do now? Did he equate illegal with immoral?

He decided he did not believe that something being illegal meant it was also immoral, but there were lines he would not cross. His failed pot deal was a perfect example. He remembered at the time thinking how stupid it was for marijuana to be illegal, anyway. And the hypocrites who squalled the loudest about marijuana were invariably the ones who claimed to be religious, and acting in defense of the will of God. He wondered, what did they think God meant by placing the plant on earth to begin with?

To give the cops something to do? Had He made a mistake? Can God fuck up?

Bonacelli's note had been instructive, in a way. It had named Lee and Kiger, but not the third man involved, a wiry urchin from New Orleans he believed was named Billy something, who was the connection to New Orleans, the man through which the original weed deal was made, and through whom the little three man drug cartel was to be paid. It was, in fact, his idea. Lee figured that fool was somehow Bonacelli's source of information, but he could not remember the guy's last name.

Lee decided he would not commit any serious felonies, no matter what the threat was. He would not participate in anything that could get anyone hurt. And he would not be forced to help steal anything from individuals. Maybe insurance companies, but he certainly had no desire to test the feds.

Finally descending into the coastal plain, he left the last hills of the lower continental United States. He allowed himself one more degree of introspection, an area that he studiously avoided, normally. His life had begun with every advantage. He was exceptionally intelligent, a good athlete, even good at art, as a child. He still incubated his ancient private desire to write, though he could never concentrate on any one thing long enough to make it work. Maybe being comfortable had made him soft.

All the stories his father had impressed upon him about Farrell family traditions, service, connection to the land, the state, country, they were all predicated on a lie. The lie of his own origins, which nobody apparently knew. Except Mama Thea, maybe, and she was practically dead. That notion shocked him again, but now he was too stressed too ruminate. He'd be on the coast soon, and had to be ready.

Diana kept glancing out the window, looking for Lee. Iris had sensed her distress, and was nervously trotting around the house, unable to get settled. Her dad did not really know the U.S. Attorney General. She made that up, and wondered how long it could work to hold off Ellis.

Diana had replayed her conversation with Ellis several times. She knew, like everyone else, that the Mafia was tied into the local economy. Had been for decades. Her own daddy had defended a bunch of them in New Orleans on gambling charges when she was in high school. It was in the paper; the other kids ribbed her about it at school.

Plus, it was Lee's birthday, his fortieth birthday, and she had gotten him nothing. She could not leave, afraid she would miss him. So, she waited.

Earlier, Lee had called Diana, gotten her strange response about her mother. Something was going on, so he had to be careful. He called Bonacelli, who said he would be at the club when Lee got there. Lee decided not to call Diana back, and hoped she had sensed the urgency of his former message. *Be there.*

It was late afternoon when he arrived in Biloxi, and roasting hot in the parking lot. *What a birthday*, he thought. He was resolved to do the right thing, if possible, but to protect Diana at the least. Bonacelli was in Lee's office, sitting at his desk, with a big canvass carry bag at his elbow.

"Crowd's a little off," said Bonacelli.

"It's early," said Lee.

"Check this out." He handed Lee a couple of pages of an article he had torn out of a magazine. "This is an article on something called a 'dow-kiet'."

Lee, still standing, scanned the article. He tossed it on the desk, said, "Brazilian tree frogs. So what?"

Bonacelli said, "Lee, grab a seat. Go on, grab a seat." Lee did, glaring.

Bonacelli propped his thick soled shoes on the desk, reclined, released the knot on his tie a little. "You are," he said, "one difficult son-of-a-bitch to do business with, Farrell, and are constantly trying my patience. Now, we can do this in an orderly way, or..."

"Listen, Bonacelli, 'business' is when two people get together voluntarily. This isn't business. This is blackmail."

"Fine. Call it what you want. Make yourself believe that you're above all this. That you really didn't do what you did. You're not really a criminal. A murderer."

"I'm no murderer."

"I'm surprised at you, Farrell. You're obviously a smart guy, even got in law school. Which I still don't believe you quit, voluntarily."

"The word 'quit' connotes willingness."

"Oh, you are a real wise ass, aren't you, Farrell? This wasn't all that long ago, was it? I bet that doll of a wife of yours wasn't very..."

"Bonacelli," Lee said, trying to control his temper, and keeping his voice steady, "if we *have* to be around each other, do me favor. Don't bring up my wife again."

"God *damn*. What is it with you southern boys and your wives and mothers? One mention, and everybody around here busts out of their overalls like superman."

Lee decided to be quiet.

"All right," said Bonacelli. "Fine. I'll accommodate your fragile ego for now. I'll even consider your being here as acceptance of our burgeoning partnership. But the girl thing, Jeez. I can't imagine caring enough about a woman to let it interfere with making money. Especially the money we're about to make."

"Why don't you tell me what the big plan is? And I'm not doing anything that gets people hurt, and I'm not doing anything blatantly stupid."

"Farrell, you're ultimately going to do *anything* I want. We both know that, so let's get around the indignant bullshit. The only reason you are alive right now is because I do need you."

"OK, Pacino, I get it. What makes me such a great partner?"

"Because I need a somebody who fits in. Having smarts is a bonus. Just don't get too smart, killer."

"I'm no killer."

"According to the law, you are. The big difference between me and you, Farrell? I know my role. I embrace it. I love it. You, you're a fucking hypocrite. A little boy with daddy's money who thinks he's above it all."

"You don't know a damn thing about me."

"I knew enough to get you here." He slapped the desk, got up, walked to the bar. "Drink?"

"No."

"We'll have to catch up on the small talk later. Let's get the deal laid out." He went back to the desk, set his drink down, pulled a wieldy leather pouch out of his bag, tossed it heavily on the desk. "What do you know about the drug Destiny?"

"Next to nothing. Hallucinogenic, expensive, some of the tourists have been taking it to try to beat the casinos, and freaking out. I had heard something about frogs a while back."

"Yeah. We've had some interesting scenes up in the hotel. Anyway, Destiny, the real stuff, is actually a secretion of our Brazilian frogs." He pointed at the article on the desk. "Hormones. It is very, very rare."

"So how do the grandmas get it?"

"They don't. The whole Destiny thing is really just a ruse. The Russians are behind it. It's mushrooms, shit like that. They make tabs out of it, sell them for a yard apiece."

"Russians?"

"Russian Mob. Organized crime."

"This is what you're interested in?"

"Fuck no. That's a street level fad, no real money in it. It'll be gone in a few months."

Lee sat listening.

"See our little frogs? They've got everything in the world against them. Deforestation, poachers, global warming. The few in captivity are kept in museum labs, a few research universities. The whole Destiny phenomenon, the real drug, is a parlor thing among college kids and scientists doing research on its effects. It started out as legit research, government funding, pharmaceutical company funding and tax breaks for R&D, in return for exclusive rights, the whole treatment."

"So what happened?"

"Politicians don't like people tripping, apparently."

"So what's your market? College kid lab rats?"

"No. The research on the drug's psychic effects was basically useless. It's just too far out. But they did run across one interesting little nugget." Bonacelli took a long drink of vodka, continued, "The subjects all claimed to have prescient visions. Absolutely accurate. Some little things, some big ones, which don't matter to us. It's the side effects we are interested in."

"What, vomiting?"

"Basically, the frog juice has a hormone that stimulates the hell out of the human hypothalamus. It makes people, no shit, after the puking and tripping is over, super strong, they can see better, hear better, better sex, everything."

"Super frogman juice. How long does it last?"

"About a week. The athlete market is just hearing about it, and these extremely rare frogs, which are the only known source of this shit in the world, are worth a fortune, right now."

"How much?

"Retail? Four million apiece. Wholesale, well, let's just say we're setting the market.'"

"What? No way. How could one frog be worth that much? Can't they just make it artificially?"

"Apparently, not yet. And the frogs are more protected than the Vatican. That's why this is an extremely short market. But there's one more thing." He tossed another article on the desk. Read it if you want, but it says that some huge percentage of all the frogs on Earth have died in the last few years."

"From what? Hippies?"

"Some kind of fungus. Why, nobody knows. The article says that these scientists are running all over the jungles, trying to save as many frogs as possible, sending them to labs around the world."

"Let me guess. You know one of these scientists."

"Bingo. The U.S. government runs a compound out in the Panamanian jungle, in the 'interior' I believe you Army boys used to call it. They're in on the hunt, for conservation purposes. But the poachers have gotten wind of the value of these little fuckers, and now, even the legit science community is having to buy frogs to save them. Our associate is the director of that compound, in Panama. He is, much like you, suspending his higher ideals in lieu of dreadful immediacy. He's selling us some frogs."

"Which you intend to…?"

"Turn into twenty million dollars. Believe me, this is the fucking score of a lifetime. "

"Why would they sell the frogs if they are trying to save them?"

"So they can buy more frogs. They get them from the source, and cheaper. This way, they can get two, three times as many before they're all dead."

"How many frogs are you buying?"

"Five."

"How much money am I supposed to be lugging around the jungles of Panama?"

"That's where our pouch comes in. "Bonacelli picked it up. It was obviously heavy, and the size of a flat football. He untied the leather strap, and poured a big pile of rocks out on the desk.

Lee said, "A bag of rocks."

"Hardly, my friend. These are uncut diamonds and emeralds. Worth a fortune on the black market, which happens to be located in Panama City."

"So why not just sell the stones? Why trade them?"

"Basic economics. They are worth a lot more the way we're doing it."

"Where do these come from?"

"That's my business. Let's just say, don't get any smart ideas. These people, the stone suppliers, would kill us both."

Lee got up, walked to the window. The normal crowd was in, thirsty and hot. He said, "And I assume your friends are not in the legitimate gemstone business."

"They're not in lower Manhattan, if that's what you mean."

"So how many people know about this?"

"Don't worry about it. Just make the trade, let me make my deal, and everybody gets paid."

"What's my cut?"

"Two million."

"Where does the rest of the money go?"

"Why do you care?"

"I care."

Bonacelli said, "Money, my friend, American *cash* money, is the oil that greases the machine of all unofficial international trade. Money goes in one end, guns come out the other. The trick is to get in the middle, where the profits are. Guns are the commodity, but right now, diamonds are the currency. Easier to handle, virtually impossible to trace. Anyway, diamonds eventually have to be converted to cash. Hence, our supply."

"You seem to know a lot of people."

"Ivy League. You meet the damndest people."

"So how did you ever manage to break into frogs?"

"Very funny, smartass. Your end is two million dollars. You still debating?"

"While you were snooping around about me, surely you didn't miss the fact that I am rich already?"

"Rich, my ass. You might be able to fool these bumpkins with that trust fund baby shit, but I know better. That property in Farrell County is so upside down, you'll be lucky if it isn't seized before next season of, well, whatever you rednecks plant up there."

"You're wrong. I was just up there, saw the books. Everything is fine."

"According to that old drunk you call a lawyer. It *will* be fine in a few years, after your flunky, what's his name? Keep? What the fuck does that mean? Anyway, if he keeps plugging away, everything will be fine in a few years. Of course, he's got to be around for that to happen."

"How can you find out everything like that?"

"Don't tell me you still think you've got privacy. Come on, Farrell. You're too smart to be that naive."

"OK, I have no choice. What do we do?"

"You take your boat to Panama. When you get there, rent a jeep, ride a chiva bus, I don't care. Go to the lab, pick up the frogs, hand over the stones, take the frogs back to Panama City, deliver them to a hotel room, you're done. You'll get paid when you come back."

"How do you know I won't grab Diana and run off with the stones?"

Bonacelli got up, walked to the bar, made another drink. "You know anything about my background?"

"Have I been investigating you? No. I read the paper. I know whatever it says."

"Please, partner, indulge me for a moment."

"If we're going to be partners, I get to use my own desk." He got up, went around, sat in his desk seat, motioned to the slowly expanding leather covered seat of the interview chair. "Give me the short version, please."

"Let's see, short version: I am an orphan, was adopted by an older couple in Chicago. My adopted father was a Polish butcher named Gorski. His wife was Sicilian, named Bonacelli. He gets up every day and goes to the slaughterhouse, comes home every night bloody and stinking. Every day, and he never, and I mean *never* has a pair of pennies. This motherfucker couldn't find a dollar if you handed it to him. So I start hating these people for adopting me, and I ran away. Fourteen years old. I started working for the Italians, in the street, later driving, in the office. Got a GED. Got my undergrad. Got my MBA, all because of my boss's connections. They - the family - paid for everything, all the way through. They were building me, you see."

"Wait, don't tell me - and then you found Jesus?"

"You laugh, my friend, but what I found was much more profound than Jesus. After Harvard, I went straight into the banking business in Chicago. V.P. of a family controlled bank. Shortly, I find out the president, my boss, is skimming the fucking skim; I naturally show the family, they snatch him. Only he blames me for the missing money. Here's the good part. They take me and this old asshole out in the lake, in a big boat, and we're both tied up. The old man, he's begging his ass off, and I'm just friggin' disgusted, thinking I had wasted all that time getting educated, and trying to figure out how to get off that boat alive."

Lee was quiet, now genuinely interested.

"So we get out, way out, they stop the boat. I figure I'm dead, and supposed to be praying, but I'm just pissed. Well, they walk us over to the back of the boat next to the little wall, the, uh…"

"Transom."

"Yes. The transom. I just closed my eyes, gritted my teeth." He stopped to take a long drink, and for effect, then said, "Somebody unties my hands, turns me around, hands me the gun. Says, 'Your ours now, kid. Do you understand?' I did. I shot that old bastard, the bank president, in the back of the head, and he flipped over the transom."

"What did you do then?"

Nothing. Had a drink. Wiped the blood off my face. It was my first time, and the fuckers didn't tell me about blowback. I had brains all the way up my arm, and they got a real kick out of it."

"Your *first* time, you say?"

"Yes. There have been others. I don't kill people unless it is absolutely necessary. When it is, I prefer to do it myself. I find it - therapeutic, in a way."

Lee had nothing to add, and wanted out of the conversation. He said, "All right, well, let's get this over with."

Bonacelli had a weird look, calm, but almost smiling. "You haven't heard the rest."

"I thought you were through."

"Well, I was answering your question about crossing me. If you do so, I will find you. If, for some miraculous reason, I do not find you, I will kill your friend Keep, his wife, and his family. I'll do it myself. I have to admit, if forced to do so, mind you, I sort of like it."

Lee tried to look normal, as the hairs on his neck and head involuntarily stood. "That won't be necessary, Nick."

"Good." Nick stood up, downed the rest of his drink on the way to the small bar. He placed the glass on the bar. "The directions to the compound and the hotel in Panama are in that bag. The hotel room will be open. Just leave the frogs there. That's it. Get your ass back up here, and do not get caught. If you *do* get caught, do not talk. That's it."

"When is all this supposed to take place?"

"Oh, right now. That hotel room will be open when you get there. Don't fuck up."

"What about my job? The Blue Stone?"

"I took the liberty of drafting a resignation letter." He pulled it out of his canvass bag. "Here it is, just sign. When you leave, lock up, and somebody will get the keys later."

"What the hell am I supposed to do afterwards?"

"Relax, Farrell, retire. Whatever rednecks do with two million dollars in cash. I may need you again sometime. Until then, good travels."

"One more thing, said Lee, "how are you getting around the Bardinos?"

"That's perceptive. How did you conclude that I was not acting *for* the Bardinos?"

"Well I assume your cut is way bigger than mine, so I understand your motivation. But a few million is peanuts compared to what the casino brings in. It's not worth jeopardizing the operation. They can't possibly know about this, and approve it."

"You're right. That's another reason for you to be motivated. They can be nasty."

He left.

As Nick Bonacelli climbed in his car in the parking lot of the Blue Stone, he thought about Farrell. He had apparently bought the whole story. Now, it was up to Flounder to do his duty. Under other circumstances, Lee and Nick might have been friends. Too bad Farrell had to die.

Lee leaned back in his desk chair, put his feet up, and tried to keep a clear mind. Bonacelli's scheme made sense, in a way. Lee had read somewhere that the illicit African gem trade was connected to funding all manner of illegal and violent activities all around the Middle East. It had to do with the feds' ability to track wire money transfers. Bonacelli's source must have some connection there. If so, he wasn't lying about the both of them getting killed, if things did not go right. Still, why did Bonacelli need *him*? Surely, Bonehead had access to all sorts of flunkies who could do his deal. And why insist that he travel by boat? Sure, he had made the trip from the coast to Panama after the screw-up at Cat Island, but that required no specialized knowledge, other than the ability to handle a boat, and navigate. There had to be dozens of people on the Mississippi coast alone who could do the same thing, and would hop at the chance for the money. It did not make sense, unless...*Bonehead planned on killing him*.

Meat knocked on the door, entered in the same motion, startling Lee. Meat said, "What's the long face about, Boss? That dago giving you a hard time?"

"Sit down, Meat, this is serious."

Lee unlocked a drawer at the bottom of his desk, where he kept a sizable amount of cash, for personal emergencies. He pulled out a roll of hundreds, and a brown envelope, which he stuffed some of the money in. He slid the envelope across the desk to Meat. Lee said, "When you leave here tonight, take this, go home get your stuff, and leave the coast."

Meat picked up the envelope, looked at it, stuffed it in his shirt pocket. He said, "What's the trouble, Lee?"

"Meat, it's more than me and you can handle. You'll have to trust me, I can't explain. You don't need to be around."

"Well, I been thinking about getting back to the Delta, anyway. Think Keep's got a spot for me at the farm?"

"Tell him it would be a favor to me. He'll understand."

Lee got up, hugged the enormous man. He said, "I'll be up here a while, if I don't see you, I...well, I'll contact you sometime." Meat left the office and the old elevator creaked under his mass.

Lee sat at his desk alone. He stared out at the club. A band was cranking up. He knew he had a decision to make. At the same time, he knew the decision was already made for him. He had to leave.

If Bonehead was really planning on killing him, someone would be watching. And listening, so he could not risk calling Diana. So, he would wait them out. Meantime, he had arrangements to make.

Diana watched the end of her favorite movie, "Wild at Heart," for probably the tenth time in her life. It was getting late, and Lee had not come home. She flipped the TV over to cable news, which announced a tropical storm had entered the gulf and was expected to become a hurricane, threatening the entire gulf coast. She and Iris stayed awake a while longer, and finally went to sleep on the couch.

Chapter 8 - Lady of the Moon

Agent Ellis was at the office early. He needed to be around in case that crazy woman Diana Farrell made any complaints, to cover his ass. Plus, he need to do something with his treasure of information, before somebody else found out about it. He started compiling his notes, collating and neatly filing all his information in an expandable brown file. He would be approaching the United States Attorney soon, maybe today, with a raft of requests for subpoenas. He was not about to sit on this matter any longer. His future now lay before him on the cheap desk in his Gulfport office; he was not about to let it go by, even if it did not include the suspicious Ms. Farrell.

Buck Carter was tired, his soul heavy with fossilized sins. So he drank. He was sitting at the bar in the Long Gravy, lights off, door locked, counting money from last night. It was eight o'clock in the morning, he was having his first Irish whiskey of the day, and he was thinking about Camellia.

She had been irresistible. She was as beautiful as the flower whose name she had adopted; her body was as perfect as it was impure. He met her around Thanksgiving, 1968, when he was strong, and young. And the sheriff. He was at the height of his powers then, mentally, physically, sexually. He was a big man, even among the physically big men of his country. The Long Gravy had been called "Daley's" in those days, was a full on casino, with craps tables on one side, blackjack on the other, pool tables for money games in the back. Poker was a round the clock affair in a locked room off to the side. As sheriff, Buck got a monthly bag of cash, carrying on the coast tradition that ran back to Prohibition.

There had been a small stage in the area now occupied by pool tables. Camellia had shown up with a bunch of call girls from New Orleans. They had done a dancing and singing routine, no mike, a crude burlesque. As "Lady of the Moon," Camellia cooed and writhed nearly naked about the little stage to a live jazz accompaniment: a horn, a bass, and drums.

Buck had fallen in love with her immediately, even though she was a prostitute. He overpowered her emotionally, sexually. She was as affectionate toward him as he her. He took her in. Or rather, set her up in an apartment close by; his wife understood his long work hours, but was ever vigilant on the subject of other women. At first, they were able to satiate each other's gulf of sexual desires. Her being underage is something he never thought about until years later.

After a few weeks, she missed New Orleans, and life there. He was increasingly uncomfortable with the arrangement, and his wife's growing curiosity. So he sent her away. Then she had shown back up, claiming she was pregnant. He was instantly pissed at himself for actually caring about the little trollop, but also at her for having the gall to bother him with such a trivial, easily solvable problem. But she would not go away, would not consider getting an abortion, an illegal activity which he could have arranged. She had actually threatened to go to the local newspaper, tell them all about their sheriff and his nocturnal rounds. Plus, white as she was, she was technically black.

It could not be avoided; she had to go. He convinced himself at the time that she was no different from all the others, whether they were no account burglars and rapists, or uppity fools from up north come south to stir shit. They did not understand the balance of things. Once the decision had been made to get rid of them, it was easy. She was just the last in a long line of what he and Cookie used to call "one way fishing trips." That was funny back in the

day, but in the end even Cookie got scared and quit. Not Buck.
He had to protect himself, and by extension, a whole lot of other
people who depended on him. So he killed her. He had done his
duty. Still did.

The thought of it rankled him. Before, Buck was a regular at
the Klan meetings. They said the South was at war. The courts,
the Kennedys, the civil rights leaders, they had to be stopped.
He'd even gone up to Hattiesburg and met with the Grand Wizard
once. Buck had been the Klan's great champion, a big man with
power, who was not afraid to use it for good. And he had been
convinced that he was *doing* good. Even the preachers said that
black people were cast out of Israel, punished for the sins of …
whoever, he couldn't remember. Still, they said white people
were made superior, by God himself. So, killing a pregnant black
girl was not something he thought was wrong, in any moral sense.

He realized, in his old age, how crazy that was. The Klan had
told him, everybody really, that anybody who wasn't white had
to be held down, that they would go crazy and take revenge if let
loose. He had fought a secret war, and lost. The thing is, nobody
went crazy. Nobody took revenge. So maybe he was wrong.

And now Cookie was running his mouth to Lee Farrell. This
was not the first time. Buck had taken him to the hospital once,
back in the seventies. The fool had dropped an oyster knife that
stuck in his foot, the one on his bad polio leg, and not taken care
of it. It got infected, then gangrened, and they wound up taking
the lower half of his leg off. Coming out of anesthesia, Cookie
had blathered all about murders and conspiracies, and somebody
shooting the head off John F. Kennedy.

Buck got up and made another drink, grunting in disgust.
Back in 1963, this skinny loser had been hanging around Daley's
for a few days, getting drunk, gambling. He had started a fight
with one of the locals about communists, and gotten his ass

kicked. Buck had arrested him, taken him to jail for a few days, gotten tired of his communist shit. He had about decided to take the little commie on a one way fishing trip when he happened to run in to one of the Bardinos at Daley's. Buck could not remember his real name, but he was the one that eventually went crazy, that the Italians called "The Raven."

This guy had been had been shooting craps around the clock, had gone down five thousand, but gradually worked his way back, got ahead, and damn near broke the place until Daley's old owner started getting to him with magnetic house dice. The Italian bastard had cleared a few grand anyway, and was buying everybody drinks by the time Buck pulled up in his sheriff's truck that afternoon.

"Sheriff," said the Bardino, "I want to buy you a beer. Or three!," he added, and everybody laughed, the way people do when they are scared of somebody.

"Well, I can't right now," said Buck, "I ain't through with work quite yet."

"Hell, maybe later then."

"Maybe," said Buck, and ordered a Coke, then headed to his truck.

"Say, Sheriff," said the Bardino, "can I ask you something?"

"Buck shrugged, kept walking. "Follow me," he said, and the Bardino did. Buck had learned from his predecessor, as his predecessor had from *his*, that the Bardinos were a fact of life, and were not to be arrested unless they killed someone in broad daylight, with a dozen witnesses. Even then, they were to be allowed to escape to New Orleans, if at all possible.

The Bardino said, "I'm looking for a guy, thought he might be up this way. You pick up any strays lately?"

"Just got one, right now. Skinny white guy with a big mouth. Thinks he's a goddamn communist or something. Oswald."

"That's him. I called the jail first. There's no record of him."

"I ain't made one, yet."

"Good. Let me have him. I promise you won't ever see him again."

A few months later the skinny little communist bastard wound up killing the President of the United States. Buck had never trusted the Bardinos again, after that. Of course, Cookie knew about that, too, and was running his mouth like a senile old fool. Between Cookie, the do-gooder newspaper and now Lee Farrell, somebody was bound to let some cats out of the bag. He couldn't believe, after all these years, he was still having to fight the same battles. There was a *war* going on then, goddammit. Was he the only one left?

He took the final half of glass of whiskey all in a gulp, threw it wildly. It shattered on the crazy old colored parquet inlays between a couple of pool tables, right where he had been standing those many years ago when he first saw her. He stared at the old, wrinkled drunk in the mirror behind the bar. He wasn't great. He wasn't right. He was just an old fool who had gotten fooled. He was wrong. Always had been, like Cookie said. And a murderer. So now he was just a coward, covering his ass.

Buck walked out of the bar, dug in his pocket for a cigarette. The water was only a hundred yards away. He watched a fishing boat pass under the railroad bridge, heading out into what its passengers thought of as a great fishery. Buck knew it was nothing but a pretty graveyard. His cell phone rang, and he recognized the number as Cookie's. Good. It was time to settle this business.

Lee woke up with Diana on his arm. For the first time in his life, he clearly saw what to do. He had always run away from everything. The Farrells, football, law school. He really believed he had the ability to be a writer, a good one, but Katrina had not only destroyed everything, it had sapped his heart. And he had let it. Now, he *had* to run.

The night before, he'd stayed at the Stone until late, closed it early. He'd gone through the old security files on the computer, found a recording of Bonacelli opening the sapphire case in the lobby. He was able to enhance the image, and see the code Bonacelli punched in. Before he left, he turned off the security cameras, opened the case, and took the big blue sapphire. He then took the rest of his money out of the lower desk drawer, all the paper cash from the day's receipts, and left the images of Bonacelli opening the display case on his computer. He had thought long about the threats Bonacelli had made against Keep. In the end, he decided that Bonacelli couldn't do a damn thing to Keep, who was one of the best shots in the Delta. There was simply no way Bonacelli or anyone else could get close enough to him and his legion of friends to do any harm. Plus, Meat would be there soon. He was comfortable that Keep Marlin could take care of himself under any circumstances.

He had screwed up everything, but he was sure that Diana was his, that their lives together was the one thing he had done right. While he had been mentally drifting the last few years, the real purpose of his life, his true ambition, and greatest accomplishment was simply his love for his wife, and their relationship. And their children, which he was, by God, going to produce. Last night, he had come in late, and Diana was sleeping on the couch. He had awakened her. He didn't answer anything, they just made love in a way that neither had ever experienced.

Now, she lay sleeping in the rusty morning light, and he was guilty. He had gotten her involved in something that was beyond his control, and she did not know it. But he could not tell her, just yet. He realized that his whole life had been reduced to this one cathartic moment. The decision was irrevocable when he took

the big blue sapphire from its case at the Blue Stone. It would
be this afternoon before anyone noticed anything, opened the
Stone. He'd have to contact Kiger sometime soon, but telling him
anything right now would be foolishly dangerous.

He would get Diana and Iris to the boat, take the damned
African stones and the huge blue sapphire, and leave. If God
let him live, he promised, he would dedicate himself, apply his
talents, from now on. He felt strangely liberated, excited.

But he knew that he could not leave without the amulet,
which *might* be adversely affecting his life. Even if the effect was
only psychological, it had to be destroyed. He had to move fast,
cursing the fact that he had left the damned thing in his place in
New Orleans. He could be there and back in a couple of hours,
long before anyone opened the Blue Stone, and saw what he had
done the night before.

So he got up without waking Diana, wrote her a note. He
reentered the bedroom, left the note, kissed her sleeping lips, then
eased his GTO out of the driveway, steering toward New Orleans.

Cookie hobbled over to his prosthetic leg, in the closet. He
hardly ever wore it any more. He was sober, a rare condition for
him, and he was about to try something else new: telling the truth.
He wrestled the damn thing on the stump below his knee. That
leg had cursed him his whole life. He had been just fourteen when
the Japs bombed Hawaii, too young to join the service, but also
unfit, his leg mangled from polio. When he turned seventeen, he
left his job cleaning tankers in the Pascagoula boatyard, and went
to join the navy.

They would not have him, but the Merchant Marines would,
and he spent the rest of the war in the galley of a vessel that
ferried supplies back and forth between bases along the gulf. The
war was still in doubt, especially in the Pacific, but the closest

Cookie ever got to a German or Japanese soldier was the constant rumors of enemy subs sinking merchant vessels in the gulf.

After the war, he went back to Azalea, joined the sheriff's department, starting on the low rung as a jailer. He had been at that job for many years, and was head of the guards by the time young Buck Carter got elected sheriff, surprising everybody. Buck was a true fire-eater; he was anachronistic, even for the time. It was 1962, the new buzzword in the Old South was desegregation, and Buck carried himself like some general of the New Confederacy, eager to fall to arms against the yankees again.

Buck had adopted Cookie, sort of as a liaison with the old deputies, all of whom were kept on, by tradition. Eventually, Cookie was Buck's main confidant, and guilty by inaction of numerous crimes involving shaking down local businesses, especially gambling houses, and a few murders. Cookie was always Buck's unobjecting, older companion, granting approval of virtually anything by little resistance, or silence.

Cookie couldn't remember if he had made up those stories about his leg, or if he just didn't correct them. Either way, the leg was just part of the big puzzle his life had become. When the pieces were all together, it was just a lie. He was no war hero; he was a coward. Until today.

Lee Farrell had got him thinking. Cookie had always sort of thought of himself as the anchor of reason, for Buck. Hell, Cookie once talked him out of walking into the courthouse and arresting a judge he did not like. He had even tried to talk the crazy bastard out of killing Camellia, and *had* talked him out of a few more. But there were at least a dozen souls besides Camellia in the gulf that did not survive Buck's rage, his crazy ideas about the South, or Cookie's meek remonstrations. Some of them were criminals, some weren't.

So he got up that morning, said his prayers, put on his leg, made his coffee, and called Buck on his cell phone. Said he was going to the newspaper and tell them everything. He figured he had a slim chance of getting in heaven, but no chance at all if he did not do this. But first, he was going to give Buck the chance to do it himself. So Buck was on his way over, and things were fixing to change.

Flounder awoke in the seat of his car, in the parking lot of the Azalea Marina. Farrell's boat was still in its slip, which Flounder was happy to see. Bonacelli had him up late last night, had come by his trailer to explain the new deal to him. It was another job, another of the dozens of promises rich people had made to him over the years; he was to be wealthy if he carried it out. Only this time, he did not have to get into an elaborate scheme, or even do any sweaty work. All he had to do was kill Lee Farrell, and bring a heavy leather pouch Farrell had back to Bonacelli. What was in the pouch, Bonacelli had not said.

So he had come out late last night. Bonacelli was certain that Farrell would be taking his boat somewhere; Flounder was not interested in approaching Farrell's house, anyway, with all the damned curious neighbors. More rich people. He drove over to the bait store, got some spicy pork rinds and a six pack of beer, and went back to the parking lot. He decided the best way to make sure Farrell did not get by was to be on the boat. If that didn't work, Bonacelli couldn't be mad. So he waited until not many people were around, made sure he had his big hunting knife, and slipped onto the boat, down to three beers.

Bonacelli woke up late. He had gotten to sleep late, after he had found the idiot Flounder and given him his instructions. Now, he reviewed the conversation with Farrell, felt sure that Farrell had believed the story about the frogs.

They were, after all, real. He had even taken the chance of making the arrangement for the frogs to be bought, in case his buddy in Saudi Arabia went behind him. The frogs, the Destiny drug, the athletic black market; they all were real, and Bonacelli imagined he could probably do the deal just like he said. Of course, there never were any Russians, that part was necessary to convince the Saudi. Hell, anything could happen to a crazy American on the way to the jungles of Panama, laden with illegal rough gemstones.

It was so simple, it made him squirm. Flounder whacks Farrell, brings back the diamonds, he whacks Flounder, and tells his Saudi buddy that Farrell was done in, and the diamonds were stolen by pirates. Lord knows there were plenty of them in the wilderness of coastal marshes off Mississippi and Louisiana. What could he say?

Lee was in the New Orleans in less than an hour. He parked in a pay lot across Esplanade from the Quarter, in the Marigny. He ran the couple of blocks to his condo on Chartres, let himself in, grabbed the amulet. He took a minute to look around, picked up a couple of books and his favorite picture of he, Diana, and Iris, then darted out to the street. On his way back across Esplanade, he happened upon old Miss Tracy and her cart. She was slowly making her way to her place on Bourbon. Lee saw her, but did not speak. As he hurried by, she turned, said, "Young man!"

He stopped, turned.

She said, "Do you remember me? You asked me a while back about some lady you were looking for..."

"Yes, and you sent me to Miss Ruby."

"That's right. How was she? Is she in good health?"

"I would say so, for her age. She's still living."

"Oh, I don't believe she's as old as all that. But tell me, was she able to help you? Did you find whoever you were looking for?"

"No, she couldn't help. But thanks, anyway." He started away.

"Just out of curiosity," she said, "who were you looking for?"

"Somebody that supposedly used to live here. Somebody named Camellia."

"Camellia! Son, I ain't trying to tell you your business, but that's who you were talking to."

"Who, Miss Ruby?"

"That's what she calls herself *now*, son. When she was young, they all called her Camellia."

When Diana awoke, she felt for Lee in the bed, but he was not there. She lay for a moment reliving last night's lovemaking, and felt, for the first time in years, that she and Lee were perfectly in love, again. She found a note from Lee telling her to pack for a long trip, that they were leaving today, and that he would explain later. He had emphasized by underlining that she should not tell anyone they were leaving, and to destroy the note.

Alarmed, she took the paper out back and burned it, wondering what was going on. She decided to pack her pictures and computer discs, since the storm was steadily gathering in the heat of the waters between Cuba and Central America. Some computer models, according to gleeful television announcers, had it scooting east of New Orleans, heading right into the Mississippi Gulf Coast, just like Katrina. While Diana packed, she wondered where Iris was, and guessed that Lee had taken her with him.

Miss Ruby received Lee in her parlor this time. He could not imagine how she had actually made it up the stairs to the rooftop deck last time they met. Lee could see her face clearer, absent the sunglasses, and he guessed she was at least eighty years old. Still, she had perfectly gray eyes, and her feckless countenance was neither inviting nor opposed to conversation. "I remember you, Mr. Farrell. You were searching for someone."

"Miss Ruby," Lee said, "I am so sorry to be bothering you this early. It's just...I am in an awful hurry, and I keep getting sent

over here by a lady, who seems to think you might know this other
lady…"

Miss Ruby interrupted, "This lady who sends you over here,
what is her name?"

"She's a palm reader, tarot, that sort of thing. She's scared to
death of you. I think her name is …"

"Miss Tracy."

"That's right. You know her?"

"I ought to. She's my half sister."

"But why…forget it. I don't need to know. Can you tell me,
I'm trying to find out about a lady who was supposed to have lived
around here, a black lady who was so white that she was what they
used to call a 'pas blanco', or something like that…"

"Pas Blanc. It means "passing for white.""

"Right. Pas blanc. Anyway, she was young, in her teens in the
late sixties, much younger than you, if you will forgive me, but
they called her Camellia. Miss Tracy, your sister, said that's what
they used to call *you*."

"Miss Tracy still talks too much, I see. We are not close."

"Yes. And apparently, Camellia was a fairly common name,
or nickname, I guess, back in those days. So, did you know this
person, another 'Camellia'? She was into voodoo, a "Mamissa,"
as they say, and apparently some kind of, please forgive me again,
a hooker. She got pregnant, and had a kid by some man on the
coast. Maybe some rich guy, or a politician. Does this sound
familiar to you?"

"Son, why are asking about this person?"

"It's personal. I just need to know."

"What would you do with the information? Would you try to
sell it, or use it against your fellow man for any evil purpose?"

"I - don't quite know what you mean. I'm not trying to hurt
anybody. I'm just trying to find out about somebody. My real
parents, actually."

"You - are you telling me that you are the *child* of this person you call Camellia?"

"Yes. Well, maybe. It's - well, it's complicated. I could tell you the whole thing, if I had time. Just please tell me, f you know, who is this person?"

Miss Ruby sat completely silent for a full minute or more, looking out the window toward Rampart Street. The corner drug dealers were just starting to stir. Lee could see her eyes welling, a little. "I...knew her," she said.

"Camellia? You knew Camellia, the one I'm talking about?"

"There were many young ladies who used that appellation, while practicing their arts. But I knew your Camellia, quite well."

"Where is she? Does she still live here? Maybe I can see her, if it's close."

"How do I know you are who you say?"

"Mama Thea. Mama Thea found me."

"I know of no one named Mama Thea."

"Stupid me. Althea Gibson was her name. Mama Thea is just what I called her."

"My. Althea Gibson." She seemed to choke, took a sip of iced tea, replaced the glass in the center of its doily, her hand shaking. "You are correct, this Camellia I knew did arrange for a child to be...adopted by a young lady from Mississippi named Althea. My acquaintance, Camellia, was distressed for many years over the fate of that child, fearing that an alligator, or coyote may have found him, taken him away."

"So she really left me out by the lake? What the hell? Where is she now?"

"What you have told me is correct, so far, Mr. Farrell, but the child would know more."

"What do you mean, more? I was a newborn! Look, I'll give you whatever you want. Here, here's a hundred." He threw the money on the table. "Now, please, tell me what you know."

"If you do not know more, then I'll have to thank you for your company."

"Lady, I...," then he realized she was talking about the amulet.

"Wait," he said. "I know what you mean." He took the amulet out of the deep front pocket of his fishing shirt, where it barely fit, placed it on the table in front of the old woman. "It's an amulet. I had it examined by an expert over at Tulane. He said it was voodoo 'hand,' and is a very powerful symbol to...those people."

"It is more than a symbol, son."

"Where's Camellia?"

"She is dead, son. Camellia died a long time ago."

Lee didn't know what to do. Mama Thea said she was dead, but he just didn't believe her. He had calculated that Camellia, if she existed at all, would only be in her fifties, if she was still alive. He let out a long sigh, slumped in his chair. Presently, he said, "What happened to her? How did she die?"

"The lady who you believe - who was obviously your mother, was very sad to have to let you go. *Very* sad. She loved you then, and she loved you all her life. But she had to do what she did, because your life was in danger. And because of you, so was hers."

"That's crap. Nobody drops a baby off at the lake, hoping the church lady remembers to show up and get him."

"It was surely far more difficult for your mother. She knew that Miss Althea Gibson would be there."

"You said she *worried* about it."

"As her - power faded, she sometimes lost faith. Listen son, Camellia was a very, very powerful Mamissa. Also very young when they tried to kill her..."

"Who tried to kill her?"

"That is not important, son. What is important, is that she used all of her resources as a Mamissa, and placed a curse on a man on the Mississippi coast. She made an...arrangement with the spirits, concentrated much energy in that gris gris, and it drained her. She declined very rapidly. She died a long time ago."

"How do you know so much?"

"She and I were very close."

"Like friends?"

"Yes."

"That must have been odd, two girls with the same name."

"It was."

"But you must have been old enough to be her mother. How were you so close, as friends?"

"I am not as old as you may suppose, Lee. I can't explain it, we were just very close. That's all I know, all I can say. I am sure Camellia is thrilled, wherever she may be, that you are in good health. Are you a good man?"

"I don't know. I think so."

"A good man should *know* he is."

"Yeah, well I'm not a killer, or putting voodoo curses on everybody. At least I'm that good. But still, I *have* to know who tried to kill her."

"Lee. Please. You must stop these inquiries now. You will place yourself in further danger."

"What do you mean, 'further' danger?"

"It's the amulet. It must be destroyed."

"I thought the thing was supposed to protect me?"

"This is not the work of men, Lee, but of spirits."

Lee started losing his temper. "I've had it with the fairy tales. Tell me what I need to know. I'll pay you whatever you want. Otherwise, I'm going to the cops, and taking that damned amulet with me. They'll probably want to talk to you, too."

"Son, I fear your curiosity may be your undoing."

"Yeah, that and the little toothy wood necklace, right?"

"I can see you do not believe in hoodoo. Yet, I notice you have made some effort to keep up with the amulet."

"Look, I *don't* believe in hoodoo, or voodoo, whatever it is. But I know other people do, and that makes people do weird things."

"Better safe than sorry, I assume?"

"Something like that. But I've got to be going. Are you going to tell me who the man was, or am I going to the cops?"

"I don't believe you are going to the police. You are very excited now, eager to go somewhere. That is obvious. But you must be very careful. You are in danger, and you must leave this gris gris with me. The spirits can be tricky, deceitful. It is in their nature to do good, but also to cause mischief. You may think you want these things, but you could lose all you love in the process. The gris gris must be destroyed."

"You can have it, if you tell me what I want."

"For your own good, Lee, leave this part of your life. What you find will almost assuredly not be what you desire."

"Your sister told me something similar that the first time met."

"She's wise."

"Just not friendly?"

"Judgmental. Very judgmental."

"Tell me who tried to kill my mother."

"Lee, I can't."

"Then no deal." He got up, picked up the amulet.

"Sit down, son," she said, in a voice that demanded compliance, and got it. "You force me to tell you these things, but you must promise me you will not use the information…"

"I know, Miss Ruby, not to hurt others. Just tell me!"

"So impatient. The man was…your father *is*…Sheriff Raymond "Buck" Carter."

Zack Ellis called an assistant U.S. Attorney in Gulfport. It was time to open the case against the Bardinos, which meant a Grand Jury, which meant witness subpoenas. And there was

another hurricane lurking, so the courts might be shut down for
an evacuation which was probably inevitable. He was not about
to sit on this any longer. At the top of Zack's list of witnesses was
Senator Ford, whose testimony would generate an earthquake in
the typically hysterical 24 hour news-based entertainment media.

Ellis was picturing himself on the talk show circuit when the
federal prosecutor said, "Did you say Senator Ford?"

"Yes."

"United States Senator Griffin Ford?"

Irritated, Ellis said, "Yes, *why?*"

"You seen the news this morning?"

"No."

"He's dead. They found him in his bed. Died last night in his
sleep. It's all over CNN."

It was getting toward noon, and Diana sat on the front
porch. She started really worrying about Lee. The storm was
now a hurricane in the gulf. It was still a couple of days out. The
television news was warning that evacuations might be ordered,
and cars were racing up and down the road in front of her house
like madness. She had burned the note as Lee instructed; now she
wished she had not, in case there was some hidden meaning or
clue in it that she had missed.

And Iris was missing. What did Lee's note mean? Where were
they going? She suddenly felt perfectly alone. She was afraid for
him, afraid of the FBI. She stared out into the gulf, trying once
again to divine the horror of Hurricane Katrina. She and Lee had
struggled through the rubble to find their home, this home, utterly
destroyed except for the antebellum chain wall that had been laid
by the unholy labor of slaves in another century.

The air was perfectly still; it was something palpable, an
opaque entity that preceded, no, *invited* hurricanes, and only
jealously yielded breath. A single drop of sweat slid off her

forehead, down the end of her nose, and she let it. Following the
flight of a single brown pelican, as it skimmed the calm sea, she
noticed a skinny, black plume of smoke rising off the west end of
Cat Island. Odd, she thought, probably a shrimper trying to get in
ahead of the storm. He must have blown an engine.

She needed to get inside, call her parents in New Orleans,
make sure they were okay. But Lee said not to tell anybody
anything. She was stymied, could do nothing but wait on Lee.
And there was something else. She laughed at herself. A nervous
giggle, really, like when she was a little girl, sitting on her parents'
porch uptown in New Orleans. She knew it was absurd. Yet,
somehow, she just *knew*. Last night, she had gotten pregnant.

Miss Ruby stared at the old amulet laying on her kitchen
counter. She was scared, and she did not care if Legba knew it.
He had drained her. Now, the gris gris must end. So she found
a meat cleaver in one of the kitchen drawers, and shattered the
amulet, with its symbols of Legba, and its ancient African human
teeth. Teeth of her ancestors.

Her first act as a mother, back in 1969, had been to declare to
the other hoodoos in New Orleans that she intended to murder
her child, to protect herself and them. It was a ruse. She had
made her deal with the powerful Legba. He promised to protect
her son, to wreak her revenge on the man she had once loved, who
had tried to drown her like a stray cat. Legba had ridden her hard
for his favors.

So she had given the baby away, just like she and Althea Jones
had agreed. Over the years, as she had dwindled physically, she
began to doubt. She wondered that the child might have been
snagged by an alligator, or any number of hungry, swampy things.
But he had not. By God, he had walked through her door, twice.
Her son was alive, and his name was Lee. He was beautiful,
intelligent, curious, strong. Like she had been, before. She

wanted to know him, and him her, so they could be together for a while, now that she was nearly dissolved. She could feel death approaching her like a loaded barge.

And she had certainly wanted to tell all of this to Lee, how she had saved him, and how he took her heart with him, and it had slowly killed her. But she decided to give him away again. She realized Lee was looking for Camellia, not her. She was not Camellia any more. Camellia had indeed died many years ago, just like she had told him.

When she was alive, Camellia had been lithe, intelligent, beautiful. She could write and converse in perfect French and English. She was a physical wonder, had matured more rapidly than her family and friends. She had been a central figure in her mother's hoodoo rituals at Lake Pontchartrain; the old folks swore she was the spitting image of the Laveaus, the mother and daughter who had talked to the spirits, and been ridden by the spirits in Congo Square and at St. John's Bayou in their distant community memories. Camellia's mother had trained her in the ways of hoodoo, and gambling, and entertaining even while she was a little girl. All of this was necessary for survival.

She was 16, on her own, and already wealthy by French Quarter street standards when she met Buck Carter. It was in a place called Daley's, on Ladnier Point, close to Azalea, Mississippi. He was solid, and tall. He was not afraid of anything, which made her feel secure. He was the sheriff, unassailable.

She was doing a small burlesque show in those days called "Lady of the Moon," which was based on the Greek Goddess Demeter, and her gift of grain to mankind. Camellia wore a grass costume made to resemble grains like wheat and barley draped around her lean form, which she gradually tore away during the show. At the end of the show she was briefly nude, and Buck had charged the stage like a wild stallion. He had to be restrained by several men. Later, he had pushed her in the front seat of his police truck, and drove away proud as a successful big game fisherman.

Their affair had been as brief and torrential as the gulf squalls that constantly buffeted the coast. He was married, but he told her he loved her. He had put her in a hotel in Biloxi. She had gotten pregnant almost immediately, it seemed, but he got crazy drunk and jealous, and kicked her out before she got a chance to tell him. When she had shown back up that August, 1969, extremely pregnant, he had first denied he even knew her. When she said she would go to the newspaper if he did not agree to support his child, her child, he decided to kill her as easily as he would have shot a deer, or clubbed a shark on the end of his fishing line.

What she remembered most about that August night in 1969, the night Buck and his crippled toady Cookie tried to kill her, was the warm temperature of the water. She had been drifting back and forth between consciousness and dreams, as the boat rocked and putted out into the gulf. She remembered seeing the ecliptic, the planets, in the broad night sky, unwashed by the light of man, or the moon. She had wondered where the moon was.

She gradually became aware that she was not in a dream, but that Buck had conked her on the head, tied her up, and put her in a stinking old wood boat. It smelled like dead shrimp on the floorboard, where her face was, and there were fish scales, a short piece fishing line, and a couple of rusted pairs of pliers next to her head. She had struggled mightily to loosen her feet and hands, but knew the effort was futile.

She was fully awake as Buck and Cookie argued about actually killing her. She knew Buck well enough to know that Cookie was not going to win. She couldn't think of anything worthwhile to say, so she didn't. She wondered how cold the water was going to be.

Buck slung her up, and over the side. She reflexively balled up, like a baby. She guessed that's how murdered people act when they are drowning. But the cinder blocks, there were two of them, hit bottom. She had balled up, and the bricks jerked her under, but the water wasn't deep enough, and she had stopped close to the lapping surface.

The two drunks had accidentally dropped her on an underwater sand bar. She held her breath as long as she could, until she had to come up, and the two killers were still there, but the tide had made them drift, and they were too far away to notice her. If she stood all the way up on the blocks, her head barely broke the surface. She stayed that way until they left.

It took her a long time to get her hands loose, and she had to hold her breath several times as she got her feet untied. She managed to make it to a nearby low marsh island of mud, sand and seashells ground by the surf. The exertion was more than her body could handle, and she had her baby right there on that unnamed, sticky spot. She didn't even know if she was in Mississippi or Louisiana.

Her baby boy was healthy and happy to nurse. She remembered thinking that he acted like the whole situation was fun, and never cried, but cooed and fed throughout the night, as she declined from loss of blood, lack of water. At first light, she saw a fishing boat, a flat one, like the one she had gotten murdered in. It was thankfully only one man, and he was solidly coonass, and not from New Orleans, and therefore trustworthy. She was strong, but sick. He had taken her and the baby back to town, to her little house, roused up a neighbor to help, and promised not to tell anyone what he had done.

Well, the devil Buck and his sidekick Cookie couldn't keep their mouths shut, and that same day rumors about Camellia getting murdered washed into New Orleans, even as Camellia

lay delirious in her bead, spewing invective and curses upon her
enemies, and most especially Raymond "Buck" Carter. She was
like that until a couple of days later, when Hurricane Camille
crushed Azalea with twenty-five foot deep water, that seemed to
kill nearly everyone who had stayed, except Buck Carter.

In the days after Camille, Buck was being hailed in the papers
as a hero for his braveness and determination in the face of, and
after the storm. At the same time, the hoodoos in New Orleans
credited Camellia with sending the hurricane into Azalea, for
revenge. She had instantly been elevated in the minds of all who
knew her to some sort of demigod, unable to be killed by man
or sea.

But soon enough, the hoodoos' awe turned to fear, and hate.
Some of her competition, other priestesses who vied for the
attention and the money that rich people in New Orleans spend
to have their fortunes told, began to claim that she was dangerous,
and that the spirits, or the sheriff up on the coast, or both, would
soon show up and do them all harm. And it was all because of the
little child, her new baby boy. She came to believe that neither she
or the baby would survive if they stayed together.

So she had made her arrangement with a nice lady she knew
from her old neighborhood, Althea Jones. But before she had sent
her precious baby away, she had invoked all the ancestral African
spirits, Legba in particular, and had worked her way through her
continuing weakness to prepare and restore the gris gris she just
smashed. She had, in her youthful rage, damned Buck Carter
and attempted to guide the Fates. She was willing to make a bad
bargain, and did.

In exchange, Legba had ridden her terribly, almost fatally.
Though her powers were sharpened, and her fame grew, she had
aged considerably over her lifetime, far more than nature could
have in the same time; Legba's ongoing patronage had been far

more of a price than she could have imagined at sixteen, yet one she had paid.

Eventually, Camellia was killed off by Miss Ruby, who went quietly into retirement as the hostess of her brothel on Rampart Street. Camellia was gone forever, and all that was left of her was her heart and brain. Old Miss Ruby could still turn boys heads, in her head. She still had rhythm, and love. She just could not show it.

She took a taxi down to the Mississippi River waterfront, by Jackson Square, and cast the shattered pieces of the amulet into the current. She immediately felt better, physically. She made her way across the square to Saint Louis Cathedral, where she place the twisted gold wire that had formed Legba's symbol on the cathedral dais. Then, she walked back home. For the first time in many years, she did not need to use her walking cane.

Chapter 9 - Destiny

Buck Carter left Cookie's house in a daze. He drove up to the Long Gravy, unlocked the door, did not turn on the bar lights. It wasn't open yet, wouldn't be for several more hours.

He went behind the bar, pulled out a new bottle of Irish. He went around front, plopped down on a stool, twisted the top off and drank from the bottle. Cookie was dead, shot by Buck's ivory handled forty-four. It had been too much weapon for the job.

And he was going to have to talk to Lee Farrell, who was bound to be moving his boat at the marina, with the hurricane coming. He took his time with the whiskey. He'd be heading out soon enough.

Speeding back to the coast, Lee's head spun. So the Camellia that Buck had tried to kill actually survived, and was his real mother? And Buck was his *father*? That meant that Jake was not just his best friend, but was also his half brother. It was too much to believe. And who *could* believe these voodoo fools? That old lady in the Quarter, Miss Ruby, or Camellia, or whatever her name was, sure seemed to know a lot, but who could believe any of it? He wished Mama Thea had told him all this earlier.

And now the damned radio was declaring a hurricane was headed in, maybe as early as tomorrow night. The place would be madness by tomorrow, as evacuations would surely be ordered. Hurricane fever on a mass scale was not something Lee was interested in dealing with, at the moment.

Then he realized the hurricane could be a gift. If he could get out quick enough, head east, toward the Florida panhandle, or Tampa, he could hold up, scoot around the backside of the storm, and be gone. He decided to go straight to the boat, get it ready, then get Diana. There was no sense alarming her any more than he had, and he was too worried about Bonacelli, the Russians, and the frigging frogs to tell her anything at the moment. Arriving at the coast, he entered merged into a madness of traffic, as people scrambled to stock up for another hurricane.

Mama Thea came awake for the first time in several days. She was sensible of the fact that she was in a hospital, believed it was in Greenville. She thanked God for allowing her one more day of life, and one more chance to ask His forgiveness for the sins she had committed during her long life.

Something was wrong with Lee. She knew it as surely as the she knew that today was her last day on this earth. She labored to breathe. It took all her energy to reach for the nurse's button by the bed. She pressed it, and waited. She had made a mistake, not trusting her son, not telling him about the evil his father, Buck Carter, was capable of. She had sent him back to the danger without warning him first. She knew that even now he was trying to find out who his mother and father were, and that he was a smart boy. He would find out, and then what would he do?

So she was going to have the nurse come and dial the telephone for her. She would call Lee right now and tell him the whole thing, if God would just give her that much strength. *Please,* she implored the Lord, *please let me live just a few minutes longer.* As she waited on the nurse, she smiled, remembering Lee when he was just a little baby, out in her tomato garden behind the Farrells' big house. She would take him out there, where he crawled around in his cotton diapers, getting the thick Delta gumbo mud caked on him from top to bottom. He used to like to dig up earthworms and sometimes, he would just eat one. She never told the Farrells that, but she told Lee, and that was one of their secrets.

She was losing her energy, so she pressed the nurse button again. She wondered if she would have the strength to talk to Lee. She needed to stay awake, but the scenes of the old days were so clear, and the hospital was so stark. So she closed her eyes, and she and Lee were cooking gumbo in the kitchen, or eating fresh sweet corn right off the husk, or fishing for white perch in the borrow pits down by the river highway. She tried to stay awake, wanted more than anything to see him one more time. But she was so very tired. She took a long, deep breath. Then she died.

When Lee got to the marina, a few boaters were already moving their vessels. Folks at the store had been giddy, starting nervous conversations with each other. All over, people were driving like maniacs, as if traffic laws were suspended. He called Diana, but all the phone circuits were temporarily overloaded, and he could not get a signal.

People were hoarding ice as if it was gold. Today, they would be hoarding up their houses, some of them getting drunk at the same time. Lee remembered how it was before Katrina. What kind of things do you save from the house? What do you leave? What if this is another false alarm?

The weather was surreal. There was no wind, and the air temperature had to be a hundred. Lee hoped Boot had topped off the fuel and oil. As he humped the supplies down the dock, he thought of all the pictures he had seen of Katrina. It was a beautiful storm from space, perfect in its huge proportions, but with a shark's eye, passionless, deadly, stupid. Hungry.

As he made a second trip to the car, Iris came running up. She had been all over Azalea looking for Lee, sensible of the crazy way everyone was acting, not wanting to miss out on anything. She had naturally gravitated toward the Miss Di. She and Lee went aboard, Lee lugging the heavy leather bag, and some ice he had picked up on the way. Lee started the diesels, and Iris headed around to the foredeck. Lee went in the head to check his fresh water flow. He would make sure Miss Di was ready, then let her idle as he went to collect Diana.

Buck Carter stepped on the boat and entered the parlor, unnoticed by Iris, who was stretched out on the foredeck, or Lee, who was in the head, or Flounder, who was snoozing under the bunk in the master stateroom. Lee heard some rustling and emerged, stunned to see Buck Carter looming, his white hair touching the ceiling.

"What the FUCK do you think you're up to, boy?," said Buck, jabbing his big finger toward Lee, a faded eagle and crucifix pulsing on his forearm. He was listing under the influence of the whiskey, and had his big pistol strapped on his hip.

"Settle down, Mr. Carter, what are we talking about?"

"You asking that old fool Cookie about somebody named Camellia. You got him all upset, and now he's...well, I had to clean up your fucking mess."

"What do you mean? What's going on with Cookie?"

"He told me you been asking all these questions. You wouldn't leave it alone. He got scared, started saying crazy shit, and now..."

"Now *what*, Mr. Carter? What have you done?"

"Goddammit! I practically *raised* you boy! I helped you get that scholarship to Mississippi State, which you *quit*. Who the hell *quits* when they're on the way to bein' a starting quarterback in the fucking *SEC*? Hell, who takes in somebody else's bastard, then has to put up with this kind of shit..."

"In the first place, *you* didn't raise me. Mama Thea did. But if you'll settle down, we've got something serious to talk about, Buck. You might be my..."

"*Mama Thea*? That old nigger in the Delta? Well, she didn't do much of a job, apparently. You ain't got sense enough to shut up when you're told."

"Call Mama Thea that word again, and I'll kick your old miserable ass," Lee growled. "Now, get off my boat." If the old man *was* his father, then he had tried to kill his real mother, too. Lee had many feelings about Buck, but none of them were affectionate.

Buck started to leave, then stopped, like he was thinking. He pulled out his pistol, turned around, and aimed it at Lee's chest. "Boy, you ain't nothing but white trash. You've had every chance, but you ain't got sense enough to be thankful." The irises in the old man's eyes were actually glowing blue. He grasped the cocked .44 magnum. He shook so badly, Lee thought he might accidentally pull the -

A brilliant blueish white roar punched the air, and Lee was on his back. For a dream instant, he imagined he was a giant laying on the floor of the parlor, and all the little bumps in the carpet under him were tiny Lilliputians collectively supporting his weight. He could not see directly, his field of vision consisted of one great red spot, and dim images on the edges. All he could hear was the rumble of the twin diesels and the heavy, fast bumping of his own heart.

He felt all over himself for blood. He felt again. Nothing wet, and his sight started returning. Lee located Buck in the same place as before, only now standing crooked and still, like a bad wax statue, with a comically horrible look on his face, and no gun. It was laying on the floor between them, where Buck had dropped it when it accidentally went off. Lee scrambled for it; Buck roared like a bear, piled on the floor, and wrestled him. Lee was surprised by how strong the old man's grip was, which Buck was supplementing by kicking Lee in the shins with his cowboy boots.

The big gun went off again, between the two men. Buck Carter slowly raised up on his knees, looking curiously at Lee, who was still on the floor. His ancient blue eyes shone like headlights through a muddy window. Then, he fell over dead.

Flounder had been sleeping up front in the small state room during the early part of the row. When the sheriff had started barking at Farrell, he awakened, and listened from a few feet away. He recognized Buck's voice, the same one he had heard bellowed down the halls of the county jail many times over the years, where he had been an involuntary guest.

Old Buck started acting like he was going to shoot Lee, and Flounder had gotten seriously concerned, not just for his own safety, but also because Farrell had the damned leather bag somewhere, and was no good dead, yet. The blast of the big .44 magnum ripped through the upper wall of the stateroom, out the bow, and made him deaf, momentarily. He now desperately looked around for a way off the boat. But there was none. He had to go back through the parlor.

So he bolted through the small galley, up the two short steps. Lee and Buck were wrestling on the parlor deck. The gun went off again, and he watched with anything but horror as he realized that somebody had finally shot the old son of a bitch. Buck Carter fell over dead; Flounder grabbed a whiskey bottle off the parlor bar, and whacked Farrell over the head with it. He stuck Buck's pistol in his belt.

He tied Farrell's hands and feet with some heavy plastic leader fishing line. He still did not know where the bag was, or what was in it, but he knew he could not stay here. So he ran out, took in the drag lines holding Miss Di in her berth, thankful that no one was in any of the nearby boats. Flounder took Miss Di out of the harbor. He saw a few people from the bridge, and waived if they did. He guessed they all thought he was Farrell, since like the damned teachers at St. Thomas always said, they looked alike. Apparently, no one had heard the shots from inside the boat, over the rumble of the twin diesels.

Lee regained consciousness in the parlor, dreamily looking at the dead body of his father. The boat was underway, and he could see out the small galley window that she was out of the harbor, in the sound.

Flounder had negotiated the boat out of the harbor and set the cruise control. He slipped down the exterior ladder from the bridge, found Farrell groggy, untied him, shoved him up the bridge ladder while he poked Buck's .44 in his back. He retied Lee's hands, and tied his feet, too. Flounder disappeared back down the ladder. As he lay on the flybridge deck, Lee scooted as far as he could, but could not see whether the shotgun was still under the dash, or not.

When Flounder went back down the ladder, Iris came around the other side, balancing on the gunnels railing, and climbed the ladder. Lee was glad he had taught her that. Iris lay behind him, flat and quiet in the shade of the dash and electronics. Lee prayed that she had figured out what was going on.

Flounder slapped the metal of the ladder, came up cursing. He had been planning on finding the pouch, which he was sure was on the boat, then getting rid of Farrell. He said, "Listen, asshole. You hid the bag good. That even bought you a few more minutes. But you can either tell me where it is, or I'm going to start shooting your fucking fingers off. He cocked the hammer back.

"I don't know why you're here, but you're no killer, Flounder," said Lee, "you can get out of this."

"Shut up, rich boy," said Flounder. "You don't know shit about me. I killed that bitch girlfriend of mine you screwed back when you were a hotshot in college. And I been looking forward to this for a long time. I'd do it for nothing."

"What girlfriend? What are you talking about?"

"You don't even remember her, do you?," hissed Flounder. "Well it don't matter now. Where's the fucking bag?" He grabbed Lee by the hair, started to pull him up.

Iris flashed from behind Lee like a ghost, first biting Flounder on the thigh, then she turned and bit him full on the ass, this time holding on.

Flounder shrieked, half out of pain, the rest out of fear, not having processed what mad appellation had come from nowhere, and was mauling his butt. He whirled and senselessly shot, blowing a hole in the bridge, which sprayed sparks. Iris temporarily let go, and Flounder took the break to wheel around and fire straight down through the floorboard of the bridge, which evidently hit the gas stove in the galley, and both he and Lee stopped moving when they heard a swoosh of flame whirling through the small starboard window below. Flounder saw the flicker of orange light, and shrieked, like a panther.

Lee furiously tugged at the line around his wrists, which had cut into his skin. Knowing the crazed Flounder was about to shoot him, he gave one great, last effort at pulling apart the leader, and Flounder's knot slipped enough to let him get a hand out.

Scratching and sliding, Iris tore into Flounder's gun hand. Lee scrambled for the shotgun, his feet still tied, as Iris and Flounder rolled around, nearly going down the ladder. Iris yowled like a hyena as she chomped on Flounder, which made each new bite sound like some mad, high canine language over Flounder's cursing. The dashboard lights went out, and Lee frantically grabbed at the wiring under the console, unsure where the gun was.

Flounder got Iris off of him, losing a shoe in the process, and was scooting around on the deck feeling for the .44 when Iris latched on again, this time on his bare heel. Flounder shrieked, then kicked madly with his other foot, catching Iris by chance in the ribs, launching her and a mouthful of heel skin over the gunnels, like a punt. Lee heard the splash, then nothing.

Flounder was rolling around on the deck, on his side, holding his squirting foot in both hands, spewing obscenities. His spastic motion made him spin incrementally with every kick of his good leg, which was gradually turning him in a circle, like a bad break dancer.

Lee found the sawed-off, flipped it open, checked the shells. He sat up, both feet still tied in front of him with his back against the hard fiberglass of the port side of the cockpit. When he clicked the gun closed, Flounder stopped his incompetent dance, and rolled up to a sitting position, stupidly facing Lee, and with no weapon.

"This is bullshit," said Flounder, like Farrell wasn't playing fair. "Where did that goddamn gun come from?"

Lee wondered if Flounder had noticed that his feet were still tied. He said, "Shut up, Flounder. Put your hands up, and tell me where that pistol is."

"It's right behind me on the floor, Farrell, and I ain't puttin' nothing up. Me and you, we are gonna work this out."

"We're going to the cops."

"Bullshit we are! They'll put your ass in jail, too! You just killed Buck Carter. Plus, I know you're up to something with Bonacelli."

"Maybe I will go to jail. Now put your hands up."

"Fuck you, Farrell. You ain't got the balls to shoot me."

"You *idiot*. You were going to kill *me*! You caught the boat on fire! I can just shoot you right now, and it would be self defense! And what the hell are you doing here, anyway?"

"Who's an idiot, Farrell? Nick Bonacelli sent me here to kill you, and get that leather bag back."

"What…"

"That's right, smart guy." Then he had an inspiration. He had brought some pictures he'd taken at Bonacelli's house of Diana Farrell, naked. He had planned on tormenting Farrell with them before he killed him. Now, he slid them out of his shirt pocket, flipped them on the deck in front of Farrell. "Guess what, Mr. Hotshot Quarterback. Bonacelli's been screwing your wife."

Lee kept the gun trained on Flounder, slowly picked up the three pictures, spread them like cards in his hand. It was Diana, alright, naked. "Where did you get these?"

"I took 'em myself. Bonacelli's been boning her for months, now. She's probably in on this with him."

"No way. That's a trick. A fake."

"No, Farrell, it's true. She's gone a lot, right? Probably tells you she's with Sarah Bonacelli?"

Lee thought, *he's right. She is always over there. But she loves me. She told me so over and over last night, like we were when we first met. Still, what he's saying makes sense.* He said, "Just get your hands where I can see them, and then you're going to help me save the boat."

"I ain't doing it."

"Listen, asshole! I will shoot you! The boat is on *fire*, in about a minute, that fire's going to get to the diesel, and then…"

"Nope. I ain't moving until we make a deal. I'm guessing there's plenty of money on this boat somewhere, and we can split it. Hell, I'd even consider forty percent, under the circumstances."

"Yeah, and then shoot me for the other sixty."

"No I wouldn't, but I can see you're willing to be being reasonable."

"For the *last time*, get your hands up."

"You know I'm right, that your wife has been fucking Bonacelli all this time, right?"

"No. I don't know. It doesn't matter."

"Sure it does. There's a dead man downstairs, Farrell. The former sheriff. Your wife is in cahoots with the man who sent me out here to kill you. What are your chances back in Azalea? Who's going to listen to you?" Flounder could see his ruse was having an effect. "Now let's split the money, and get out of here."

"There isn't any money, fool, and don't mention my wife again." Still, he wondered. *Could it be possible?* "Now get up," he said.

Flounder did not reply, only sat with his shoulders slumped; he had a dejected look on his face, was looking down, like he was anything but scared, or mad. He just looked disgusted. Then, he spun around, grabbed the .44, which was on the deck behind him, rose up on his knees. When he raised the gun, his head exploded, and his body flipped backwards over the ladder, onto the fishing deck.

Lee dropped the empty, smoking sawed off shotgun, frantically untied his feet, the roar of the fire bursting out of the parlor, now, licking up to the bridge. He looked all around the water for Iris, but could not see her. They were now by Cat Island, the boat still running on auto pilot. He hit the ignition kill, and the flaming vessel stopped its forward power, drifting aimlessly off to starboard.

Lee jumped onto the aft deck, nearly onto Flounder's quivering body, took a deep breath, ran into the parlor and grabbed the pouch, which now also contained the big sapphire and a stack of cash, out of the microwave in the galley. He came hopping out of the parlor, his shirt smoking, and dived into the water. Fire was rapidly overtaking the Miss Di now, her decks moaning and expanding, like a living thing. As Lee struggled away, she finally listed to port, the hot fiber of her outer hull coming into contact with the water, making a long, high groan, causing a plume of steam. Then she rolled over and sank, hissing.

The next morning, Diana was crazy with worry. People were racing up and down the road outside, getting ready to evacuate. She finally called the cops, who nonchalantly suggested that she not worry, that Lee probably got drunk with his buddies at a hurricane warm-up party, and slept on a couch. Under normal circumstances, she would agree. But he had left the mysterious note, which she could not tell them.

She dug around, found Zack Ellis' card and called the number. Maybe the jerk had seen her ruse and gone after Lee anyway. A cool female voice answered, "FBI."

Diana was expecting Ellis to answer. She said, "May I speak to Zack Ellis?," which immediately seemed too casual to her.

"Who's calling?"

"A friend. This is a personal matter."

"I'm sorry, miss, but Agent Ellis is not in today, and we do not expect him in for some time."

Diana said, "Can you tell me where he is?"

The operator, or agent, who had not identified herself, simply said, "No."

After a while, Diana could see Coast Guard boats and helicopters buzzing around. She flipped on the local news, which was saying Cookie's body had been found, and Buck Carter was missing. Diana did not know what to do, and felt like she could not leave. So she stayed busy, doing unnecessary things in the house.

Then the Coast Guard found the Miss Di, or what was left of her, sunk off the west end of Cat Island, and visited her. The water there was only ten feet deep, and everything in her melted and warped hull had been roasted in a diesel pyre. They said they found parts of the dead bodies of Buck Carter and Lee. Fire and sharks had not been artful with either body, one of which was headless. Still, they said, several witnesses at the Azalea marina had seen Lee taking the Miss Di out the day before.

The hurricane lurched across the open gulf, vacuuming heat from its surface into her maw. It formed an eighty mile wide eye, dark as it was perfect, that sucked a thick blister of saltwater up in 175 mile an hour winds. It tacked between Havana and Cancun, made a graceful northerly turn, and prepared to spread itself along the same path as its succubus ancestors Camille and Katrina. Then it paused. People along the coast scrambled like a pile of ants as it meandered in the northern gulf for a day, then two.

Three days after Lee Farrell, Buck Carter, and old Cookie were found dead, the hurricane quietly dissipated, sending surfable waves all along the Redneck Riviera.

The cops found Buck's pistol and Lee's empty shotgun, both roasted in the Miss Di's wreckage. Obviously, Farrell's head had not gotten shot off before he killed Buck, so they deduced that Lee Farrell had killed the old sheriff, then blown his own head off. A dozen people saw Buck Carter, drunk in the parking lot of the marina, apparently heading for Farrell's boat. Several more saw Farrell leaving the marina at the helm of the Miss Di. The coroner said as far as he was concerned, you had a murder suicide. Lee Farrell had just gone crazy.

But they couldn't figured out a couple of things. First, the old man's gun had been fired five times, and Buck's partial torso apparently had only one bullet hole in it. The old man Cookie, who had been buried in the pauper's cemetery behind the Catholic church, had a hole through him and another bullet from the same gun in his kitchen wall. Who killed Cookie? And what happened to the other three bullets?

Second, what happened to the big old sapphire that used to be in the case at the Blue Stone? Leaving Nick Bonacelli opening the case on video at the Blue Stone had been cute, but Bonacelli could not be tied to the crime. The sapphire was not on the boat, or in Farrell's house or car, which they searched. Amateur treasure hunters and maritime scavengers had practically dug a new shallow harbor around the wreckage site of the Miss Di, and had found nothing.

What was recovered of retired Sheriff Raymond "Buck" Carter got a huge funeral, with a state police honor guard. That same day,

The Mississippi Sound ran a front page article, written by Charlie
Roark, entitled Mass Murder Possibly Connected to Cronus?,
which was several columns of old rumors about Buck Carter's
connections to illegal gambling when he was sheriff, and new
ones about the ownership structure of the Cronus Casino and its
possible ties to the Mafia. It finished with a gaggle of innuendos
and an ominous suggestion that the FBI refused to comment.

For weeks, the coast was atuttle over the multiple murder and
apparent suicide that had so many conspiratorial ramifications. A
news entertainment television show ran a segment on the story,
but suspect veracity had already muddied the subject, along with
threats of libel suits. The story almost immediately died as far as
the national trash media was concerned.

FBI Special Agent Zachary Ellis was still in shock over the
news of the death of Senator Ford when he found out about the
deaths of Buck Carter and Lee Farrell. He took his first personal
leave since joining the FBI. His grief was real, not for the loss of
life, but because he figured Ford and Farrell to be the linchpins
that held his case together. No case, no leverage, no glory. When
he came back a few days later, he got summoned to Washington.

Ellis was relieved of his current duties, and placed in a special
unit in Honolulu, Hawaii. His Bardino files were taken, and he
was instructed to forget about anything he heard or learned in
Mississippi. His new job was to monitor Japanese businessmen on
golf courses all over Oahu, and he soon got his handicap down to
single digits.

One day at work Charlie Roark got a call from the
Entertainment Director at the Cronus Casino. He was invited
on a "celebrity" fishing trip, sponsored by the casino. Flattered,
he showed up. The other celebrities apparently all had conflicts,

which was fine with Roark, who loved the attention. So he made a big scotch drink, and chilled out in the parlor as he, the boat captain, a deckhand, and the head of security at the Cronus cast off in the casino's big high roller cabin cruiser.

A few miles into the coastal shipping channel, Roark went out on the fishing deck. Slugging down his second drink, he was happy the casino bastards were finally giving him some damned respect. He nodded at the security guy sitting next to him in a fishing chair. He could not think of the guy's name to save his life. When they got out of sight of land, Roark noticed a couple of big, concrete cinder blocks on the deck, next to the transom, and wondered what in the world they could be for.

Nick Bonacelli had been questioned in his office about the video at the Blue Stone. He laughed it off, and the cops said they were just curious, apologizing for taking up his time. They all got comped rooms at the Cronus.

The Saudi was more curious, but the papers made it clear that Farrell had just gone over the edge. Besides, the Saudi had pre-approved the whole sordid scheme, and could not complain to anyone without getting killed, himself.

Bonacelli was the only person in the world who knew that at least one more person was supposed to be on Lee Farrell's boat. Nobody important noticed that Flounder was missing, and Bonacelli quietly had his car towed a couple of days later. He had secretly spent thousands of dollars recently trying to locate the asshole; who knew Flounder had the balls to kill Farrell and the old redneck former sheriff, then run off with his diamonds?

And he had the new problem with his crazy wife. He soon decided to let the Flounder problem lay for a while; the Bardinos were more curious than ever about his daily activities, and there would be plenty of time for more necessary killings later.

Still, he could not get over the nagging feeling that Farrell had somehow managed to fuck him.

Boot never had believed the body in the boat was Lee's. That, and his instinctive ability to avoid serious trouble kept him away from Lee's funeral. When he found out through the hustler grapevine that Flounder was missing, he smiled to himself, packed his few belongings, and hitched a ride with a girl named Esta, and headed to Austin, Texas, knowing he would probably see Lee Farrell again.

Dahlia wondered at the news of Lee's death when she read it in the newspaper. She did not believe for a moment that Lee Farrell had killed himself. It was obviously a setup, and Lee had gotten killed by fooling around in someone's business, probably the Mafia.

She had seen Sarah Bonacelli a few times in the club where she now worked, the "Persian Kitty." Sarah was talking about moving down, working there. They both agreed to look for an apartment, if that happened. Sarah could make a ton of money at the Kitty, or anywhere else.

Once, when Dahlia was in the dressing room, she noticed her first gray hair. She skipped her next dance, went to the bar and got a drink, which she uncharacteristically paid for. Back in the dressing room, she frantically mined her head for others. Something made her think about Lee, and she cried until her makeup ran all over her pink sequined g-string.

Petrino "Pete" Mallini strolled down Carondelet Street in New Orleans' Central Business District. He just had lunch with his crazy uncle The Raven. It had been necessary; they met periodically to talk about whatever did not need to be discussed on the phone. Pete always insisted on meeting his uncle in a bustling, open place, where they would draw less attention.

Most of the talk was mundane, but his uncle had said one thing that got his attention. The Raven had an oldish street thug in his employ, a steroid and speed freak who was cheap help, yet violent and disposable. A perfect bill collector, in other words, and just as full of shit.

From TV, Pete knew about the spectacular deaths of Lee Farrell and the old Mississippi sheriff, just like everybody else. The Raven's guy claimed that he was in on some kind of amateur drug deal several years ago that involved both dead guys, Farrell and the old sheriff. Pete brushed the guy's story off as low gossip.

The thing is, the Raven did not know too much about the family's recent dealings with the government, or how these events might or might not be related. He wondered whether Bonehead had anything to do with the deaths. Bonehead was too smart to be trusted. He was not a real member of the family. He had always been expendable.

But Pete Mallini had greater worries than the curious coincidence of the deaths of an old sheriff and some loser named Farrell up in Mississippi. The Bardino family's old partners in the spook end of the U.S. government were calling again; this time they were planning to go back south, into the gulf and the Caribbean, and finish some old jobs. They needed the family's help again. But they especially needed the family's secrecy.

Walking, Pete chuckled at the thought. Sure, it was tough balancing the money, and the personalities, and the killings, when necessary. But his job was made a lot easier by the simple fact that he ran an organization that permanently held Uncle Sam, the United States government, by the balls.

He was not about to let anyone go off grid and screw it up, especially Bonehead. But he had to be careful, too. There was this business with Senator Ford. He had gotten sentimental, was planning on going on the fucking news and telling everything he knew about, well, everything. He had to be put down. But doing a U.S. senator is never easy, not even for the Bardinos. So he had to lay low for a while. Dealing with Bonehead, if necessary, would have to wait.

Sarah Bonacelli was afraid she may be in love with Diana. But ever since Lee disappeared, Diana was not really talking to anyone. Sarah had never even considered loving Nick, but he had been tolerable before he moved to Mississippi. Even though their sex had always been good, he had just gotten too intense.

She knew he used to sneak home at lunch, peek out the bay window. She had never told Diana about it, but it got her excited, sometimes. Nick did not know about the half a dozen or so other women Sarah had slept with since college. Somehow, he was too fucking eager.

But that was all past. She could no longer picture she and Nick together at all. She was going to go to an attorney, get a divorce. New Orleans looked like a great place to start over; she had been there several times during the year and had found that the French Quarter, and Uptown were just as gloriously bawdy as she imagined. It was a town that an artist, or a stripper, or both, could get along indefinitely. Especially one with a good alimony settlement.

Jake Carter resigned his position as D.A. With his father dead, he had no real ambition to be a politician, or even an attorney. He mulled around for a few months, trying to figure out what to do. He finally reopened the Long Gravy, stuck in a little kitchen, and was doing good business.

He was in the kitchen, working on gumbo. He had to make it once or twice a week, depending on how big the evening crowds were. They bitched about having to pay for food, instead of getting it for free, like when good old Buck was around. But the dart league nights were busy, and people were generally getting in a better mood, four years after Katrina.

Good old Buck. Since he died, Jake got to sit back and think about him. He had been a hard working man. Jake could not remember a time when he saw the old man sitting around. He was a hard drinker, hard talker. He never gave up his anachronistic way of using the most offensive ways to talk about people he didn't like. Jake could never understand his father's generation and their ridiculous hatred for other races, especially African Americans. It was just crazy, and Jake had tried to talk sense into the old bastard several times.

But Buck held on to his hatred like a life raft. Like he thought that if he ever let go, he'd drown. Or have to admit he was wrong. Jake's dad had been a hardass in every possible way, and therefore, Jake guiltily admitted to himself, easy to not miss.

He emptied cut bell peppers and celery into the gumbo. He never believed that Lee Farrell had killed his dad, at least not on purpose. And how Lee had died was so uncharacteristic that it made the absence of the lout Flounder all the more suspicious. Hell, they always looked just alike.

Either way, he didn't know, and didn't need to know. Flounder was working for Bonacelli. Bonacelli worked for the Bardinos. That made it none of his business. If Lee was alive, he'd get in touch. If he wasn't, he wouldn't. Jake dumped in andouille sausage, stirred the pot.

Now, when he thought of Lee, it was always like they were in high school. Out at the island, fishing, sailing, chasing girls. Like they were real brothers.

Several months after Lee died, Kiger got a box in the mail at the Blue Stone. According to the flushed cocktail waitress who helped him, it contained had fifty thousand dollars in cash, and a computer generated, unsigned note that said, "See you one day. Ocho." He knew it was from Lee.

Years earlier, Kiger had gradually started losing his eyesight. The doctors said it was a rare degenerative disorder, but Kiger always figured it was punishment, somehow. He had lost his sight completely. Lee had always managed to help take care of him, and for that, he would never be betrayed.

So Kiger took the money, quit his job, and eventually made it to Miami. Then he found a retired rum runner from Marathon Key willing to get him and his wad of undeclared cash to Ocho Rios, Jamaica.

Camellia reclined on her rooftop deck with a glass of tea in the sunny northern French Quarter. Destroying the gris gris had the gradual effect of removing decades from her countenance. Some of her customers had recently remarked how much she resembled her retired great aunt, Miss Ruby. Camellia, flattered that they all assumed she was much younger than her fifty-something years, let them think so.

When Buck Carter died, the newspapers claimed that Lee Farrell had killed him, then himself. But Camellia knew that was not true. Legba had been patient, accomplished his task. She had paid by giving herself to him for a generation. All debts were satisfied. Camellia placed her tea on a linen doily, rose, glided to the black iron rail.

Looking down Rampart, and around the Quarter, she always expected to see Lee. One day she would, and this time, by God, she would tell him the truth.

Lee Farrell leaned against the back of his stool at the Balboa Yacht Club, outside Panama City, Panama. He was at a long outdoor bar, overlooking the Bay of Panama, and the Pacific Ocean. The club was on the Pacific end of the Panama Canal, practically under the Bridge of the Americas, the only decent way to drive from North to South America.

He got up, walked over to where a guy was playing the acoustic guitar and singing, solo. There was a tip jar, he dropped in a five. The singer nodded at him, and started in on a song by Jimmy Buffet. Lee went back to his cane bottomed stool, and ordered a mojito.

He'd quit having nightmares, ironically, after the nightmare scenario with Buck Carter. And he'd apparently killed his father, the father of his best friend, his half brother, Jake Carter. He had come to accept these things as true; what Mama Thea had told him dovetailed with the story he heard from Miss Ruby and Buck's own actions. Old Cookie was just wrong about Camellia, and Buck killed him for it. That meant Buck thought she was dead, too. Somehow his real mother, the mysterious Camellia, had survived Buck's murderous rage, saved Lee's life, then gone off and died, like Mama Thea said. He would never know her.

The day he died, Lee knew the smoke from the Miss Di would have the Coast Guard out quick. With Flounder dead, he'd changed his mind about going to the cops. So he swam the short distance to Cat Island, lugging the heavy bag. He fretted about Iris, spent hours scanning the water and looking around the island to see if she had made it. When the Coast Guard showed up, he had to hide. Maybe, by some miracle, she made it. Maybe.

That night, he mercifully found an unsecured skiff at one of the island's few fish camps, and got back to shore. He managed to hitch into New Orleans that night, in all the hurricane panic, and checked into an uptown hotel under a different name, paying with cash.

The hurricane had been barreling toward the area when it came to a complete stop. Then it turned southeast, away from any land. It died off as quickly as it had boiled up, and people started acting like the civil law was in effect again. Lee stayed in New Orleans for a couple of more days. He saw on the news how he had gone berserk and killed the old sheriff, and maybe Cookie, too. He knew he couldn't stay in New Orleans, but if he went back home, there was Bonacelli. And the cops. And Jake, who would be wanting to know why his best friend just killed his dad. Who would believe that killing Buck *and* Flounder was self defense?

Then, there was Diana. She was undoubtedly naked at Bonehead's house in those pictures. But the fact that Bonehead himself was not in the pictures made him wonder. Could she actually be screwing the guy? There was just no way to know, and he had to make a decision, get the hell out of New Orleans. So, he found a cargo captain at the docks willing to let him stow to Panama, for cash.

He had enough money to live. More, really, than he needed in Panama. And he was careful to sell only a few of the rough stones at a time, just enough to steadily fill his new numbered bank account. He eventually bought an old Bertram boat, refit it, and was running charters. His new name was Mike, but the locals and the endless stream of Americans he ran charter fishing trips for called him "Pop" for no reason he was particularly aware of. It suited him fine.

His life had been nuts. Twice, he'd gotten away with murder, even though he had not actually murdered anyone. Hell, they were all trying to kill *him*. And he had won. As far as anybody knew, he died off Cat Island, a day after his fortieth birthday. He wound up with all the money, a cool place to live, and a new identity.

But he had lost Diana. And she meant more than anything else. As time passed, he forgot about any of their problems, how she seemed to always expect more of him than he thought he could perform. How he'd gone to law school for her, not for him. How she always looked down on him, in a way, because he wasn't really a blue blood, just a bastard, an adopted urchin, a usurper hanging out with rich people by pure chance. But she loved him, anyway.

And he had not been fair to her. His preoccupation with Dahlia seemed like a stupid joke now, but there was a time when he thought he might actually love her. But he came to realize that Dahlia was just a dream girl, one that could never exist in reality. A rented diversion, who he never had to see in mundane circumstances. Like she was a character in a movie, always perfect, always unobtainable.

No, Diana was his one true love, the girl of his life's secret story, the one who should be with him when he ran off to the tropics. Still, every time he started to try to contact her, he stopped. It was something Jake had said, the last time they talked: *are you and Diana OK? Like, getting along?* What did that mean? What else *could* it mean, but that she was up to something? But Bonacelli? It just did not make sense.

After a while in the tropics, he'd quit wondering if the damned amulet ever really meant anything at all. Diana, Mama Thea, and Iris were all gone. Jake probably hated him. And he was a wanted man, facing murder charges, There was no way to go but forward. He had to learn some way to live, to survive, without slipping into madness. So he'd been writing in the skinned up travel journal on the bar next to his drink. He finally figured out that the best subject he knew, and the weirdest, was his own life. So he changed the names and dates, and was writing it all down. The story was so bizarre, nobody would ever take it as true.

Taking a sip, singing in his head along with Mr. Buffet, he looked to the north, under the bridge, up the Panama Canal, toward Diana. Toward home.

Diana grabbed her wide straw hat as wind coming off the gulf threatened it. She was reading a book about Greek mythology, and reclining in a beach chair on the sand across the highway from her house.

Iris sat on the beach next to her, staring out toward Cat Island. Iris had shown up wet, tired and hungry two days after the Miss Di sank. But she recovered, and now she got up and scooted around to Diana's other side, where she licked the new face of Althea Diana Farrell, who giggled. Diana had the baby exactly nine months to the day after Lee disappeared.

She had cried at Lee's funeral, like they were really burying him, but she thought that she knew the headless partial body in the cemetery behind the Episcopal church was not Lee, at all. The coroner had not bothered with the expense of a DNA test, since plenty of witnesses had seen him get on the boat and leave. Diana could have requested an autopsy, but if it really wasn't Lee, he surely would not want everyone to know.

When Boot had called and told her that the lowlife Flounder was missing, she *knew* Lee was alive, and wondered why he had not come back. Did he really have some part in those murders? Was he afraid that he could not prove his innocence? Had someone told him about her and Sarah? Did he even know that she loved him? Had she ever really made that clear?

She could not go to the police, believing that any circumstances that caused Lee to essentially run away could only be made worse by getting the cops involved. So she went about her life. Keep Marlin made sure the money continued to come from the farm. She tended to her house, changed the baby's clothes, went to the grocery store, cooked, visited her parents. She and the baby slept together, in her and Lee's bed.

Iris looked up at Diana, who patted her head. Iris settled down, crossing her front paws toward the water. She fixed her gaze on Cat Island and beyond, the endless Gulf of Mexico, waiting on Lee.

21123201R00168

Made in the USA
Middletown, DE
19 June 2015